LIES WE SING TO THE SEA

for mum, for everything

LIES WE SING TO THE SEA

SARAH UNDERWOOD

HARPER TEEN
An Imprint of HarperCollinsPublishers

HarperTeen is an imprint of HarperCollins Publishers.

Lies We Sing to the Sea

Copyright © 2023 by Sarah Underwood

ISBN 978-0-06-323447-5

Typography by Corina Lupp

23 24 25 26 27 LBC 5 4 3 2 1

First Edition

for mum, for everything

"Death shall come to you from the sea, and your life shall ebb away very gently when you are full of years and peace of mind, and your people shall bless you. All that I have said will come true."

—Homer, The Odyssey
Translated by Samuel Butler, 1900

I

ANOTHER FEAT OF GODS AND HEROES

Leto

A silent maid braided Leto's hair into an elaborate crown for her execution.

Her knees smarted as she knelt on the rough flagstone floor of the little room. Her arms, pale but for the bruises already blooming there, protested and cramped against the rope that bound them, wrist to wrist, behind her back.

The maid pulled Leto's head sideways and pushed in yet another pin, scraping the sharp metal against her scalp and drawing thick strands of dark hair taut. Leto gritted her teeth and blinked hard, furiously avoiding the gaze of the hulking guard standing watch at the only door. He was fully armored, a sword strapped at his hip and his features obscured by a shining bronze helmet.

Leto fixed her eyes instead on the flickering light of the fireplace. The scent of the burning incense hung in a choking fog and filled the room with a close, oppressive heat. Sweat ran in rivulets down her neck—over the terrible black scales that had risen on the skin there, marking her for slaughter—and disappeared beneath the neckline of her gown. The carefully arranged curls about her face were already damp and frizzy.

Some sacrifice. It was a bitter thought. Perhaps Poseidon would be so disgusted that he would simply send her back.

From the corner of her eye, she watched the maid—her mouth

full of pins, brow furrowed—empty a handful of tiny white flowers from a linen-lined basket. She checked each carefully for crushed petals, then began to weave them deftly through the plaits at Leto's brow.

It was the first time someone had done her hair in years.

There was little occasion for intricate hairstyles anyway. Leto's mother had died when she was ten, and since her father had followed a few years later, Leto had been forced to make her own money. The work had not been hard to come by at first—Ithaca's common folk still flocked to the house of the last royal oracle—but she did not have her mother's talent for it, and the few brief snatches of the future that Apollo granted her were infuriatingly ambiguous. Her remaining customers were those that could be satisfied by spectacle, by the theatrical slaughter of a rabbit or the wild rolling of eyes that Leto had soon perfected. There weren't many of them, but they paid enough silver to keep her from starving.

As for her hair, a ribbon to keep the longer strands from her face normally sufficed, though she supposed it would not stop it getting caught in a hangman's noose.

This braid, she reasoned, briefly surprised by her own practicality, *will do a much better job.*

A sharp knock on the door broke the near silence of the room. The maid started and snatched her hands away from Leto, glancing nervously toward the guard. He hadn't moved an inch.

"Quickly." The guard spoke for the first time since Leto's arrival. His voice was low, gravelly, and strangely flat. "It is almost time."

The maid nodded and reached for another handful of flowers.

The hairs on Leto's arms prickled. Under the smooth material of the ceremonial gown they had dressed her in, her heart quickened and fluttered like a trapped bird. Something heavy and unpleasant settled itself like a great pressure on her chest, squeezing her lungs, hitching her breath.

Shuttered in this unfurnished room, it had been impossible to keep track of time. The sound of birdsong and the first rays of light streaming in through the tiny window had told Leto that the sun had risen, but beyond that, nothing. It might have still been early morning.

Now, though . . . *It is almost time.* She knew exactly what it was almost time for. The sacrifices took place at noon, when the equinox sun had reached its peak in the sky.

It was not dying she was afraid of, for she had long steeled herself against the idea of it, but what lay beyond.

In her seventeen years, she had led a decidedly unremarkable life. Some of the more superstitious townsfolk still whispered of her mystical powers, it was true, but Leto had vanquished no monsters, thwarted no criminals, bested no cheats. She had only been kissed twice. The afterlife waiting for her would not be an unkind one—for there was little to recommend her to damnation—but she would certainly not find herself in the company of brave heroes like Perseus, Heracles, or Odysseus. She would not see her mother again.

Apollo had not even deigned to grant her a vision of her own demise—the night before the guards had arrived to claim her, she had dreamed of a girl with golden hair and eyes like the sea.

Her thoughts of greatness were vain and stupid, of course. But still, Leto had always hoped, in the way little girls do, listening open-mouthed to tales of heroic deeds, that she would one day be remembered as extraordinary.

She could still feel the prickle of scales around her throat,

the mark that had appeared mere days ago and brought it all to a lurching halt. The truth was plain to see: Poseidon had chosen her. There was no escaping it. No one would remember her now.

For a moment, she wondered which of her neighbors had noticed the scales, had sold her to the royal guard. She didn't blame them—her fate was already sealed, and at least the bounty would give them a few more silvers for bread.

The knock came again, louder this time, as the maid forced in a final pin.

"For gods' sake," snapped the guard. "Are you finished?"

"One last thing," said the maid. This time, when she reached into the basket, she pulled out a leather cord, knotted roughly into a loop. From its center there dangled a tiny silver coin. The shape was instantly familiar. An obol. "For Charon," said the maid solemnly.

Leto had been expecting it, but still, the sight of the metal set her stomach rolling. The dead were customarily buried with money; this single obol would serve as payment to the ferryman to bear her soul across the Styx and the Acheron. Her *dead* soul.

The maid carefully eased the necklace over Leto's braids. She felt it fall underneath the gown, to rest in the hollow between her breasts. She bit her lip; the metal was cold, startlingly so, where it lay under the folds of pale fabric.

The guard scoffed as the maid straightened, fumbling with her basket of pins and battered petals. "Organize your things. I will escort you out." Perhaps he wasn't the superstitious type. He eyed the leather cord with disdain and, when he caught Leto watching him, flashed her a sly, mocking grin.

Leto shuddered. As she did so, her eyes caught on a sudden reflection of sunlight. A reflection, she realized, that stemmed from the flat of a shining blade. Obscured from the guard's view by the yellow fabric of the maid's chiton was a pot of dressmaking pins and a great pair of bronze shears.

Leto's pulse surged as she gazed at the shears, hardly daring to believe her luck. How the maid had missed them, she didn't know. But the blades looked new—sharp and shining and perfect for cutting through troublesome restraints. The gods had handed her a lifeline at the eleventh hour.

"Come on then," grunted the guard to the maid. Leto's head snapped up again. "Is that everything?"

Leto's eyes darted between them. As soon as the maid stepped forward—or, gods forbid, turned back—either she or the guard would notice the dropped shears.

Leto made a split-second decision.

She pitched herself forward onto the shears, concealing them beneath the masses of her skirts. "Don't leave me!" she cried out. "Don't let me die!"

The maid, with distress plastered over her huge, doll-like features, turned and flinched at the sight of Leto on the ground. "I—" she began, reaching toward Leto.

"Please!" shrieked Leto, thrashing her body side to side. If the maid got too close, she would almost certainly spot the forgotten shears. Leto willed wild tears into her eyes and bared her teeth like a cornered dog. "I don't want to die!"

The maid made a whimpering noise.

"All right. That's enough." The guard abandoned his post and covered the distance to them in two massive strides. "You"—he slapped a heavy hand down onto the maid's shoulder—"out. Wait in the corridor. I'll deal with this."

She didn't need to be told twice. Clasping the basket of flowers to her chest, she fled.

"And you." The guard regarded Leto dispassionately. "Pull yourself together," he snapped. "Have some dignity."

Leto made pointed eye contact and let out another melodramatic howl of sorrow.

The guard made a noise of disgust. "Very well then," he said. "Stay like that." He turned, kicking up a cloud of dust from the half-swept floor, and marched from the room. The door clicked shut behind him, and Leto was left alone.

There had been a time earlier, whilst the maid had been meticulously tailoring the white ceremonial gown to Leto's hollow frame, when Leto had familiarized herself with her restraints.

For some minutes she had occupied herself with rolling her bound elbows and wrists experimentally, searching for a position which didn't set them prickling painfully.

After this time—during which she had succeeded only in contorting herself further—she had resigned herself to discomfort. The ropes were simply too thick, the knots too tight and elaborate.

But now, apologizing silently to the maid, who would doubtless be punished for her oversight, she exploded into action.

Or, more accurately, though it wasn't quite the daring escape she would have preferred, she shuffled, rolled, and twisted herself painfully into action.

The hardest part was getting the shears into the right place. Her hands were sweaty and shaking. They slipped and fumbled on the handles, sending them clattering to the floor more than once. The slightest of sounds in the corridor behind the door left her frozen in place, holding her breath and counting down until the footsteps faded or the scurry of mice quieted.

At long last, she managed to ease the blades into position against her bonds. She worked her hands carefully back and forth and felt the ties begin to loosen. The sound of each thread breaking was like music to her ears—the most beautiful she had ever heard.

At last, the thickest part of the rope was sawn through. With more strength than she knew she possessed, Leto tore the last stray threads apart. The bindings broke with a snap and fell away. They had barely hit the ground before she had staggered upright, almost tripping over the too-long gown as it pooled like spilt milk over her bare feet. Her legs, tired from kneeling for so long, shook and nearly buckled underneath her. Disoriented and completely devoid of a real weapon or plan, she staggered toward the door, then came up short at the sound of footsteps on stone outside.

Right. She turned and lurched toward the window, the light filtering through it beckoning her forward.

It was not yet so far into spring that crops were sprouting and the goats were producing milk by the barrel. The winters always left Leto with a perpetual knot of hunger in her belly, but today she was grateful for it. Had her slight frame been any larger, she would have stuck fast in the narrow window. Instead—twisting and turning and scraping her hips so closely to the stone that blood bloomed on her skirt there—she managed to make it through, depositing herself on a patch of sparse grass and dry soil. She struggled to her feet and peered up at the great mass of stone that had been her prison.

When the Ithacan guard had first come for her, with splintering force on the door of her house in the early hours of the morning, it had been dark outside—and they'd blindfolded her for good measure—so her sleep-addled mind had been unable to follow the many twists and turns they had taken through her home village of Vathi, then out onto the sprawling hills that surrounded it. She had assumed she was being kept in some remote dungeon, some squalid cave where the rest of Ithaca could forget all about her. But now, she recognized where she was immediately.

Blinking against the harsh sunlight, Leto looked grimly up at Vathi's Northern Guard tower. Then, her heart sinking unpleasantly into her stomach at the sound of a muffled clatter, she turned to look at the group of armored soldiers loitering on the ground in front of her. The soldiers looked back with identical expressions of bewilderment plastered over their faces.

For a moment they gazed at each other, the prisoner and her jailers. Most of the soldiers had their helmets off, their heavy sword belts discarded at their feet. They had clearly not been expecting company; some of them looked half-asleep. Perhaps they *had* been asleep—that would explain why Leto had not heard them from her cell.

How foolish she had been, to think that her only escape would not be guarded. How naively hopeful.

At last, one of the soldiers very slowly retrieved his sword, clambered to his feet, and leveled the blade at Leto. He cleared his throat cautiously. "And where do you think you're going?"

Shit.

The tower stood atop a great hill. Leto could see the brown, sloping rooftops of Vathi, so near she could almost have reached out to touch them. Freedom was tantalizingly close; she could not let it escape her. Not when the alternative was to die like an animal, for a kingdom and its wretched royal family that deserved nothing from her. Not after they had failed her so badly. Not after they had failed her mother.

So, though she knew she was caught, that she couldn't outrun a soldier on a good day, let alone battered and bruised and dressed in a ridiculous ceremonial gown, Leto gave it a go. Praying to every god she could remember offhand, she spun on her heel, barefooted, and ran.

She had made it barely four paces before a hand caught her by the back of her gown and hurled her to the ground. Her leg twisted underneath her, and she fell on it hard. Pain shot up from the impact; as if from a great distance, she heard herself cry out. She tried to pull herself to her feet and had made it onto all fours before something solid hit her across the back. She crumpled again.

"Get her on her feet," barked a familiar voice.

Hands under her armpits hauled Leto upright. Her leg buckled under her weight and she sagged like a rag doll. Dizzy with the pain that thrummed through her leg and ran down the full length of her spine, she squinted at the hazy figure in front of her.

The guard from Leto's room knelt down slowly. His helmet was off now, and he moved his exposed face very close to hers. With a deliberate spite, he smiled. It pulled taut the narrow scar that ran from the middle of his cheek, down and over his chin and neck, and disappeared under the breastplate of his armor.

"Dear me," he purred. His eyes were the blue of a cloudless day and they flashed with malice. "Did you get lost?"

There were several things that Leto had never done in her life, nor dreamed of doing. But given that it seemed near certain that she would be dead by the evening, she abandoned any sense of self-preservation she had ever had.

"Die," she snarled, and spat in his face.

His smile vanished. He drew his hand back, then brought it forward with a speed that sent the air whistling around it as he backhanded her across the face. Hard.

Were it not for the two guards flanking Leto, supporting her body between them, she would have gone reeling backwards into the dirt. Her cheek smarted and she tasted the metallic warmth of blood. She debated spitting *that* into his face too, but before she had evaluated whether the brief satisfaction would be worth another beating, the guard had straightened and turned away.

"Take her to the beach," he said. "I'll make sure I'm there to watch her die."

II

IN A FIELD OF FLOWERS

Mathias

Prince Mathias of Ithaca did not become aware of the most recent attempt on his life until nearly a week later, when his mother informed him over breakfast that the perpetrator—a fisherman by trade, apparently—was to be hanged.

"Wonderful," said Mathias after a deliberate pause. He stabbed his fork into a grape and eyed it murderously. "Will that be before or after we execute his daughter?"

Such attempts always saw a sharp increase in the weeks before the vernal equinox, those weeks in which the first of the girls woke up to Poseidon's mark on their throats. Their desperate parents, husbands, siblings, lovers would descend on the palace with all manner of blades and poisons and the occasional explosive, and make for the queen and her son. As if it would do them any good. As if Mathias had a say in any of it.

He mashed the grape into a pulp on his platter.

His mother pursed her lips and laid down her knife. It was one of the rare occasions that the hall wasn't bustling with courtiers, that they were as close to alone as they ever were, with just two guards flanking the table. Even Olympia was not here, alternately adoring and irate. This lack of audience meant that the queen was a little less patient, her temper a little quicker to rise. "Really,

Mathias," she said sharply. "You of all people should understand why we must do this. After Selene—"

Selene. The sound of her name was almost too awful to bear. It brought with it the sound of whistling wind, the churning of an ocean that had risen from its bed, the memory of what happened when Ithaca failed to pay Poseidon's price. The air felt like salt water in his lungs; he fought down the sudden, violent urge to gasp for breath. His mother was right, of course, and he hated it. The marked girls had to die. If Mathias didn't do it, the sea would claim them itself, would ravage the land, destroying everything in its path, until it found each and every one of them.

He was on his feet before he realized it.

"*Mathias.*" The same thing happened every year; somehow his mother was still surprised by it. "Are you even listening to me? I—"

"I need to make sure the preparations have been finalized," he said, refusing to look at her. He didn't need to see the disappointment in her face, not today. They had very different ideas of what it meant to be a prince—what it would mean, once he finally came of age and took the throne, to be a king. "They'll be taking the girls down to the beach soon. They'll be expecting me there."

The queen sighed and took a long drag from her cup. "Very well then."

Mathias didn't wait for her to change her mind. He thrust his chair back into place and strode across the hall toward the great wooden doors that marked the only exit, holding on to the circlet of gold on his brow to stop it slipping.

"Make sure you practice the blessing," his mother called after him. "Not that it matters to me, darling, but perhaps there is an . . . *expectation* for a future king to speak clearly. Besides"—her voice softened—"I know you can't stand to stumble on the words. You were ever so upset last year; I hate to see you like that."

Mathias gritted his teeth and wrenched the doors open, slipping through the gap before his temper frayed too thin and he snapped back. What did it matter what was expected? It was not as if his people would be there to hear him; they were all barred from the hangings and had been ever since a spate of failed rescue attempts some ten years previously.

But of course, they were not the audience he cared for. The audience for whom he *must* get this right. Twelve girls were about to die for Ithaca, and he would be damned by every god there was before he let their sacrifices go unhonored.

As she always did, the queen had arranged for a chariot. Mathias ignored it pointedly when he reached the stables, raising a hand to silence the harried-looking groom that had hurried over. "My horse," he said deliberately. "That's all."

To his credit, the groom did not argue and returned a minute later leading a charcoal mare by her halter. Clearly, they had been expecting Mathias to refuse the chariot; she was brushed, and a crimson saddlecloth had been draped across her back. She sniffed at Mathias eagerly.

"Hello, Sthenios," said Mathias, taking the halter from the groom. "No honey for you today, I'm afraid."

Sthenios gave a disapproving snort, but she stood obediently and allowed Mathias to swing onto her back.

"Come on then." He drove in his heels. "How fast can you go?"

Very fast was the answer to that question. Sthenios had been a gift from Athens, the kingdom of his betrothed, and she was the finest horse in Ithaca's stables. Within mere minutes, they were up on the hilltop, taking gasping breaths of the thick, hot wind. Mathias pulled Sthenios into a walk. A winding path stretched out before them, meandering aimlessly toward the sea before reaching its conclusion at a narrow strip of sand to the east. The hanging beach.

Its original name had been erased by hundreds of years of tradition. Mathias doubted anyone alive even knew what it was; twelve girls had been hanged there each year for centuries now. Thousands dead, sacrificed to appease—if only temporarily—the ever-rageful Poseidon.

There was no escape for any of the marked girls. The sea would find them wherever they fled on the island, and to try to leave was just as hopeless. Poseidon, always watchful, would blow over their boats and drag them to the depths. There were countless tales passed down through the centuries: of storms so sudden in their violence that they could only be the work of the earthshaker himself; of the wretched shell of a fishing village on the north side of the island, the houses smashed into pieces by raging tides; of dead girls upon dead girls upon dead girls.

Mathias did not need reminding of the consequences of the sea god's wrath; they were laid out before him.

The hollowed-out bones of the landscape were achingly familiar. He knew every contour of the hills, every gleam of the sky as it danced on the ocean. Here was the patch where he had picked daisies with Selene, weaving them into child-sized crowns and balancing them atop her windswept black curls until the sun burned low on the horizon. And there—hidden now by the twisting roots of some starved, wizened bush—was the spot they'd leave them, hoping that the wilting flowers would tempt nymphs out from their trees.

If he was ever afraid—if a bird startled too quickly from its perch, if a wolf howled in the near hills—Selene would hold him close, ruffle his hair, whisper in his ear, "Do not be afraid, little brother. No one will hurt you. Not while I am here."

The daisies didn't grow here anymore. The sea had razed them all to the ground, drowning, smashing, and salting the earth beneath its path as it fought to claim what it was owed. Even now, nothing but tough shrubbery grew there.

Mathias shut his eyes tightly and forced the memories of Selene away. It had been his fault, his mistake. But he would not make the same error again. He spurred Sthenios onward.

There was some part of him that hoped the hills would go on forever, but soon, Sthenios's hooves met sand instead of soil, and they were there.

The beach stretched out in front of him, flushed gold in the early morning sun. It might have been peaceful were it not for the neat rows of armored guards, their hands resting on the hilts of their blades. The damp sand almost glistened, beckoning him toward the sea and toward the rough wooden scaffold that had been erected on the shoreline so that the waves lapped against its posts. Easier, then, to cut the dead girls down into the water. Sensible. He swallowed hard.

Twelve identical nooses swung in the low wind. Twelve girls in simple white gowns stood beneath them, their backs to the water—water that Mathias could have sworn had begun to swirl in anticipation.

He slipped from Sthenios's back and walked slowly toward them. Someone had laid down a rich, plum-colored carpet for him to stand on, lest he dirty his boots. He longed to kick it aside in a ridiculous display of temper, but such things were unbecoming of the future king, so he pushed the desire down and took his place in front of the gallows.

Alexios had offered, as he did every year, to take his place, to dress in Mathias's armor and wear his helmet to hide his face. As he did every year, the leader of the guards had looked almost disappointed when Mathias had turned him down. More than once, in the years after Selene's death, Mathias had almost accepted. Poseidon did not care who conducted the sacrifices, only that they were made. But it was not Alexios's duty to bear, not his burden.

Besides, Alexios had sacrificed enough for Mathias, had saved his life at just twelve years old and taken a dagger to the face for his trouble. Now, he stood to Mathias's left, his features impassive and a meticulously sharpened blade clutched between his calloused hands, ready to slice through the ropes that held the platform up and send the girls swinging to their deaths.

"Your grace," said Alexios quietly. "The first order?"

Mathias forced himself to look down the line of girls, to meet their frightened eyes and pray that they saw in his all the pain, the anger, the sorrow that echoed through his hollow chest. Not that his feelings would matter much to them when they were dead.

He nodded once. At the signal, a guard swiftly ascended the gallows and began to loop the nooses around the girls' black-flecked throats. The smallest, a trembling girl with wide black eyes, made a soft noise as the rope came to rest above her collarbones.

"Any issues?" Mathias murmured to Alexios, looking away.

The guard smiled grimly. "Nothing to be concerned by. We had to . . . *escort* one ridiculous boy home—his little sweetheart is here—but aside from that, it's been a quiet year. They know they can't afford to anger the earthshaker."

Mathias nodded wordlessly. Yet another failed land harvest had left his people hungrier than usual, and they knew as well as he did that the sea was their salvation. Maybe that was why the betrayals of the marked girls had been faster this year, why all of them had been turned in well before today.

"Oh," Alexios added, his expression souring, "there was an incident with the sacrifices—one cut through her bonds and tried to run, stupid girl. But she didn't get far. She'll be hanged with the rest."

Some mad part of Mathias thrummed with disappointment. He lifted his head and looked again down the line; which girl had been selfish enough, *brave* enough, to try? But then the guard positioning the nooses was jumping down onto the sand again, and it was *time*, and the girl that had made her madcap attempt, whichever one she was, was condemned to die alongside the others.

Mathias cleared his throat and began: "Blessed twelve. In Ithaca's name, I thank you for your sacrifice." Several of the girls were already crying, their frightened eyes shining and their lips trembling. Mathias swallowed. It was necessary, he told himself forcefully. And the alternative was far worse.

"In Zeus's name, I honor you. In Hades's name, I beg for you a soft welcoming to his kingdom."

Someone scoffed loudly.

He had been expecting the sobbing—it happened every year, and it appalled him the same every time—but this was new. He peered at the girls, searching their faces for some disdain, some derision, and found nothing but fear.

He opened his mouth to continue just as his gaze fell on the last girl in the line. Half-hidden behind her neighbor, such that he had not seen her clearly until now, she stood with her back perfectly straight, chin up, as she glared at him with a look of such revulsion and hatred that, for a moment—forgetting every word of the speech he'd been forced to recite since the age of fifteen—he could do nothing but stare back.

Her face was gaunt and pale, her cheekbones hollows that spoke of a hard winter. The ceremonial gown hung straight down from her shoulders; her arms, pale and peppered with bruises, were bound behind her back. One of her eyes was swollen half-shut, her hair was a frizzy, dusty mess, and someone had forced a gag between her teeth. Still, the eye that was fully open was clear-sighted and full of stubborn pride.

Cut through her bonds and tried to run, stupid girl . . . She'll be hanged with the rest.

So, this was the would-be escapee.

"Your grace," hissed Alexios. "The blessing."

Mathias could not look away from the girl, from that fierce determination in her eyes. It was the same look that Selene had given him on that fateful night, the last time he had ever looked up at his sister's face. If she were alive, she would be here in Mathias's place, and he would be safely back at the palace. A foolish younger brother, not the future king. Knowing nothing. Caring for nothing.

He cleared his throat and forced himself to speak again. "And in Poseidon's name, great lord of the seas, tamer of horses, shaker of the earth, I, Prince Mathias of Ithaca, sentence you to die, so that your brethren may live to prosper."

The girl's face twitched. That one tiny, vulnerable movement sent a vicious throb of guilt through Mathias's chest. A girl like that—proud, furious, *afraid*—did not deserve to die like this. Dishonorably, like an animal.

The guilt returned again then, stronger. His mother would have scoffed to see him like this: moved to weakness by a pitiful, broken girl with fire in her eyes and a proud curve to her back. She did not deserve this, of course not. Nor did any of the eleven others that stood alongside her. But Ithaca would drown if they were allowed to live, and a choice between them and every other soul on this wretched island was not a choice at all.

III

BY WORD OR DEED

Leto

Leto glared at the prince, baring her teeth as best she could with the gag in her mouth, and prayed furiously that he could not see through her anger to the pain, the weakness that lay beneath. The long walk had not been kind to her injured leg. The guards had seemed to care little for her comfort—and, indeed, why would they? She would be dead within the hour.

The tears had threatened to come then, hot and fast. Leto had wiped them away furiously on her shoulders as she staggered and limped her way over the loose gravel and snapped twigs, pausing every few steps to roll her ankles and bite back low noises of pain until at last, after what felt like hours, they had arrived.

Now, she did her best to keep the weight off her injured leg as she stood atop the gallows. It must have been made new; the wood was rough and caught on the hem of her gown as she swayed in the humid wind. The smell of pine had been comforting at first, now it was suffocating, nauseating.

The platform swayed beneath her feet—it was held up by thick ropes, looped over a high, horizontal beam, then knotted tightly around stakes that had been driven deep into the sand. Once those ropes were cut, the platform would fall, she would follow, and the rope around her throat would yank her back up. Perhaps her neck would break.

The prince cleared his throat yet again. His tanned olive skin was slick with sweat; it plastered his curls to his forehead, made him shine like gold in the sun. His eyes flicked back and forth across Leto's face.

For a wretched coward who let his people starve in their beds, he was shamefully lovely, like a portrait, all hard lines and smooth skin with eyes and brows and lips in worshipful arcs of charcoal. His voice, despite the shaking, was soft and musical when he spoke. "As you leave this life, may your bodies be as the waves, may your bones be as the sand, may your souls fly free as the gulls and watch over us. Oh, great Lord Poseidon, accept this offering."

His voice cracked on the last word. Then, "I'm so sorry," he said. A hushed murmur from the guards told Leto that this was not part of the script. "If I could do anything—" He broke off. His eyes, still fixed on Leto, were wide and pleading.

She could almost have forgiven him. But at the last moment, as he dropped his chin in a reluctant nod, as his guard raised his sword and brought it down in a glittering arc toward the ropes holding the boards steady beneath her, the prince looked away.

Coward.

The platform gave way underneath Leto's feet and she was suspended in the air for a dazzling, terrifying moment.

Then, Leto fell and the rope caught her.

She had expected pain, but it was far fiercer than she could ever have imagined: instantaneous, incomparable. It caught her in a sensation partway between pressure, ripping, and an extraordinary burning. Had her breath not been trapped by the knot around her throat, it would have been torn from her in a shrill cry of shock and agony.

Though she had sworn to herself that she would not struggle, she felt—rather than willed—her legs spasming and kicking. Her feet danced a frantic pattern in the air, and even as white spots began to tremble at the edges of her vision, she tried desperately to call out through the wad of fabric between her teeth. For whom, she was not sure. Her mother, perhaps, long dead. Her father.

She tried to gasp but she could not—the iron grip on her throat would not yield. With each moment it grew tighter, and the pain grew fiercer.

Leto felt consciousness slipping between her fingers like fine threads and allowed herself to welcome it. The pain dulled, her legs stilled.

The last thing Leto felt, before the waves rose up to swallow her whole, was the peculiar sensation of being watched. Not from the land—by the prince and the rows of his guards—but from the water. Then, the pain reached a dazzling, shattering crescendo— and stopped.

Oh, she thought, *it is over*, and died. There were flowers in her hair and the ghost of a smile on her lips; her body fell limp like a snared bird.

◈◈◈

On the shores of Ithaca, gentle waves lapped at the smooth stones. A distant gull cried out and another, closer, answered. The leaves of trees bristled in the breeze and the air hung in a haze thick with the scent of salt as a procession of soldiers cut the dead girls from their nooses and set them to rest—first floating, then dragged under by the weight of their gowns—in the receding tides.

As the current pulled her away from Ithaca, the little island she had spent her life always plotting, planning, *hoping* to leave,

Leto sank quietly under the water, her eyes closed, her neck marked starkly by the rope and the scales beneath it.

And somewhere, beneath the surface, something—*someone*—stirred.

IV

THE BITTEREST TONGUE

Mathias

The room that was highest up in the palace was Selene's, so that was where Mathias went to hide once the hangings were over and the girls had been set out on the water to be claimed by its currents.

The furniture in the room was undisturbed, exactly as it had been the day she had died. Her maids had been redistributed to the kitchens or the stables or let go from the palace entirely, but Mathias had arranged for one to stay on to sweep the floors, to brush out Selene's gowns and mend the holes that the moths left in them. It was an unnecessary, indulgent expense. Eventually, the gowns would be beyond repair, but for now they hung neatly in her wardrobe, all jeweled blues and golds and shining whites, slowly decaying.

Mathias sat in the chair at the window and gazed out over the hills that lay beyond it. Here, in Selene's quiet, empty quarters, was the only place he was ever truly alone.

At this very moment, even, he was supposed to be with his mother, recounting the hangings for her, as if they really changed from year to year. But the queen had stalked off to *somewhere* to brood with her ladies, which suited Mathias just fine; there was little he wanted to do less than recall the faces of the girls he had condemned, the girls whose bodies were lost now to the seas and the god that ruled them. Still, the eyes of the twelfth girl—bloodshot and blackened and *angry*—would not leave him be. He had ordered her death, and he didn't even know her name.

It would do him no good to dwell on it, he had learned that by now. He returned his attention to the hills and the towns and the great wide sea that lay beyond them.

The ships were returning to the docks with great fanfare, laden down with heaving nets of fish. The meager patrol that Mathias had dispatched to the harbor had returned, beaming, with stories of laughing children clinging to their mothers. The crops still would not grow where the sea had razed them all those years ago, and the goats wandered farther each day from their flocks in pursuit of something—anything—to eat, but for once, Ithaca had *hope*. Hope that the sacrifices meant something, that this sudden bounty of wrasse and bream and bass meant that they could still earn Poseidon's favor, that the sea god had not forgotten them. The fish had cost him far too large a share of the pitiful treasury, and bribing the sailors—to claim that they'd caught it themselves, that it hadn't been ferried down by foreign fishermen from the prosperous seas north of Ithaca and Cephalonia—had cost almost as much.

It was a precarious thing, a deception that teetered on a knife's edge, but it hadn't failed.

Yet.

The sacrifices would haunt his dreams for weeks; at least he would not have to watch his people struggle on without hope too.

He took a long drag of wine from the chalice clutched in his hands, then set it down at his feet. The chalice had been cast from pure silver, another of those ridiculously indulgent expenses, but what would Ithaca's noble visitors say if they were served wine from tin cups and bread from battered wooden plates?

The near-empty treasury was a persistent worry. It had been

a small comfort when a messenger had arrived from Athens to declare that Mathias's fiancée, the princess Adrasteia, was preparing to depart her kingdom and would be arriving on Ithaca within the year. His father had arranged the match when they were children—indeed, Mathias had never met her—and his mother had encouraged him to quietly dissolve it in the months following his father's death. He should marry a nice, local girl, she had said, one of the noblewomen in her court, perhaps. Mathias knew exactly who she had in mind. But he had heard the rumors of the dowry that Adrasteia brought with her. If they were true, he would have enough gold to feed his people for a year.

And gods, if he didn't owe it to them.

Mathias fumbled again for the chalice, then cursed—loudly; the sound echoed around the chamber as he knocked it to the ground. Wine spilled over the marble tiling.

He jumped to his feet and cast about wildly for some solution to make itself apparent. When no such thing occurred, he made for the heavy wooden chest he knew still held Selene's blankets. He'd once pirated the lot for the construction of a fort. When Selene—dripping wet from a bath and wrapped in a clumsily bound chiton—had found him, she had shrieked at him loudly enough to bring even their father running.

He threw the chest open and pulled out a goat-wool throw. Something had been caught in the loose weave and it fell to the floor with a dull thump; he paid it no heed as he returned to the pool of spilt wine and mopped it up as best he could.

The wine had run in between the tiles, and the blanket in his hands was not entirely effective at absorbing it. When the curls of wool were saturated with red, he gave up. He would have to send the maid up later. He massaged his temples with his fingers. Some king he would be; he could not even clean up a pool of spilt wine.

He turned despondently back to the chest, belatedly remembering that something had been hidden beneath the throw, that it had been hurled to the floor, and that it lay there now: a bundle of papyrus, the sheets battered at the edges and held together with a slip of white ribbon.

Selene had worn ribbons just like it in her hair. She had been wearing them the day she died, the day she stood in this very room and—

Mathias snatched the bundle up. It was no use thinking of that day, no use remembering how the wind had whipped Selene's skirts up and snatched her obsidian curls from her braids. He had cried enough times over those memories, had learned a hundred times over that the gods would not hear his desperate pleading. Or if they did, they did not care to honor him with an answer. He marched back to his post at the window and flipped the first page over.

It became rapidly apparent that it was a journal.

The entries were made out in Selene's carefully curling script, the margins filled with drawings of flowers. The seasons were marked at the top of each section. As he gazed at the first, his heart gave a nauseating lurch, and his vision slid rather alarmingly out of focus. His hands shook as he collapsed back into his chair, upsetting the chalice again.

The last days of winter four years ago. The year that Selene had died.

Springtime is coming, read the entry, *and Ithaca will receive her gladly. There have been too many troubling reports of late: of children shivering in their parents' arms, of animals starving out on the hills.*

The altars lie empty; Ithaca fills its belly before that of the gods. If the goddess Demeter is good and well pleased with the return of her daughter, she will bring a much-needed respite from this suffering.

But, of course, as one challenge to our prosperity falls, another, greater, rises.

As much as I plead with Father, he refuses to search for a way to break this shameful curse. He will not bring another oracle to Ithaca. He will barely allow me into his precious library, though he seems quite happy to receive Mathias there.

Mathias blinked at the paper. His name was a vicious slash of ink; he could all but hear Selene speaking it out loud. She had resented him, he had always known it—that he, the younger child, would not have to suffer the same expectations, the pressures, that she did—but there was something else in the angry lines of the words here.

Men, the entry continued. *I cannot help but wonder whether they would care so little if the curse claimed the sons of Ithaca, as well as the daughters. But it is no matter. I will see this wretched piece of our history drawn out, whether they will help me or not.*

I swear it.

In the following pages, she had made notes, written names, scribbled maps and marked them with furious crosses. Extracts of verse—prophecy?—had been annotated and underlined. One page read only *Twelve by force? Not the marked girls—Who?* Mathias let the bundle drop into his lap.

Selene had wanted to break the curse. That in itself did not surprise him. But she had thought that he did *not.*

He clenched his hands into fists.

There came a sound of crumpling paper. Mathias looked down. A slip of papyrus had fallen and caught in his sleeve; as he moved, it shivered and threatened to come free. He plucked it up and cast a weary eye over the page. It, too, was marked in Selene's hand—messier than that in the journal; there was an urgency in the scrawl.

Mathias, said the first line. *I am going to die.*

Oh gods. A letter. A letter to him, from Selene. From Selene, who had known what fate awaited her, who had known that she would not live past that godsdamned equinox.

He could not bear to read it; he longed to cast it aside, to pretend that he had never discovered its existence, but his body would not allow it. His fingers stayed curled into the parchment, crumpling in the edges, and he found that his eyes could do nothing but move along each line and *read.*

> *Mathias. I am going to die.*
>
> *Our mother will not hear of it, nor our father, but we all know what fate awaits me. I have read the records from centuries past, from those few times that the marked girls were not sent to their deaths. The sea came for them, Mathias, and it will come for me.*
>
> *If this is the path the gods have chosen for me, then so be it: I will go to meet my end, and I will go bravely.*
>
> *I wish I could say I have lived a complete life, that I am content with my lot, but the truth is that I am not. I have left a great many things unfinished, and I can only pray that you, little brother, will take them up when I leave.*
>
> *This curse must be broken. It must. I am certain that it can be done—I do not believe the gods capable of inflicting such cruelty without some secret for release. They are not so unkind as that. The solution is here, I know it. I have left—*

Here, the letter ended, with a violent line of ink that bisected the paper. Selene had been interrupted before she could finish it, that much was clear. There was a rust-colored stain in the lower corner; Mathias did not care to examine it more closely.

He returned his eyes to the ocean, that treacherous expanse that fed Ithaca and destroyed her in the same stroke. Somewhere out there, tugged onward by the currents, were the dead girls, their hopes and dreams and fears lost to the seas.

They would be the last twelve.

He had sworn it the year that Selene died, and the year after that and the year after that. But—he was ashamed to admit it even to himself—he had never *done* very much to make it so. This time, it would be different. It had to be, because Selene had set him this task and he could not fail her. Not again. Carefully putting the letter aside, he lifted the remaining sheets to his face and examined Selene's notes closely.

The final lines of her letter were burned behind his eyes. *The solution is here, I know it. I have left—*

The maps were faded, her handwriting almost illegible, but one thing was clear: somewhere, in the scrolls that filled the library or hidden within the dizzying labyrinth of wine cellars and tombs that lay below the palace, was the answer Selene had searched for.

Mathias was going to find it.

V

WHITE BONES AT DAYBREAK

Melantho

There were twelve bodies in the water.

They always found their way to the island of Pandou eventually, though the seas that stretched for miles around it were invariably still and silent. Melantho would have been foolish to think that it was the natural currents that had brought them; she had been there long enough to know that nothing found its way to Pandou unless it was meant to.

They had been adrift for months, but they were hers now. Hers to tug ashore and bless and bury and weep over until the last dregs of summer were sipped from the skies.

She waded into the shallows fully dressed, shivering as the water turned her skirts sodden and the first tremblings of the change wound their way up from her ankles. By the time she reached the first girl—a little thing with fine hair pulled back from her slack features—Melantho's eyes were sharper, the sound of shrieking gulls clearer.

The water twisted around her thighs and pulled her deeper, that restless reminder that she was Poseidon's creature, that this was where she belonged.

She did not need to peer at her reflection in the water to know that her olive skin had faded to a greenish grey, that emerald scales had bloomed on her legs, her hips, the tops of her shoulders, and

the crests of her collarbones. The yellow of her hair would be a deep green now, like strings of seaweed hanging about her face, and the glint of her eyes would have vanished into a pool of ink.

A monster.

Melantho swallowed hard and reached for the dead girl.

Her grey eyes were wide and staring, her mouth open, her lips blue. Twelve years old perhaps.

Melantho closed her eyes carefully and began to pull her toward the shore.

The first one of each year was always the worst. Once Melantho had pulled the girl up onto the sand, combed the seaweed from her hair, and commanded the water from her sodden gown, she swallowed down her grief and returned to the sea. The second was easier. The third, easier still.

Even so, by the time she had eleven girls laid out on the beach, their hair combed and gowns dry, her throat was raw from sobbing, her vision blurred. Each of these girls had once had a life of her own, a family, memories and sorrows and hopes. Now, all they had were necklaces of scales, battered coins on leather cords, and the ragged scars of the rope.

She stepped into the water for the last time, opening her arms as the waves brought the last girl in to meet her. Soon, all twelve would be buried, with honey and wine and the coins resting on their chests. Soon, they would lie undisturbed beneath the soil of Pandou with a thousand others, would feed the flowers which bloomed in the graveyard and the great fig that threw them into shadows. Soon, Melantho would be alone again and—

Melantho froze, her hand outstretched toward the twelfth girl's face.

Her eyes were already closed, and she was beautiful, but that was not what set Melantho's heart thrumming wildly in her chest.

This one was not like the others; she was different in a way that was horribly familiar. Her pallor was not quite right for a dead girl; there was a flush in her cheeks, her lips were pink. But that was not the worst of it. Slowly, a different hue was spreading out over her skin, smoothing the freckles and sun-flush and the canvas of mottled bruises into an unblemished grey. Then, the scales began to appear.

Melantho recoiled.

No. Not now.

How long had it been since the last? Seventy years, perhaps, or more—it was not so easy to keep track after three centuries. However many years had sidled by her since Thalia, since that wicked, foolish girl, it did not matter. It could have been a century and still, Melantho would not have been ready for this.

Thalia had been the eleventh of the hanged girls to change, to be offered to Poseidon and spat back, intact, into the seas that surrounded Pandou. Melantho had still had time then. But that made this girl, her face now the color of the rocks that dotted the shorelines, her cheeks dusted with scales like patches of moss, the twelfth. The *last*. And just like that, her time had run out.

The water *felt* her anguish. From the places where Melantho's hands met the water, ripples burst outward, rocking the dead girl back and forth. Her hair spilled out around her face; it had been a rich brown when Melantho first saw her, but now it was green— the shine of the sea on a moonless night.

It was happening whether Melantho wanted it or not. She took a deep breath, forcing herself to calmness. The water stilled about her, as if it held its breath with her.

The girl opened her eyes.

For a moment, she gazed blankly upward. And then she screamed.

Her eyes were huge and round and fixed unwaveringly on Melantho's as the awful, wrenching sounds tore free of her throat and split the still sky. A heartbeat passed before the girl seemed to recognize where she was—lying on her back in the shallows. Another beat, and she was splashing backwards, putting as much distance between them as she could.

If that was her reaction to seeing Melantho, then Melantho was not looking forward to the screaming when the girl caught sight of herself.

The change was complete by now, of course. The girl's skin was grey and green and inhuman; her eyes were pools of black, her hair like a swirling torrent of seaweed.

Melantho waited until the shrieking petered off and the girl, at last, commenced gulping down great lungfuls of air between the harsh, painfully dry exhales. She kept her voice low, calm. It was the voice she used on the rabbits she trapped before she killed them. "Are you all right?"

The girl's chin snapped up. "Am I all right?" she blurted. She looked horrified. Perhaps she had not realized that Melantho could speak at all.

Melantho shrugged, deliberately casual. She had done this enough times to know that the girls, in all their bewilderment and bemusement, would watch her for their cues. If she was calm, they would let down their hackles enough for her to walk them up the beach to the caves that were her home, to set them down on a log with an apricot to watch Melantho roll out pita dough and bake the soft loaves on the fire.

If she allowed her fear to show—as she had, admittedly, done the first time and the second, and possibly the third too—the girl's answering agitation would stir up the waves into a frenzy.

So Melantho smiled at the girl, who had folded her arms across her chest and was glowering at her as if Melantho had tied her noose herself. It wasn't too far from the truth.

"You must be cold," she said, hoping that the girl could not see through her false, soothing smile. That she would not glance too far up at the beach and see the eleven linen-wrapped bodies there. "Come ashore. We have much to talk about."

She would do this right. This girl would not catch a glimpse of all that fluttered, caged, in Melantho's chest. All Melantho's guilt and fear and sorrow would stay there until this girl set off from Pandou, as all the others had, and made for Ithaca with one goal in mind.

To bring the prince to the sea. And to let it swallow him whole.

VI

BIRDS OF THE SAME FEATHER

Leto

Leto woke abruptly in the blinding sunlight.

Her body felt weightless, as if she were floating. Every limb was numb with a peculiar cold—one that didn't *feel* like cold, one that throbbed underneath her skin and threatened to burst through it, to shatter her into pieces of jagged terra-cotta. She tried to swallow, but her throat was raw and parched.

She blinked hard as her eyes adjusted to the light and brought the world swimming into focus about her. She looked up into a blue sky, swirled with flocks of starlings. The moon was a pale face peeking through wisps of cloud.

And someone was standing above her. Someone that was not human.

Leto took in the ash-colored skin, the sopping green curls, the flat black, white-less eyes, and screamed. She spluttered and splashed and thrashed her arms wildly about as she sought to put as much distance between her and this—this *creature* as possible.

Then, she—because the creature certainly *was* a she, all smooth curves and a neat, tapered waist under a sodden chiton the color of a rose petal—actually *spoke*.

And Leto replied.

Stupid. This was how idiotic mortals found themselves tricked into the servitude of the gods. Leto scowled and folded her arms in front of her, thrusting her chest forward in what she knew was a pitiful attempt to look intimidating.

The monster didn't seem to notice. "You must be cold," she said. "Come ashore. We have much to talk about."

Much to talk about? Leto's head was spinning. Her neck, too, was aching persistently, the dull throb of a bruise.

Automatically, she lifted her hands to the source of the pain.

"I wouldn't do that," warned the creature-girl. But it was too late.

In a perfect circle about her throat was a patch of sore, ragged skin, like the healing scab of the wound from a slipped knife. Nausea swelled in her stomach as her mind flooded with sudden clarity. The wound was not that of a knife—it had come from a rope. She had been *hanged*.

She had *died*.

And someone had seen fit to save her. Or at least, they had not cast her into Tartarus quite yet.

She stared up again at the creature-girl. Surely, she must be standing in the River Styx, waiting to be rowed across to Hades, where she would be set before the judges of the Underworld. But the dead did not enter the river, so how could Leto be immersed now in its waters? She listened hard for the sound of a ghostly boatman or the baying of a three-headed hound. Nothing.

She had always imagined that the dead found themselves exactly where they needed to be. She knew the rituals; at twelve years old, she had ensured they were carried out over the body of her father. She would have done the same for her mother— vanished when Leto was barely ten years old—if her corpse had ever been found.

Milk, honey, water, wine. Prayers. A coin.

Leto knew that she would have received nothing like such

careful attendance. The bodies of the hanged girls were left to Poseidon, though there would, perhaps, have been prayers.

She cleared her throat. She would not allow herself to cry. "Am I dead?" she asked flatly.

"No," said the girl. "You are not."

"Why?" A foolish, childish question. But it was all that Leto could think to ask. "I was hanged. I should be dead."

"You were," said the girl. "I will ask you again—come ashore with me. There is much to be discussed, and I am sure that you would be more comfortable somewhere warm and dry, with something to drink. Something to eat too, if you feel well enough."

Something to *eat.* The thought of it almost made Leto trust her. Almost. But she had learned the hard way that she must always be quicker to turn to suspicion than blind faith. Had always checked over the food she bought in the market, argued over the price. Trust did not keep you alive.

She shook her head. "If I am not dead, then we are not in Hades, I suppose. So where are we?"

"Pandou," said the girl.

"Pandou?" *Everywhere.* A strange name for a strange place. She looked around again, more slowly. She had not noticed it at first, but now she found that she could pick out strands of peculiarity amongst the tapestry that made up Pandou. They stood facing each other in the ocean—she could taste the salt on her lips—but the tides were not moving in and out as they did on the shores of Ithaca. Instead, the water swirled in aimless circles about the girl. And the birds, the starlings she had seen when she'd first opened her eyes: they were wrong too. They followed the same loop in the sky over and over and over, their cries whipped up by the wind and carried away. "Which of the gods made this place?"

The girl's eyebrows shot up. "Poseidon," she said, as if she were so shocked by the question that she had forgotten to lie.

Poseidon. So this was where the sacrificed girls went: an impossible island in the middle of the ocean.

Hope sparked in Leto's chest, as perilous as a flame in the wind. *Mother.*

Because it had not been fever that had taken her, nor starvation, nor any of the other ills that plagued the people of Ithaca. She had disappeared the night before the spring equinox in the year that Leto had turned ten, and she had never returned.

Her father had refused to believe that she had been chosen by Poseidon. She had been too old, he had raged; this was the work of the queen who hated her. The other villagers had believed him too, had joined him in searching the hills for a sign of their beloved oracle. But over time, the search parties had grown smaller, less frequent, until only Leto's father remained, roaming the hills at night while his daughter shivered at home, locked in her room.

But he had not been able to find his wife. And once he realized that he never would, he had simply given up.

Here, perhaps, was a chance to discover the truth.

Leto realized then that she had been silent for too long, lost in her own thoughts.

The girl was frowning. "Come ashore," she said again. "I know it must be overwhelming. Dying, living, the changing—" She broke off with a horrified little gasp, her hand flying to her mouth.

"The changing? What—" Leto followed the girl's gaze down, to the place where Leto's toes were pressed into the damp sand.

"I misspoke. I didn't mean . . ." the girl was speaking, but Leto hardly heard a word. The silt had settled again; the water was clear and cool.

Leto's gown was all but transparent in the water, and beneath it, her legs were covered almost entirely with smooth and shining moss-green scales. They started, greyish, at her toes and bloomed with fantastic color as they swirled themselves up her calves and over her thighs. The only patches of skin left uncovered—between her toes and in the creases behind her knees—were a smooth and unblemished grey.

Through the damp, clinging fabric of the gown, she could see where the scales stopped at her hips, dipping underneath her navel. The skin there, too, was unnaturally grey. Leto stretched out her trembling hands, twisting them this way and that. Every inch of flesh was wrong, a mottled green or stone grey. At her elbows were more patches of green scales.

She was a perfect mirror of the girl standing before her.

A monster.

Her throat contracted. She could not breathe; she could not think. She gasped for air as her legs trembled beneath her and threaten to give. The water was writhing around her, as if it somehow felt her anguish.

A moment later the girl was by her side, catching hold of her arms and gripping them tightly. She forced Leto still, supporting her torso even as she sagged, breathless.

"I'm here," she said. "I've got you."

Leto barely heard her. She twisted against her grip, tears dripping down her cheeks, gnashing teeth which felt suddenly huge and awkward in her mouth.

"For Zeus's sake." The girl dropped one of Leto's arms. Released, Leto lashed out blindly. The girl dodged her easily and slapped her across the face.

In shock, Leto bit down hard on her lip. The coppery taste of blood was followed an instant later by the pain. She snapped back to her senses with a thin yelp and cupped her face with her free hand. Blood—miraculously red, human blood—dripped into her palm as she swayed on the spot.

The girl released her other arm, and Leto pulled it protectively against her chest.

"Sorry," said the girl. She looked ashamed. "Sorry, that was not meant to happen. I didn't know what else to do. I didn't want you to panic."

"Panic?" Leto's voice was a squeak. Her eyes were burning, her lips trembling as she forced the words past them. "I—what's *happened* to me?"

"Come ashore," said the girl for the third time. "Please. I will explain everything."

"I can't." This was not precisely a lie. Leto's legs had ceased their shaking, but now they seemed entirely incapable of movement. In fact, she couldn't feel them at all, and her vision was slipping sideways and a great rush of blood was surging through her veins and—

And then she was standing on the shore, water dripping from her hair, and the girl was there beside her as the wave that had carried them retreated and dissolved back into the sea.

"How did you. . . ?" Leto trailed off. "What sort of creature are you?"

The girl scowled. "I am human."

Leto looked her up and down slowly, taking in again that slate-grey skin and the smatterings of little green scales and the *eyes*. The eyes were the worst part. Or was that the ring of dark scales around the girl's throat, a mark Leto would have recognized anyway? The mark of Poseidon. She forced herself to speak. "You're not like any human I've seen before."

"Look closer," said the girl. She raised her hand sharply and Leto flinched away instinctively. But the girl did not strike her again. Instead, she closed her eyes and brought the hand arcing down through the air.

The water that drenched her shivered and rushed away from her skin in a fine mist. Somehow, the girl was controlling it. How could she be human with a power like that?

Leto recoiled from the spray, squeezing her eyes shut, until at last it relented enough for her to turn back and peer through her eyelashes at the *thing* standing before her.

Her breath left her all at once.

Where the monstrous creature had been, all green and grey and black, there now stood a girl.

A *beautiful* girl.

She was dressed in a loose, pale pink chiton slashed short above the knee to reveal thick, muscular thighs and ankles covered with a shifting layer of scales. Her skin was a rich, Mediterranean tawny, her braided hair like spun gold. Poseidon's mark had vanished from her throat, leaving only a faint scar behind. Leto met her eyes. They were the perfect color of spring grass.

She was, quite simply, one of the most extraordinarily lovely girls Leto had ever seen.

"Do you see?" said the girl. "Human. You and I both."

"I—" said Leto. But she was barely listening. Her mind was swirling instead with the fragments of a memory. A memory of a memory of a dream. *The night before the guards had arrived to claim her, she had dreamed of a girl with golden hair and eyes like the sea.*

The girl that now stood before her.

Leto exhaled slowly. *This* was what Apollo had been showing her. This was who she was meant to find.

"I know you," she said. "Who are you?"

"My name is Melantho," said the human-but-not girl, and smiled. It made her twice as pretty, if such a thing was even possible. "I suppose I have been expecting you."

Leto frowned. Was Melantho being deliberately elusive? "If you—if *we*—are human," she said, gesturing down at herself, "then why—?"

"Oh," said Melantho. "That is the end of a long story. One I hope to tell you very soon. For now, though, would you feel more . . . comfortable if I changed you back?"

"Yes." Leto did not need to think on it; the word had passed her lips before she had truly processed what it was that Melantho was saying. She could change *back*. She may have been changed—cursed, perhaps—but she could still *look* human.

Melantho laughed. "As you wish."

She made another of those smooth, easy gestures with her hands. A strange sensation—not unpleasant but not *entirely* pleasant either—enveloped Leto as mist rose from her body and dissipated into the sea air.

Despite herself, Leto glanced downward. Relief washed over her. Under the ripped hem of her gown, her legs were pink and freckled. Her arms, too, exactly as they were meant to be—though when she automatically lifted a hand to pat the skin there, the scales on her neck remained.

"Oh," said Melantho. Something in her voice sent a shiver up Leto's back, set the hairs—*gods*, she had never been so grateful to see the stubbornly dark strands—on her arms prickling. "That is better."

Then, to Leto's very great surprise, Melantho stepped forward and embraced her, crushing her against her chest. Her skin was cool despite the sun, the muscles underneath as hard as rock. "Welcome," she said into Leto's hair. Something was off about her tone; Leto had the peculiar feeling that she was hiding her face deliberately. "I am very glad to meet you."

Leto gave her an awkward pat on the back.

"I don't know your name," said Melantho, still speaking into Leto's neck. Leto could feel her breath on the sensitive skin that dipped beneath her collarbones. It was a little too close.

Leto shoved her away. "My name is Leto." Somehow trading it away felt like giving something up, peeling away a final layer of protection.

Melantho released her and stepped back, her eyes shining. There was a faint ring of black around the green, a lingering reminder that—as human as she might look—she was something *other*. "Leto," she said.

Leto's new body betrayed her yet again. She had always thought her name simple and plain, nothing like her mother's. *Ophelia.* But Melantho said it with such elegance, such *reverence* that, for a moment, it felt like a name worthy of an oracle.

She cleared her throat. "That's me." *That's me?* Idiotic. She was an embarrassment.

Something softened in Melantho's face. When she smiled— the smallest twitch at the corners of her mouth—it looked genuine.

"So," managed Leto. "The story? You said that you would tell me."

The smile faltered. "Yes," said Melantho. They were still facing the sea, gazing out over the idle currents, but now Melantho looked back at the island in a quick, furtive movement. Leto followed her gaze—and froze. Scales bloomed on the skin of her calves again, as if the monster inside her was threatening to burst out.

Bodies.

There were eleven of them, laid side by side on the white sand with their ceremonial gowns fanned out about them. If that had not betrayed their identities, Leto would have known them from the rings of black scales around each of their throats.

The other sacrificed girls. All of them dead.

She had prepared for this from the moment she had first seen their faces, as they shivered in a row on the hanging beach. She had *known* that they would die, but her own awakening had planted the tiniest seed of hope within her, a seed that now withered and shriveled until it had vanished entirely.

"Leto." She was vaguely aware of Melantho at her side, calling her name. She caught hold of Leto's wrist and *squeezed*. "*Leto.*"

"They're dead." It was all that Leto could manage.

Melantho loosened her grip. "Yes," she said simply.

Leto knew what happened to bodies left to the elements. The way the skin seemed to loosen, the limbs to contort. It could have barely been a day since their deaths. But how could so much have changed in a day? "How long?" she whispered.

"It—it has been a while. It is almost autumn."

"Autumn?" Half a year, flown by as if it were nothing. It wasn't possible. Leto shook her head hard. "But they look . . . perfect. How can they be—"

"They're dead, I assure you. I suppose it is Poseidon's magic that preserves them. Sometimes the sea gives a girl back. But most years"—Melantho paused, her voice thick—"it does not. There has never been more than one in a given year."

Leto whirled on her. "This has happened before?" Again, that

wild, ridiculous hope flared in her. She still did not know if she believed the story of her mother's death, that she had been chosen and hanged as all the rest were; it was simply too *convenient*, that the disobedient royal oracle had been sentenced by Poseidon to die. But if it were *true* . . . her mother could be here.

"Eleven times before," said Melantho. "You are the twelfth."

Leto looked about them, gripped with a mad sense of expectation. "Where are they?"

"Gone," said Melantho.

"Gone? All of them?" Her hope left as quickly as it had come. *If* her mother had come here, *if* she had lived, then she was gone all the same. What was the value in knowing the truth of her disappearance if the story would always end with her death?

"I am sorry," said Melantho. "But you must understand, there has not been a changing in decades. The task that we dedicate our lives to is not an easy one. The changed girls . . ." She broke off. When she finished, her voice was softer. "We do not tend to live very long."

Leto stared at her. Their task? It was all too much. "How did this happen?" she said at last. "The sacrifices, the—what did you call it?—the changing? And *you*. I don't *understand*."

"Let us start at the beginning," said Melantho. As she spoke, she took a strand of gold hair between her fingers and twisted. Her eyes were fixed on the sand, their bright color hidden beneath long, curling lashes. "I suppose it all began with a queen. Her name was Penelope, wife to Odysseus, and she had twelve maids."

VII

WHAT MORTAL TONGUE

Melantho

"Each had been handpicked as a child," said Melantho.

It was a story she had told many times over, practicing and twisting and sanding down the rough edges until the words spilled smoothly off her tongue. She had refused to say more until they had left the beach though, had led Leto to one of the caves that opened onto the shore, and now they sat side by side in front of a crackling fire. She watched Leto carefully—the tension in her shoulders, the knotting of her fingers.

The girls did not always react well—Thalia, bold, brave, *beautiful*, had lunged for Melantho and tried to throttle her; Sofia had howled at the sky for hours—but this one *had* to. Ithaca's future depended on it.

And so did Melantho's, though she would not allow herself to linger on that. She had been alone for too long. She would be alone again if Leto failed in her task, left to her wandering and her hopeless, wretched tears. Left to kneel at the place she had buried Thalia and to count down the centuries as they fell away from her.

But now was not the time to think of her own fate. She returned her attention to the girl sitting beside her.

Leto pressed her hands toward the heat of the flames. She had protested, as Melantho had drawn her toward the caves, that the dead girls should be buried first, but Melantho had dismissed her easily. The girls would not decay, not here. They never did. In the earlier years, Melantho had left them on the beach for days, weeks even, unable to face their slack, grey faces. When she returned to them at last, they were always just as she had left them.

Perhaps the plots in her makeshift graveyard were not filled with bleached bones but with rows upon rows of preserved bodies. Untouched by time, so perfect that they might have been sleeping had they not been lying so still.

Leto cleared her throat.

Melantho snapped her head up to meet Leto's gaze, her thoughts already slipping away from the girls that lay dead on the beach. She would bury them in the morning; for now, her priority was the *living* girl sitting beside her, with deep brown curls spilling over her shoulders and eyes like storm clouds.

"Sorry," she said hastily. "Where was I?"

"Handpicked," said Leto.

"Right. Yes. Of course. The queen wanted the prettiest, the cleverest, the fattest," said Melantho. "Their mothers, slave women or servants or whores, traded them away for a gold piece each and never saw them again."

Them. The lie was so easy, close enough to the truth to be believable. Far enough that Leto would not look at her in that way the first girls had before they left Pandou and did not return. She could not meet Leto's eyes, though, as she lied to her, so she stared into the fire instead as she continued.

"The king had been absent for years, forced to fight by an oath he swore as a young man. Many believed him dead—many, in truth, would have wished it—and they flocked to the queen to clamor for her hand. She rejected them, claimed that she would not marry until she finished weaving a shroud for her dying father-in-law, so they turned their attention to her maids instead. But it was not the *hands* of the maids they sought."

Leto's face twisted in disgust, the perfect mirror of the emotion that surged through Melantho's chest. She could still see Eurymachus's leer as he pressed her into dark corners, the way Antinous's head had snapped about at the sound of her footsteps in the corridor, the way he'd smiled at her before turning back to the maid he had pinned against the wall, her skirts around her waist and her face streaked with tears.

Melantho tasted bile on her tongue, acrid and foul.

"The king returned in the end, of course, and killed the suitors." She spoke frankly. If she did not, she would not make it through her tale. "They had never had a hope of marrying his widow; she was too devout. She had her maids unpick the shroud every night. But the king could not stand that such men had lived in his palace, walked his floors, so he commanded his son to kill the maids that the suitors had raped. They were sullied, you see. Unclean, unworthy of living a moment longer. He suggested the sword; his son chose the rope. Hung them all from the rafters like game birds, then had his men toss their bodies in the sea." Now she smiled and looked up. The light played off Leto's skin, and she shone like the moon on a clear night. "A mistake. For Poseidon is lord of the sea."

Leto leaned forward. "He objected to their senseless murders?"

Melantho could not help the laugh that bubbled up in her chest. "If only it were that. He had a grudge against the king for a historic slight, nothing more. But he took this act as an opportunity, and thus was born the curse of Ithaca. And thousands of girls are dead as a result." How easy it was, to shift the blame. Poseidon's curse. Poseidon's only.

"That cannot be all," said Leto. Somewhere, from the distant shadows of the cave, Melantho could hear a scuttering as if of footsteps. Rats again. They were a constant plague. Leto frowned. "If he was pretending to care so much about the lives of innocents, why would Poseidon ask for more death?"

"Gods feed on the terror of mortals," said Melantho. "Where there is no fear, there are no prayers. But you are right. That is not all. Poseidon hoped to turn the people of Ithaca against their king. Twelve of their women would be killed each year—and the king himself would be forced to command it—or the sea would rise up to drown them. Only one way to end it all." She looked up then, straight into Leto's eyes, begging her to stay calm, to understand.

"We need to kill the prince of Ithaca."

VIII

THE SONS OF PRINCES

Mathias

When Mathias's father had been alive, he had often disappeared. And when he did, Mathias had always known where to find him.

After his father's death—from a wretched disease in his lungs, one that had eaten him from the inside out until every breath came with a soft spray of blood—the library had been sealed. For what felt like the hundredth time, Mathias stood in front of the doors and examined the thick iron bolts and rusting locks that bound them shut. His mother's orders, of course. She had always hated it—hated the perpetual chill and the smell of parchment and the creeping, persistent damp that tarnished the silver and left new clothes smelling faintly of musk.

Mathias ran a hand over the mottled, age-warped wood of the doors. Then, he walked away.

To his great shame, he had not tried to find another way into the library during the few short years that had followed its closure. This was justified, perhaps; he did not wish to anger the queen with such a deliberate act. The things he did quite by accident enraged her enough. Her fury alternated with a cloying, almost smothering affection that was equally disconcerting.

He examined Selene's journal again, pausing at the very center of the corridor. In the months following his discovery of it, he had spent every spare moment poring over its pages. Still, those times were few and far between, and most of the notes were scattered and near indecipherable, so it had taken him this long—the whole of the spring, most of the arid summer—to find a way into the library. One that did not involve having the doors smashed in, that was. Despite his best efforts to avoid her, he was sure that his mother had noticed his skulking about the palace, and she would most certainly notice *that*.

But Selene had always been cleverer than him. In one passage, she described eavesdropping on one of their father's meetings here. She described a hidden entrance, a doorway she could creep in through, undetected.

He does not make it easy for me to learn. He is angry, I suppose, that his eldest daughter will take the throne, and not his eldest son. Perhaps he forgets why—forgets that, for many years, when his ancestors could not produce sons, it was their daughters who ruled us. I think that he would see it changed if he could, and that is why he keeps me out. It is no matter. I have found my own way in.

Mathias considered the smooth surface of the wall. Then, deliberately, he swiped his thumb over a mark on the marble, a curl in the stone that might have been a flaw to someone who did not know better. He stepped back as the hidden panel clicked open and torchlight fell on the room concealed behind it.

⦚⦚⦚

Inside the library, the hours melted away.

It must have been morning again when Mathias awoke, his face pressed into the wood of a tabletop, his stomach knotted with a furious hunger. For a moment, his mind was fogged with panic. Where was he?

His lamp had almost burned out; it illuminated the curl of a scroll.

Oh. He blinked the fog of sleep from his eyes. Of course.

The library did not feel quite right without his father there. It was not the smell of mold as the scrolls that hung from the ceilings slowly rotted away, nor the empty seat of his father's great wooden chair. It was the absence of *life*. There were no cake crumbs, staling, forgotten, on a side table. The light of the lamp at Mathias's side did not spill off half-drunk cups of ouzo or catch on the thick lens of his father's eyeglass. He had always used it to hold his place in the piles of papyrus. All small things, but Mathias had not realized that he would miss them.

Even the cats, lithe little creatures that could find a way into anywhere, did not come here anymore—and why would they? There was never anyone down here to sneak them slivers of meat and spill goat's milk into saucers for them to lap at.

Mathias stretched his aching muscles and leaned over the wooden table, the shine of the varnish hidden beneath a good inch of dust. He retrieved the first scroll from the teetering pile he had collected. Gods, there were hundreds.

He'd examined the tags of each, had started off with collecting every reference to *curse,* to *hanging,* hells, to *Poseidon,* and now, he was regretting it. He'd cleared half the library, and it had only just occurred to him that he actually had to read them.

He tugged apart the leather cord that held the scroll and pulled it open.

He caught the first words—*it has been said*—before the wretched thing disintegrated in his hands.

He shook the pieces from his tunic with a curse.

He had known that the library was deteriorating—his mother

had expressly forbidden him from wasting precious gold on its upkeep—but he had not realized how bad it had become. It would be impossible to find anything on the curse when every scroll more than a few decades old was moth-eaten, moldering, or had been shredded into yellowing scraps to build a mouse's nest.

The next scroll he opened, to its credit, did at least stay in one piece. But its contents, which his father had tagged simply as "hangings," were an alphabetized list of tapestry weavers. The third, "Amathus's curse," was a filthy extract that sent heat rushing to Mathias's cheeks. The fourth, which he'd only picked up because it looked so comparatively well kept, was beyond pornographic. He threw it onto the reject pile and buried his head in his hands.

It was hopeless. It would take him years to read everything, and with each springtime that passed, the blood of another twelve girls would be on his hands. He gazed despondently at his father's chair. If the king were here, he would know where the scrolls that Mathias needed were hidden. Perhaps he'd even have read them.

But the king wasn't here. He was dead, his eldest daughter was dead, and all he had left behind him was one moldering library and a useless heir.

Mathias took a deep breath. His father was not here to be disappointed in him; sitting around sighing would do him no good. He picked up yet another scroll. This one hadn't been tagged at all, but Mathias had recognized it the moment he saw it. It was one that he had often found his father buried inside, one that the king had always slipped into a sleeve when he caught Mathias watching. Mathias peeled it open.

It was full of burned scraps of parchment.

Mathias bit back a curse. The words that had once danced over the paper were smudged with ash, entirely unintelligible. Whatever it was that his father had pored over so studiously—and had concealed from Mathias so zealously—was gone now. In a fit of temper that would have made Selene laugh—she always had found Mathias's childish tantrums so very amusing—he tossed the pieces into the fireplace, empty of both flame and fodder, and scowled at the blackened hearth.

As he leaned back, a fragment of paper, the edge burned and blackened, fluttered to the filthy flagstones. Mathias would have tossed it into the grate with the rest of the ashes had it not been for the name, inked in an elegant hand, that topped the scrap.

His name.

He brought it up to his face and read: *The prophecy of the royal oracle on the occasion of the birth of his grace, the prince Mathias.* The rest of the looping script had been burned away, all but a single word.

Death.

Mathias read it carefully. Once, twice over.

He got to his feet and strode from the library without looking back.

Mathias had spent his entire life within a few miles of the palace, save for infrequent trips to visit the nobles in the far north of the kingdom or the tranquil moments when his mother had come down with one of her headaches and Mathias could take one of the horses up to the tops of the cliffs and pretend that he never had to return.

Unfortunately, his mother did not have a headache today.

Mathias hadn't even made it to the gates that led to the stables, his riding boots in hand, before Alexios accosted him with her summons.

"You weren't in your rooms last night," said the guard after he'd delivered the queen's message. A meeting with her advisors, an emergency. "Where were you?"

"Walking. Couldn't sleep." There was no reason to lie to Alexios, and yet the words slipped from Mathias's lips as easily as the truth would have done. More easily, even. He dropped the riding boots to the ground and scowled.

He was not sure why this interruption vexed him so greatly. He had been expecting the queen's summons, after all; in the last week, piracy on the Ionian Strait had claimed three vessels loaded with silks and leather—silks and leather that Ithaca had already paid for with the gold it barely had. Something needed to be done.

Still, it was with a great deal of reluctance that Mathias allowed Alexios to lead him back into the palace, glancing despondently over his shoulder as the gates vanished around the first corner. It would be sundown before the queen released him again, far too late to make the journey up into the hills and back again. The temple to Apollo there—dilapidated, all but abandoned—had once been the haunt of Ithaca's last royal oracle. She had made all her prophecies there.

Which would certainly include the prophecy she had made when Mathias was born, the prophecy that had been burned away until *death* was all that remained.

His mother waved him over to her as he entered the meeting rooms. "Here," she said imperiously, waving a scroll in his face. "This is everything we have lost, Mathias. You will have to send out some of your guards to see to these pirates."

Which guards would that be, Mother? Ithaca's army was barely a hundred men now. On the occasions when they needed more—the hangings, the festival before the equinox that seemed to cost more every year—they had to hire the sons of farmers and blacksmiths, put swords in hands that rarely wielded anything but a hammer or a battered pitchfork. Mathias sighed. "I will see what I can do."

The queen smiled, her eyes raking over his face. "Make sure that you do. We cannot *afford* this, Mathias, you know that."

He bit down the retort that had leapt to his tongue. Perhaps his parents had been a little loose with their gold, but Ithaca's most severe troubles had not begun until the last year of his father's life. Until Mathias had made the most foolish decision of his own.

Smooth, warm olive skin, black eyes, a circlet of gold on her brow. Selene had been the perfect heir, would have been the perfect queen. He dropped his chin. "Yes, Mother."

"That princess of yours will be arriving soon," she said. That was the way she always referred to Mathias's Athenian fiancée: with searing indifference. "Before the spring. I have had word. I know you insist on seeing through your silly engagement, and you know my feelings on that—"

"I do," said Mathias. He did not cling to his betrothal just because it was the honorable thing to do. He had no true allies in his mother's court; his sisters were gone, Olympia hung on the queen's every word, and all the rest treated him with a kind of desperate veneration. To have a *partner*—someone who treated him as her equal, who did not want from him more than he could give—was almost too much to hope for. Mathias hoped for it all the same.

His mother was watching him with visible displeasure. "Well then. How do you expect to impress her if all of our wealth is lost to the seas? How do you expect to shower her with gifts? How do you expect to feed the household she will doubtless bring with her? Spoiled brat."

She muttered that last part quietly enough that he knew she spoke of the princess rather than of him. If she wished to insult him, she would say it loudly, to his face, without the slightest of qualms. A king, she would say, could not be brought low with words alone. "Yes, Mother," he said again.

The prophecies of the last royal oracle of Ithaca would have to wait.

IX

A BREATH OF AIR STIRRING

Leto

"We need to kill the prince of Ithaca."

Leto blinked at Melantho. "What?" she said. Surely, she must have misheard, because beautiful girls with skin like honey and eyes like the trees did not smile like *that* as they proposed a murder.

Hell—Leto frowned and felt salt crackle on her cheeks—even girls who did *not* look like that would not suggest such a thing.

In the myths and the legends that she had grown up on, the girls did not—well, they did not do very much at all besides an awful lot of weaving. Like Leto's own namesake, they mothered the children of gods if they were unlucky or cast spells of transformation if they were incomparably wicked. A thousand ships were launched for them, not *by* them.

Leto had always wanted *more*, had always prayed for it. Here, she supposed, was her punishment for her hubris.

But Melantho was watching her with a quiet wariness and when she spoke, her voice was calm and level. "It is what Poseidon asked for; it is the bounty that he demands. The prince, his *life*, is all that binds the curse to your kingdom, and his death releases Ithaca, releases *you*. It is the only way, I assure you."

Leto opened her mouth to protest. The death of a prince. It was an awful, ungodly thing to contemplate, and yet . . . She remembered his beautiful, *cowardly* face with its high cheekbones and perfectly full lips and black eyes that had darted away as the ground fell into nothingness beneath her feet. The empty words he had spoken, looking straight at her. As if he cared about the gods and their cruelties, their curses. As if he cared about her.

The voice in the back of her mind sighed, the huff of a feather caught in the wind, and said, *Would killing him really be so bad?*

Leto ignored it. "I cannot kill someone," she said. She pretended not to notice the tremor of doubt she could hear in her own voice; she squared her feet in the sand that covered the cave floor in a fine layer. She was not sure if she was lying or not, if her protest was rooted in truth or in some peculiar sort of obligation. You were *supposed* to object to murder.

She plowed onward: "You're asking the wrong person. I can hardly slaughter a pigeon without blanching and I do that every day." That was true, in a way. It wasn't the act of killing itself that repulsed her—that was quick, painless even. It was the thought that death was what it took for Apollo—if it really was the sun god who had offered her those pitiful visions, or just some other god taking pity on an abandoned child—to acknowledge her. To answer her questions, to reveal to her those brief glimpses of the future.

Melantho's face twitched. Leto had thought she would argue, would launch into some impassioned speech about destiny and the greater good, but she merely arched a single golden brow and tossed her hair over one freckled shoulder. "Every day? Do you have a vendetta against pigeons?"

Leto laughed, surprising herself. "I read the entrails. It is . . . not an exact science, but people will pay double for the perceived authenticity."

Melantho grinned. "You will have to read for me sometime,

even if you are a self-confessed charlatan."

"I am not," Leto protested. "My mother—" She broke off at the thought. How quickly the subject of the prince had receded to the periphery of her mind, and with it the question of her mother. She would not find her mother here, and it had been foolish to hope. But she had a new reason now to discover how she had died and who had killed her, if it had been Poseidon or the family that she had worked for. The family that had cast her out without a single piece of silver the moment she had outlived her usefulness as their oracle. The *prince's* family.

"Melantho," she said carefully. "Do you remember them?"

If Melantho was alarmed by this sudden turn in the conversation, she did not show it. "Remember who?"

"The dead girls."

Melantho cocked her head, birdlike. "You will have to be more specific. This island has seen a lot of death in its time." A pause, a skipped heartbeat that could have been anything if Leto had not been observing Melantho closely enough to watch her look up, quickly, and blink into the light with eyes that shone a little brighter than before. "As have I."

"A woman," blurted Leto before she could convince herself to say nothing. She still did not know what she believed, whether her suspicions were just the fantasy of a suddenly motherless child. "Seven years ago. She would have been thirty, thirty-one, perhaps?"

Melantho frowned. "That is older than they usually are. But I suppose not unheard of."

"Yes." Young enough that the lie was plausible, that eventually the Vathi folk could believe the death of Ithaca's last royal oracle was not a deliberate attack, that it was *fate*. Leto hated that gods-damned word.

"Anything else? Hair color? Eye color?" Melantho's frown was deepening. "How old would you have been anyway?"

"Ten," said Leto. "And I suppose she would have looked a little like me, given that she was my mother." She could not bear to meet Melantho's gaze. She forced herself to stare at light filtering in through the cave entrance, as Melantho herself had done mere moments ago.

"Ah," said Melantho softly. "That is not so much to go on. My memory is not so sharp as that—"

"She had a birthmark," said Leto. It had been a brushstroke in brown, a crescent that framed her face, running from the corner of one eye to the curl of her lip. Leto's father had said it was the waxing moon, but her mother had said it was the last sliver of the sun before an eclipse blotted it from the sky.

A solar eclipse, she would whisper against Leto's cheek, holding Leto's fist inside her own, *is an omen. They say it foretells the death of a king.*

"A birthmark?" Melantho's voice tugged Leto from her memories. Her hands stung; without meaning to, she had clenched her fingers into her palms. She let them fall slack. Her roughly cut nails left stark white crescents in their wake.

"On her face," said Leto. "Like this." She drew the shape on her cheek.

Melantho shook her head. "I do not remember all the faces," she said. "I think I would have remembered that—but I cannot be sure. There are so *many*."

There was a bitter taste in Leto's mouth. If only she could find the truth herself. If only she could *see*.

She had tried, of course she had. Had piled together every ridiculous thing she could find—bread, meat, wine, clothes, every little trinket that the gods might want from her—and had set them alight. Had squeezed her eyes shut against the smoke, had asked, had begged Apollo, then, later, every one of the gods in turn to show her something. Anything.

The gods had not answered.

There had been moments where she could have sworn there was something—a lilting melody, the creak of a door, the gentle press of a hand against her cheek—but then the sensation would be gone, and Leto would be left alone again to shriek in frustration and wonder whether it had been the whisper of the gods in her ears or an echo of her own wretched memories.

"Leto?" Melantho's voice jerked her from her thoughts. Her distress must have been clear on her face; Melantho reached toward her, frowning. "Leto, are you—"

"Don't," she interrupted. If she had to answer that most innocuous of questions—*are you all right?*—she knew she would burst into pitiful tears. And Leto did not allow herself to cry, not over her lost mother. Not anymore. She straightened herself abruptly and met Melantho's eyes. "You were telling me a story, I believe? Poseidon asked for a prince?"

It did not matter how her mother had died. If the royals had killed her themselves, as her father had always suspected, then they were responsible. And if she had died at Poseidon's command, as the curse continued, as—if Melantho spoke truly—the prince lived on, then they were responsible.

Perhaps the gods were not punishing her, after all. They were *rewarding* her. Granting her the vengeance she longed for in her heart.

To her relief, Melantho did not press the matter further. "If only. In return for the twelve maids, for Poseidon swore that they were devoted servants of his, he wanted twelve from the king that

condemned them. Twelve from his line. Twelve men, for the king had never been one to value women much."

Leto blanched. "Twelve?" she managed. She had only just steeled herself against one. Against the idea of wanting it at least. An eye for an eye. But *twelve*. "But you said—"

"Eleven are dead," said Melantho flatly. "A century or two's worth of the foolish and the unlucky." She watched Leto closely as she spoke, as if waiting for her to stagger away, horrified. "So one remains."

There was something awful and unspoken written in her eyes. Leto had seen that look before in a soldier who came to her to beg for her help. The gods had forsaken him, he said; could she reach them for him?

She had not been able to.

"You killed them," said Leto softly.

"*We* did. I do not deny it—I am alive for a reason," said Melantho. "As you are now. I suppose we should be grateful that we were all condemned to the rope rather than the blade. Poseidon might have struggled to restore headless corpses, but a strangled girl is much like a drowned girl and he breathed life back into our bodies as easily as you or I would blow out a candle. We do not age. We cannot sicken, nor can we starve." She paused, then, as if it were an afterthought: "But we can die." There was a great weight to the words, full of love and fury all at once. Fury and a quiet, careful sadness which said *some things are best left buried*.

So Leto left them in the ground. "It will be easy enough," she said. "A blade to the throat, a drop of poison in his wine." He deserved it. He *deserved it*. She shaped her hatred into something wickedly sharp, something deadly.

After what his family had done to hers? Well, why *shouldn't* she take her revenge? She smoothed out her skirts, the material stiff with salt and crackling under her fingertips like papyrus.

"Perhaps," said Melantho. "Perhaps it would be easy. But there is a caveat. His death is a gift to Poseidon, so he must die in the sea and at the hand of one of Poseidon's chosen. If it were not for that, we would have bribed the sailors at the harborside to try their hands at it. But if it's hard for a commoner to walk into the palace, it's a thousand times harder for him to walk out with a prince under his cloak. And"—she arched one golden brow—"his demise must come within a given period: one that begins the moment that the first girls are marked and ends at sundown on the spring equinox. The day of the hangings."

Leto frowned. "But . . . that is rarely more than two weeks. And how will I know when the first girls are marked? There is no fixed time for it."

Melantho shrugged. "Poseidon always was one for dramatics. He reveled in the uncertainty, perhaps. Or maybe he thought that the people would rise up to save their own once they knew *exactly* what they had to lose. They didn't, of course." She flashed Leto a quick, grim smile.

"Perhaps they didn't know," said Leto. "Or they did not believe it." She wasn't quite sure whether she believed it herself, and the evidence was sitting before her, looking at her with grass-green eyes and a golden flush on her cheeks. "So," she ventured. "How will we do it?"

"Ah," said Melantho. Something shifted in her features; she looked away from Leto to stare fixedly at the far wall. "That's another thing. I have been here too long, far longer than I was meant to. I am bound to Pandou now, as it is bound to me. This task, I am afraid, is yours to bear alone."

X

THE WANING OF MOONS

Leto

The skies of Pandou were bright with the midmorning sun. It set the sand afire with its light, its heat.

Melantho had awoken early to bury the dead girls, so when Leto stood again upon the shoreline, there was nothing there but miles of white sand and shards of seashells.

Seashells and Melantho at her side as they strode into the sea together.

Melantho urged her to be patient, to allow herself time to adjust. They could not kill the prince until the first girls were marked—until those last awful days of winter—so waiting would not hurt. But Leto had smiled at her, taken up her hands, and said, "*This* is what I have been waiting for." Now the change started the instant that her toes met the surf. That strange prickling that climbed and wrapped its way about her thighs. "Do you get used to this?" she bit out, through the shivering it brought with it.

"Yes," said Melantho. She turned and flashed Leto a bright, wicked grin that should have been a warning. "But it's always easier to do it all at once. To take the plunge."

There was something deadly in Melantho's eyes, something that sharpened as black spread out from her pupils and swallowed the irises, the whites. It should have made her monstrous. It didn't. Leto frowned. "Why are you looking at me like—?"

Melantho struck, swift as a viper. The sea lurched beneath Leto's feet, a wave cresting up from the shallows. It ripped her from Melantho's side and tossed her up in the air. She had time to take a wild, gasping breath before she smashed back down into the water.

The sensation that enveloped her body would have been easy to confuse with cold. The difference was subtle at first, then so blatant it was incredible. Instead of slowing, Leto's heart began to pound faster. Instead of seizing up, her limbs flooded with energy. She had never felt so alive. It was so astoundingly different from any experience with the ocean she had ever had. Her lungs didn't burn from lack of breath and it took her a moment to realize that they didn't need any. When she opened her eyes, she found that she could see *everything*. She could pick out every dazzling thread of light in the water, every shift in the current.

And there was Melantho. Grey-skinned and black-eyed, her hair a swirl of emerald and obsidian around her face. She grinned, her teeth sharp and shining. The last days of summer sun broke, glittering, through the surface; they had months until the equinox. Months to think on it all, to plan the death of a boy with black eyes and a golden crown. Leto grinned back.

The days melted away into the sea-foam. Perhaps the illusion that hung over the island extended as far as the endless circling of the sun and the moon, to time itself. Or perhaps it was Leto herself that had changed.

Each morning, she would wake early and spend the day out at sea with Melantho. Before winter ended, before the equinox marked the start of a new season and the end of twelve innocent lives, Leto would have to swim through the invisible barrier that hid Pandou from the world beyond and set off for the Ithacan palace to kill a prince. Until then, there was so much to learn: how to direct her movements through the water, how to send her power sprawling out over miles, to understand the changes of the tides and the shifts in the currents caused by merchant boats as they crossed from Sami to Vathi and back again. Then there were practical matters: how to flush the water from her skin and clothes—she was decidedly unsuccessful there—and how to pull it along with her wherever she went, to shape it. How to keep her eyes sharp and her mind quick. Melantho made her test the limits of her powers over and over, so she would understand how far she could stray from the sea before its power deserted her. She learned to catch hold of it from farther and farther away. When she finally set off for Ithaca, she must be perfect.

"You're not very good at this," said Melantho during one such lesson. Autumn had arrived in earnest, the leaves that blew in from the sea shifting from green into a riot of red and gold, even if those that grew on Pandou never changed. Melantho plucked the petals from a daffodil—like everything else, the little yellow flowers on the island seemed to defy the seasons; they grew everywhere—as Leto failed yet again to shape seawater into a bird.

Melantho waved her arms and sent a herd of watery horses galloping over the surf. "You're not trying to *sculpt* it. Just *tell* it what a bird looks like."

"How," said Leto, through gritted teeth, "am I supposed to do that?"

"For gods' sake," said Melantho. "Look at your *posture*." She strode toward Leto, reaching out for her.

Leto wasn't sure what she expected—perhaps that Melantho would reposition her arms or straighten her back. Instead, she moved, quick as a flash, so she was behind Leto and pressed herself flush against her, catching Leto's wrists in her hands. Leto stiffened for a moment; then her traitorous body relaxed against Melantho, curved into the shape of her. She forced herself to exhale.

It was like that sometimes. Melantho's hand would linger on her shoulder or their hips would brush together as they walked, and Leto's soul would *sing*. It knew that Melantho was the key to her future, perhaps. That Leto's legacy would be entwined forever with whispers of a girl with golden hair and freckles that covered every inch of her olive skin.

Well, not every inch perhaps. Leto hadn't exactly checked.

She caught herself blushing furiously, heat surging through her cheeks.

Thank the gods Melantho had not noticed—she was too engrossed in the task at hand. "Do it like this," she said. Her breath disturbed the light hairs over Leto's ears as she moved Leto's limbs with her own, guiding them through the air. "*Tell* the water what you want it to do."

Leto was barely paying attention to the task at hand—every muscle in her body felt taut. Her brain could only focus on the feel of Melantho's skin against her own. Half-heartedly, she tried it. *A lark*, she told the water.

Incredibly, it worked. The waves surged and from the crest flew a little bird, each of its feathers perfectly formed in the surf. It spread its wings and circled the two of them, spinning dizzyingly quickly over their heads.

The sound of Melantho's laughter was ringing in her ears, and Leto was beaming, stunned by her own achievement. She had never felt quite so accomplished—that was, until the foaming creature disintegrated without a moment's warning and crashed down onto them, drenching them both.

"Oh, *damn it.*" Green and black scales peppered Leto's arms where the water touched her.

"Thank you for that," said Melantho, her face pinched in playful chastisement. She picked a damp strand of hair off her face and tucked it behind her ear. The daffodil had been tugged from her grasp; its petals littered the sand.

"Sorry," said Leto.

"Don't apologize," said Melantho. She was smiling, flushed with both emerald and gold in the sun. "I am not afraid of a little water. Let's try that again. A whole flock this time."

She curled her fingers over Leto's as the water surged in toward them.

It was easy, at times like this, to forget *why* they trained. Easy to imagine that they would stay on Pandou and live only in moments like this—with daffodil petals at their feet and the wind tugging their hair back from their faces. To pretend that Leto would not soon leave and Melantho would not *stay.* Leto stole a look at her. Would the breaking of the curse free her from Pandou's grip?

And if it did, would she want to spend that freedom with Leto?

Leto welcomed the waves as they hit her. She tugged power from the water, felt it thread its way through her veins. This would all end soon, as it had to, with the death of a prince. She would do well to remember that.

Leto closed her eyes, raised the hand that would wring the life from him, and let Melantho slip through her fingers.

Leto soon found her favorite place in all of Pandou. It was a mile or more from the shoreline, a place where, at last, the shallow seas spilt out into the great expanse of the Ionian Strait. A rock surged from the water there, a perfect vantage point from which to look out over the swirling currents and to watch the merchant ships shuttling goods between Ithaca and Cephalonia. If Leto climbed all the way to the top of the rock and stood on the outermost edge, she could feel the push of Pandou's boundaries, could lay her palms against them and feel them flex in time with the waves.

Sometimes she would feel eyes on her back and would whirl about, her lips already upturned in a half smile, expecting to see Melantho pulling herself up from the water. But the rock would be empty, and Melantho would emerge some while later from the ocean with her soaking chiton pasted to her body and a little net of fish held aloft.

Today, though, the feeling was absent. Leto squinted into the sun beyond the boundary. "What *exactly* would happen if I went through?"

Melantho was sprawled farther down—she always refused to go to the edge, preferring instead to spread herself out where the rock plateaued, her face tilted up to the sun—and she eyed Leto warily before she replied, "Nothing, I suppose. Thalia, and the others before her, they could always find their way back."

Thalia. That was the last girl that the sea had spat back. Melantho barely mentioned her.

She supposed that was because Thalia was dead.

Leto did not wish to speak of her. She summoned a ball of water to her hand and burst it into a thousand droplets. "Can I try?"

"Leaving?"

"And coming back. That's part of the plan, isn't it?"

Melantho's face went blank. "I—of course it is."

"It seems like a good time to be working out the finer details, then."

"I didn't think we'd agreed on *any* details, actually. I was going to wait until you were a bit more"—Melantho waved vaguely in her direction—"competent."

"I am *competent*."

Melantho sighed. "Fine. The plan."

Leto beamed. "The plan."

"The first step will be breaking into the palace. Do you think you can—"

"Easy." Leto had been waiting for this—stewing on it, over and over, in the sleepless nighttime. It was a distraction from the thought of Melantho, sleeping one cave over, just a ragged wall of stone separating them. "The baker's daughter works in the palace. She gets up early every day to heat the bakery ovens—her father is a drunk, he's useless. She doesn't wear the same chiton to the palace, I suppose she doesn't want it to get floury. I could wait for her to leave, sneak in—"

"Steal the chiton and then sneak into the palace under the guise of a maid." Melantho nodded approvingly. "You don't think you'll be recognized?"

"Do *you*?" Leto spread her arms wide and grinned. Her clothes were damp, clinging to her skin. Was she imagining it, the way Melantho's eyes caught on her thighs, her breasts? She reveled in the fullness of her body; there was a *substance* to her now that she had never had before.

A long pause. "I don't know what you mean," said Melantho. Her cheeks had gone pink.

"You think I look the same as I did, do you? You don't think I've tanned, you don't think I've put on weight?" She shifted her body, looked coquettishly over her shoulder. "I swear my scars have gone too." All of them but the rope burn still marring her throat. She did not wish to dwell on that now.

Melantho's hand drifted to her hairline. "They do that. The water doesn't just heal us of new injuries—it takes the old ones as well. Although, if it's a really big scar . . ." She cleared her throat. The slightest of shadows passed over her features. "Anyway, you look different. But I would still be careful about it. Maybe we could lighten your hair, or—"

Leto feigned insult. "What's wrong with my hair?"

"Nothing! It's lovely. It's just, it's—well, it's *your* hair. If we were going for unrecognizable . . ." Melantho trailed off. She frowned even as the shadow lifted again from her eyes. "You're being difficult on purpose, aren't you?"

"Not at all. But here's the part of the plan I'm stuck at—what do I do once I'm *in* the palace?" Leto leaned carefully back, pressing as much as she dared against the boundary to the outside world. It wasn't easy—her stomach muscles protested as she engaged them—but she was convinced it made her look excellent. "Drug the prince and drag him out? Threaten him?"

"Seduce him?"

"*Seduce* him?" Leto had half forgotten about the barrier behind her already; she flailed dramatically and—

Toppled through.

The wind pulled a shriek from her throat as she reached out, desperate to catch hold of something before she spilled into the waves below. Her fingers met warm flesh. A moment later, an iron grip wrenched her to a halt.

Melantho had caught her.

She hung there, panting. "Gods," Leto managed to say faintly, her eyes on the sky. A storm was brewing; that was peculiar. It had never stormed on Pandou before. "It's going to rain." She looked up at Melantho with a rueful smile. Or at least, she tried to.

Melantho was gone. Where she should have been—where the rock should have been, where Pandou should have lain beyond it—was nothing but air and sea spray.

The lower half of Leto's body had vanished. She could feel Melantho's fingers gripping hers, but her own outstretched arm seemed to have been cut off at the wrist. "Melantho," she said faintly.

"Leto." Melantho's voice seemed to be coming from very far away. "Can you hear me?"

"I can. Pull me back—"

"Good," Melantho interrupted her. "Listen carefully. When I let go, you might not be able to hear me anymore. But that's all right. Don't try to listen, don't try to look. Follow the *feel* of Pandou—your powers will always lead you back here, all right?"

"What?" Leto's voice was a squeak. Her fingers were cramping, were slick with sweat and slipping.

"I'll see you in a minute, then." Melantho let go.

᪣᪣᪣

The water beyond Pandou was *cold*.

As Leto hung there, suspended in disbelief and the swirling current, power surged through her body. "Ridiculous," she said to herself, and the words were a string of bubbles. She reached out for the ocean, waited until she could feel it singing in her veins, then, with a flick of her wrist, propelled herself forward.

Going through the barrier did not feel the same the other way. Leto scrunched her eyes shut, turned her head with a wince as she prepared for impact. But none came.

She opened her eyes. There was nothing there—nothing but the blue of the sea and the distant, swirling grey of the sky.

Pandou was gone. She tried again, and then again, flinging herself every which way as she searched and searched and searched for the place where truth became myth, where the real world broke off into a timeless place that was as lovely as it was utterly lonely.

She surfaced, shaking the water from her face. The obol that she still wore about her neck, threaded on its leather cord, had come free from her clothes. She clutched at it.

What had Melantho said? Follow the *feel* of it? What did that even *mean?* But there was little else to try—after all, there was nothing but ocean for miles and miles around her, no sound but the wind and the shrieking gulls that spiraled above her.

She closed her eyes again and reached out, traced her toes through the water and caught hold of the threads of the tides with her fingers. There was so much *more* here than there had been on Pandou; she could feel every wave that crested around her, the movement of every shoal of fish flitting beneath the surface, and—

There. Something stronger, something she could cling on to. Something that felt familiar, comforting, that pulled her in.

She drifted into it and allowed it to lead her on until, as if from nowhere, it appeared. A shimmer in the water, a distortion that surely could be nothing else. She lunged for it, one handed. She could have cried with relief at the little shiver that went through her as her fingers disappeared through the gap. A moment later, the rest of her followed, and she was back in the waters of Pandou, blinking up into the sun.

"There you are." Leto spun in the water to see Melantho, still stretched out on the rock. She was clapping slowly. "You took your time."

"I *found it*," she crowed. "Look, I'm back!"

She beamed at Melantho, who rolled her eyes. "I can see that."

Leto only smiled wider. "I'm going to do that again."

So she did, over and over and over until she was certain that she could do it blinded. On the final time, she backflipped out of the water purely because she *could*. Her very soul seemed to sing with power.

She flung herself down, triumphant, and grinned down at Melantho. "Your turn."

"I *can't* go through, and you know that," said Melantho flatly. She raised her hand and caught the spray before it hit her, reforming it into a tight, swirling ball, and tossed it into the ocean. "I've been here far too long, and I belong to the sea god now. While I am Poseidon's creature, Pandou is my home. My prison."

"But if you could?" Leto knew she was pushing it.

Melantho sat up abruptly. "Does it matter? You will need to leave soon. We should be thinking of that instead." It was always easy to see when her temper was beginning to fray—the water around them would become agitated, start to lash against the sides of the rock. That ring of black about her irises would darken, the spring-grass green eaten away by the something *other* that always lurked beneath the surface.

It did not frighten Leto anymore. Melantho was as lovely in stone and emerald as she was in peach and gold. Still, she pushed the subject no further and returned to watching the merchant ships and the fishing boats and the pods of dolphins that harried them across the strait, blowing bubbles and arching out of the water with high-pitched squeals.

XI

UNDER THE SHADY GROVE

Mathias

Mathias had convinced himself that the temple of Apollo would hold all the answers. Now, as he walked inside, the tentative spark of hope in his chest flickered and died.

Somehow, the last of the summer days had flown by in a whirl, frantically harvesting the sparse crops, slaughtering and salting, the thrill of relief when the shoals of fish had finally, truly, come to Ithaca. Autumn was gone just as quickly.

He gritted his teeth. He had been distracted by his duties, of course, and the preparations for his Athenian bride's arrival, but he could hardly understand how it had taken him so long to make it here. And how he had pinned so much hope on it.

It all seemed ridiculous now.

The temple had been *wrecked*, torn apart by two decades' worth of looting and fierce weather and sheer neglect. Feeble rays of sun worked their way through holes in the bowed ceiling. Anything of value was gone; the ground was littered with smashed pottery, animal bones, and cracked paving slabs where the weeds had grown through.

"Oh," said Olympia quietly. She had caught him just as he was sneaking out through the palace gates and hadn't ceased pestering him until he admitted where he was going. And *then*, once he'd told her—justifying the journey with some hastily concocted story of reconnecting with the island's history—she'd presented herself rather forcefully as a willing companion.

"Oh," Mathias echoed.

They stood there, side by side, for a moment. A soft wind curled its way through the columns, stirring up the hem of Mathias's robe and sending a chill across his knuckles. He flexed his fingers, made a hard fist, let his fingers fall slack again. If he tried to speak, he knew his voice would break. This was not a temple anymore. It was a tomb—a grave for the gods that Ithaca had all but turned from.

Olympia fidgeted beside him. She had never been much good with quiet. Before everything—when Selene was alive, before his younger sister, Hekate, was sent away—Olympia could be relied upon to resolve every fight, to dry tears with some well-timed quip, to cartwheel down the passageways until they were ringing with laughter again. They did not share blood—her brother was Alexios—but they had grown up together. She had always felt to him then like just another of his sisters.

Now he didn't know what she was. She would no longer tolerate his teasing, she followed his mother about like a lost duckling, and sometimes he would catch her looking at him with a fierce sort of longing that made him nervous.

Eventually, she spoke, clearly unable to take the silence a moment longer. "Did you think it would be like this?"

He shook his head without looking at her.

"Shall we go, then?"

"*No.*" He surprised himself with the intensity in his voice. No. He could not leave, not while there was still some tiny chance of finding something here, something that could explain that scrap of burned parchment so many months ago and the scrawled word upon it: *Death.*

"What shall we do, then?"

He had no real answer for her. He shrugged helplessly and kept his eyes fixed on the shattered stone beneath his feet.

"Suit yourself," said Olympia. "I'm going to look for gold. I bet there's *something* left." She strode purposefully toward a partially collapsed alcove. "Let me know when we can go."

There was nothing to do but follow her lead.

For what must have been the best part of an hour, Mathias searched, relentlessly ripping the last remnants of the temple apart as he searched for something, *anything*, that would lead him to the answers. Nothing, *nothing*. Not a single scroll or tablet. Eventually he managed to retrieve a battered little bronze cup which had been wedged into a crack in the floor, but its surface was unadorned and useless. There was no trace of the oracle that had known the truth of Mathias's life, the oracle who had vanished from the palace before he had learned to walk. She was dead now. He knew that much.

Occasionally, he caught Olympia looking his way, shifting impatiently as she pretended to examine some piece of shattered pottery. She was an ever-present reminder that Mathias should not be here. That he should be back at the palace, preparing for the arrival of a girl he had never met, a betrothal celebration he had never cared for less. And then the sacrifices that would follow it— his throat thickened with guilt. He was the only one that his people could rely on to save them, and he had barely discovered anything. Maybe the princess Adrasteia would change things; maybe she would slip into place at Mathias's side, the place that had been emptied over and over until Mathias learned to equate love with loss.

He stared hard at the bronze cup in his hand, tracing the dented surface with one finger. Maybe Adrasteia would like him. Maybe she would *love* him.

Maybe he would lose her too.

He startled at the touch of a hand upon his sleeve. "Mathias," said Olympia. He must have reacted too strongly; she was already withdrawing from him, already smoothing the injured curl of her lip. Had he always recoiled from her like this? He could hardly remember. "Can we go back? There's nothing here."

"Just one more thing." There was a note of desperation in his voice, audible even to him.

He stepped carefully over an upturned pedestal and knelt in the center of the room. There had been a statue of Apollo here once—Mathias could still make out the patch of stone where it must have stood, where the moss was just a little thinner—but that, too, had been lost. Still, ignoring Olympia's questioning look, he gazed up to the place where he thought Apollo's face might have been and prayed.

His prayers were never the sort of thing that he could put into words, never clear or tangible, just a whirring display of aching feelings and hopes and memories of Selene's face swimming before his eyes.

Sometimes, he would glimpse the chubby face of his younger sister, Hekate, who had been bundled off to Crete within weeks of Selene's death. She had been seven years old then; he'd thought her a mere baby to his fourteen.

She'd be eleven now.

Seeing her again, on an Ithaca that did not sing for her death— that was something he would pray for, something he would pore over scrolls for hours and days and weeks for, if it meant that she could come *home*.

If not that, at least Adrasteia would bring with her the gold that Ithaca so desperately needed. At least he would be able to feed his people for another year, two years, to distract them as best he could from the deaths of their daughters.

Mathias rose to his feet and returned to Olympia. "That's all," he said. He dropped the bronze cup to the ground without watching where it fell. "Let's go home."

◈◈◈

Olympia was notably happier once they'd left the temple and set off across the hills to the palace. She threaded her arm through his and skipped along beside him. Night was falling—always faster than Mathias expected, even as the days grew longer and the springtime crept closer. As the *hangings* grew closer. They followed the light of the moon and of the distant torches.

"That place was terrible," said Olympia with a brightness that was almost bewildering. "Although I suppose I did not expect it to be much better, given it was really the old oracle that maintained the temple and drew the villagers up here. Now she's dead, and her daughter too—"

"Her daughter?" Mathias almost tripped over a rock. He straightened hastily, before Olympia could notice. "I didn't know she had a daughter. Or that her daughter was *dead*." How was it that everyone else always seemed to know so much more about Ithaca and its people than he did? He was meant to be *king* soon.

"The queen told me," said Olympia with a tone of great superiority. Her hair blew about her face as she turned to look at him. "The oracle's daughter was one of the marked girls this year. She was an oracle herself, working out of Vathi, although a rather shabby one at that." She frowned, dark brows knotting over dark eyes. "I'm surprised you didn't know—apparently there was a whole *saga* with that one. She tried to run, but Alexios caught her before she got too far, of course. He told me she held on, though. That she died slowly."

He could not help it—Mathias flinched.

He had not known that, had not found the strength to watch as the battered and bruised girl took her last desperate breaths. He had turned away as soon as Alexios swung for the rope. How long had she struggled, choking for air? Had her eyes been blown wide, the fear and panic visible even through the swollen lids—

"Mathias?"

He took a sharp breath. He had not realized that he'd stopped walking, but he found himself frozen in place, every muscle painfully tense. "Sorry, I—I didn't know."

Olympia narrowed her eyes. Her arm was still looped tightly through his. "The oracles in that family have done nothing but hurt ours. You should be glad."

Ours. He could think of nothing to say to that. He looked away from her, out across the hills. The damage that the sea had done to Ithaca was subtler in the winter; he could almost have believed that the desolation was a product of the cold, the short hours of sunlight, the barrenness brought on by Demeter's longing for her lost child. Beyond the fields, faint pinpricks of firelight flickered in the coastal villages.

A sudden resolve caught him almost entirely by surprise.

"Olympia," he said sharply. "Did you say the oracle—the girl—that she was from Vathi?"

"That's right." If she was alarmed by his tone, she did not show it. "Her and one other, I believe. Why do you ask?"

"Two from one village?"

A note of petulance crept into her voice. "I'm telling you what I know. You may question Poseidon if you think it is unfair."

"I am going."

There was a long, bewildered silence. He looked pointedly away from Olympia, who was glaring at him with disbelieving, probing eyes. "You are going . . . where, exactly?"

"Vathi." Perhaps it would mean nothing—certainly, he could not bring the dead girls back to life—but he could at least pay his respects, could try to learn their names, include them in his prayers. Then, he might stop dreaming of a girl with hollow cheekbones and fierce, furious eyes.

"They hate you in Vathi," said Olympia. It was clear that she thought him quite mad. "You are a symbol of everything they despise. Your wealth, your power, your beauty—"

"And they have no idea what I look like," said Mathias. "Since my mother rarely allows me out of her sight. So none of that will matter. Here," he said, pulling the circlet of gold from atop his head with his free hand. "You'll take this back for me, won't you? And make my excuses to the queen if she asks."

"She won't ask," muttered Olympia, but she took the crown from him nonetheless. "Your clothes are far too fine, still. You'll never fit in." A pause, then her tone softened. "Are you going to do something ridiculous?"

He gently disentangled their arms. "Possibly."

XII

WHERE DWELL THE SOULS AND SHADOWS

Melantho

Melantho could not stop thinking about Leto's mother.

It was a strange thing to fixate on, admittedly—especially when there was so much else to think of—but she could not forget that early conversation, the hope that had flared in Leto's face. *Do you remember them?*

Sometimes was the truthful answer.

Sometimes, their features swam through Melantho's head as she dreamed. She would see them lying in the water with their open, staring eyes fixed on the sky. In her dreams—at least the ones that were not so bad—they stayed like that, gazing at the moon above them. In the bad dreams, they would stare at Melantho. Grey lips would tremble, shape words.

Your fault.

She *wished* that Leto's mother had been amongst them. It had been months—the world beyond Pandou was well into winter now, if the quiet skies and empty seas were anything to go by—and yet she returned to the thought often, wished that she had *something* to offer other than a shake of her head, a sympathetic press of Leto's hand.

Still, she remembered nothing of the woman Leto had described, and as the days melted over and over into cool, starry nights, she resigned herself to the thought that she never would.

On one such night, they sat side by side in front of a smoldering fire and toasted bread over the glowing logs.

"What was she like?" Melantho asked, addressing the soot smudged over her bare foot.

The stick Leto held in her hands—normally capable and steady on a knife or a stone or a bird's neck as she snapped it—quivered. "She?" she asked, though Melantho could tell from her voice that she knew already.

"You said that your mother looked like you," she offered. "She must have been beautiful, then." It was an easy compliment. From the corner of her eye, she caught the twitch of Leto's lips.

It shouldn't have filled her with the joy that it did. She was sure she'd sat with some of the others like this, had made them smile before she sent them off to kill a king. There were few she truly remembered now—only a few had come back after their first mission. Thalia had, and Hebe had, but not after the second time she set out, and so had Timo—

No, no. That was one girl Melantho could not stand to recall. She returned her attention to Leto who, with an expression of drunken happiness, was speaking of her mother.

"She *was* beautiful. And clever. A wonderful storyteller, and seamstress and . . . everything, really." If there was a note of bitterness in her voice, it was lost to the swirling, cyclical winds that stirred the sea. "The village folk adored her, came to her every day and clamored for her prophecies, even when they did not need them."

Prophecies? "Your mother was an oracle?" Melantho eyed Leto dubiously. Leto had mentioned as much once before—or had begun to. Melantho had made the natural assumption that she was a fraud. *True* oracles were few and far between. "She could see the future?"

Leto sat up straighter. In the light of the dying embers, she seemed to glow. She might have been Hestia, tending to her hearth. Or Aphrodite. Melantho felt heat surge up her cheeks. She ducked her chin swiftly as Leto went on, her scrap of bread still pressed to the coals. "The future, the past, the present, she could see all of it." Then, as if it were an afterthought: "She passed that down to me. Supposedly."

A true oracle. In the flesh. Perhaps that was why Poseidon had chosen her.

In all her life—and it had not been a short one—Melantho had never met an oracle. Leto seemed to shine even brighter now. There was *power* in those grey-brown eyes. Melantho leaned into her and asked, in a conspiratorial whisper, though there was no one else on Pandou to overhear them, "How much can you see?"

Leto looked away and shifted uncomfortably. "That depends, I suppose."

"On what?"

"How much Apollo wants to show me."

"Right." Melantho dropped the subject and reached for another piece of bread. Still, she could not push down the feeling that raced through her, like tendrils of lightning stroking tree branches bare. *Hope.* Leto was the last girl; she would kill the last son of Ithaca. The end of the curse was in sight and Melantho could, for the first time in three hundred years, dare to wonder what would happen then.

If there was a future ahead for her, a future where she was not chained to the soil of Pandou, to the ground that held a thousand of her dead, each one a regret that weighed Melantho's heart like lead, then perhaps Leto could tell her.

What path lies ahead of me? she wanted to ask.

And then: *Will you walk it with me?*

She asked Leto the very next day. They were standing at the shoreline, letting the sea lap over their toes, and Leto was trying not to turn green. Melantho had insisted she learn to push away the sea and the magic it brought with its touch—Leto could not walk up to the palace grey skinned and emerald scaled after all—and was now doing her best not to burst out laughing.

Leto's face was twisted with concentration as her scales—patches of emerald that dusted her cheeks and the tops of her bare shoulders—faded in and out of existence. She threw her hands up, the grey flesh flecked with the sea spray she was meant to be forcing away from her skin. "This is impossible!"

"Is it?" Melantho smiled as Leto turned to her and lifted her eyebrows. She knew that her own eyes would be green, that her hair—where it fell in fat coils over her shoulders—would be gold under the sun. It was the easiest of instincts to push back against the ocean as it fought to claim her. Only her ankles—washed with salt water—stayed stubbornly grey-green.

"Not for you, perhaps," muttered Leto, squeezing her eyes shut. Pink bloomed on her cheeks, the green scales replaced with a spray of brown freckles so perfect that they might have been painted on. Melantho fought back the urge to run her fingers over them, to check her fingers for flecks of tawny, to see if they smudged.

"There are things you can do that I cannot," she said reasonably. Leto's eyes were still shut; Melantho forced her voice to be calm, unwavering. "The gods show you things. Did—did they ever show a way that I could leave? Or perhaps you heard something, on Ithaca. A legend or—" She trailed off.

Leto cracked one eye open and watched her, her expression

inscrutable. "I don't know," she said at last. "I'd never even *heard* of you—or Pandou for that matter. The gods showed me something once, but . . ." She cleared her throat and averted her gaze. "Well. Never mind that. I didn't understand it. And I'm sure that I've had many other visions that I've not understood, that I've forgotten almost as soon as I saw them. Besides, Ithaca has done its best to forget the curse. If there's a way, a way *out* for you, I don't know what it is."

"Perhaps you could ask," said Melantho.

"Ask?" Leto frowned. As her concentration lapsed, the green flush had risen again on her cheeks. "How would I—oh." The realization dawned on her face. "You mean the gods. You want a prophecy."

It had been a mistake to ask—Melantho could see it in every line of Leto's face as it crumpled. But still, she could not suppress the longing to *know*. Leto was the twelfth, so she was Ithaca's last chance; those were the terms of the bargain that had been made three centuries ago. If Melantho could go with her, protect her, do *everything* within her power to make sure that she succeeded . . . then perhaps, Melantho's past would unhook its claws from her skin and at last, *at last*, she would be free.

"Please," said Melantho, and was ashamed of the depth of the longing in her own voice. "You told me yourself that your mother was an oracle, that she passed it down to you. You wouldn't have told me that if there was no chance, would you? If there's a way—"

"I'll do it," said Leto, stepping away from the water's edge. She looked very tired all of a sudden, the shadows under her eyes darker. "Or at least, I can try. Do you have any incense?"

"What for?" Incense was not the sort of thing that washed up on Pandou. Still, perhaps they could burn some of the herbs that grew wild at the top of the island, or the flesh of an overripe orange.

Leto chewed her lip. "I don't know, really. It's what I remember about my mother. Whenever she came home, she always smelled of incense. And whenever I tried to see, whenever people would come to me with their questions, having the incense always seemed to help." She laughed sourly, drumming her fingers against the top of her thighs. "It made the whole thing a little more believable. That, and the pigeons."

Melantho leaned toward her. "What sort of things would you see?"

Leto shrugged. "It wasn't always the same. Sometimes I'd see faces or places, but mostly it was small things. I'd see a color, or hear a snatch of song, or smell something. The week before the bakery caught fire, the baker's wife came to me—she was pregnant, due any day—and asked whether her child would be healthy. But I couldn't see anything. I could just smell burning. She died in the fire."

"And the child?" ventured Melantho.

"Turned to smoke and ash with its mother, I suppose," said Leto. "So what I saw was the truth. I just didn't know what that truth was. I know that my mother used to have visions, *proper* visions, a whole scene or a full prophecy. Ones that *rhymed*. The clearest thing I ever had was—" She broke off abruptly, a flush of pink rising in her cheeks as she looked away from Melantho's face.

I know you. Those had been the first words that she'd said to Melantho. And the way she had averted her eyes earlier . . . *The gods showed me something once.* Surely it was not too bold to think that Leto had seen *her.* That their paths had always been destined to meet. "What was it?" Melantho asked. The words were an exhale.

Leto looked at her. Her irises were the hazel shine of a lark's wing. "I saw you."

"Me." A delicious kind of warmth unfurled in Melantho's chest.

"You were standing there, looking at me. I didn't think much of it, really, just a dream, but after the mark appeared—" Her hand went to her throat, her eyes widening as her fingers brushed the scales there, as if she hadn't intended the movement at all. She dropped her hand into her lap again and shook her head. "I don't know why I did it. Perhaps I thought it wasn't true. But I lit all the lamps, got out all of my mother's silks, and I asked Apollo what was intended for me. I suppose I thought perhaps you were a goddess." If her cheeks had been pink before, now they were crimson. "Because I thought you would save me. Not because—"

Melantho couldn't stop the smile that stole across her face. "A goddess?"

"I don't know! I just—I didn't want to die. Look"—she made as if to stand—"are we doing this? Do you wish me to unlock the secrets of your past, your present, your future?" She tried for a smile that didn't quite reach her eyes.

"Was that how you used to tempt your hapless customers?" Melantho lightened her tone as best she could. She didn't know much of fate, but she suspected that a miserable oracle's predictions were likely to be lacking in optimism.

To her intense relief, Leto smiled. A *real* smile this time. "More or less. I'd wrap myself up in scarves and beads and things, try to deepen my voice. There's nothing less credible than a twelve-year-old oracle."

"Well then," said Melantho. "I will fetch the incense."

There was no incense to be found, of course, but Melantho pulled as many herbs as she could find and set them smoking with a heap of oranges and fat apricots.

Leto sat cross-legged on the sand and breathed in deeply. But for the ring of scales at her throat, she was entirely human again, now that the sea no longer wound its tendrils up her thighs. She murmured something in a low voice, the words so rapid that Melantho could not discern a single one. The smoke thickened around them.

Leto's hands were claws, the nails dug into the suntanned skin of her thighs. Melantho had looked away before, embarrassed, as Leto flaunted her new fullness, but now she could stare unnoticed. She was so different now from when she'd first arrived. She had not just shaken off the greyish pallor of death; the hollows in her cheeks had filled, the shadows receding from beneath her narrow rib cage, and her skin was the brownish pink of a ripe peach and flecked with freckles.

Melantho reached out to catch a strand of Leto's hair—loose strands whipped up in the wind, brown turned to brass in the sun.

Leto's eyes flew open. They were blank and unseeing, fixed on Melantho's face in such a way that she did not feel that she was being looked at, rather looked through. She was not one to be unnerved by such things, but the emptiness in Leto's expression made her shiver with unease.

Leto blinked, her eyes clearing, and the feeling dissipated.

Melantho leaned in eagerly. "What did you see?" Perhaps this would be it, perhaps Leto would speak the words that would release her from the bonds of uncertainty.

Leto stood up. "Nothing," she said, and began to walk back up the beach toward the caves. "We shouldn't have tried it."

"What do you *mean*, 'nothing'?" Melantho jumped to her feet and raced after Leto. It could *not* be nothing. She would not permit it. Leto did not turn until Melantho reached her and caught her by the arm, pulling her to a stop. "What do you mean?" Melantho repeated. "How could it be nothing?"

"I didn't see anything that would help us."

"You must have seen *something*."

"I did not."

"Don't lie to me, Leto! That isn't fair. You know it isn't. I have been stuck here for longer than I care to recall. I have been *alone* for decades. *Please*." She softened her voice, relaxed the grip of her fingers on Leto's arm. "What did you see?"

Leto huffed out a breath and Melantho thought suddenly, impulsively, of Thalia. She would need to tell Leto that story eventually, tell her of Thalia's life and of Thalia's death and of how she had loved her. *Not yet*, said the voice in the back of her mind, the part of her that hoped, foolishly, that she might love Leto as well as she had loved Thalia. Better, even.

"Please?" she asked again.

"A ship," said Leto flatly. "I saw a ship, burning, and I watched as its sails were consumed by the fire. The air was full of ash and it smelled of *rot*. There is death on the wind, Melantho. It is coming."

XIII

THE ILL-OMENED NAME

Mathias

The hanged girls had come from all over Ithaca, each plucked from some rural village that Mathias had never seen before but as a scrawl of charcoal on some fading map. Some were more than a day's ride, no matter how well fed and rested Sthenios was. Others were little more than a cluster of ramshackle houses crouched like a mouse in a valley, so that it would take him hours of fruitless circling to spot them.

Still, over the past few months, through almost the whole of the barren winter, he had managed to visit ten villages. In each, he searched for the families of the chosen girls. Some had left, fleeing from the places of their grief, and some of the girls had never had families at all. But where he could, he followed directions to their homes and left small tokens tucked into the crevices of their entrances, to be discovered when he was long gone. With Ithaca's treasury empty as it was, he could not give much, but he could still give *something*—a gold piece or two; each visit eased the guilt that clutched at his heart.

He'd ended up saving Vathi—the one place unlucky enough to lose two of its daughters—until last.

When he'd first set out, racing down from the temple in the hills, he had come to an abrupt halt half a mile from the moldering village gates. A woman had stood before him: a grey, frail little thing, bent double over a walking stick and dressed in a ragged blue peplos. Its hem was dark with mud, and her feet were equally filthy, clad in sandals so ancient they might have fallen apart at her next step. Olympia had been right to doubt his flimsy disguise. The old woman had taken one look at Mathias—even without the gold on his brow, the fine quality of his clothes was obvious—and fallen to her knees. He had thrust his smallest ring into her hands, stammered an apology she had been visibly baffled by, and fled back to the palace.

Now he stood in the same spot and took a deep breath. He had learned his lesson, and it was only now that he *almost* felt prepared to face Vathi. He was not dressed in finery today, but in a stained guard's chiton he'd stolen from where it hung, drying, in the palace laundries. His wrists and fingers were bare of his usual rings and bracelets, his ears and forehead unadorned. The only gold he carried was tucked into a leather purse at his waist. This time, he would not run. This time, he would learn the truth. The truth about *her*. He had not been able to forget the proud tilt of her chin and the hatred burning in her expression.

Inside the village gates—which were in such atrocious condition that they hardly seemed to have a point—he strode up to the first person he saw: a girl perched behind a sparse display of leather sandals.

"Hello," he said. "Might you have a moment to answer a question?"

"Is the question about these sandals?" She didn't look much older than Mathias himself, twenty or so, and she watched him with warm interest. Her dark hair was bound in a practical braid over one shoulder.

"I—er, it's not. Sorry." Mathias cast an eye over the shoes. The craftmanship was flawless, the stitches neat and tiny, but nothing could distract from the poor quality of the leather itself. Doubtless it was left over from making far finer pairs sold to a far richer clientele. These would be worn through in a season.

"Then why are you asking me? I can't feed my family answering questions, can I?" Her tone was gently mocking. When he met her eye, she raised a flirtatious eyebrow.

Mathias hastily returned his attention to the sandals. "The hangings, last spring. There were girls taken from Vathi—I was hoping to learn their names. Perhaps you could be so good as to point me toward their homes too?"

Silence. Even the soft, dry wind seemed to have ceased its blowing.

Mathias looked up. All the warmth had gone from the girl's face. Her jaw was set, and when she spoke at last, every word seemed to choke her. "*Cressida*. Why do you want to know about my sister?"

He had not prepared for this. Before, some helpful villager had always pointed him in the direction of the hanged girl's grieving family. When they'd questioned his motives, it was so easy to lie— he was a man of some god or other, wishing to spread their word and their mercy on Ithaca. But now, looking into the stricken face of Cressida's sister . . . "Was she an oracle?" he blurted.

"An *oracle*? No she was . . . she was *twelve*. What good would a twelve-year-old oracle be?"

Mathias ducked his head. "I apologize. The other girl from Vathi. She was the oracle, I suppose. I didn't mean to—" He stopped himself midsentence and took a deep, calming breath. He could still salvage this. He was going to be *king*. A king should know how to speak to his grieving people. But Mathias's mind had gone almost perfectly blank; he could think of nothing to say to Cressida's sister as the silence between them stretched on and on. When it surpassed agonizing, he forced his lips to move. "How much for the sandals?"

"The *sandals*?"

Mathias fumbled for his purse and offered her a gold coin. There was no use in hiding money in the doorway of her family's house now. "Will this cover it? No"—he took another—"will this?"

She stared at him in astonishment.

"I'm truly sorry." He scrambled. "I only wished to know about the oracle. Her name." The twelfth to add to his nightly prayers, his useless apologies offered to the sky.

"I have no idea." She narrowed her eyes. "What's it to you anyway? Why do you care so much?"

Mathias dropped the coins onto the table. "I don't. I just— thank you. And I'm sorry." He hurried away, cheeks burning with shame.

He did not turn back, even when the girl shouted after him, "You didn't take your sandals!"

❧❧❧

The next three people he asked did not know the name of the oracle girl, either. When the last, her face twisted with suspicion, pressed him further on *why* he was here, her voice growing steadily louder and the eyes on them growing steadily more interested, Mathias fled back to the village gates. Mercifully, the pitiful sandal display—and its owner—were gone. He leaned against the gatepost and buried his head in his hands.

He had outstayed his welcome today, but he *would* return. Next time, he would find what he needed. He *would*. He *must*.

But it was impossible to stop the doubt creeping in. Perhaps this was a curse, one sent down by the gods as punishment for his sheer uselessness. Perhaps he would never know anything more about the dead oracle, nothing but the way she had glowered at him in the moments before he had condemned her.

"Are you going to move?"

"Hmm?" Mathias turned. A man stood behind him, his hands fisted on the handle of a wooden cart. Mathias, standing in the gateway, was blocking the path ahead. "Oh . . . sorry." He moved aside.

The man grunted and heaved the cart forward.

"Wait." Mathias caught him by the shoulder. This was his last chance. "Just one thing before you go. The Vathi girl offered to Poseidon last spring. What was her name?"

The man carefully lowered the cart handle to the ground. He frowned, wiping his hands on his faded chiton. "Cressida?"

Mathias fought to keep his expression level. "Not Cressida—the other. There were two."

"Ah." The man scratched his chin. "The oracle girl, that's right."

Mathias let the silence stretch out between them for longer than strictly necessary. "And her name?" he prompted.

"Er," said the man. "Her name. Well. I wasn't . . . I don't, that is—I'm not superstitious like that, you know? The gods. Seeing the future. I can't say I had anything to do with the little oracle. Not many of us did. Barely saw her, only at night, skulking around after the nesting birds. Took us all some time to even realize that she was gone. She kept to herself, she did, after all that business with her mother. Then her father, poor man." He shook his head grimly. "Drove himself mad with grief."

Mathias had hardly listened to these last words; he was open-mouthed and dumbfounded. Eventually, he managed to collect himself, to ask tersely, "It took *how long* to realize that she was gone? That she was *dead*?"

"I told you." The man's voice was defensive now. His shoulders had gone up. "We didn't have much to do with her! I could hardly tell you what she looked like. It was one of her regulars that realized in the end, when she'd not shown up for a few appointments. She was like *you*—all angry and saying we hadn't taken care of the girl. As if we don't have our own to look after."

"I'm not angry," said Mathias automatically. Every organ in his chest seemed to be twisting itself in knots. He could hardly breathe.

"Right," said the man. "Is that everything, then? Only, I've got to—"

"That's all." Clearly, there was nothing else to be learned. Mathias forced himself to incline his head respectfully. "Thank you for your time."

The man acknowledged Mathias's thanks with a grunt, then continued on his way, pushing his cart and whistling tunelessly.

Mathias slumped against the gatepost again. Of course, he had fallen at the final hurdle. He had learned the names of eleven, of every girl that had died the previous spring, all except one. All except *hers*. Would there ever be a night he did not dream of her, furious and nameless? The hollows of her cheeks, the twist of her mouth—

"I am loath to disturb you, young master, but did I hear you asking after the oracle?"

A man had materialized in front of him. A stooped, ragged

man with hair that fell past his shoulders and pale, waxy skin. He looked as though he rarely stepped outside. He *smelled* as though he rarely bathed.

Mathias found his tongue. "Yes. You knew her?"

"Knew, knew of. What is the difference?" The ragged man waved a dismissive hand. "I know many things. Funny what people will say when they think you cannot hear them. But my walls are not thick." He nodded his head toward the nearest house. It was small and ramshackle, the wooden door barely clinging to its frame.

"What did you hear?" Mathias took a step forward, his heart leaping.

"Oh . . . all sorts. But my memory is not what it once was. Perhaps you could give me a little something to . . . remind me?" The ragged man eyed Mathias's purse significantly.

It was the easiest thing in the world to tug it open and withdraw a fat gold coin. "Her name," said Mathias eagerly. "Do you remember her name?"

"Ah, I might. Yes . . . it is coming back to me, yes!" He caught the coin that Mathias tossed him and grinned through his broken teeth. "Yes! I have it!"

"Well? What is it?"

The ragged man took a fistful of Mathias's chiton and yanked him closer. Waves of greasy hair covered his eyes. The smell was extraordinary. The remaining coins in Mathias's purse clinked together as dry lips moved against his ear. "The last oracle . . . they called her . . . *Ophelia.*"

With a dramatic flourish, the ragged man released him, swept himself into a low bow, and vanished into his little house. The door rattled on its hinges as he slammed it behind him.

"Ophelia," repeated Mathias into the empty air. He smiled wide, something like hope catching in his voice as he spoke her name again: *"Ophelia."*

Mathias was back in the safety of his own rooms, collapsing into his favorite chair, when he realized that his purse had been stolen.

With the name Ophelia ringing in his ears, he examined the cut string still tied to his waist and found that he could not bring himself to care.

XIV

BUT NOW THE STORM-WINDS

Leto

Days turned to weeks, winter went on and on, and the ship did not materialize. Perhaps Leto had imagined the omen, the smell of decay ripe in her lungs. Still, she could not forget it; she watched for it every time she stood on the shoreline as her impending departure grew ever closer. But the seas beyond Pandou stayed empty and she found herself desperate for distraction, to *plan* what they both knew must come next.

Melantho, clearly, could not forget it, either. She was a little quieter, a little slower to smile and to lean in with some private joke, but the changes were small enough that Leto could hope to have imagined them.

"How did you know there was a prince of Ithaca?" she asked a few days later, pushing her toes into the sand of the beach and squinting against the fierce glare of the sun.

Melantho shrugged and looked up from the daffodils she was plaiting together to make a clumsy yellow crown. "You would not be here if there was not a prince to be killed. It has always been that way."

"But you weren't *certain*, then?"

"How could I be? Who would have told me? Only the dead come to Pandou."

"That's not true. I came."

"And you were dead when you came, weren't you?" Melantho grinned. "At least, you smelled like it."

Leto let out an indignant shriek and shoved her away. When Melantho had righted herself and leaned back in, smiling, Leto cleared her throat and spoke. "I bet there's a way out."

Melantho stiffened. "Of what?"

"Of Pandou," said Leto. "For *you*, not just for me. I'm convinced of it. Poseidon cannot always be watching, can he?"

Melantho looked down at her daffodils again. "We've talked about this. If there was a way out, I'd have found it. Trust me. I've been searching for a long time."

Leto reached out and stole a daffodil. "*I* haven't, though." She lightened her voice, made it teasing, flirtatious. The flirting was not *serious*; it was only to endear herself to Melantho, to have her agreement. Nothing else to it. But there was something hidden beneath Melantho's pretty smiles that spoke of something darker, a grief, a *guilt*. Perhaps that was why she hesitated. Perhaps, despite everything she had said, she did not really want to leave at all. "I've barely mastered leaving for myself. You must be curious; you surely cannot object to trying again? Besides, I am certain I'm cleverer than you."

"Are you?" Melantho raised a golden brow. "That is a bold claim." She lunged for the daffodil, but Leto yanked it out of reach, grinning.

"See? I saw you coming. Twice as clever, if not three times."

"Or was that a cleverly devised distraction?"

Melantho raised her hands and twisted them. The sea rose up like a striking viper, wrapped a shining tendril around Leto's waist, and tossed her out into the deep water so fast she barely had time to shriek before she was under the surface, her skin green and grey in an instant. She caught on to her power and righted herself with a sweep of her hands.

From beside her came the distorted sound of laughter. She twisted to look at Melantho diving in after her, already reaching out to grab Leto's hand. Her face was split in a delighted smile. In the water, through Leto's changed eyes, Melantho was even more dazzling. Her skin had returned to green, to grey, but Leto's gaze caught on every curve of her slender torso, the roundness of her strong thighs, the sharp slant of her cheekbones. Her muscular arms moved gently through the water as she pushed it up against their bodies, keeping them suspended and still.

Leto rolled her eyes and brought herself up to the air. A moment later, Melantho surfaced, shaking the water from her hair.

"How's that for victorious?" She grinned, wiggling her fingers so the sea churned around them.

"You are ridiculous." Leto raised her own hands; a wave formed at her command and carried them gently back to shore, depositing them in the sand so that they lay side by side.

Melantho dropped her head back and laughed, her throat and the scales there bared to the sun.

Leto watched her quietly.

She could have sworn that she could see the gods etched into the freckles that spilled across Melantho's cheeks, stars scattered across her chin and the marred flesh of her neck, disappearing beneath the soaking and clumsily draped fabric of her gown.

Melantho shook her head, breaking the spell. "You still think you're the cleverest?"

Leto shrugged. She couldn't stop smiling; her cheeks were beginning to ache. "A display of brute force hardly proves otherwise."

Melantho's mouth fell open in perfect mock outrage. "How dare you!" She jumped to her feet, raised her hands to strike again.

The daffodil crown had fallen from her head. It lay on the sand in a peculiar loop, a shape that tugged at Leto's memory and set her stomach rolling uneasily. But then Melantho was diving at her, kicking up the sand, the water was following her, and the crown was knocked, buried, torn in half.

The next time that Leto asked, Melantho relented. They had been lost for too long in winter; the springtime was coming soon. Too soon—if Melantho's reading of the skies and seas was correct, the equinox was in three weeks' time. Leto's departure, then, only a week away. It took only a small reminder of this—and of the deaths that the changing of seasons would bring—and the escape attempts began. Perhaps Leto was flattering herself, but she sometimes allowed herself to think that there was another reason that Melantho had agreed, would spend her moments alone lingering on the memory of how Melantho's face had twitched when Leto reminded her that they might only have a week left together.

To her credit, Melantho bore Leto's experiments with good humor. She swam with Leto to the bottom of the sea and watched, with an exasperated half smile, as Leto pushed and poked at the entire perimeter of the barrier, searching for a place that did not bear the telltale shimmer, or flex, threateningly as she pressed against it before slipping through—then back again—with a now-practiced ease.

She did not comment when she caught Leto squinting out at the seas beyond Pandou, watching for a ship that might—perhaps—still appear as she had foreseen. Nor did she complain when Leto summoned up the greatest wave she could to fling Melantho into the air, hoping, perhaps, that she could be to the barrier as stones fired from a ballista were to a particularly high city wall. But Poseidon's cage seemed to be all encompassing, all enclosing. When Melantho slammed into the barrier for the fifth time, Leto could have sworn she felt the sand beneath her feet shaking, as if Poseidon were laughing.

Her final plan was the most brilliant, she thought: *bubbles.*

She'd come up with it first after watching dolphins as they blew rings of bubbles through the shoals of wrasse, blinding and bewildering the little fish and herding them into the dolphins' waiting jaws. The sea would be a churning mass, and it was impossible to follow the individual animals as they twisted and surged forward with startling speed. If they did not draw too much attention to themselves—if Poseidon was not watching so very closely—then perhaps one girl would appear much like another when she was surrounded in a frantic multitude of bubbles. Maybe *two* girls would be hard to distinguish from *one.*

It did not work, and she returned again to her contemplating.

At last, Melantho begged for it to cease when she caught Leto sharpening a poorly constructed axe at the base of a slender olive tree.

"Like a battering ram!" Leto protested, but Melantho would not hear any more of it.

"How many times do I have to tell you?" she sighed, "Poseidon does not let go of what is his so easily. You will have to go without me. And soon."

Leto scowled. "How soon? Three days? Two? You're not giving me any *time.*"

"It is not me! Do you think I would do this if I had an

alternative? I would keep you here forever if I could, if it meant that you were ready when you left, if I could be sure that you would succeed! But twelve girls will die on Ithaca *soon*, Leto. *You can save them*." She was glaring, chest rising and falling rapidly.

"When, then?"

Melantho threw her hands up. "I can't force you to go. But time is running *out*; Poseidon is not going to wait for you to be ready! And there is not much left for me to teach you. Nothing essential anyway."

Leto looked her up and down—golden hair, golden skin, eyes like the flesh of an underripe olive. The graceful curve of her neck, the tension in her fists. She was shaking. "What about the ship?" she asked quietly. What if it came—came with fire and death as she had foreseen—once she was gone? And why had she seen *that* when she was searching for a way for Melantho to escape? They were linked. They had to be. The ship and Melantho's way out were one and the same.

"Leto, I—" Melantho looked away. "I can't come with you. Please. You have to—"

"Tomorrow, then?"

"What?"

"Tomorrow." Just speaking the word out loud solidified the resolve in her heart. "You're right. I have little left to learn here, and I cannot be selfish. I will leave in the morning."

Some part of her wanted Melantho to refuse. To cling to her wrist and weep and keep her for her own. But Melantho just ducked her head, clasped her hands together, and smiled softly. "Tomorrow, then."

XV

TOWARDS THE SUNSET

Melantho

It had been seven decades since the last changed girl had died, and the pain had only just begun to relent a little. Still, Melantho always tried not to think of Thalia.

She would try not to think of Thalia's smile and her laugh, her rashness, her habit of tossing her dark hair when she lied—which was a lot. Then she would try not to think of the way that Thalia's eyes had been wide and bewildered that last time she had come ashore, with that wretched guard's spear thrust clean through her rib cage.

But every day of every year in those seven decades, Melantho had failed.

She lay on her back in the dark of the caves and listened to the distant dripping of water. That was another thing about living forever: nothing ever seemed to change. Each day she would walk through the same tunnels, glance up at the same ceilings and the same glittering array of needle-shaped rock above her. And then, every so often, she would catch her hair on a stalactite that had grown a little long and realize that ten years had passed and one hundred and twenty girls had been brought to Pandou and buried under its soil.

All but one.

Something fluttered in Melantho's chest, the tiny wings of hope left trapped in Pandora's box. Leto—still asleep, no doubt, on the other side of the stone wall—had awakened something within her, something she had not felt in a long time. Even the island itself seemed to be stirring.

"*Melantho.*" The shout ripped the silence into pieces.

Melantho swore, loudly, shooting to her feet, her eyes barely open before she had dropped into a defensive stance, her fingers groping for the knife she knew would be strapped at her hip. It took a moment for her to recognize the face of the figure standing in the cave's entrance—Leto, her cheeks pink, her eyes frantic, and a bundle of rope clasped in her shaking hands.

"Did you just tell me to eat shit?"

Melantho relaxed her stance. "Never," she said slowly, "do that again. For your sake as well as mine."

Leto ignored her. "We've got to go!" she panted, doubling over with her hands on her knees as she drew in deep, gasping breaths. "Now!"

"What?"

"The ship," said Leto. She was already turning around; her hair was a wild mess. Melantho longed to tease apart the tangled curls.

"The ship?" Melantho frowned at her. Surely, she couldn't mean—

"The ship," said Leto again. "The burning ship, the ship I saw! I *knew it*! I knew we couldn't go without it. It's here! You have to see it, Melantho. It's here and I understand the vision. We need to go now!"

She caught Melantho's wrist and pulled her along as she ran back toward the beach.

"You see?" panted Leto as Melantho's bare feet met sand. She was grinning, her finger outstretched toward the pale sails of a ship, a smudge of white on the horizon. The bay was thick with fog. Melantho could see little else.

"I see it," said Melantho. There must have been something she was missing, something that made this ship different somehow. She had rarely seen Leto so excited, besides the time she had come across a turtle in the shallows and sat there, a grinning statue under the sun, and watched it until it paddled lazily away. "It's a ship." *And it isn't burning.*

"It's an Athenian ship," said Leto significantly. "I swam out. The insignia is Athenian, I am sure of it. It is the Boeotian shield— they stamp it on all their coins. I *know* it."

"Ah," said Melantho, ". . . so?"

Leto whirled on the spot and seized Melantho's hands. Her fingers were feverishly hot; she was radiant in her joy. "The prince is engaged to an Athenian princess," she said. "If that is her ship— and I am convinced that it is, because there is simply no other explanation for my having seen it before, for the gods having *showed me*—then we have found our way in."

Our way. Melantho couldn't look her in the face. "And you are certain of it? That ship is not burning."

"It will be soon," said Leto, her words rang with such confidence that Melantho almost—almost—trusted her. "I will strike the flints myself if I must. And when it is, when those sails are swallowed in flames, we will strike. *Together.* You are coming with me. The princess will hardly know what has hit her."

She was glorious, divine in her joy and her certainty. But she was going to fail.

Still, Melantho narrowed her eyes at the ship, at the shadows shifting in the fog behind it. It could not hurt to let Leto try this one last time. And when it did not work, she would still leave today, as they had discussed, and she would go alone.

Because this was their final chance.

Melantho did not want to destroy that chance—did not want to risk Poseidon's wrath by escaping his careful bounds. She was not *meant* to go. It was not the destiny that he had intended for her.

She knew all too well that those who meddled with fate seldom met a pleasant end.

"A princess," Melantho repeated. If Leto was somehow right, then a princess of Athens could be most useful. "It is not a bad idea. We can adapt our original plan. You could be *her* maid or her tailor—can you sew? And then it's a matter of seduction—princes have always loved to dally with their maids."

But Leto was already shaking her head. "No," she said, smiling until Melantho could see the eerily pointed tips of her canines—they had lengthened, sharpened as she spoke, as if her powers over the ocean, and the monstrous form that came with them, had sensed that they would be needed.

"I won't be her maid," said Leto, and her fingers tightened over Melantho's. "A maid can only get so close to a prince. No, I won't serve the princess."

She smiled. She was extraordinarily lovely. "I'm going to take her place."

"And *then* seduce the prince?"

Leto let go of Melantho's hands abruptly. "What is your obsession with seduction?"

"What else could you do?"

"Oh, I don't know. How about *stab him*?"

Melantho shook her head, doing her best not to show her alarm at this sudden display of violence. "But he must die in the sea—"

"I can stab him anywhere, as long as it doesn't kill him too quickly." Leto waved a dismissive hand. "We can talk about it on the ship."

"Leto, I can't come to the boat." Melantho heard the frustration in her own voice, tried to temper it. "You know I can't."

Leto's smile did not slip. "I know you don't think that you can," she said gently. "I have another idea, a final idea—I have been contemplating it for some time—but you will have to trust me. Will you trust me?"

Now, her smile did fade a little. She peered up into Melantho's face with wide eyes—eyes that flickered between black and grey as the water fought to make it her creature and Leto, stubborn as always, refused to allow it. Her hands were clenched into anxious fists.

Melantho sighed. "What is this idea, then?"

Leto inched forward so that there was the barest wisp of space between them. Melantho swallowed as Leto tilted her head conspiratorially and whispered, "Do you remember that olive tree?"

XVI

THE MERCY OF THE WINDS
AND WAVES

Leto

"Is that a raft?" Melantho's face was twisted with bewilderment as she beheld it. "Leto. Did you think I have never tried a *raft*?"

Leto felt something drop in her chest. Perhaps it was not quite as brilliant a plan as she had thought.

She bit her lip then spoke, haltingly. "I think, maybe, you did not try a raft like *this*."

Melantho stayed silent as Leto outlined the plan. They would sit atop the raft together, taking great care not to touch the water, and instead of driving it forward with the powers they commanded, would use a hastily carved oar to paddle themselves to the boundary.

"So long as the water does not touch us, we remain human," she finished. "We are not Poseidon's, then."

"I suppose when I built a raft before, I was not so careful." Melantho frowned. "But why can't you just use *your* powers? You can leave anytime, Poseidon's creature or not."

"Because"—feeling a little ridiculous, Leto lowered her voice—"I swear—I swear I feel him *watching* sometimes. When I first entered the water, every time I go back into it, and every time we tried to leave before. Whenever I use my powers, he sees it. I *swear*. He will see me, and he will see *you*."

"I believe you," said Melantho gravely. "I feel it too."

"So you will try it, then?"

"I will. But if it does not work, you must go alone. You must leave me today. Promise me."

"I swear it," said Leto.

It would work. She swore her second oath as she dragged the raft to the shore and carefully helped Melantho climb atop. *It will work.* It was a slow process, one they did not have time for, but failure would be ruinous; every time she thought that the water might touch them, she would leap back onto the sand, heart pounding.

It would work. It had to. Because whenever Leto looked at Melantho, her heart danced a frantic drumbeat and her fingers curled and the little voice in the back of her head said, *If you leave her, you will never forgive yourself.*

At last, they managed to launch: dry, human, unwatched. Leto pushed the paddle into the waves and carefully moved them away from the beach. She could not look at Melantho, could not bear to face the derision that she knew should be written in every one of Melantho's features. It was a ridiculous, frantic mess of a plan and yet, it was the only plan they had.

"I think this might work," said Melantho after some time.

"You do?" Leto turned to her, bewildered, and found that Melantho was smiling—actually *smiling*—at her. Her cheeks had dimpled, her eyes were bright. "Really?"

"Are you going to keep asking me that?" Melantho's smile widened. She reached toward Leto's face. A shiver ran up Leto's body, rendering her stiff, immobile, bewildered as Melantho caught up a handful of her curls. "And you were right, by the way." She twisted the loose strands into a messy braid.

Leto swallowed. "I—What?"

Melantho nodded toward the ship. "It's burning. As you predicted, no?"

"Wha—" The question froze on Leto's lips as she whirled wildly to face the boat, her hair slipping free from Melantho's grip. The raft rocked beneath her but she barely noticed it. The ship *was* burning; Melantho was right. It was as Leto had seen before, as she had *known*. And yet, some part of her had doubted the truth of her vision, had thought it was just another piece of the elaborate joke the gods seemed to have been playing on her for her entire life. Seeing the crimson flames reaching up—as if they could lick at the sun with their burning tongues—unfurled something in her heart. She had made a prophecy, a real one, and it had come true. At least, most of it had.

One part to go.

Her resolve strengthened into a blade of iron. "Come on then. We have a boat to catch."

"Let us hope," said Melantho softly, taking up her own paddle, "that Poseidon will keep looking the other way."

XVII

THE LIGHT OF THE SUN

Melantho

When they broke through the barrier at last, it was to a sky full of flames. Melantho clutched Leto's hand in hers and breathed in air that was thick with salt and tasted of ash.

Behind them, Pandou fell.

Melantho did not need to turn, to look, to know it. She *felt* it, an appalling ache in her chest, a shrieking in the water about her as the island that had been her home for years, for *centuries*, let out a low, dying moan and sank into the ocean from whence it had been wrenched. A peculiar understanding washed over her. Without her, there was nothing to keep it there. It had been tied to her, as she was to it, and now it was unmoored, unneeded.

Thalia had been buried there. Timo too. And thousands upon thousands of others, dragged down to the depths with the trees and the caves and every hope and dream and fear that Melantho had left there. But Melantho did not fall with them.

She had lost everything she had ever had.

She had never felt freer.

Leto's hand tightened over hers—a warning—and Melantho looked up sharply. They were barely a hundred feet from the ship with its heaving wooden sides and its great white sails.

At least, they had been white once. Now, they were a mass of flickering orange and plumes of black smoke as they burned.

The Athenian crest—the Boeotian shield, Leto had said—that had once adorned the sails was a tattered, smoking wreck. As they watched, the sails fell into ash and were gone.

With them, the fire faded. Perhaps the crew had been able to beat down the flames before they burned through the deck.

"There," said Leto softly. "Do you see that?"

Melantho followed the line of her outstretched finger to another vessel—a little, battered wooden thing that was all but lost against the bulk of the Athenian ship.

"Pirates," said Leto. She was smiling slyly. *How can you be smiling?* "That does not bode well for our princess, I think."

They were free of Pandou now, and it did not matter if the gods—if *Poseidon*—turned to watch them again, but Melantho still shivered as she watched Leto thrust her hand in the water. Its power answered her call and surged up her arm in spirals of green and black. If Poseidon knew of their escape, he could not be angry. Perhaps it had been a deliberate oversight; perhaps he had always meant her to be free. The hairs on Melantho's arms stood on end as, with another wave of Leto's hand, the ocean moved them forward.

As they neared the wreckage, the water grew murky and treacherous with shrapnel. Something blackened bobbed in the water before them, something that emitted a smell that was curiously familiar to Melantho. It stirred an ancient memory inside her, a long-forgotten instinct that shrieked, *Run.*

Leto gagged. "Is that—"

It was. Melantho realized a moment too late what the smell was, where she had tasted it on the air before. She opened her mouth to speak. *"Stop."*

Before the word had left her lips, there came a sudden surge in the currents, and she could do nothing but watch as slowly, appallingly, the half-burned, half-melted features of a girl spun to face the white skies.

"Gods." Melantho recoiled from the dead girl, her throat burning. "Leto, are we—are we too late?" She turned to Leto, whose fingers were squeezed so hard around her own that they had lost all feeling. Her grey-green features were drawn tightly together, and she had bitten into her lip so hard that it dripped ruby over her chin.

"I hope not," she said grimly. "We had better not be."

She did not move that Melantho could see, but the water about them *twitched* abruptly. An instant later a wave rose up from the depths below them, scooped Melantho and Leto up, and bore them upward. The familiar feel of Leto's power surrounded Melantho; she breathed it in deeply.

"Do you have a plan?"

"Don't die." Leto let go of her hand and the water bore her away.

Panic fluttered in Melantho's chest. *Plans* were what kept you from dying. It was the decisions made in haste—in anger, in fear, in *grief*—that went wrong. Melantho knew that better than most, had paid for it more dearly than others ever would.

Now was not the time to think on it.

She had passed the smoldering side of the boat at last and the wave deposited her on the wooden deck. She reached to steady herself on a fat wooden barrel—one of a great pile of the things, all stamped with that now-familiar Athenian crest—that was leaking golden-brown liquid. A splinter pierced the sole of her bare foot.

Melantho had little time to react to this new irritant—other than a hissed curse to whichever god ruled over splinters—before the deck lurched dangerously beneath her feet and sent her sprawling.

The burned wreckage of the mast broke off with an appalling wrenching noise and the ship lurched again, righting itself in the water. Melantho crouched beside the barrel, breathing hard. A hand closed over her arm and she lashed out instinctively, her blow connecting with soft skin.

"*Ow,*" said Leto, clutching her cheek. She had already returned to her human form—despite the circumstance, Melantho felt a dull thrill of pride. "What was that for?"

"What are you *doing?*" hissed Melantho. "*Get down.*"

They were going to be seen, be caught, be *killed* before they had even reached Ithaca's shores. Melantho had no idea how to fight, had never defended herself. Had never been *able* to defend herself.

"Why should—" Leto broke off with an expression of great alarm and ducked down next to Melantho. There was an angry red mark on her face where Melantho had slapped her. "There they are." Her voice was thick with horror.

Together, they peered around the edge of the barrel.

They came—four of them, dressed in ostentatious finery—onto the deck with great bravado, whooping and cheering with open jugs of wine clutched in their fists. "I had thought Athens a great military power," crowed one. There was a gash across his cheek oozing dark blood. "Clearly, I was wrong."

"Careful," said another, a slight boy with pale brown hair that flopped over his eyes. "Don't let the girl hear you say that."

"What's she going to do? Shout at me? Stamp her slippered foot?"

"Iason thinks she's a witch." Another of the pirates—a huge man with a straggly, grey beard—laughed raucously. "Be careful, lads, or she'll hex you."

The small pirate must have been Iason; he scowled at his companion's words. "She is a witch, Captain. You mark my words."

"A witch?" breathed Melantho, forgetting herself for a moment. The things they could do with a *witch*. "Do you think they mean the princess? You didn't say she was a witch."

Leto, a tangle of warm limbs at her side, snorted. "There's no such thing as witches."

Melantho turned to her, arching her brows deliberately. *Some people say there's no such thing as oracles*, she wanted to say. *Some say that dead means never coming back.*

The pirates—thank the gods—stopped her from saying anything so foolish. As she opened her mouth, there came a great racket, one that swelled in volume and ferocity as a fifth pirate dragged a struggling girl from belowdecks.

"*You bastards*," she shrieked, punctuating each word with a wild kick at the pirate's shins. "*I'll kill you.*"

He held her tighter, pulling her hair until her head stilled.

Melantho drew in a sharp breath. The Athenian girl could not have been much older than twenty. Her olive skin was smooth and unblemished over high cheekbones and a blunt, strong jaw. Her lips were full and symmetrical, her gnashing teeth were straight and white, and she had astonishingly long and luscious lashes. Her royalty was impossible to conceal; every feature sang of wealth and power, of a line entwined with the prosperous lands that bordered the Aegean Sea. Not that any of it would help her now.

"That's her," Melantho said. She could not tear her eyes away from the princess. The pirate with the beard had stepped forward with the peculiar sort of arrogance that marked him as their leader. He ran a filthy finger over the princess's cheek. She snapped at him and he whipped his hand away just in time with a curse.

"Where's the other?" he asked, stroking thoughtfully at his beard.

"Killed her," said the new arrival. The girl in his arms howled like an injured animal and let out a stream of curses so filthy that a proper lady would have blushed.

"Killed her?" the captain looked disappointed. "A waste. She could have been useful."

"There's still this one."

"All right," said Leto softly, her voice cold. "That's enough."

"What?"

Melantho turned just in time to watch Leto rise to her feet, grinning, and holler, "There's one here too, if you can catch her!" She shot Melantho a glittering smile, turned on her heel, and charged across the deck toward the pirates.

"*Leto.*" Melantho was standing without meaning to, still half-concealed behind the barrels as she caught at the sea's power and prepared to unleash it on the men before her. She had known Leto could be impulsive—stupid, even—but not *this* stupid.

The pirates did not spare Melantho a single glance; their eyes were fixed on Leto, who advanced on them with nothing to protect her but that bright, lovely smile. "Come on!" she called. They had not drawn their swords. They were watching her with quiet bemusement. "*Come on.*"

The one called Iason seemed to like his odds better with her than he had with the princess. He drew his blade and leveled it at her. "Would you like to taste my steel, little girl?"

"That depends," she said brightly. She had almost reached them. If Melantho had not known what to look for, she might not have seen the tendrils of salt water weaving their way through the planks of the deck, curling their way around Leto's ankles and scattering green scales over skin that was suddenly pebble grey.

"On what?" said Iason.

"Are you a good swimmer?"

Leto raised her arm and the sea rose with it. A wave towered over the boat, swaying, then darted forward and snatched Iason up. He flailed, trying to find purchase where there was none to be had. Leto had come to a halt just out of reach of the remaining pirates. She cocked her head. "Apparently not."

When did she become so powerful? A fleeting thought, swiftly replaced with a darker one: *I could do that too.*

A burst of energy surged through the wave and it swallowed Iason. When Melantho reached out, tentatively, she *felt* his fear as the sea pulled him down, down, down.

Leto was kind—drowning was not a quick death, but death from *pressure,* as the sheer weight of the sea crushed Iason's organs and sent his eyes bursting from his skull, did not take long.

Leto reached out a hand toward the remaining pirates and curled her fingers inward. An invitation. "Who's next?"

෧ ෧ ෧

The next three pirates met their fate without protest.

Leto had killed one, and Melantho, having forced herself to charge forward at last, had dispatched two more. The first two men she had ever killed, and yet it affected her so little she wondered whether her time on Pandou had rendered her heartless. If only she had encountered Eurymachus like this, or Antinous. She would have destroyed them.

She had never used her power in such a way, but it felt *right* as she flung them out into the ocean without ceremony. The fish would eat well tonight.

Two remained: the captain and his burly lackey, the princess still clenched in his massive arms. She had stopped struggling so violently. She watched Leto and Melantho with wide, black eyes, her mouth half open.

"Two against two, then." Melantho had left the talking to Leto; now she spoke her first words of the battle. They had both managed to stay human looking, besides the scales that crept up their ankles, dodging the surges of water as they lashed over the boat's edges. "I suppose we are even, at least in that regard."

The captain curled his lip. "What are you?"

Leto had asked her that once, soaking wet and terrified. Melantho opened her mouth to retort, but Leto was faster. "My name is Leto," she said. "You should remember that for when they ask you in Hades how you came to be there."

"My name is Damianos," he snarled. "You should recall the same." Melantho had not spotted the little knife strapped at the captain's hip. Stupid, foolish. She called up a wave from the sea too late, *too late*. She could only watch as he yanked it free and threw it with appalling strength at Leto.

The smile slipped from Leto's face. She brought her hands up—the water with them—but the knife slashed through both and buried itself in her breast.

Leto made an awful shrieking, gasping sound and dropped to the deck. She clutched at the blade where it protruded from her skin—higher than Melantho had thought, closer to her shoulder, close enough not to be fatal, thank the gods—and twisted her bloodied hands over the hilt. "You—fuck—" she began.

Melantho caught the glint of the second knife in time.

"Leto!" she screamed.

Leto looked up, her face slackening in a sudden, infant-like fear as the second blade whirled through the air toward her. It would have hit her in the heart, would have felled her in a single moment, had Melantho's wave not surged over the edge of the boat and knocked her aside. She cowered on the floor, her hair a dripping mess of green and black and brown in a pool of blood and salt water. The sea was changing her already, her skin flickering from peach to stone and back again.

She would be fine. She had to be fine.

The captain smiled. It was clear that he did not think Melantho a threat. He looked like Eurymachus; he looked like Antinous. He looked like Odysseus.

Nausea, sudden and violent, surged in Melantho's throat, choking her. She was seventeen again, helpless, defenseless—

No. The thought was followed by a peculiar, rippling calm. *No.* Melantho had watched Eurymachus die, had watched Antinous die, had scrubbed their blood from wooden floors. Odysseus, too, was long dead. And Melantho was *not.*

"I'm going to kill you," said Melantho pleasantly, smiling at the captain. This was why Poseidon had granted her these powers. For men like these. She hurled herself at the captain.

A moment later, the sea followed suit. A great tendril burst from the surface—a spiraling arm of water that towered above them, blocking out even the sun. The captain's eyes widened, his lips parted, he turned to run as the wave—*Melantho's* wave—came smashing down on top of him. The deck flooded.

Was he alive?

Melantho didn't wait to find out. She twisted her fingers and tugged, leashing the ocean like an unruly stallion. Then she lashed out again, tearing her arm up through the water that was now waist deep and sending a ripple of energy out toward the other pirate, the one who still had the princess clutched in his arms as he gaped stupidly at Melantho. She had changed entirely; she could feel it. She was a monster. It felt better than she could have imagined.

She smiled as the wave knocked him clean off his feet. He struggled to regain his balance as the deck surged beneath him, the water sloshing over the sides. The princess had freed herself from his grip and staggered away from him with an admirable determination. Melantho had expected her to be some frail, weak-wristed thing, but there were coals smoldering in the princess's black eyes as she held herself up against a great splinter of wood buried in the deck. She scowled as she tugged at it, as if to check that it was secure.

The pirate had steadied himself. He reached for the sword strapped at his hip.

"Idiot," said the princess. It transpired that she had not been pulling at the wood to check it would hold. She had not *wanted* it to hold. Her smile was victorious as she yanked it free and, dancing forward with a startling elegance, plunged it into the pirate's side.

He crumpled.

The princess spat on him.

Melantho would have liked a moment to take in the sight of the dead man—because the life had already leached from him as he lay in a spreading pool of blood—but the sound of heavy, lurching footsteps behind her heralded the return of the captain.

Damn. She had been praying that the wave had killed him.

She turned to him with her hands raised.

XVIII

IN THE LAIR OF A LION

Leto

Leto staggered to her feet.

The water that surrounded her sang to her as it knitted her wounded skin back together again. The pain, when she had pulled the knife free, had been extraordinary, but the little blade was a welcome weight in her hands.

Melantho stood near the princess, her own palms raised as the pirate captain advanced on her. The fog had begun to clear around them—a concern, as they might be spotted from the shores soon, which was a complication Leto did not wish to handle. She allowed herself to revel in the glow of sunlight on Melantho's skin. She was glorious. She could have been Athena in the moment before striding into battle.

Leto might have been content to watch her tear this wretched man limb from limb, but they did not have the time. She considered the knife in her hands, testing its weight. She was not so blind to her own incompetence that she thought she could throw it, that it would hit its mark in the center of the captain's back and send him sagging to the wooden deck.

Sometimes, the simplest way was the best.

She padded softly forward.

The captain heard her at the very last second. He started, turned, his face a mask of surprise as Leto slipped the knife in between his ribs and twisted, hard. His blood was a spray as fine as the lightening mist; his pupils were huge as he fell to the deck.

Leto did not wait for his heart to stop. She called the waves to her and they carried him out into the ocean as the last of his life slipped from between his fingers. She had killed three men today. She took a deep breath. One more. One more boy, with golden skin and a golden crown, and then she was free.

"What," said a sharp voice, a voice that curled with the accent of the mainland, "in the name of *every single god*, just happened?"

Leto had almost forgotten about the princess. Now the realization was a crushing weight in her chest, a pressure that squeezed tighter and tighter and a voice that whispered, *Here, this is where it stops being easy.*

Because they would have to kill the princess too.

⑥ ⑥ ⑥

Leto had frozen where she stood, gazing at the girl as understanding slowly dawned on her. They could not let her live, could not risk her telling anyone what she had seen. Leto had not hesitated much with the pirates who had held her—they had known the risks they were taking, they had *deserved* it—but this girl's only crime was being rich. Being a target.

It was not *fair*.

Leto knew that her guilt would be painted over her every feature, saw her own trepidation reflected in the princess's wide, black eyes as the girl hooked a fist into her chiton, pulling the hem off the damp, soot-covered deck. She took a wavering step backwards and then another.

"You are not here to save me, are you?" she asked. She did not sound surprised by this. She sounded *tired*, resigned.

Leto opened her mouth to speak and found that she could not. This girl was innocent; she was young, she was beautiful, she had everything to live for and—

And she had just thrown a knife at Leto's face.

"*Shit*," Leto yelped, and dived out of the way. The knife—Leto had no idea where the princess had found it; if she hadn't been so startled she might have been impressed—missed her by an inch and sailed over the edge of the boat.

"Oh, don't do that." It was Melantho. Leto had almost forgotten about her; she had been too occupied with contemplating the appalling task ahead of her. The familiar set of Melantho's jaw was a welcome sight, even if there was a peculiar blackness in her eyes. Melantho would know what to do.

Melantho did not look at her. She frowned at the princess. "What's your name?"

The princess frowned back. "I think you know my name."

Feeling left out, Leto frowned too. She did not like way the princess was speaking to Melantho, the arrogant assumption that they should know who she was. Even if she was technically right. "*I* think you think you're more famous than you are."

The princess tossed her head. "My name is Princess Adrasteia, second daughter of King Elpidios of Athens and Queen Antigo—"

"Adrasteia, then," interrupted Melantho. Her voice was surprisingly soft. Leto recognized the tone and felt her heart sink. Melantho, too, did not want to kill the girl. But one of them had to. "I won't lie to you, Adrasteia. We are not here to help you."

"To kill me?" asked the princess. Her voice was admirably calm. Flat, cold. "Hold me to ransom?" She laughed. "I can assure you, my father will not pay half as much as you are hoping for."

"We don't want *money*." The words had tumbled from Leto's

lips before she could stop them. It was an instinct, one that was not so easily unlearned. Sometimes the noblemen and women of Ithaca would come to her seeking her fortunes. They would look down their noses at her; their words would *drip* with the insinuation that she needed them far more than they would ever need her. That she needed their *money*.

They were right. That was what made it hurt.

She scowled at the princess. "We're trying to save people, *actually*."

The princess raised an eyebrow. "How heroic. And where do I come into it?"

"You don't," said Leto. Her sympathy was fading, scrubbed away by the look of lazy superiority spread across Adrasteia's fine features. "I suppose you were right—we did know who you are. And who your betrothed is. The prince has never met you, has he? He's got no idea what you look like, sound like. You're nothing to him but a royal seal and a chest of gold, two things we can very easily take from you."

She wasn't sure where her anger had come from, but it ebbed away very suddenly as her words landed, as Adrasteia's eyes widened in something that might have been genuine fear. "You want to *pretend* to be me?" Her eyes narrowed as fast as they had flared open. "You want to marry the prince?"

"We want to kill the prince," said Melantho. Her voice was clear and candid as she took a step toward Adrasteia. "It is . . . necessary. It will alleviate a great amount of suffering, you must understand. There is a curse—"

"I am nothing to the prince," interrupted Adrasteia.

Melantho blinked. "Pardon?"

Adrasteia turned to Leto now. She looked away hurriedly,

struck suddenly by the fear that Melantho would notice her admiration of the princess, and then found herself wondering whether or not Melantho would *care* that she admired the princess. She felt very hot.

"I am nothing to the prince," said Adrasteia again, and Leto seized gratefully upon the words.

"No," she said, "and—"

"And he is nothing to me," said Adrasteia abruptly. "I will help you."

"You—what?"

Adrasteia shrugged a shoulder. "It's that or die, I suppose?"

Leto gazed at her blankly for a moment, then turned helplessly to Melantho. Adrasteia couldn't help them, could she? Their plan was already so vague, so hastily concocted, they could not risk discovery by bringing the princess along with them.

"You can't come with us," said Melantho.

Leto exhaled with relief. There, she no longer had to make the decision.

"I don't want to," said Adrasteia. "You'll let me go. And I'll keep my mouth *shut*. I swear it, in the name of every god there is." She smiled, sly and secretive and . . . hopeful. "There is a world I want to see before I am inevitably engaged to some other prince in some other land that I do not wish to be tethered to. Here." She yanked at the heavy gold bracelets around her wrists. "You'll need these. There's a chiton in one of those trunks for the equinox festival—do wear it, it was expensive. And my seal ring, and the letter from my father. I have drafted a reply already, confirming my arrival. It is very rude, but you can finish it off and send it. I don't care."

Her smile had become a grin. She thrust the bracelets into Melantho's hands and set about tugging off a fat silver ring.

Leto looked at Melantho. Melantho looked back.

"Well?" said Adrasteia.

Melantho offered Leto the bangles.

Leto accepted them.

She slipped them onto her wrists. They were plain, nothing like the elaborate earrings in Adrasteia's ears or the dazzling array of rings that adorned her fingers. And they were *heavy*; they clattered together as she turned her hands this way and that. She could not understand why Adrasteia wore them.

"What are *those*?"

Leto raised her head in alarm at the sharp, furious sound of Melantho's voice. Melantho had suddenly lunged for Adrasteia, had caught her wrists up in her hands and was glowering at them.

Leto followed her gaze.

Adrasteia's olive skin was smooth and perfect, brushed over with a delicate smattering of dark brown beauty marks. Her fingers were soft and uncalloused, the sign of a girl who had never done a day's work in her life, but her wrists were circled with raw, red marks. Leto had seen marks like that before on her own wrists— the bite of the ropes that had bound her as her hair was braided, as she was sewn into a white gown. Her breath left her all at once.

"The pirates?" she managed.

Melantho replied before Adrasteia could. "These are old," she said very quietly. "Aren't they?"

Adrasteia nodded.

"*Why*?" asked Melantho.

The wind whistled around the smoking remnants of the ship. Adrasteia did not speak for several moments. Then, "My father believes that I should like to be married. I believe that I should *not*. He is not the most persuasive of men, you see, so he felt obliged to trial a— Well, a more *compelling* method, shall we say?" Her smile was bitter.

Leto gaped at her. As ridiculous as it was, she had never considered that the princess would have been anything but willing to travel to Ithaca, to marry its beautiful, craven prince. And she had certainly not considered that Adrasteia's father would disregard his daughter's wishes so easily, that he would clap her in irons and force her across the seas against her will.

"And what *should* you like?" asked Melantho.

"What?" Adrasteia's eyes widened and flicked, briefly, to Melantho's face. Then, apparently finding that Melantho was *not* joking—as Leto had known she would not be—she smiled. A real one this time. "I should like to go to Delphi, to meet the oracles there. Then I should like to go farther, out onto the seas that are as yet uncharted, to find the islands that are always shrouded in mists, the ones that you cannot find unless you know where you are going. They say there are witches there. I should like very much to meet one."

"I suppose," said Melantho, "that your father would not allow that."

"He would not."

"And you believe you will find your witches?"

Adrasteia smiled, sharp and vicious, and jerked her head at Leto. "I see that mark on your throat, creature. Whatever you are—nymph, demigod—"

"*Human*," said Leto, just as Melantho had said to her once. "I am human."

"I don't believe you," said Adrasteia. "But it is no matter. There are stranger things to find in this world than a girl with a fish throat—"

"Excuse me?" The scales ringing her neck were not *fishy*. She had not seen a fish with scales that glittered like obsidian, all greens and subtle purples in the sun.

"Well then," said Melantho hastily. "You promise. You won't breathe a word of this to anyone, will you?"

Adrasteia's smile widened. Leto caught a glimpse of something lurking behind the princess's eyes, a vicious sort of pleasure, a wickedness, and an *understanding.* Caged birds, she supposed, learned to recognize the sound of each other's songs.

"I will say nothing to anyone," said Adrasteia. "Besides, my crew are all dead."

"I'm sorry," said Melantho.

Leto said nothing. The crew had been dead when they'd arrived. She had no obligation to be sorry. Besides, Adrasteia did not sound *sad.* She sounded thoughtful, as though pointing out a scuff on a tiled floor.

"I'm not sorry," said Adrasteia. "Every hand on this ship is— was—loyal to my father. Every one of them betrayed me. Well, perhaps one did not, but . . . I suppose it does not matter now. I will not follow in their footsteps. *I* keep my word. I will swear it again, to every god that will listen." She reached, swift as a viper, for Melantho's waist, for the knife thrust through the tie there.

Leto started, made to stop her. Melantho did not move.

Adrasteia pulled the knife free and dashed it across her palm. Blood dripped onto the deck. "I *swear it,*" she repeated. "No one will ever discover what happened here today. Not from me."

"Good," said Melantho. "Good." She had been tense, coiled, ever since she had sighted the marks of Adrasteia's bondage. Now she relaxed, straightened, took the knife from Adrasteia, and wiped it clean on the skirt of her chiton. "We can take the ship's rowing boat—I assume it has one?"

Adrasteia nodded.

"Good. There is a boat that the pirates left, a small one. It will take you to the harbors of Cephalonia. You will make your own way from there; I think that you are clever enough to make it to Delphi unharmed. Take what you need from here, leave the rest for us." A pause. "One last thing. How many days is it until the spring equinox? We have been . . . away awhile, you see."

Adrasteia raised her brows but did not press Melantho. "Eleven days."

Melantho winced. "Eleven. Right. Thank you."

Leto listened silently. They were letting Adrasteia go, then. And in a matter of days, once the first girls were chosen, they would try to kill her fiancé.

Here was one life spared at least.

A last thought lingered: that it might be the only one.

XIX

THE SUN EITHER SETS OR RISES

Melantho

When they were done with this, Melantho never wanted to set foot on a ship again. She was sure Leto would agree with her.

They stood on the deck facing each other. Adrasteia's trunks were loaded into the rapidly sinking ship's rowing boat, the last of the bodies cast overboard. Adrasteia would be on Cephalonia by now—Melantho had helped her into the pirates' abandoned boat and commanded the sea to take it across the strait, but she'd finally lost her connection with the boat, so there was nothing left to do but pray that the princess would keep her word. Leto had shed her torn chiton and changed into one of Adrasteia's extravagant gowns. Before leaving, the princess had found her a small chest of cosmetics, had darkened her brows and eyes, stained her lips bloodred. Still, Leto did not look particularly regal; she was grim faced and very wet. "You think she'll find her witches?"

"I don't see why not."

"I still don't believe in them. Even after"—she waved a hand at Melantho—"all this. It's just *impossible*, isn't it?"

Melantho smiled. She wanted to sweep Leto's hair back from her face—it had fallen from its braids again—and remind her that there were more extraordinary things in the world than she could imagine. She wanted to brush a thumb over her full bottom lip.

Instead, she ran a hand over Leto's shoulder, the thick fabric there. She knew that the skin underneath was still pink and puckered, but it was healing. "We should sink the ship," she said. "Someone will find it if we do not. We cannot take another chance, we cannot—"

The trapdoor in the center of the ruined deck banged open and something—*someone*—clambered out.

A girl. She had not seen them yet; she was facing the wrong way, her shoulders hunched inward, as if she were in pain.

She was dressed in a soaking, yellow chiton, the material plastered to her slight frame. She must have been hiding belowdecks, cowering behind some jewel-filled trunk or other as the rest of the household was slaughtered. Now she swayed unsteadily on her feet and blinked into the sunlight.

"Princess?" she called.

But the princess was gone. Melantho saw the horror in Leto's face, the crumpling of her brows, as the realization dawned on her and knew that it would be reflected in her own. Adrasteia's words rang in her ears: *"Every hand on this ship is—was—loyal to my father. Every one of them betrayed me."* Which meant that they could not let this girl go. They had already risked too much.

Leto's hands shook, her mouth twisted with indecision.

Melantho moved.

It should not have been so easy to take the maid in her arms, to pull her close, to thrust the knife into her chest. But it was. The maid died without a sound.

It was only then that Melantho saw the wound that had already opened the girl's belly to the sea air, a wound that would have doubtless killed her. Struck by one of the pirates, surely.

Melantho stared at it wordlessly, then walked to the edge of the boat—ignoring Leto's voice, the frantic question in it—and vomited over the edge.

◉◉◉

Leto had stayed on the deck as the boat began to sink. Melantho watched her silently.

She could not seem to look away from the spill of blood on the wood, the place where the maid had taken her last bubbling breath.

When she was done with her retching, Melantho had cast the dead girl out onto the sea with a gold piece taken from the princess's chest. That would be more than enough to buy her passage across the Styx, to the afterlife waiting beyond.

Melantho hoped that it would be a kind one.

"Leto." Melantho walked to her. She should say something. Words of comfort, perhaps. But what was there to say? They stood there, side by side, until Melantho could stand the silence no longer. She reached for Leto's shoulder, pulled back at the last moment, turned again to leave. "It was necessary," she said. There were rings on Leto's hands, part of her princess guise, fat gold things studded with gems. Melantho wanted to pull them off one by one and toss them into the ocean, wanted to fall to her knees and say, *Gods, is this what it feels like? To kill an innocent? I did not know.*

Instead, she said, "Breaking curses is never as simple as you hope."

Leto did not reply.

"Come on," said Melantho, gentler this time. "We should go. The ship's rowboat isn't in good shape, either. We'll be lucky if it makes it to shore."

XX

THE FAIR FIELDS

Leto

Melantho's prediction had been correct. The remnants of their escape boat, peppered with holes and filled with water, did not last long. By the time they glimpsed the Ithacan shores, it was about as far from seaworthy as was possible. Melantho had thrown herself over the side without a word and swum beneath it, using her powers to keep it together as best she could. It had been a relief to watch her go; Leto had not been able to find the words to say to her anyway.

I understand. But she *didn't*, not really.

Each of the pirates had *earned* their fate. It had been but a small task to convince herself that they deserved to die, to fling them from the ship and let the ocean do the rest for her.

The maid, though—

She had been dying; Leto had seen it in the set of her shoulders and the shake of her hands before Melantho had embraced her. But she had been innocent still. And now she was dead.

Returned to Ithaca at last, Leto watched grimly from the harbor as the boat finally sank below the surface. Melantho resurfaced nearby, baring elongated canines, ash skinned with hair like the depths of the sea. She heaved a final trunk onto dry land.

They had taken only as much as they could fit in the ruined boat—some gowns, a few jewels, not remotely as much as they needed for their charade. They would have to find some excuse for that later. For now, Leto was too exhausted to do anything but clutch at her shoulder and wonder at the speed at which the wound had stopped bleeding and closed over into a puckered scar. There was almost nothing left of it now, hidden beneath the wide shoulders of one of Adrasteia's chitons. "How are we going to explain all this? We come alone, with half of Adrasteia's possessions missing."

"The truth: attacked by pirates," said Melantho. "Followed by a daring escape, of course."

Leto could only force herself to smile. Her belly was a flutter of nerves.

"Your hair," said Melantho. "It's wet."

"Oh," said Leto. She could wield the sea like a blade, command it to throw grown men out into the dark water, but the *subtler* things were still a challenge. She had not *quite* perfected the art of commanding the water from her hair without leaving it dry and painfully frizzy. "I hadn't thought about that."

Her dismay must have been plain. "Let me do it," said Melantho.

Obediently, Leto bowed her head. Melantho ran her hands carefully through the strands, teasing the knots apart and pulling shining threads of water away. At last, Leto's own dark-chestnut curls fell loosely around her face. Melantho brushed them back and tucked them carefully behind her ear. "There," she said.

They were dangerously close together, closer than they had been since Leto had looked into Melantho's future and smelled death in the air. But perhaps Melantho thought that the prediction had already been lived out. The pirates were dead, after all. The maid too.

Leto could believe that it was over.

Melantho had not moved away. Her eyes were fixed on Leto's, burning into them.

"My chiton is still wet," said Leto softly. "A princess wouldn't turn up soaking wet."

"Don't be ridiculous. You won't be turning up soaking wet. Here," said Melantho. She reached out to run her hands over Leto's waist. The fabric shivered—or was that Leto herself?—under her touch and dried. Melantho paused, her hands brushing Leto's hips. "That's better."

Leto looked down at the chiton, then back up to Melantho. She swallowed. "It doesn't fit me."

"It's undone," said Melantho. Without warning, she caught Leto by the waist and spun her around, pulling the skirts into place and tugging the sash tight. The moment that had hung between them was shattered. It was a startling relief, though the feel of Melantho's hands through the thin material sent another peculiar shivering up Leto's back. It must have been colder than she thought.

Leto opened her mouth to speak. The words seemed to lose themselves before they reached her lips. "I—" she managed, clearing her throat and turning so that Melantho's hands skimmed over the tops of her hips but did not let go. "How do I look? The makeup?"

Melantho's eyes moved slowly over Leto's face. "There's something on your cheek," she said at last.

"Oh." Leto reached up.

"I've got it." Melantho withdrew her hands from Leto's hips; their absence left the flesh there prickling in the cool wind, but Leto barely noticed it as Melantho reached up and swiped her thumb deliberately over the skin at Leto's cheek. "There," she said. "Beautiful."

Melantho was becoming gradually less green as the water dried from her skin. The scales faded from her throat, to be replaced with that red, raw scar. They were so close to each other that Leto could have counted the freckles appearing in a tawny spray over Melantho's nose. She could pick out the red patches on Melantho's lips where her teeth had dug in. It would be so easy to just lean forward and—

They both jumped at the sound of some distant horn blowing. A herdsman, calling in his flock, perhaps, or a sailor signaling his ship's arrival to the shore.

Melantho looked away. There was a pale pink ribbon in her hand; she knotted it deftly over the mark at her throat. Leto frowned at it. The mark of the rope was not what gave her pause— its sister curled over her own skin—it was the fact that it was the *only* blemish. There were no scales there, nothing to mark Melantho as one of Poseidon's chosen few. But that did not make sense. The only girls that washed ashore on Pandou were the hanged girls, Melantho had made that clear enough.

Perhaps the passage of time had stolen the scales—would Leto's own eventually fade from her throat? She brushed her hand along their soft edges.

Melantho's voice yanked her from her thoughts.

"Come on," she said shortly. "We shouldn't be wasting our time here." With a single sharp movement she sent the water spinning out from her own chiton, her own skin. Her hair sprang back up into golden curls. She turned and began up the path to the palace, leaving Leto to loop a thick golden necklace about her neck and follow.

She shook out her skirts as she went to hide the flush of green that still lay beneath them.

XXI

FALL TO, AND WELCOME

Melantho

They reached the palace gates as the afternoon sun began to cool.

Melantho had managed to convince two Vathi boys to carry the bags for a silver piece each. She should have been outraged by their blatant swindling, but she was too nervous and exhausted to care. The sun was punishingly hot and being out of the water had Melantho on the verge of collapse. She had not left Poseidon's domain for centuries; Ithaca felt like another world.

Leto didn't look much better. The walk in Adrasteia's heavy, elaborate gown had sent rivulets of sweat cascading down her neck. The princess's careful makeup was melting down her face.

"Excuse me," Melantho panted to the guard manning the gate. He gave her a doubtful look. "This is the princess Adrasteia of Athens," she said, indicating Leto, who managed to raise a limp hand in greeting. Her face was beet red. "She would like to request an audience with the prince."

The guard's doubt morphed into blatant disbelief. "Princess?" he repeated.

Leto straightened, patting down her sweat-dampened curls and conspicuously angling her hand to flash him the assortment of heavy, bejeweled rings and the silver signet. Melantho fought down a smile. Leto looked like Thalia had when she'd returned once from

Ithaca with a chest of jewelry: a bloodstained child playing at dress up. She'd been dripping in gems for months until she'd managed to lose them all.

Sometimes, Melantho would find a stray ruby set in a battered silver ring and the memories would grip her throat so tightly it felt like choking. Thalia had taken so many risks. Idiotic girl. Now, though, the grief was not so fierce, tempered by the sight of Leto puffing her chest out and rising up on her toes. "You were expecting me, I assume?"

The guard's eyes were fixed on the rings. His hesitation was written over every feature, but Melantho knew that he would not risk his position by refusing entry to a princess. Clearly, he knew it too; he dropped his head in a swift bow. "Your grace, welcome to Ithaca. You and your men may enter."

"My men?" Leto's voice rose. The panic was clear in her expression.

"These are not ours," said Melantho quickly, gesturing back to the boys that were still loitering with the bags. "They were helping us this far. We were set upon by pirates on the strait, you see. Our men are—" She lowered her chin and blinked up at the guard through her lashes. "They are all dead."

"Dead?" The guard's voice squeaked. It was almost possible to see the thoughts churning through his mind: Would Adrasteia be angry? Would she blame Ithaca?

"Thank the gods you are unharmed," he managed at last. Melantho could only hope that his thoughts did not cross the final gap to ask *how* she was unharmed.

He turned to beckon forward two soldiers standing at their posts a little farther up the way to the palace. "This is the princess Adrasteia," he told them. "There was an attack. Her escorts are dead. Take her bags and alert the staff to her arrival. Remind them that the princess must have every comfort. Make sure her suite is ready within the hour. Alert the queen. And her maid—"

"Stays with me," said Leto firmly, and the words sent a thrill through Melantho's chest.

"As you wish," said the guard shortly. "This way."

"Thank you," said Leto, turning to flash Melantho a grin.

The back of her hand brushed against Melantho's as she started forward, tossing her hair as she went. It took all of Melantho's strength not to grab that hand and never let it go. She stood still for a moment, breathing deeply, looking back over her shoulder at the sea she had left behind. The next time she stood on the shore, she would be accompanied by a prince. And he would die there. Melantho had sworn it to herself. The curse would not claim another girl, not while she still drew breath.

The boys who had carried their bags had already left, racing back down the track, their silvers held aloft as they whooped. Then, as though the gods wished for their introduction to go as disastrously as possible, it began to rain.

The prince was not there.

It was typical, thought Melantho mildly, watching Leto examine their new suites, that no sooner had *one* thing gone right than the rest had fallen apart. The prince had disappeared, judging by the muffled whispers of his staff, and none of them were quite sure where he'd gone.

She had done her best to hide her apprehension as a silent manservant had lead them through the palace, keeping up a commentary in his bland, nasal voice. *This is the gallery, of course, and here is the armory. And here, another gallery. Another armory.* Melantho had not listened closely.

The rooms were all the same: studded with intricately carved klinai—couches made explicitly for reclining whilst pretty handmaids offered around plates of cheeses and grapes—each of which boasted a fine array of silken cushions.

The challenge had not been telling them apart from one another, of course, because Melantho knew this palace like the back of her hand. It was distinguishing them from what they *had* been once that was hard. Trying not to remember the things she had seen in this corridor, the horrors she had witnessed in this little meeting room. The blood she had smelled here, the rank scent of a dead man as he emptied his bowels.

For the most part, Melantho had kept her eyes on the floor.

Leto had been quiet until they'd reached their rooms and she'd seen the luxury within. There was a sprawling sitting room, within which Melantho could count three separate tables, two desks, and at least twice that number of chairs. Then came the bedroom, hidden from view with a heavy purple curtain.

"These are . . ." Leto gaped at Melantho. "These are all for me?"

"Us." Melantho threw herself down on the bed. The *one* bed.

On Pandou, when the nighttime brought to mind thoughts of Leto—of her eyelids fluttering closed, her mouth parting, how the skin of her belly would feel pressed against Melantho's—Leto herself had always been safely slumbering a cave away, but to *share*? Melantho was not sure that she could bear such vulnerability, such prolonged *closeness*. She ducked her head, afraid that her expression would betray her thoughts. The layers upon layers of coverlets were a masterpiece of gold threads and red dyes atop a mattress so soft she sank half a foot into it. She plucked a feather out of one elaborate pillowcase and examined it closely. "Goose feathers. Lovely."

Leto did not respond nor did she appear to have noticed the situation with the sleeping arrangements. Perhaps she did not *mind* the thought of sharing a bed, did not even consider that it could have been an issue. Melantho swallowed, her throat peculiarly dry as Leto examined every single part of the room in minute detail. There was agitation etched into every inch of her face, singing from the set of her shoulders and the sharp movements of her body. She wiped away the ruined makeup and yanked at the gold necklace; Melantho could see the edges of the scales that were hidden underneath.

Melantho watched her silently. Centuries on Pandou had gifted her one thing at least: patience.

"For gods' sake," Leto snapped at last. "We have to do *something*. Could we go to the sea? Practice? Pray? *Something*."

It was difficult not to be amused by her impatience. Melantho rolled over and pushed her face into the pillow. The thought of the sea, though, made her heart ache. She missed the feel of it already, the rush of power that came with Poseidon's curse. Without it she felt *heavy*. Tired through to the very core of her bones.

Or was it something else that pained her? Something else that had her shrinking in on herself, her heart racing faster and her mind swimming with memories of hands and faces and voices and—

No. This wretched palace had been the site of her destruction once; she would not allow it to break her again. She breathed in slowly before she spoke.

"Should we not wait for the prince?" Her voice was muffled by the pillow.

"I don't give a single damn about the prince," said Leto, her voice dripping with faux amiability. "And I don't intend to. It is much harder to kill someone you care about, even if their death will save countless lives."

Melantho lifted her face slightly so that she could speak more clearly. "What is there to *gain* from us leaving now? And what is there to gain from meeting the prince anyway? We cannot even *try* to kill him until we are certain that the first girl has been chosen for sacrifice. So what is the *point*?"

Leto scowled at her, eyes flashing. "The *point*," she bit out, "is that this is the man that had me killed!"

"What does that have to do with it? You can't confront him about it, can you?" Melantho kept her voice level, her tone calm. She would not argue about this.

It wasn't as if Leto could get up to much mischief anyway. The prince was away; his servants had confirmed his absence. They would just have to wait.

"I won't know until I see him," said Leto. "Perhaps I will discover something useful." Suddenly decisive, she snatched up one of Adrasteia's traveling cloaks and threw it over her suntanned shoulders. She marched across the room to the door and paused there, her hand resting on the bolt, and threw Melantho an expectant look. "Are you coming?"

Melantho bristled. She wasn't sure what it was, but there was *something* in Leto's tone that tugged at her nerves. It pulled memories to the surface that she had quietly, carefully buried over the years. "No," she said sharply. Would everything here remind her of that life long ago? Perhaps it was not a question of *if* she must face it but *when*. And she was not ready—not yet.

She shook her head at Leto. "There is little point in snooping around."

"And there is *no* point in *sitting* around," said Leto. "*I* am going to look for the prince's rooms. I am sure there is something to discover there." She opened the door, slipped through, and let it snap shut behind her.

Melantho pushed her face back into the pillow. She should have known it would be like this. Leto was so young, her hatred still burned fierce and bright; she was impetuous and impulsive and—

You are afraid. Because you do not wish to lose her.

It was Thalia's voice that spoke in her mind: sly, sharp, knowing. Melantho made a furious noise—half a shriek, half a groan—into the goose feathers. It was only natural for her to feel protective of Leto. She was Melantho's last hope, *Ithaca's* last hope.

That was all it was.

She rolled over and occupied herself with finding patterns in the marble ceilings.

She had not been at it long before the doors to the chambers banged open yet again. Sharp footsteps sounded on the stone floor. Melantho picked herself up off the bed and stuck her head into the main room where Leto was standing, arms crossed, her face tight with irritation.

"That was fast," said Melantho. And then, though she could read the answer in Leto's face, "Did you find anything?"

"I got lost on the way back, had to accost a servant. You know, there aren't many at all, but they *still* manage to make sure that the prince's door is guarded," said Leto. "No chance I'd be able to get in. But, you know, I'm fairly certain that his chambers are directly below these ones."

"Oh, well, that's a—" Melantho broke off as Leto marched right by her and thrust the room's shutters aside in a single movement. "Shame? Tell me you're not going to try to go through the window." She was beginning to think that Leto might have been *more* impulsive than even Thalia.

The Thalia in her mind—that part of Melantho that still belonged to her—spoke again. *See, you* are *afraid to lose her. Just as you lost me.*

"I'm not going to try to go through the window," said Leto as she went through the window.

Melantho should have followed her. Should have thrown herself forward and caught Leto by one narrow wrist.

But Thalia's voice in her ear was not stopping, and other voices were joining it now and a sadness and a hopelessness and a *terror* was racing its way through Melantho's bloodstream until she was all but paralyzed by it. Then, it was all she could do to listen to the sound of scrabbling on stone outside the window and hope that she was not making yet another mistake.

XXII

CHILD OF MORNING

Leto

It was not so very difficult to climb down the side of the palace. Nor, admittedly, was it as simple as Leto had hoped. The moon was all but concealed behind dark grey clouds, hiding her from suspicious eyes as she clung to the rough stone, but the surface was slippery with rain and kept leaving pieces of grit painfully embedded in her fingertips.

She inched down carefully, her gaze fixed on the place below her where the stone gave way to a window. And that window, she hoped, would lead her straight into the chambers of the prince. She was not sure exactly what she hoped to find there, but she could not stand—as Melantho seemed so able to—*waiting*. Some part of her had expected Melantho to follow her. Some part of her had been disappointed.

Perhaps she would discover some convenient hiding place, some illicit secret they could use to their advantage when the time came. And that time would be *soon*.

Her swinging foot tore at a patch of ivy and sent a spray of foliage into the courtyard below.

Leto froze. There were not so many guards about the palace; she had noticed it distinctly already. There would not be one in the courtyard, surely—

Ringing out above the gentle pattering of rain, there came the

sound of footsteps. Not fast enough to be a run, but not slow enough to be the walk of a man who had no cause for alarm. Someone had heard something, seen something. Leto flailed about hopelessly. The window was still too far below her to be an easy refuge, and there was nothing in the courtyard below but a bubbling fountain that spilled into a wide marble bowl. Ithaca's fountains were salt water and fresh water in equal measure.

Please, thought Leto, a silent prayer. *Let this one be salt.*

The guard had appeared below her. He was staring at the heap of fallen ivy. He was scratching his chin, he was lifting his eyes upward to—

Before he could catch sight of her, Leto thrust one hand out toward the fountain. For a split second, nothing happened; her heart dropped in her chest and her throat tightened. Then the fountain moved.

It surged and spiraled on her command, spraying water wildly. Somehow, the droplets reached far enough to soak Leto's chiton, despite the distance between them. She cringed away with a muffled curse, releasing her hold on the water. It sank back into its usual docile bubbling. She heard the guard cry out. "What the—"

Leto grinned, victorious. She could already picture Melantho's delighted face, all her long-suffering patience vanished. *A saltwater fountain, Leto?* she would say. *Yes, I suppose that is part of Poseidon's domain. You're a genius.*

Beneath her, the guard looked wildly around for some explanation of the fountain's peculiar exhibit. But he did not think to look *up*. At last, shaking his head, he disappeared around a corner and Leto returned to the task at hand—getting into the prince's chambers.

Though scaling down the last section of the wall was

awkward—her damp chiton kept snagging on the rough stone and her hair caught in loose foliage more than once—she made it to the window of the room, pushed open the shutters, and all but fell through. She dropped to the tiled floor with a thud. Struggling for balance and narrowly avoiding upending a little vase brimming with yellow daffodils, she stumbled wearily into the empty room.

It became very apparent very quickly that the room was not, in fact, empty.

Somebody's possessions were distributed haphazardly over the low wooden surfaces, and Leto registered with a rising feeling of dread, the somebody was staring at her in blatant astonishment with a half-tied chiton slung low on his muscular torso and wet curls pasted to his forehead. Water dripped over his chest.

She would have recognized him even if this had been their first meeting. He was the spitting image of each of the hundreds of royal portraits hung about the palace—with wide, burned-coffee eyes, curling lashes, and full, feminine lips. Beautiful, for a dead man walking.

Prince Mathias, it appeared, had returned from his travels.

"Ah," said Leto, taking a half step back. This was not how she had imagined this going. He was meant to be *away*. And she was not only disheveled, but she had failed to reapply Adrasteia's heavy makeup. What if he recognized her? No, she reminded herself, surely not. She had been a skinny starving thing when they had last met, with a gag jammed between her teeth and a black eye. Still—"Wrong room, I should think. Sorry."—she turned smartly on the spot, thrust the shutter aside, and made to step from the window. *Gods*, she thought to herself, *what am I doing?*

The prince seemed to agree. "Gods, what are you *doing*?" he sprang forward and pulled her away from the opening with one hand. The other held the strip of material protecting his modesty very firmly in place. "Who *are* you? What on earth are you doing?" He narrowed his eyes at her. "Why are you *wet*?"

Leto declined to point out that he was also wet. "I was . . ." She grappled for an appropriate excuse. Her skirts were not *that* wet, just peppered with the wild spray of the fountain and occasionally marked from the damp slick of the stones. Perfectly justifiable. "I was taking a turn about the palace, near the fountain. It was behaving very strangely, you see."

The astonished look remained firmly in place on Mathias's lovely face. But there was no recognition there. Somehow, though it should have been a relief, it made her feel . . . disappointed. From the way he'd spoken, spoken *directly* to her, before he'd commanded her death, she had thought he might remember her. Clearly not. A good thing—his recognition would have complicated things, might have ruined the whole plan. She shouldn't have wanted it, but . . . No. A ridiculous thought.

"The fountain was behaving strangely," Mathias repeated. "I do believe you have answered just one of my three questions and presented many more. Now, who *are* you, before I call my guards in?"

Leto straightened. She must have looked a state. From the corner of her eye, she could see several leaves which seemed to have taken up residence behind her ear. "I am Princess Adrasteia of Athens," she said. "Pleased to make your acquaintance."

If that had been an answer Mathias expected, he did an excellent job of acting like it was completely astounding. He dropped her arm hastily and stepped back a pace. "Pleased to meet you too, Princess," he said smartly. "I am Prince Mathias of Ithaca. Do all the royal family of Athens make a habit of scaling the outsides of palaces like wall lizards and dropping in on unsuspecting young men?"

"Just me, I think." Leto smiled apologetically. Gods, what was she going to tell Melantho? "I was hoping this was my room. Which is where I'd quite like to be, incidentally. So if you'll excuse me I'll just . . ." Again, she moved toward the window. Again, Mathias lunged to stop her.

"I don't think I can allow you to lizard any further about the palace, I'm afraid," he said quite firmly. "Perhaps you'd like to use the door. I believe most prefer it."

"Right. I'll—" Leto averted her gaze from him and sidestepped across the room. As she reached the door, she paused with one hand on the bolt. Would she be able to find a servant to direct her this time? She was not looking forward to the prospect of wandering around the corridors for another hour. "You wouldn't happen to know how I'd get there, would you?"

From the look on Mathias's face, it was very clear he wanted nothing less than to explain to a damp and possibly deranged girl who had crawled in through his window how to get back to her room. In fact, Leto suspected he would rather not sleep in the same building as her. She couldn't blame him. She was impressed he hadn't already summoned his guard to execute, or at least evict, her. "Give me one minute," he said at last, and ducked behind a large wooden screen.

He emerged a few seconds later in a loose grey chiton, properly tied this time, rubbing the discarded one through his hair. "This way," he said, pushing open the door and disappearing down the corridor.

Leto picked up her skirts and hurriedly followed.

Climbing one window down was not so easily undone from

inside the palace. The corridors seemed to be lined with endless doors, and it seemed like the only staircase on the whole floor was a mile away. Mathias also moved very quickly. He barely paused except to helpfully point out the passage that would take her to the dining hall, so when he finally deposited her in front of a familiar door, her underarms were damp with sweat and she was breathing far too quickly for a faux princess.

"This is the one." Mathias indicated the door with his head. "And this"—he pushed it open and waved her inside—"is how I would suggest you enter and leave in the future."

"Thank you," said Leto, louder than necessary, hoping that Melantho would hear and know not to emerge from the bedchamber or to say anything untoward. "I'll bear that in mind."

"Good." Mathias looked for a moment like he wanted to say something else. He reached to take Leto's hand and pressed it gently to his lips. Leto gaped at him. She couldn't think of a single occasion in which anyone had actually kissed her hand. It seemed so ridiculously formal. But of course, she was a princess now, not a child masquerading as the voice of Apollo. She would do well to remember it.

"I am glad you are here." Mathias smiled at her. "Good night then, Princess."

He emphasized the word *princess* with some amusement, as though he still couldn't quite believe it. Not entirely surprising, since it was categorically false. Realizing she was still gaping like a gormless fish, Leto tried to think of a suitably regal response. "Uh" she managed. "You may call me Leto, if you wish."

"Leto?"

Shit. In all her embarrassment, she had forgotten her guise. She scrambled for an explanation. "A nickname," she said. "For my . . .

close friends. A secret to stay between us?" He would not recognize the name, but perhaps others here would. She needed to be more careful—there were more than just twelve lives at stake, after all. Her crime of deception, of infiltration, would not go unpunished if she were discovered.

The prince's smile was surprisingly sweet. Leto had never seen such a symmetrical face. It was like he had been carved, meticulously beautiful as he was, to stand in a temple as a likeness of Hermes or Apollo. "Leto," Mathias echoed. "I will do my best to remember that." He released her hand, turned smartly, and vanished around a corner.

"Goodbye, then," Leto said to the empty corridor, dazed. The thought returned to her very suddenly that this was the man who had sentenced her to the rope. Given all that had occurred since then, she had almost forgotten that she had actually been hanged. *And* died. And that it had been *his fault*. If only she could have her revenge here, now, before she humiliated herself further. But Melantho had been clear—they had to wait until the first girl was marked, or the prince's death would be for nothing.

XXIII

ON ONE AND ALL OF THEM

Leto

It was not the servants bustling in with clean linens and hot water that woke Leto the next day—Melantho had, with a careful word, barred them all from the chambers—but the sun streaming in through the gap in the shutters she must have left open. She groaned, covering her eyes, and let the previous night's memories wash over her.

Their acceptance to the palace, manipulating the fountain—and from such a distance!—the prince and his strange farewell. The *prince*—Leto bolted upright, heat flaming in her cheeks. Gods, she had managed to cast their encounter from her mind for a moment but now it reemerged in hideous detail. She covered her burning face with her hands and groaned.

At her side, Melantho stirred. Leto had not told her of what had transpired between herself and the prince; she had not been able to face the shame of it. Besides, Melantho had already been half-asleep when Leto came in, curled in a deliberate, irritated ball on one side of the bed.

Leto had not thought much of the sleeping situation until she realized that it would be the bed or nothing. The bed *with* Melantho. She'd kept a careful distance as she had slipped under the sheets, closed her eyes tightly and forced herself into uneasy sleep.

She did the same now, clenching her eyes until there was no light at all filtering through her lashes.

She was an idiot. It was not proper at all for a supposed princess to be exhibiting herself so outrageously. Perhaps she would be thrown from the palace after breakfast. After all, how could the royal family continue to entertain her after they heard such a tale? She needed to be more careful; if she were cast out, killing Mathias would go from a difficulty to an impossibility. And twelve more of Ithaca's innocents would die.

A knock sounded from the sitting room. Gods, that could not be Mathias, could it? What would Melantho say to that?

Leto jumped to her feet and sprinted out of the bedchamber. "Correspondence for you, Princess," said a pretty maid, nodding toward a scroll tucked underneath a platter of breads and compotes as Leto opened the door a crack and peered out at her. "From the prince. He returned last night."

That is brand-new information. Leto schooled her face into an expression of neutrality. "Thank you, just . . . leave it there."

The maid's eyes narrowed almost imperceptibly. "Here, Princess? On the floor?"

"Yes," said Leto.

The maid clearly did not care enough to argue. She knelt gracelessly and placed the pile of breads on the flagstones. As she stood again, she glanced over the sliver of Leto that was visible between the door and the marble walls. Her face twitched. "Enjoy your breakfast, Princess," she said, then marched away.

Leto noticed belatedly that her arm was covered in thumbprint-sized bruises and shallow scrapes. She retrieved the breakfast tray swiftly, hoping that the maid had not noticed the matching scratches that marked her chest. Her climb had not left her as undamaged as she had hoped.

She placed the tray on the nearest table and turned to bolt the door. Turning back, she caught a glimpse of herself in the wide bronze mirror on the far wall and cringed. Even if the maid hadn't noticed the scratches, it would have been hard for her to avoid noticing the state of Leto's *hair*. Her dark brown curls had frizzed out so violently she looked deranged, and she could see at least one twig matted against the side of her face.

She pulled the scroll open mutinously. Now the servants would think her a madwoman as much as the prince did. Or worse, they would realize that she was an imposter. She forced herself to take a deep, soothing breath. It was no matter. The first girl would be marked soon. Leto had only to wait a few days before their condemnation. Before she . . .

Well, it did not bear thinking of.

The letter was written in a very elegant hand which, though beautiful, was unreasonably difficult to read. Leto held it very close to her face.

My dear Adrasteia, it began. *It was a great and most unexpected pleasure to meet you last night. It is not often that I return from diplomatic trips to find foreign princesses clambering on the rooftops. Although I did enjoy your visit greatly, I am sure you will agree with my sentiment that a more traditional introduction may now be in order. I have several matters to attend to this morning, but I hope that you will consent to lunch with myself and my mother at midday, as well as some of the court ladies.*

You may send your answer with my guard, Alexios, who will call upon you after breakfast. I eagerly await your reply

*and, if you agree to it, dining in your company. Perhaps I can
give you a more formal tour of the palace than the one you
seem to have given yourself.*

My very warmest welcome to Ithaca,
Mathias

He had added a scruffy addendum. *You may want to brush your
hair before this one. The queen will greatly prefer it.*

Leto read it twice, becoming more infuriated each time.

The whole thing had an air of smug amusement. She could *see*
his wry smile in every word.

Scowling, she reached for one of the blank scrolls neatly rolled
on the room's writing desk and scrawled a reply.

Most esteemed Prince, she began, then crossed it out. *Mathias.*
She wrote, *You must have mistaken me for someone else. I have never
even heard of a rooftop. As for my hair, it is always immaculate,
Adrasteia.* Her scowl deepened as she crossed it out again. No one
had ever bothered to teach her the etiquette of royal communica-
tion. It was unusual that she even knew how to read and write, but
her mother had insisted she learn from the moment she was old
enough to hold a reed pen.

Her final attempt was simple. *Dear Prince Mathias,* it read.
*Thank you for your kind invitation. I look forward to dining with
yourself and the queen. Yours, Princess Adrasteia.* She stared crossly
at her own messy postscript: *You may want to wear all your clothes
for this one. I'm sure the queen would prefer that too.*

She doubted that Mathias even read his own correspondence.
She wondered what Alexios would make of it.

Deciding she didn't care, she rolled the message up and secured
it with a ribbon. Her knot was as scruffy as her handwriting. She
scoffed and tossed it down on the desk with Mathias's original letter.

"What is that?"

Melantho's voice was thick with sleep as she padded into the room in her thin nightdress and yawned. To Leto's great relief, she made no move to snatch up either scroll to examine their scathing contents.

Leto avoided her eyes. "The prince has summoned me," she said. "His man will be here within the hour, I suspect, to collect my reply." She paused. "*Should* I reply?"

Melantho shrugged, her nightgown slipping off one shoulder. She'd drawn her hair into two braids, like ears of yellow wheat. She looked very young. "We will have to convince him to come to the sea with us one way or another—it cannot hurt to be kind to him now. Is that jam?" She had spied the breakfast tray; her face lit up. "I adore jam."

"You can have it all," said Leto.

"I shall," said Melantho. "You should brush your hair."

🌀🌀🌀

There came a sharp rap on the door shortly after Leto and Melantho finished breakfast. They had not managed to finish everything, so Leto had carefully wrapped the remaining pastries in linen. They would still be good later.

"I will answer it," said Melantho, rising from her perch on the bed. Leto was still idling in front of the mirror there; having finished removing the twigs and leaves from her hair and oiled it back into its curls, she was now dithering over her choice of chiton. Even with half of it left aboard the princess's sunken ship, she had never had such an *expansive* wardrobe—nor such an expensive one. She felt overdressed in everything, and they were far heavier than she was used to.

"Thank you," she said, pulling one around her. She examined her reflection closely. The chiton was pale blue, the edge embroidered with curling yellow flowers. Above its carefully shaped neckline, her hair was neat, the scar at her throat hidden beneath a thick gold collar; she should have looked beautiful. But her face was pale and wan. She pinched at her cheeks to bring the color into them, then set about applying charcoal to her eyes.

"I like that one." Melantho smiled, absentminded, and picked up the scroll Leto had prepared. "You look nice in blue."

She vanished into the main room. Leto heard the door open and Melantho's clear, cool voice. "Alexios, I presume."

The reply was short and harsh. "Yes."

Leto froze. She knew that voice. It caught at her memory, then her throat; the air thickened in her lungs and become like molten lead.

Slowly, slowly, she crept from the bedchamber and into the sitting room.

Melantho was standing by the open door, frowning up at a large, dark-haired man. *Alexios*, she had said. Leto shivered, positioning herself safely behind a solid-looking chair. He was not an ugly man—far from it, in truth—but she could not look at him without a swell of nausea in her abdomen, a low throb of recognition. Her hand twitched, her fingers aching to brush over the raw scar and the scales beneath the collar at her throat. Melantho cleared her throat and dropped the scroll into his massive hand. "My lady's reply for Mathias."

"It is Prince Mathias to you," said Alexios shortly. He had startling blue eyes, which flickered with interest as they moved past Melantho and fell on Leto where she stood, half-concealed behind the broad back of the chair.

She met his gaze, looked into those bright, lovely blue eyes, and for a moment she was lost in the memory of kneeling with a mouthful of blood on a hillside as she was sentenced to die.

There came a little sound, one that she might have dismissed as the gusting of the wind had she not felt the air pass her lips. She could taste her own fear in the air. Melantho had noticed, thank the gods, had stiffened and half turned. She knew then that Leto was afraid.

"Well," said Melantho hastily. "I am sure that *Prince* Mathias will appreciate your haste in delivering this response. Good day." She tried to shut the door but the guard surged forward, blocking its path with one huge, leather-booted foot.

They looked at each other, silent and still, then he withdrew his foot with a peculiar abruptness and the door lurched closed.

"What an unpleasant man," said Melantho, turning back to Leto.

Leto stood very still in the center of the room. Her heart was not just racing; it was twisting violently inside her chest as if it were trying to free itself from her rib cage.

"That man," she said carefully, "is head of the royal guard. That man tore me from my home. That man watched me die."

❧❧❧

The next knock on the door, an hour or so later, announced Mathias. The prince was dressed in a frankly alarming mustard yellow, but he smiled warmly as Leto opened the door with Adrasteia's letter of introduction—and the hastily finished missive for her family—clutched in her hand. She did not really know why she was bothering with the latter: it would be delivered far after her work here was done. The journey to Athens was not such a quick one—the messenger would have to travel first by boat, then by land—and she did not intend to stay on Ithaca long. But some small part of her had felt a kinship for the princess; she could, at least, give her more of a head start.

"You're early," she said automatically. She had still not shaken off the shock of seeing Alexios.

Melantho had been frantic with questions, had wanted to know *exactly* how Leto knew the guard, whether he had looked at her long enough to memorize her features, whether he would recognize her now. But Leto had been curiously unable to answer. It had felt as if her lungs were shrinking in on themselves, catching every word before it could form on her tongue. She had fled back to her wardrobe wordlessly, trying her best to ignore Melantho's gaze boring into her back.

Now she took a sharp breath and forced herself to smile back at the prince standing before her. He, at least, clearly did not recognize her for who she truly was. That was the effect of fine jewelry and dresses and more food than was just enough to live.

"I wanted to make sure you made it to the dining room safely," said Mathias, offering her his arm. Leto took it. His skin seemed to shine like gold. He belonged in a temple, a beautiful statue with offerings rotting at his feet. "Without taking a detour over the rooftops."

"Very funny," said Leto. In the shock of the previous night, she had been uncharacteristically pleasant to him. But seeing Alexios had brought back every feeling of resentment, *hatred*, for this boy and everything he stood for. As soon as she had a chance, she would end his ridiculous, charmed life. She tossed her hair. "Besides, I am quite confident of my way now, thank you."

"Really? Lead on, then."

"Of course." Leto stuck her head through the frame and examined the corridor carefully. It was easier to be cold and unkind when she was not so hopelessly lost. She had known that the palace would be vast and grand—you could see its columns from Vathi—but it was even more overwhelming inside. Every corridor seemed the same, a labyrinth of marble and columns and grandeur so wasteful it left a bitter taste in her mouth. "Left," she said at last, trying not to let her face betray her frustration.

"Nice try," said Mathias. "It's right. I knew you'd need my help."

Leto looked sideways at him. "I could have asked a servant."

"You could have," said Mathias, "and it would have been equally effective, but you would not have the added benefit my presence offers."

"Which is?"

"The pleasure of my company, of course." Mathias smiled winningly.

Leto laughed, then almost immediately felt bad about it. How quickly she had allowed herself to relax. She glanced over her shoulder at Melantho, who trailed them quietly, a *little* closer than she should have been. When she caught Leto looking, she arched her eyebrows, a quick movement that said, *Do you need my help?*

Leto turned back. No. Melantho did not speak of her past often—and when she did, she was sparing with the details—but it was clear that it had not been a kind one. She had done more than her fair share. Leto would not make her do it all again, would not send their ruse crashing to the ground with her own sharpness, her lack of polish. Until the time came, until she found a way to get Mathias to the sea, alone, she needed to be more careful.

Mathias shot her that lovely smile again and she forced herself to smile back.

XXIV

PREY TO THE BIRDS AND
WILD BEASTS

Mathias

Mathias had ruined his engagement already.

Somehow, at some point between the bewildering events of the previous night and now, walking through the corridors at Adrasteia's—at *Leto's*—side, Mathias had managed to commit some grievous misstep. All her warmth was gone, every smile she offered him pained, false. Her pretty maid had tailed them wordlessly; every time he glanced over his shoulder, he caught her glowering at a tapestry or scuffing her shoes over the marble floors with an alarming intensity.

What had he *done*? Was it the letter? It had been a touch informal—but Leto had been far beyond the boundary of impropriety when she'd clambered through his window in the middle of the night. Perhaps she was merely embarrassed. Or perhaps she had learned one of Ithaca's shameful secrets. There were certainly enough to go around: the empty treasury, the missing princesses—one dead, one all but exiled—and the meager guard. Or, worse even than that, perhaps she had learned that in just ten days, he would be overseeing the executions of twelve innocents. But she would know that already, wouldn't she? Or had the world beyond Ithaca forgotten their curse so easily? The doubt made him twist his fingers together; his neck felt hot.

"I heard you were attacked by pirates," he said. A servant had informed him this morning. Perhaps that was the reason for her coldness. Yes, that must be it; now that the thrill of escape had faded, it had left her shaken and afraid.

"I—" Leto stumbled on a flagstone, lurched into him, then recoiled away just as quickly. She kept a tight grip on the letters in her hand. She cleared her throat. "Yes."

"How did you manage to escape?" Beyond his fear of her rejection, beyond his longing to return to the ease of their parting the night before, he was genuinely curious. If her entire escort had been killed, her possessions stolen, how had *she* survived?

"Oh . . . uh. I suppose the gods were looking favorably on us. Athenians are a devout people."

Was that an insult? If it was, it was not a subtle one. Mathias knew the whispers, that Ithaca had turned from the gods. *You would too*, he wanted to say, *if the gods did nothing but slaughter your people.* He settled on "Oh." Then, "What are those letters?"

"One is from my father," said Leto. "For your mother. The other is from *me*—I will need your servants to send it on to Athens for me. I would ask my own men but, well . . ." She trailed off pointedly.

"Of course," said Mathias hastily. "I will see that it is done."

It was almost a relief to arrive at the dining hall and usher Leto inside. His mother was seated at the head of the table. She raised an imperious eyebrow at him. She had already waylaid him that morning to ask after his fiancée's dowry, the gold that Athens had promised would come with her. He could see it in her face that she had not forgotten. Gods, he had to keep Leto away from her.

"Sit here," he said quickly, pulling out the nearest chair. It was close enough to the queen as to not be impolite, but far enough that she could not—

"No, no," interrupted the queen. "That will not do. Come *here*, my dear." She nodded at the seat to her left. It was not empty; Mathias's cousin Melina looked up from her plate with an expression of startled delight. She was on her feet in an instant, dropping into a careful curtsy before backing away from the queen at great speed.

His mother gestured again for Leto to sit in Melina's now-vacant seat. Olympia, on the queen's right, watched the exchange silently, her eyes flicking between Mathias, his mother, and his fiancée in turn.

Melina was normally not *quite* so clear in her discomfort; the queen must be in a particularly bad mood today. Even Olympia was avoiding her gaze, though he could not fail to notice the smug curl of her lip, her delight that Melina had been displaced and she had not.

Not that the queen would ever banish Olympia from her seat, of course. Not while she still liked to remind Mathias what a suitable match Olympia would make for him if only he would end this tedious Athenian interlude once and for all.

"Brilliant," muttered Mathias.

"What was that?" asked Leto.

"Nothing," said Mathias hastily. "I suppose we should do as my mother bids. She must have lots to ask you, after all." Then, almost as an afterthought, he lowered his voice. "She is intolerable. I'm sorry." It was a satisfying, secret betrayal. He reveled in it.

The horror on Leto's face was an apt reflection of that which he kept concealed. The queen had made it clear a hundred times over how little she thought of this match. Perhaps Leto had already heard the whispers of it. Something in her face reminded him of his sister. Not Selene—for once, though he seemed to see her everywhere these days—but Hekate, so young, sent to her marriage on Crete.

As subtly as he could, he reached over to take Leto's hand, to press her fingers comfortingly as if to say, *Don't worry, I will be here.*

She snatched her hand away without looking at him, held up her letters like a shield. She squared her shoulders, and this time he *did* think of Selene, and it made his heart ache. "How bad can this be?" she asked. "I'm sure the queen will love me."

XXV

BY FAIR MEANS OR FOUL

Leto

"The queen hates me," declared Leto.

The lunch had been appalling. Beyond appalling. She could barely stand to think of it; she had fled as soon as it was polite—or at least *possible*—to do so, leaving Mathias behind with barely a goodbye. Melantho, thank the gods, had a fantastic memory and had led them back to their chambers with ease.

Now, Leto launched into yet another rant, the third of the evening. She had cleared a path between the room's three tables—and their twelve accompanying chairs, all distinct in their shape or the careful embroidery of the blankets draped over them—and had commenced pacing up and down it like a caged animal. "She asked *three times* after my dowry, each time even more obvious than the last! I mean, we knew that Adrasteia was all but *sold,* like some prized heifer, but I didn't realize it would be this bad! I cannot dance around the issue forever, but I cannot tell the queen that no replacement will come for her precious gold, can I?" She looked to Melantho.

"Oh dear," said Melantho for the third time from where she lay on the bed, gazing at the ceiling. There was a shimmering ball of salt water floating above her palms—the contents of the waterskin she had filled from the fountain below the moment that Leto told her of its saltwater contents. Presently, she was amusing herself with forming it into a little bird. With a flick of her fingers, she sent it winging across the room to Leto.

Leto glared at it. "Did you hear what I said? She hates me. Can't stand the sight of me. Apparently, Adrasteia and Mathias were engaged as *children*—all arranged by the king, of course. The queen had nothing to do with it. Did *you* know that she was from Sparta?" She was not sure why she was so upset. The queen did not *need* to like her, after all. But something about the sneering curl of her lip and the way her eyes had moved slowly over Leto, savoring her discomfort, set Leto's blood boiling. Some of her clients had looked at her like that: the poor oracle with her thin frame and her rickety little house tucked into one of Vathi's ramshackle streets. She would always give them a worse fortune than the cards or the smoke or the entrails predicated. She would hope that she was right.

"I did not know that she was Spartan," said Melantho wearily.

"Well, she is. And Adrasteia is Athenian."

"How awful."

"The queen acts like I am personally responsible for *that* conflict!" Melantho's bird was still flapping about her head. Leto snatched at it irritably. Her fingers passed through its crystalline body with ease and it fell at once into a shower of fat droplets, soaking the carpets at her feet. Where she had touched it, color bloomed in an instant; the skin of her knuckles flecked itself with tiny emerald scales. A tiny burst of power shot up her arm.

"You killed my bird," said Melantho, her tone sepulchral. She sat up. "I'm sensing that this . . . situation with the queen is vexing you."

"It is!" Leto had reached the far wall. She spun on the spot and raised an accusing finger at Melantho. "She was always fawning over that wretched Olympia with her pretty eyes and her perfect hair and her table manners, acting like I'm some unpleasant creature that's crawled in from the latrine! You know, I don't think she wants Mathias to marry me at *all*."

"And why is that an issue?" asked Melantho delicately. "You are aware that you don't *actually* want to marry him?"

It was a fair point. Leto ceased her pacing. It wasn't like marrying Mathias would benefit her much, not when she'd inevitably be harried across the continent for his subsequent murder.

"It's an insult to Adrasteia," she said at last. "She came all the way from Athens, just for—"

"Just for us to sink her ship, steal all her possessions, and send her out into the world with nothing but the clothes on her back," said Melantho. "She could be dead by now for all we know. I would suggest that not being liked by her future mother-in-law is the least of her issues."

"It is an insult to *me,* then," said Leto. "Surely you care about *that*?"

"When it is coming from the queen of Ithaca?" asked Melantho. "No, I do not. It is my experience that the words of the queens of Ithaca are worth very little." She frowned, her eyes unfocused for a moment. Her voice softened. "Do you think she believed you? I heard some of your answers to her questions. They were . . ."

"Terrible," said Leto flatly. Her manners had been just as dismal. She had hardly listened to a word Mathias had said to her, the names of his court. She had simply had too much to think about besides names: how to sit, how to smile, how to spoon soup into her mouth without hunching over the table but also without spilling it over her chiton. Out of nerves, she had been drinking wine much faster than she was used to. She had caught Mathias eyeing her with distinct alarm more than once and had been forced to make a concerted effort to put her cup down. She was not looking forward to the upcoming equinox festival at all; there would be twice as many names to remember, twice as many eyes on her, and she would be expected to *dance*.

And the *questions*. Gods, she had never told so many lies in such a short space of time. She'd done her best to imply that she had a poor relationship with Adrasteia's parents—a half-hearted excuse for knowing nothing of them at all—and had mostly filled the time with ridiculous chatter of fountains and taxes and how *very* harrowing her journey had been and how she very much wished to rest in her rooms.

Not that she *could* rest now. Her heart was a fluttering bird in her chest. "It was *awful*," she pronounced again, and collapsed into a chair. "How long do we have to wait until we can get this over with?"

"Well." Melantho hesitated. Something in the twisting of her fingers betrayed her—she was hiding something.

"Well, what?" Leto narrowed her eyes.

Melantho sighed. "I did not want to tell you today. I thought we could discuss it tomorrow, but—"

"But?"

"I cannot tell you if you keep interrupting me! It might not be anything, but I overheard something when I was walking to the laundries. I—"

"The laundry? Why were you going there?"

"Half your clothes stank of smoke. That's what salvaging things off a burning ship tends to result in. Are you *going* to let me finish?"

Leto offered Melantho her most apologetic smile, then covered her mouth with her hands. She widened her eyes significantly: *go on.*

"Thank you." Perhaps Melantho was trying to sound stern, but the lift of her cheeks and the shine of her eyes betrayed her. "I overheard a maid complaining about washing bloodstains off a guard's chiton. And *then* another maid said to her, 'Well, you'd better get used to it. There's eleven more to go, and they never come quietly.'"

Leto's blood seemed to still in her veins, to freeze then shatter into needles that pricked at her insides. "*Eleven more to go,*" she repeated. "The first marked girl?"

Melantho nodded. "It must be. What else?"

"We could do it tonight then?"

"Tonight?" Something dark passed over Melantho's features. She blinked rapidly. "I did not mean—that seems unnecessarily hasty. There are still ten days to the equinox. We might want to give ourselves a little more time to prepare."

"Then we do it tomorrow," said Leto. It was a relief to say it out loud. The nightmare could be over, almost as soon as it had begun. "I cannot pretend for much longer. We will end this tomorrow."

⑨⑨⑨

They came up with the plan together. It was simple: an invitation dispatched to the prince for a romantic walk along the Ithacan cliffs. Lovely, very suitable, *very* close to the sea.

Perfect.

By the time she woke up the following morning, Leto had wholly convinced herself that she would not spend another day in the palace. Mathias would be toppled from the cliffs, claimed by the sea, and no more girls would die on Ithaca. Not for this.

And she and Melantho would flee the kingdom the moment it was done. Where would they go then? The whole of the world would be opened to them, and they could see it together.

Her dream was shattered by another note from Mathias. He had already begun to do away with many of the formalities that had adorned his first letter. Even his curling script seemed a little less embellished as it spelled out the words,

    My dear Leto, I would be delighted to accompany you to the cliffs. But it is too far to walk there and back in a day—I have asked for horses to be prepared instead. I hope you will agree that it is a suitable compromise. I am eager to see you again. Mathias

Leto glared at it. Horses. Wonderful.

Leto had ridden a horse barely three times before. Each time she'd been tossed from her seat—or, though it was not so dramatic, perhaps she had merely fallen—before she made it out of the paddock. As a rule, horses did not like her. She'd heard they could smell fear—and she believed it.

"Look at this." She thrust the note at Melantho.

"I'd rather not, thank you." Melantho continued twisting her hair into a plait, her fingers working deftly to catch up every stray golden curl and knot it into place. Her eyes were soft, though, when she threw Leto an approving look. "It is from the prince, I assume?"

"Unfortunately, yes," said Leto. "He does not wish to walk, he says it is too far. He wants to go *riding*."

"Oh," said Melantho. "Well, I suppose it will get us there faster. Is that bad?"

"It is *disastrous*," said Leto. "I cannot ride."

"I can," said Melantho brightly. "Though I confess, it has been a long time. There weren't so many horses on Pandou to practice on."

"One would have been enough." Leto marched over to her trunks and began extracting dresses at random. She had no idea what a princess would wear to ride. "You don't suppose I can use my feminine wiles to convince him to walk anyway?"

Melantho laughed loudly. Leto shot her a furious look—

Melantho had finished braiding her hair, and she had nothing to do now but observe Leto as she suffered.

"What?" asked Leto sharply. She threw a balled-up chiton at Melantho's head.

"You look positively *tragic*," said Melantho, catching it and smoothing the creases from the fine fabric. "It can't be *that* bad, you know. Besides," she added, leaning in, conspiratorial, shielding her mouth with her hand as if there were spies hiding in the walls just waiting to catch them in their crime, "we are still going to the cliffs. Remember, they are *very* steep, and the terrain is so *very* unsafe. Even for a prince."

Leto paused with her hand on a pale violet peplum. Was she imagining something else in Melantho's voice, hidden beneath the idle threats? "I am just a princess." She kept her voice sweet, almost flirtatious. The plan would still work. It had to. "And you are just my maid. How could we be expected to help if he were, say, tossed over the cliff's edge? We would be helpless."

"Helpless," echoed Melantho. "Tragic, really. And the sea is so very deep—"

"And so very *wide*."

"It would be quite a feat to recover his body," said Melantho. "Near impossible, I should think."

"I should think that you are right."

For a moment they stayed like that, frozen, smiling at each other. If Helios had driven above them, painting the sky with his brilliant light, he would have seen two beautiful girls, caught up in the glow of youthful adoration.

But if he were to look closer?

Well, he would see that the nightshade was as deadly as it was lovely.

XXVI

THE MOST ILL-STARRED
OF ALL

Melantho

Melantho trailed behind Leto as they descended the final flight of stairs into the courtyard, doing her best to look meek and innocent. No one would suspect her of plotting a murder, not in this plain chiton the color of fresh mint, with her eyes lowered to the ground.

Mathias, waiting for them in front of the fountain, greeted Leto with a blinding smile. "You look beautiful."

Melantho had told her the same as they'd walked from their rooms together.

She had braided Leto's hair carefully, firmly pinning back the loose strands, and insisted she wear Adrasteia's largest, most elaborate earrings. Anything to distract Mathias and tear his mind away from questioning Leto as she convinced him toward the cliff's edge. She knew how high the cliffs were, how far—*too* far—the sea would be, so she had sewn a waterskin into the chiton at the pocket; full of fountain water, it would grant Leto a taste of her powers if she needed them. Enough to lend her a little extra strength—the strength she would need to overcome a human prince.

Melantho had been granted less freedom in choosing Leto's necklace; the thick metallic band around her neck was one of the few that covered the ring of scales which clung so determinedly to her skin. She had persuaded Leto to perch a circlet of twisted gold over her head. Even now, she was struck by its glow against the brown of Leto's hair and, more alarmingly, how reminiscent it was of a crown.

Melantho did not have fond memories of those who wore crowns.

Still, as she looked at Leto, a peculiar feeling of comfort settled itself on her chest—one that, at first, she could not place. When it did come, the realization came slowly. She felt . . . safe. She was not waiting for Poseidon to punish her anymore. When was it that she had realized that he was not coming for her, that perhaps he had always known she would break free from his prison? Perhaps she was always meant to be here.

She twisted her hands together to hide the trembling of her fingers. If they succeeded today, then it would be over. Years, *hundreds* of them, saved and spent and lost to a curse that could be broken in an instant by a girl with spiraling brown curls and eyes like the wood of an ash tree and a twist of gold on her brow.

Please. She was not sure who she was praying to. *Please, let this work.*

She did not wait for an answer—the gods had never seen fit to bless her with such a thing—as she returned her attention to the girl and the boy walking ahead of her.

"So, horse riding," Leto was saying conversationally, smiling forcefully up at Mathias. "Is that something you've done a lot of, historically?"

Melantho resisted the urge to roll her eyes.

"I . . . suppose so?" Mathias frowned. "Have you?"

"Not at all," said Leto. Her false smile widened until, from where Melantho was standing, it could almost have been a grimace. "I'm terrible."

"Well," said Mathias bracingly, "here is an opportunity to

improve." He was so very *earnest*. Melantho had not expected it. She had been waiting on a boy like her own prince, the boy she had loved as a brother, the boy who had betrayed her. But where Telemachus had been all sharp words and fits of violent temper, Mathias was soft-spoken and his eyes were gentle as he smiled back at Leto.

Melantho wondered if there was a snake in there somewhere, waiting to strike.

"Wonderful," said Leto darkly. "I can hardly contain my excitement."

"I suppose you traveled exclusively by chariot in Athens?" asked Mathias. Melantho drifted closer, watching the shift of his broad shoulders beneath his chiton.

He was tall, towering over Leto, and was corded with muscle that Melantho knew would have come from years of swordplay— not that this princeling would ever see battle—and archery and horse riding and all the sorts of things young men did whilst their sisters labored over their needlework. It would not be an easy task to pitch him over the edge, but Leto was stronger than she looked. They both were—they would not have survived this long otherwise.

So many others had not.

Mathias and Leto had reached the edge of the courtyard. Ahead, Melantho could glimpse lush pasture, carefully clipped short, and a groom attending to a stocky pony.

"Yes, by chariot," Leto said idly. It took a moment for Melantho to remember what they had been talking about. Traveling. How very dull. "It's not quite so rustic in Athens, you see, so we are a tad more civilized in our transportation."

She was clearly making it all up as she went.

"Rustic," repeated Mathias thoughtfully. "Was that your first impression of me?"

Now *that* interested Melantho. She had discussed the prince very little with Leto in the brief time since their arrival—after all, she did not want to seem *jealous*. Still, she could not help but wonder if Leto thought of the prince the way that some of the maids clearly did.

Melantho had heard the serving girls giggling in the laundries when they did not think she was listening—or perhaps they did not *care* whether or not she was listening; she was only another maid, after all. They mooned relentlessly over his eyes (black, like the night itself!) and his lips (perfectly arched, like the bow of Eros himself!) and even his slender hands, laden with their gold rings and carefully polished fingernails.

They were hands that had never seen a day's labor, the hands of a man who had everything. Melantho disliked his hands almost as much as she disliked him, though admittedly this was mostly on the principle of the thing.

The other maids, of course, thought they were very elegant.

Melantho hoped that Leto did not.

Ahead, Leto deliberated for a moment. "You are not what I expected," she said eventually.

How so? Melantho frowned.

"How so?" Mathias sounded genuinely offended.

Leto shrugged. "I prefer you now," she said, "if that is a comfort."

It was not. Not to Melantho. Why should Leto prefer him now when she was mere hours from killing him? She could see no reason for it.

The injury in Mathias's voice did not change. "Still"—he

pressed Leto—"I cannot see why you should have thought unfavorably of me. I thought I behaved quite well, given I had just been surprised wearing nothing but a half-tied chiton. I do not like to be half-dressed in front of strange women. It is not a situation I find myself in often."

Melantho tripped on a cobblestone, almost pitching herself into a low, meticulously shaped shrub. She was grateful then for the soft soles of her sandals—they meant that she felt every stone in her path keenly, but they did not clatter against the ground as she stumbled and righted herself hastily.

Neither Leto nor Mathias seemed to notice her. Perhaps they had forgotten about her entirely. Breathing deeply, she resumed her eavesdropping. When had Leto seen Mathias *half-dressed?*

"—think I make a habit of it, do you?" Mathias sounded indignant.

Leto stopped walking. She turned to look him full in the face and, as she did so, she caught sight of Melantho, close behind them. *Too* close.

Melantho fought the sudden, frantic urge to hide. Leto knew she was here, knew she would be listening. Leto's eyes flicked back to Mathias.

"You cannot expect me to believe," she said, a peculiar stiffness in her voice that Melantho could not identify the source of, "that with a court full of ladies hanging off your every word, you have never—"

"I am *betrothed*," said Mathias shortly. "To *you*, I might add, and my mother expects that I behave accordingly." He took a short breath, then continued with a softer voice: "Are your parents the same?"

"Yes," said Leto.

Did it hurt to lie like that? To alter her history with a single word? Melantho had not known her parents, not really, but she had heard Leto speak of her own mother often enough, knew that some small, secret part of her heart still longed for her.

"I think they would prefer for me to be under somebody else's supervision," continued Leto.

Mathias laughed. "I can well believe that. Do you climb about the palace in Athens too? Is that why they sent you all the way here? I think this might be the only place far away enough for us not to have heard the rumors that I assume are spread of all your escapades."

Melantho caught herself scowling and smoothed her face out quickly. What on *earth* were they speaking of? Surely it must be the night before, when Leto had clambered down the side of the palace, when she had shamefully remained behind. No, it couldn't be that. Leto would have told her. But what had Melantho missed while she was falling into the shrubbery?

"Absolutely not," said Leto indignantly.

"I am teasing you," said Mathias. He turned and entered the pasture, Leto following his lead. The groom Melantho had spied before was guiding the pony into carefully crafted wooden stables, from which another emerged holding the halter of a sleek charcoal mare.

"It's nice," said Mathias, in such a low voice that Melantho had to strain to hear him, "to speak to someone who understands. Decisions are always being made for me. I feel like my life is moving at a gallop and I am always running to catch up."

Gods, he was just like all the young men that Melantho had once known. Did he think he was a poet? Melantho would mimic him later, back in their suites, and Leto would laugh and smile, and say—

Melantho's stomach lurched. They would not return to their

suites. They would never set foot in the palace again, not after they had sent Mathias hurtling from the cliff's edge. They would have to flee from Ithaca, far beyond any of the Ionian Islands. Melantho shivered and looked up.

The groom had handed Mathias the halter of the charcoal horse, and now Mathias was offering it to Leto.

She took it tentatively. "Good boy."

"She's a girl," advised Mathias.

"Good girl." Leto patted the horse's nose. Its nostrils flared, scenting her.

Leto's eyes were wide with dismay. Melantho would never have taken her horseback riding.

"That's it," said Mathias, smiling. "Look, she remembers you."

Leto frowned. "Remembers me?"

"Sthenios comes from the Athenian stables—a gift from your family." Mathias's smiled slipped. "They told me she was a favorite of yours, but I suppose—"

"Oh! *Sthenios!* Oh, I didn't recognize you!" Leto's voice was just a little too bright. Melantho's fists were tight and tense; she gritted her teeth. Would Mathias see through the lies? "Oh, she's grown!"

Mathias laughed, delighted. "She has! She eats more than any of the others." Melantho allowed herself to relax.

Mathias was still grinning as he fitted a halter over the head of his own horse, a colossal black stallion which snorted and pawed at the ground. He checked its grip swiftly, tugging on the leather straps with a practiced ease. Apparently content with the fit, he dropped the halter. The horse stood obediently still as he walked the few paces back to Leto. "Can I help you up?"

Melantho saw Leto's cheeks flush. "We won't ride too fast, will we?" she asked anxiously as Mathias pushed her up and onto the saddlecloth. She sat in an uncertain straddle, so precarious that Melantho could not help but think that she might slip off at any moment.

Two more horses were brought out. She saw Leto shoot them a curious look. "Are we expecting company? I do not think Melantho needs *two* horses."

Mathias laughed. "No—well, yes. Alexios was going to—"

"Alexios?" Leto's voice was high and panicked. Melantho stiffened, her hand outstretched toward the horse she had decided would be hers. If Alexios was ever going to recognize Leto, it would be here, in the blazing sun, out in the open with nowhere to hide.

Melantho looked around wildly. What could she do, what could she say, to convince the prince that he did not need his guard, to protect the precarious guise Leto wore? Perhaps she could startle one of the horses, or—

"Alexios?" This time, Leto's voice was calm, careful, even . . . sultry? She leaned into Mathias; if Melantho had not been appraising her so closely, she might not have seen how she wobbled in her seat. "Your guard, if I remember correctly. You think you need protecting from me, do you?"

"I—"

"Perhaps it could just be you and me. And Melantho, of course—we cannot go without *any* chaperone, that would be improper, but—" Leto laughed softly. "Well, do you not think it would be a little nicer? I do not enjoy an audience; it makes me feel as though I am performing. But if we are to go alone, I know I can be entirely myself."

There was a long, stunned silence. Melantho balled her hands into fists.

"Well then," said Mathias at last. "I—yes. I see what you mean.

Maybe I'll, erm." He twisted in his seat, like a bewildered child. "Will you tell Alexios that I no longer have need of him when he comes?" There was something lingering in Mathias's voice as he addressed the groom, something Melantho did not like. She ignored it as best she could, returning her attention to her horse. She did not bother to check her halter as Mathias had done—she would hardly know what to look for anyway—but she took a moment to stroke her hands over the horse's short grey fur and look into its wide brown eyes.

"We are both creatures of Poseidon, you and I," she breathed into its ear. "Be kind to me. I am out of practice." That was the legend, of course, that Poseidon had wrought horses from the frothing crest of the ocean's waves. The horse did not seem to know this; it shifted underneath Melantho when she sprang lightly onto its back and whickered irritably. Her chiton had a slit on one side, which meant she ended up flashing the lingering groom a great expanse of her thigh. He went very red and scurried back into the stables.

Leto and Mathias had ridden on ahead already, apparently having forgotten all about her. She spurred her horse on harder than she might had done usually—a mistake she paid for almost immediately when it lurched forward and almost tipped her from her seat.

"This is horrible!" she heard Leto cry from up ahead. "It is so *uncomfortable!*"

"You sound like my sister!" Mathias called back. He was a confident rider; he pulled ahead with ease.

"How many sisters do you have?" Leto bumped up in her seat with every stride her horse took.

"Two," replied Mathias. Something had changed in the set of

his shoulders. He pulled on his horse's reins so the great stallion slowed into a trot.

Leto followed suit, bringing her horse up next to his. Melantho fell in close behind them. Riding was easier than she remembered; perhaps her transformation had granted her better balance.

"How wonderful," Leto said. If Melantho hadn't known better, she would have thought that Leto was genuinely interested. "How old?"

"Hekate must be, oh, twelve now?" Despite the tension in his arms, his back, Mathias's voice was soft. His fondness for his sister was clear in every syllable. "And she's an absolute nightmare! Desperate to travel all over. Last I heard, she wanted to be a witch." He laughed, relaxing at last and launching into some story of his sister's escapades. They had left the palace grounds and started on a rough track that led over the hillsides and toward the cliff.

Leto turned to Mathias and smiled; the lift of her cheeks creased her eyes into grey-brown slits. For once, Melantho was glad to ride behind them. It meant she did not have to fake a smile herself.

Twelve years old.

It was awfully young to lose a brother.

XXVII
A DUST UPON THE PLAIN

Leto

After some time, during which Mathias recounted to Leto what might have been his and Hekate's entire childhood, they came to a place in the track where the path curved sharply to the left.

Before the turn, it ran barely an arm's length from the cliff's edge. Below was a great expanse of ocean. Something about the sight sent chills through Leto's body as she pictured herself leaning over and pushing Mathias from his seat and over the edge. She could almost see the way his expression would change, from lazy contentment to surprise and then fear. One push and the curse would be broken.

Melantho had been sullen and silent behind them, but she had relaxed gradually as they traveled farther from the palace. Now she rode with a joyful wildness, tossing her yellow curls in the wind—they had come loose from her braids—and grinning into the sun that sang above them. It painted her skin gold, and her eyes flashed the green of the grass beneath the horses' hooves. With a gesture from Leto, she would sober herself in an instant. She would help Leto commit murder.

To Leto's right, caught between her and the cliffside, Mathias was still talking about his sister in that bright, loving tone. They were barely three paces from the bend. Two paces. One pace.

If Melantho had seen the opportunity, she did not show it,

did not raise her brows meaningfully at Leto, did not signal that it was *time*. Time to turn to the boy at her side, with his delighted, youthful smile. The boy who had watched Leto die, the boy who loved his sister.

Leto breathed in sharply and turned away from them both. Her stomach rolled, nausea forcing its way up her throat. She could not do it. They had not thought it through, not really, and now the plan's many flaws become apparent. It was too risky. What if Mathias didn't fall all the way to the sea? He had to die in the ocean. Melantho had been clear about that. What if he hit his head on the descent; what if his cloak caught on the skeleton of a long-dead tree?

Leto forced her eyes down, searched the low-lying shrubbery intently, though she was not sure what she was looking for. Dotted about the hard ground were patches of yellow flowers. Daffodils, like the ones Melantho had worn in her hair on Pandou as they'd planned to kill a prince.

Leto's hands shook where they gripped the horse's reins.

And then they were around the bend, the cliff face disappearing from view as Mathias chattered on beside her, blissfully unaware of how close he had just come to death.

◈◈◈

They soon reached the highest point in the hills.

Ithaca lay splayed out before Leto, all orange rooftops and swathes of parched grass. The path was barely a path anymore; in the final stretch of their journey, they had followed nothing but the contours of the land. They'd woven back toward the cliff's edges again—she could hear the sea. Its call was almost irresistible.

Somehow, Leto had become even worse at horse riding since

they had begun. The saddlecloth slipped about under her with every slight movement, and there seemed to be no righting it. "I thought Poseidon was the lord of all horses," she hissed at her mount. "Aren't you supposed to listen to me?"

Melantho, now riding at her side, shot her a wry smile.

Her horse flicked its ears and sped up. Mathias was showing off ahead, galloping his stallion away and then back again at top speed.

The saddlecloth slipped again, and it took all of Leto's strength not to fall. "I hate riding," she hissed to Melantho. "It is a wretched activity for idiots."

"I like it," said Melantho. "I think you would too, if you were not so terrible."

"I am *not*—" Leto began, but she broke off as the saddlecloth moved again, farther and faster than it had before. Melantho hadn't noticed her discomfort; she grinned and, never one to shy from a competition wherever one could be found, galloped after Mathias with the clear intent of overtaking him.

Leto's seat grew progressively unstable. "Mathias," she called ahead at last, slowing the horse to a trot with some difficulty. "Melantho, wait a moment!" she pulled hard on the reins "Stop, you damned thing. I—"

Two things happened then, almost at once. First, her horse tossed its head against the reins and came to an abrupt stop. Second, barely an instant later, the saddlecloth slipped off completely and sent her sprawling sideways.

"Oh, fu—" She smashed face-first into the dirt, the saddlecloth landing in a heap atop her. The horse whickered in satisfaction, lowered its head, and began to graze.

Leto groaned. The impact had knocked the breath from her and the noise she made was so pitiful it was embarrassing.

Her shout had not carried far enough: Melantho had not even slowed. Indeed, she and Mathias were the barest of smudges up ahead by the time one of them remembered her. Mathias wheeled his horse around and caught sight of hers—now riderless. His lips formed frantic words, the sound of them whipped away by the hilltop winds.

As they charged back toward her—Melantho ever so slightly ahead—Leto set about freeing herself from beneath the heavy cloth. As she did so, her eyes caught on the saddlecloth strap—on the buffed leather studded perfectly with round metal pins and the neat cut which bisected it.

Leto gaped at it.

The strap hadn't broken. It had been deliberately sabotaged.

Shit. It must have been Melantho. She must have known that Leto would be a coward, that she would turn away at the pivotal moment. Somehow, she'd found a way to unseat Mathias, a way to make him vulnerable. She must have done it when she'd gone to fill up the waterskin from the fountain. But she'd not predicted that Mathias would offer away his horse; she'd accidentally caught Leto instead.

She had to hide it. Mathias had overtaken Melantho, and he was seconds away, his hair whipping back as he neared her. His face was creased with worry. Leto cast wildly about for a solution; then, finding no other alternative, she hefted the bulky saddlecloth up into her arms and heaved it over the edge of the cliff. It tumbled, buckles flailing wildly about, and caught on a shrub some quarter of the way down. It would have to do. She slumped down to the ground again.

"Leto!" Mathias had dismounted—thankfully, he had been turned away as she threw the saddlecloth—and he dashed to her side, pausing to tie the horses' reins together. "What happened?"

Melantho, a mere moment behind, tossed herself from her seat with an impressive grace. They reached Leto at the same time, Melantho jostling Mathias in a way that could have been played off as concern, or panic even, had her eyes not been so hard, her pink lips not drawn into such a thin line.

Leto ignored it. A dull ache began to build through her right side. She would be bruised beyond belief by the morning. "Damned horse," she managed, teeth gritted. "I hate riding."

Melantho helped her into a sitting position. Mathias, eyes wide with concern, peered over the cliffside at the cloth which swung in the breeze like a large, leathery bat. "Gods," he said. He looked as if he wanted to throw up. "At least you fell the other way. I can't imagine if you hadn't—" He broke off.

"But I *did* manage," said Leto, patting him gently on the arm. Good that he was distracted by thoughts of her safety. It gave him less time to wonder how on earth the saddlecloth could have freed itself from the horse's back and flung itself toward the sea. Less time to notice the tension in Melantho's thighs as she rose into a crouch, her sharp eyes taking in the scene before her.

They were alone, at the edge, the sea churning beneath them.

Mathias was unarmed, crouching at Leto's side.

A rider had been thrown from a horse; if they returned to the palace, it would be easy to say that it had been Mathias. That he had slipped over the edge before they could save him.

Mathias still looked alarmingly unwell, his face an unappealing shade of grey. "And are you hurt?"

"Of course she's hurt," snapped Melantho. "Your horse threw her!"

"W-well," stammered Mathias, taken aback. "Technically, Sthenios is Athenian. . . ."

Leto stared. Melantho did not often speak so sharply. From the expression on Melantho's face, she had realized this too. She flushed pink, lowered her eyes. "My apologies," she said. "I was concerned—"

"You were right to speak so," said Mathias, recovering admirably. "I have hurt your mistress. Your friend."

"I'm not hurt—it's just my pride, I think." Ignoring the looks that Melantho was throwing her, Leto lifted her arm to examine it. She hissed through her teeth at the surge of pain. "And my elbow." She pulled the sleeve of her chiton up and peered at the blotchy skin underneath. "Oh, look at that." She twisted her arm and blood dripped onto her skirts. "I'm bleeding."

"I knew I should have brought another escort." Mathias cast about them wildly. "We need to staunch the wound."

"*I* am here," said Melantho.

"It's only a bit of blood. . . ." Leto trailed off as Mathias pulled his chiton taut in his hands and began to tear a strip from the bottom. "Never mind."

Melantho's eyebrows had shot up and all but blended into her hairline as Mathias began to wrap the strip of fabric about Leto's arm. "Gods, this looks bad."

The wound really was not that deep, but Leto kept her mouth firmly shut and allowed Mathias to continue to fuss over her. At last, with an expression of great satisfaction, he knotted the makeshift bandages tightly. "All done," he said. With the torn strip missing, his tunic was laughably short. It barely reached the middle of his tanned, muscular thighs. For some reason, it was impossible to look away.

"Now, perhaps, is the time to think that you should have brought another escort," said Melantho. Her voice was level, emotionless, but she regarded Mathias's exposed skin with disdain.

"I think you are right," said Mathias. His pallor had returned to its usual warm golden tone, but the worry hadn't quite left his eyes and his lips, usually curled up, were a flat line. "We should be getting back."

He stood fluidly, then reached down to pull Leto to her feet.

They were very close to each other, closer than they'd ever been before with all the decorum and etiquette of the palace. Flushed with sun and exercise, his hair damp, Mathias was beautiful. Leto opened her mouth to say something, then closed it again, the thought evaporating before it had even begun to form.

This was where she *should* catch hold of him and send him tumbling down to the churning waves below. She did not.

Mathias was looking at her, his expression unreadable. "Leto . . ." he began.

She narrowed her eyes at Mathias, whose peculiar, penetrating gaze was still fixed on her. What was happening? Why had she frozen? Why could she not look away? This was *Mathias*. He was ridiculous and royal and cowardly. She was meant to kill him. And Melantho was watching them.

Which shouldn't have mattered. Why did it matter, then? Leto's mouth was bone dry, and her tongue felt like lead.

"Yes?" she managed, the words caught up and lost as the wind whipped about them. The horses tossed their heads impatiently, but Mathias did not seem to notice, or if he did, he did not care.

"You are . . ." he began again, and took a step forward. He was so close now, his chest brushing hers, that Leto could pick out every thread of gold in his dark eyes. She fought down the urge to step away. If he only came a little closer to the edge—

"I think, that is, I am, I have to—"

All of a sudden, he was leaning in to kiss her.

She had never expected him to do something so *bold*—and in front of Melantho? She was too surprised to do anything else; she slapped him.

Then, ripping open the waterskin at her waist so that the fountain water dripped down her leg and sent a surge of power through her body, so that she felt the familiar prickle as Poseidon turned his eyes to her, she tried to throw him off the cliff.

XXVIII

THE MEMORY OF SORROWS

Mathias

Mathias could have sworn that his fiancée had just tried to kill him.

She had slapped him first—a hard, stinging blow that hurt him far more than he cared to reveal—and then she had caught him by the shoulders and forced him toward the edge of the cliff.

She was surprisingly strong, her grip firm and unshaking, and even now, he could not help but feel that she could have succeeded. *Would* have succeeded, perhaps, if her golden-haired maid had not made an awful noise, a gasping, panicked inhale, as she tripped over something—though Mathias never did work out what it was—and went hurtling forward.

Leto had released him instantly. She had caught her maid—*Melantho*, that was the name she had called out—and pulled her into her arms. Mathias had stepped rather hastily away from the edge. It might have been a trick of the light, of the sun as it spilled through the cloudless sky, but watching the girls with the peculiar feeling that he was intruding, he could have sworn that Leto's eyes were filled with tears.

Now, though, he doubted even that.

Because of *course* Leto had not tried to kill him. She had simply reacted to his advances with a great panic, a panic he should have expected, because he had acted without a shred of decency or respect or honor, and he was thoroughly ashamed of himself.

He imagined what Selene would say, how she would frown at him and bunch her thick, dark brows together. She had always done that, on the few occasions when she'd caught him trying to flirt with the maids, and had chastised him so thoroughly he'd felt ashamed for days.

She would have liked Leto, would have liked her apparent disdain for tradition and decorum. She would have taken Mathias aside and told him that Leto would make an excellent wife. That was, if Leto would still have him, a wretched prince to a wretched kingdom.

She would not even look at him now, as she and Melantho rode side by side in his wake.

∾ ∾ ∾

Later, Mathias slumped over the library table and breathed in the scent of moldering papyrus.

The true scale of his failures was beginning to sink in; the first of the marked girls had been found—Alexios had relayed the news to him upon his return from the cliffs—and Mathias had still not found a way to break the curse that would kill her. He had wanted to visit her, to offer what little, futile comfort he could, but Alexios had responded to this suggestion with scathing incredulity and a pointed question: "What would the queen say to that?"

Alexios was right; his mother would certainly not approve of his sentimentality. And now that he had considered it, Mathias was not certain his presence would be anything but unwelcome to the wretched, condemned girl. It would be a selfish thing, one borne entirely of guilt and the fading memory of another girl: Ophelia, the oracle's daughter—furious, fearless, *dead*.

Mathias pushed his face into the wooden tabletop and groaned.

He would find no solace, no aid in Leto, either. At least he would be permitted a single day in which, humiliated, he could hide away here without facing his scathing bride-to-be. The following day, though, his mother had organized a dinner for all the Ithacan nobles to celebrate their prince's betrothal. As the prince, he really ought to attend.

And as the prince's betrothed, Leto would also be there.

He did not know if he would be able to face her. He had been so convinced of what he saw in her eyes—attraction, admiration at the very least—and yet she had rejected him so swiftly and so sharply that he knew now he had been entirely mistaken. Perhaps he should have dallied with the serving girls as Alexios had so often encouraged him to do. Then, he might not be so thoroughly clueless when it came to affairs of the heart, to matters of *emotion*.

Mathias had never been very good at knowing what it was that people were thinking. The only person he'd understood—or *thought* he'd understood until she showed him how very wrong he was—was Selene. And Selene was dead.

He cast a despondent look at her journal. The sheets were scattered on the table beside him, evidence of his desperate, useless search for something, *anything* that would enable him to break the curse. The nearest sheet was some kind of riddle. *Twelve by chance, twelve by force. One by choice.* She'd written the words a dozen times in different orders, half of them crossed through. The page was littered with question marks and ink blotches. Maybe the riddle meant something, but Mathias could not make head nor tails of it. He could never distinguish the useful words from those that were merely the everyday musings of a furious girl. He was useless, foolish.

If Leto did not want him now, he could not imagine how she

would feel when she watched him oversee the execution of a dozen innocent girls for the first time. No matter how much she knew— or didn't know—of Ithaca's plight, he imagined that she wouldn't view this in a particularly favorable light.

It was possible she'd grow to despise him as much as he so often despised himself.

He had not done *enough*; his mother had been keeping him occupied with his duties, sending him on diplomatic trips around the island and demanding lengthy written debriefs. He *had* tried to follow the trail of Ophelia's mother, of Ithaca's last royal oracle. She had written of his death—or at least, *someone's* death, who would be significant enough in his life to be included in his prophecy— and she had lived in the palace, after all. But she'd been cast out more than a decade ago, and it was hard not to feel that he was wasting his time in investigating her. His own death was not an urgent concern.

That, perhaps, was why he had not returned to Vathi, though he considered it increasingly often. After all, that was how he had learned *her* name. But there were just nine days until the equinox and he could not think of her now, could not waste more time in Vathi. Even if a peculiar feeling had begun to unfurl within him, a feeling that he was missing something, that he had been deceived somehow.

His mother was still insisting that they celebrate the spring equinox, as if it were anything but an omen of the deaths that shortly must follow. Year on year, she invited every noble family from the kingdom—and several from beyond—to dine and drink and dance with them. It took place two days before the true equinox, of course, so the visitors were all long gone by the time Mathias rode down to the hanging beach and condemned twelve girls to die. Before twelve families had yet another reason to grieve and rage at their ineffective rulers. This was a time for politics and scheming, as much as it was for delighting in the new springtime. The day itself was not so important.

The queen would not listen to Mathias's protests, so he reveled in small mutinies. The palace was full of bustle, of servants running back and forth with oil lamps and great swaths of fabric, and tradespeople brought up from the villages to make repairs. When Mathias had found a blacksmith wandering the halls on some frivolous errand for the queen, he'd had the man strike down the bolts that held the library's ancient doors closed.

His pleasure at their destruction had been short-lived; the petty rebellion was all but meaningless. Leto would not stay beside him if the curse continued, once she had witnessed its reality and the part he played in it. And with her, she would take the support, the military power, the *gold* of Athens.

A tiny piece of his heart—a part that he had thought had died when Selene had—would go with her too.

XXIX

AS AUTUMN WINDS WHIRL THISTLEDOWN

Leto

Later, after they had all ridden back—Mathias had taken her horse and cantered bareback, which vexed her greatly by sending her pulse racing higher than the riding itself did—Leto stumbled back into her rooms and threw herself onto the bed.

"That did not go as planned," she said to the ceiling. She longed to ask Melantho *why* she had stopped it, why she had lunged for Leto with such reckless force. There must have been something Leto had not noticed, something she had missed. Something that meant it would go wrong. Or perhaps she had talked herself out of it the same way that Leto had: the cliffs were too high, the sea too far. They could not risk Mathias's life like that, not unless they were certain that it would work.

And there was something else too. She was not sure if she had imagined it or if her pain-addled mind had conjured it up from the air—a vision.

It had been fleeting, gone in the blink of an eye.

No, she must have imagined it. She was not so talented an oracle that visions simply *came* to her; they had to be begged from her god, wrenched from him with muttered prayers and burned offerings and the glistening guts of an animal spread out over her table.

Still, she could not stop seeing it, could not ignore it where it clung like a brand to the periphery of her every thought. An image, a moment, something that had not yet come to pass. Something that *would not* come to pass because Leto would not allow it.

Melantho: ashen, gasping, dying. Lips parted, long fingers clutching her scarred throat. And her eyes—wide and green and fearful.

No. The gods were cruel; they fed on fear, on pain, on desire. Leto's heart had already ached with all three. They already had what they wanted. The vision was a figment of her own imagination; the gods had no reason to send it.

She cleared her throat, forced herself back into the present moment. "We can try again, can we not?"

Melantho said nothing. Leto felt the bed dip under her weight as she sat at its edge, but she was not quick with a careful, scathing comment as she usually would have been. Leto rolled over to look at her. Melantho's face was tight with worry, her hands were fisted in the skirt of her chiton. She had rarely looked so somber, even in the early days on Pandou as she had slowly, carefully told Leto of her tragedies.

Leto sat up. "What is it?"

Melantho would not look at her. "I did not trip," she said flatly.

Leto blinked. "What?"

"*I did not trip,*" repeated Melantho with a great force. "At the cliff top, when Mathias tried to—well, when you tried to drive him over the edge. You stopped because—"

"Because you stopped me!" said Leto. "Didn't you? Or you fell—"

"That is what I'm trying to tell you," said Melantho. "I did not fall. I did not trip or stumble or any such thing. I was pushed.

Someone, some*thing* pushed me. I have felt it before, Leto—the touch of a god. And I felt it today."

Leto shook her head. "I don't understand."

Now, Melantho did look up. She fixed Leto with her clear, piercing gaze and *stared* at her so intently that it was uncomfortable. "You don't believe me." It was not a question.

"What, no, I—"

"Don't bother lying." Melantho waved her off with one elegant hand. "I do not blame you."

"I *do* believe you."

"You don't need to." Melantho drew in a deep, calming breath and wrapped her arms over her knees, huddling in on herself. "I know it sounds ridiculous. I am not sure if I believe it myself. I could have imagined the feeling of *them,* of the gods. Perhaps it was only the wind, or the heat, or—or something else. Perhaps I was merely surprised." She shook her head hard. Her voice was suddenly lighter, and her eyes searched Leto's face. "You know, there is something else to talk about."

The vision. She knows. Leto cast about for some excuse. "I—"

"I *am* correct in thinking that Mathias tried to kiss you?"

"Oh." *Oh.* She felt her face go hot.

"He *did*." This time, Melantho grinned, a real smile. Leto could see its truth in the dimples at the corners of her lips, the way her cheekbones lifted and squeezed her eyes half-shut. She was lovely, laughing, she was *alive*. It would do Leto little good to imagine her otherwise.

Leto smiled back. "You would have thought he'd wait until we were alone at least! He must have been quite confident I would accept him. He did not even dismiss you."

Melantho let out a little squeal of mirth. "I would have liked to see him try! I would not leave your side for *anything*, not if it meant missing *that*. Did you see his *face*? He looked like he had swallowed an entire lemon."

Leto laughed. She could not help it; Melantho was right. The shock on Mathias's face, however brief, had been stark and very, *very* funny.

As they descended into another fit of laughter, allowed themselves to fall into a lightness that burned away the fear and the doubt, and then, at last, wrapped themselves in bedsheets and extinguished the last of the lamps, Leto realized that she had not mentioned the cut strap to Melantho. She could have teased her, reminded her to be more careful in the future—*I have already been killed once; I do not wish to experience it again.* She would laugh, softly, to make it clear that she was not angry. Melantho would smile, relieved. She would apologize in a low voice, and Leto would tell her *exactly* what she could do to fix it.

She shook her head.

No, this was not the time for flirtation, for inventing scenarios in which Melantho leaned forward, as she had on the Ithacan harbor, to press her thumb to Leto's cheek. In those dreams, Melantho did not pull away. In those dreams—

Leto pinched herself, hard. Another day, perhaps. She looked up at the ceiling again, at the marble hidden beneath a cloak of darkness. For now, she had more important things to think about.

Like how she had nine days left before the equinox. Nine days to prove herself to Melantho, to show that she could succeed. That Melantho did not have to devise another scheme to aid her, to cut another saddlecloth strap, to help break a curse that she had already lost so much to.

No, it was Leto's turn, and she had nine days to lure Mathias back to the sea, after she had rejected him. And slapped him. And tried to toss him off a cliff.

Nine days. She was painfully aware of Melantho lying next to her in the dark, the shallow sound of her breathing. It would be enough.

It had to be.

XXX

NOTHING BUT DEATH

Melantho

Leto hardly ate a morsel at the betrothal feast.

Melantho knew this because she had been watching her ceaselessly since they arrived. They had been forced to postpone their murder attempts while Mathias vanished to *somewhere* and ignored both of the flirtatious notes Leto had sent to his rooms. Instead, they wasted an entire excruciating day lounging around their apartments, staring into the middle distance, and pretending not to think about their failed effort. About *what* had caused it to fail. Melantho was not so sure in her recollection, now, not quite so convinced that something *other*, something not quite earthly, had sent her lurching forward.

Or perhaps she just did not wish to consider what it would have meant. Either their information had been wrong, and the first girl had not yet been marked, or she *had*, and the gods simply did not wish to see them succeed. Or perhaps they just did not wish to see *Melantho* succeed. Eight days left, then seven, each one wrapped itself around Melantho's heart and did not let go.

Tonight, Melantho had wrapped Leto up in a chiton the precise color of a rose petal and woven a handful of ribbons through her braids. The last, she had knotted carefully around Leto's throat.

Mathias had beckoned Leto to the head of the table, and she sat stiffly between him and his mother. Every time Mathias made a pathetic attempt at a joke, or looked at Leto for a moment too long, or even jumped to his feet to intercept a servant and offer her a dish of asparagus, the queen would shoot Leto a sideways, irritated sort of look and take a long sip of her wine. Her eyes were dark. Melantho wanted to slap the expression from her angular face.

Instead, she stood at the wall, glowering, next to half a dozen of the other servants. The flagon in her hands was empty, but she had no intention of refilling it. She had served her time, half a millennium ago; she would not be reduced to a serving maid again.

Her stomach growled as a serving boy passed with a stack of figs the size of a small goat. Gods, she had forgotten how torturous it was to stand by as nobles stuffed themselves with meat and wine, tossing the scraps of bone and gristle to their dogs. And watching Leto flirting with the prince of Ithaca wasn't helping much, either.

As if on cue, Mathias burst out laughing, shaking his head of black curls and reclining in his heavy wooden chair. He was very pretty to look at, extraordinarily so; he could have been carved from stone and breathed to life by Aphrodite herself. Melantho hated him.

"All right there, darling?"

One of the noblemen had managed to extract himself from his bench—no mean feat, if the vinegar on his breath and the redness in his face was anything to go by—and had clearly deluded himself into thinking that he could persuade her into conversation.

Melantho turned the full force of her scorn on him. "Can I help you?" she asked, injecting every ounce of cold hatred she felt for him—for the gluttony that surrounded them, for the prince, for the whole damned palace—into her voice.

He leaned into her. He smelled even worse up close, of garlic and watered-down red wine.

Melantho hated him. She did not know him—she did not need to—but she already hated his thin, twig-like fingers and his watery blue eyes and the way they crawled over the curl of her hip with a luxurious slowness. She hated the gold and jewels that hung around his scrawny neck and all but threatened to topple him over. She wanted to smash the flagon in her hands across the back of his skull, wanted to watch the redness drip from between his fingers as he clutched at the wound. She wanted to spit in his face. A peculiar fury had bubbled up within her, bringing to the surface years and years of hatred and resentment and—

Sadness.

Melantho sagged.

The memory—soft, quiet, aching—pressed its fingers against her mind and begged to be allowed entry. It was easy to remember Thalia, the press of her lips, the curve of her arms, the splintered shards of her ribs as she'd died. But Thalia had not been the only one; there were other shadows that gathered in the corners of the room with hers, other ghosts that curled themselves into the eaves and whispered against Melantho's ear.

Timo's whispered the loudest. Melantho could not block it out, not this time. The memories—the recollections she had fought so hard for so long to bury—lunged for the surface. She could not catch them; they slipped through her fingers and burst in front of her eyes.

She had stood against this wall with Timo once, had clutched Timo's tiny fingers between her own. Timo was too small to pour well, her wrists and delicate forearms too slight to heave around platters, so Melantho had convinced the queen to allow her to hover behind Melantho and learn.

Timo had been a shadow with olive skin and hair that frizzed around her face like smoke no matter how much she oiled the curls and tried to pin them down. Melantho had been a surrogate sister to her, had protected her from the leering noblemen that dined in the halls.

Her protection had been worth very little in the end.

"Hey!" A clammy, repulsively warm hand closed over Melantho's wrist and dragged her back into the present.

She blinked fast, forcing back tears that had been left unshed for too long.

"Let. Go." Each word was as much of a threat as she dared make it.

He did not. "A young, pretty little thing like you shouldn't look so glum." He leered. "Give me a smile, hmm?"

Another servant was passing by with a platter laden with a fat roasted pig.

Melantho smiled; she knew she looked lovely.

"That's better," crooned the noble.

She lunged for him, sending the both of them spilling backwards into the servant. Grease, hot and pungent, went flying; it burned Melantho's wrist and the pain was so startling, so sobering, that she could have wept. The noble was moaning in a crumpled heap on the floor.

"Oh, *sir*," Melantho crooned, pulling herself off the flagstones and kneeling above him. "Are you well? You just *collapsed*."

His wrist was pinned beneath her knee, hidden by the flowing skirts of her chiton. He moaned.

"A doctor!" she called, pressing down *harder*. Something gave way with a soft *crack* and the nobleman's eyes rolled. "For the nobleman."

She stood in one smooth, fluid movement. "Excuse me," she

said to the servant they had collided with. "I think I should change my clothes." She did not wait for him to answer; she turned on her heel and marched toward the closest door.

As soon as it slammed shut behind her, she let the tears come.

Timo, dead. Agathe, Timo's bright-eyed little sister, dead. Callidora, dead. Euphrosyne, Hebe, Stamatia, and the rest. Sofia, Thalia—so, so many of them. How easy it had been to forget them. How awful to remember.

She had stayed quiet for so long, she had thought she was forgetting, somehow, but now she howled her grief to the darkening skies and yanked at the suddenly suffocating ties of her chiton so that it fell from her frame the moment she made it back to Leto's rooms.

When these seven days were over, when Prince Mathias of Ithaca lay dead at the bottom of the ocean, Melantho would leave Ithaca. At least, she would try. If she survived, if her life was not so hopelessly entangled with the curse as she had always suspected, she would buy passage to Sami on the first ship she could find.

She would never come back.

XXXI

FIERCE AND FULL OF FURY

Leto

Between one long moment and the next—the time in between having largely been filled with a scuffle of movement as Leto knocked her wine over—Melantho had vanished. Leto scoured the hall for her once, twice, then a final, third time before reluctantly concluding that she was truly gone. The crowd of servants had been slowly thinning out as the feast in front of them did—emptied platters of meat and cheese and fruits cleared away silently—so she supposed Melantho had finally been dismissed.

This was not necessarily a bad thing; Melantho's face had been growing steadily darker as the evening went on, and Leto had been too focused on blending in with the nobility to think up a way to save her. A thousand scenarios had run through her head, each resulting in the exposure of her lie. Someone would notice that her voice was not the smooth, Athenian drawl of Adrasteia's, or that her eyes were no match for the princess's, with their deep mahogany. Or they would ask her a question about her supposed homeland, and she would flail so spectacularly that it would be obvious to everyone present that she did not belong at their table and that she was not who she claimed to be.

"What are you thinking of?"

She was jolted from her thoughts by a gentle touch on her wrist and Mathias's soft, low voice in her ear. She had not realized how close he was; when she turned to look at him, the movement disturbed his carefully arranged curls. A single perfect ringlet lifted and settled again.

She blinked. "I—sorry, what?"

"Never mind." His smile was blindingly lovely. "Maybe we should get some air. It's hot in here, isn't it?"

"Is it?" Now that he'd mentioned it, she was suddenly, overwhelmingly aware of it. The warmth of so many bodies, and the dying embers of hundreds of lamps, had rendered the room positively *stifling*. She took a breath of thick, humid air and almost choked on it. "Yes, air. Can we?"

He stood in an easy, fluid movement. The chairs were shockingly heavy—Leto had discovered that after she had dropped a fig beneath the table and been totally unable to push herself back far enough to reach for it—so she waited for him to help her up. Standing made her head spin. She'd either been sitting down for longer than was advisable or had drunk more wine than she had realized.

They walked close together. Too close. Mathias led her by the arm, one of his hands curved beneath her wrist while the other rested against the small of her back, a chaste enough touch to be proper, yet intimate enough to leave her almost breathless.

She looked back as they left. The high table seemed largely not to have noticed their departure, but there was one notable exception: the queen, stock-still, her arms crossed over her chest, and jewels shining upon her brow, was staring after them. Despite the heat, Leto shivered. In the flickering lamplight, the queen's glare was sharp enough to draw blood.

Outside, she took great gulps of the cool evening air and leaned as far from Mathias as was polite until her light-headedness receded. When she was finally confident in her own stability, she detached herself from his arms and sidestepped hastily away.

"Better?" Mathias propped himself against the nearest column.

"Much." She offered him an appreciative smile. "Will they mind that we've gone? Your mother, I mean, and the others?"

He shrugged. She had never noticed it before, how he moved like a performer on the verge of dancing. "They're about to turn the room over anyway."

"For what?"

Mathias was saved answering by the slapping of footsteps nearby. A moment later, Olympia materialized beside them, looking distinctly irritated. When she caught sight of them, even with the careful distance separating them, her expression soured further. Leto could guess why; from the first meal she'd taken with Mathias's court, Olympia had been almost territorially possessive of Mathias. She was always tapping at his shoulder, pulling at his sleeve, doing anything she could to divert his attention from Leto to herself. Another time, Leto might have found it funny, that Olympia clearly thought her a rival. As it was, she just found it irritating.

Olympia tossed her carefully oiled curls over her shoulder and addressed Mathias, ignoring Leto completely. "Are you missing the competition?"

He put a hand to his chest and feigned injury. "I would never."

That seemed to appease her. She cracked a smile. She really was very pretty: tall, with a boyish figure and strong jaw. She wore a deep blue peplos, and her wrists and throat were looped about with gold. "Good. I'll see you in there." She strode away.

Mathias cocked his head back toward Leto. "Ready?" The movement sent the light flashing off his earrings: fat, golden hoops that Leto could have lived off for a year were she still in Vathi. For a brief moment, she felt a peculiar, aching longing for the little village. She may have been out of place there—an orphaned girl, hiding her face behind an oracle's silks—but even that had not come close to how *wrong* she felt here.

She swallowed down the feeling. "Ready for *what*?"

"Let's make it a surprise—I think you'll like it, truly. Come on. Do you trust me?" He offered her his arm.

She forced herself not to scowl. Mathias's trust, his affection, was vital. "I suppose so." She took it and allowed him to lead her inside again.

❧ ❧ ❧

Within those few short minutes, the great hall had been transformed.

The long tables had been emptied of food and drink and carted away somewhere; the floor had been scrubbed clean of wine stains. The lamps that had burned down had been replaced, and the space was brightly lit once again. Emptied like this, its vastness took her breath away.

It took her a moment to understand why the tables had been cleared. In their place, a dozen axes had been driven into the wooden floorboards by their handles, marking a straight path to the heavy, painted target against the far wall. A handful of finely dressed noblemen were gathered at the nearest axe, bows in hand, deep in discussion.

"Oh." Mathias sounded pleased. "They haven't started, that's good."

Leto could not hide her curiosity. She let go of Mathias and drifted closer. "What are they doing?"

"It's tradition for special occasions," said Mathias. There was a playful glint in his eye and the grooves of his lips were wine dark. "To remember Odysseus's return and his feat of strength in stringing the great bow and shooting an arrow through the twelve axe-heads. A show of love to his wife and to his kingdom."

Something in Leto's chest did a peculiar, disappointed sort of flip. Odysseus's return held another significance. It was also the day that he had ordered his wife's maids hanged, that Poseidon had cursed Ithaca in their names. Of course, Ithaca's people did not remember that particular aspect of their history, but the hangings were just seven days away and Mathias had not yet mentioned them to her. Did he think his Athenian bride was naïve to the hangings? And if he did, how long did he intend to hide it from her?

"Odysseus's return?" she ventured. She could not reveal that she knew more than she was expected to. "I seem to recall some history there?"

"Oh." He shot her a brief, guilty glance. "Well, it is the most exciting thing to happen in Ithaca's past, I suppose. The bards like to embellish it."

Leto forced a smile. *Exciting?*

"Come on, we'll get the best view from over here."

He led her to the head of the hall, where the queen stood with a cluster of women in jewel-toned peplos. She almost stumbled when Mathias came to an abrupt halt still several paces away from them.

"A little privacy," he said, in answer to the look she was giving him. "I am tiring of company."

"Perhaps I should go?" She should probably find Melantho anyway.

"My apologies. I spoke vaguely. I am tiring of company that isn't yours."

She shot him a surprised sideways look. A flush of pleasure unfurled itself in her stomach. "Well—"

"Oh!" he interrupted her. His eyes lit up. "They're starting!"

She turned back to the axes. The men had organized themselves into a jostling queue. As Leto watched, the first—a huge, dark-haired man with hands the size of dinner plates—raised his bow and, with a dull grunt, fired an arrow toward the axes. It passed through the head of the first, the second, moving so fast Leto could not keep track until it clipped the head of the ninth and went spiraling off course.

It thudded into the handle of the tenth and stuck there, vibrating. A murmur went up from the assembled spectators. The queen clapped politely and a handful of her ladies hastily copied her.

"That wasn't that bad," muttered Mathias. "Most don't make it past the eighth."

"Oh," said Leto politely. A second archer was moving into position. His arrow, when fired, hit the first axe and fell to the ground.

The third, then the fourth competitors took their turns without success. It was the fifth, a lithe, boyish member of the Ithacan guard, whose arrow first struck the target.

Mathias huffed out an anxious breath. "Oh good. I was hoping one of ours would get it."

There must have been upwards of forty men competing, but even once each had tried their hand at it, only three arrows had made it to the target. The watching ladies had lost interest by the twentieth; even Leto was watching servants filing in with more wine when someone shouldered past them into the room and captivated her attention completely.

Olympia had returned.

Leto could only stare. Olympia wore a chiton in the men's style, loose and short, showing off the lean muscles of her calves. In her hands was a longbow, its arrows slung across her back. She had pulled her loose curls up and removed her gaudy jewelry. She looked *fearless*. Leto could almost imagine her as one of Artemis's huntresses, running unchecked across the wild places of the world.

Leto was only half surprised to see her striding not toward the queen and her ladies but toward the cluster of competitors. She offered a small, encouraging smile. A gesture of peace.

Olympia's eyes slid, unseeing, across her face and found Mathias's instead. He had not noticed her entrance; he was fiddling idly with the clasp of a bracelet and humming tunelessly under his breath. Olympia set her jaw and marched up to the shooting line.

She nocked an arrow in a single fluid movement, pulled the bowstring taut, and looked again at Mathias.

He was still not looking. Leto elbowed him in the ribs and tried for a smile again. This time, as Mathias looked up with a small, injured noise, Olympia saw her. Her shoulders stiffened. She broadened her stance and held Leto's gaze, her face impassive. She was still staring at Leto as she loosened her grip on the bowstring, as the arrow went spinning away, passing neatly through the gaps in the axe handles, and slammed into the center of the target. Leto felt her smile slip from her face.

Mathias whooped. Olympia grinned, baring her teeth with feral joy.

Mathias insisted upon accompanying Leto back to her rooms after the rest of the competition, which somehow had ended pleasantly enough. Olympia had walked away with the champion's prize—a fine new axe head of her own, which she accepted with a brilliant smile.

Mathias was glued to her side as they strolled through the corridors. Exhausted, a little drunk, and with no *immediate* plans to murder him, Leto was happy enough to entertain his rambling narration on the short walk as he pointed out the various tapestries and the finest of the views from the windows. After all, if she was going to convince him to accompany her to the sea, she needed him to trust her.

It was also, she had to confess, useful to have a guide. She *still* hadn't quite learned her way around, and the corridors looked very alike in the low flicker of torchlight. But Mathias navigated the halls easily, tugging her by the elbow down passageways so narrow Leto would never have noticed them without him.

They paused at last at the beginning of another unfamiliar corridor, lined on one side with a great number of marbled busts. The other side boasted yet more tapestries. The few closest to Leto depicted a very vicious battle. A central figure was contorted in the throes of death, an arrow piercing his ankle.

Mathias followed her gaze. "The Trojan War," he said in a tone that suggested Leto should have known it by sight. She did. Everyone did. A decade of needless death and destruction architected by the gods themselves. "These tapestries tell the story of Odysseus, you see."

"Oh, yes," said Leto politely. Surely, now he would tell her of the curse. Would his face crumple in familiar guilt as he spoke the words? Would he look away from her again at the worst moment?

"My ancestor," continued Mathias, oblivious to her expectation.

"Look, here he is." He moved toward one of the busts depicting a stern-faced man with a mass of curls and thick beard. He looked to Leto for approval. She forced an expression of neutrality, even as her stomach turned.

"And here is Telemachus," continued Mathias. "Then I confess I do not know the rest by heart." He laughed uneasily. "But of course, these are the legends of Ithaca. Are they well known in Athens?"

Was he . . . *testing her*? Finding out how much she knew of the curse? She would not give him an easy way out; she wanted him to look her in the face and tell her everything. Leto cleared her throat. "I confess," she said, "I know few stories from your western islands. If they are common in Athens, they have sadly evaded me. My mother preferred to tell us tales with what she viewed as teachable moments."

This was actually true. Leto's mother had always taken care to ensure that her daughter understood all the risks and evils of the world—narcissism, curiosity, and ambition were her particular favorites—and how to avoid them. She had, unfortunately, neglected to teach how to overcome such risks once unavoidably ensnared. A few more tales of heroes and battles might have served Leto well in her current predicament.

Something shifted across Mathias's face. Resolve? "Well, you should know, really. This will be your kingdom soon. But then"—he averted his eyes—"you will be expected back at your chambers, will you not? I will not have time to tell you everything."

Leto's mind went briefly to Melantho, but she dismissed the thought easily. She had to know what he would say to her. Besides, this was research. If Mathias knew too much of the curse and its origins, then he would be quicker to suspect them, more wary of the ocean and its power. Melantho would understand. "I am not needed," she said. "And I have time if you do."

"Well then," said Mathias. He offered Leto his arm, though his eyes would still not quite meet hers. "Will you allow me to explain to you the contents of these fine tapestries?"

Leto took the proffered arm. Mathias's skin was very warm— she could feel the heat through the thin fabric of his tunic. The blood that ran through his veins would be cold soon. What would it feel to look upon him then? Would he be as lovely in death as he was in life? Would she grieve for him?

"I believe I will," she said.

Mathias was a surprisingly excellent storyteller. He began where the tapestries started—the end of the Trojan War—and launched at once into the epic tale of Odysseus and his decade-long struggle home to Ithaca.

Though Leto had not remembered them at first, she recognized some of the tales, though Mathias's renditions were far more engaging. His version of Odysseus's encounters with the cyclops Polyphemus, in which he put on great booming voices for each character, had her laughing more genuinely than she had since she first arrived at the palace.

"—and Odysseus tells Polyphemus, 'My name is Noman!' and blinds him. In agony, Polyphemus bellows out to the other cyclopes, 'Noman has hurt me! Noman has blinded me.' So they shrug and leave him to his bawling." Mathias grinned.

"But surely he did not need to name his attacker?"

"Ah, that is the beauty of these tales," Mathias reassured her.

"They fall apart under the slightest of probing. Fantasy cannot always be as robust as truth."

"You mean that the stories are not true?" If Mathias believed them fiction, then surely he did not know of the link that joined Odysseus to Ithaca's curse. The link to Mathias himself.

"Oh, no, they are true," Mathias persuaded her swiftly. "Though embellished a little by the returning hero, that's all. Besides!" He pulled her along to the next panel, depicting a retreating ship narrowly avoiding the path of a great boulder. "This story is certainly true in one way or another—see, here is Odysseus sailing away from the island of the cyclopes."

"Which makes it true?"

Mathias nodded. "Oh, absolutely. You see, Odysseus is arrogant and desperate for fame and recognition. As he sails away, he calls out to the blinded cyclops, 'You have been bested by King Odysseus of Ithaca.' Then Polyphemus almost crushes the whole boat with a rock, which would have been an unfortunate end for Odysseus, but he misses." Mathias beamed excitedly at Leto. "Now here comes the pivotal part. The cyclops goes crying to his father about this Odysseus of Ithaca and his father gets *angry*."

"Poseidon," said Leto flatly. It was always Poseidon. If not, it was Zeus.

Mathias looked triumphant. "*Exactly*. Poseidon now *hates* Odysseus and makes it his life's mission to ruin him."

"And that's why you still sacrifice those girls to him every year?" She could not help it. He did not seem in danger of stopping his story, did not seem any closer to discussing the curse with her. Perhaps she had misread the look in his eyes, and he was hoping to conceal it from her a while longer.

Mathias's delighted demeanor vanished in an instant. He

stared at her with an expression of such shame and horror that she felt positively wretched.

"I—" he began. "No. That is not why. I was not certain you knew of our island's curse at all."

He *had* been hiding it from her. Fury, startling in its ferocity, burned her throat. She said sharply, "I know a little."

"Oh," said Mathias, and said nothing more.

Leto felt a surge of indignance. How *dare* he be evasive? Did he truly think he could hide from her the lost lives of hundreds of innocents? In such a grand palace, filled as it was with its statues and tapestries and vases, she had not seen the slightest sign that any of these girls were remembered or mourned or even acknowledged for the great sacrifices they had made.

She was one of those girls, no matter how hard she tried to forget it. She scowled at Mathias. "I have the right to ask," she snapped. "When I first heard that you oversaw the ritual hanging of innocent young women, I was led to think the worst of you. And why should I not?"

Mathias looked appalled. "It is a shadow that lies over this kingdom. If we fail to fulfill our obligation to the sea god, his wrath is incomparable. We have—*I have* tried to deny him. You must understand, Leto, that there are villages that once existed on Ithaca that exist no longer. Each was destroyed the moment that Poseidon realized he would not be receiving his bounty." The tentative truce that existed between them had vanished. He would not even look at her; he balled his chiton up in his hands and stared intently at the tapestry. "So Poseidon came to get it himself."

Leto had seen the razed section of the island enough times. Mathias was speaking the truth now.

"And the curse cannot be broken?" she probed. Perhaps he

knew. It would certainly erase the eventual guilt of killing him if he had known his death could save the girls that had died alongside her—the ones that had not come back as she had.

Mathias shook his head. "Not that I know of." He looked suddenly at her with a great intensity and caught up her hands in his. "Leto—you must know. If there were a way, if I could rid my people of this grief, I would do so. I swear it to you. You must not think ill of me. I have been *trying*. . . ." He seemed to run out of words here; his mouth continued to move helplessly but no sound emerged.

He was frantic for her approval. It should have made her feel *something*—a boy this beautiful, desperate to earn her affection— but she felt nothing but dread and anger and a grief that bubbled up inside her and threatened to spill over.

Leto said nothing. So he knew nothing. Nothing that would help her, nothing that would explain what had happened on the cliff tops—the scene that had flashed before her eyes, the invisible force that had pushed Melantho toward the edge. She pulled her hands from his grip and let them hang at her sides. "I think I will go to my chambers," she said. "I have a sudden headache."

Mathias looked crushed. "Yes, of course," he murmured, dropping his eyes. "Behind the last tapestry is a passage that will take you there directly. It is what I had hoped to show you here. Your maid may be able to help with your headache. I . . . I wish you a swift recovery." He nodded to her, then turned and walked away before she had a chance to answer. For a moment, Leto listened to the echoing sound of his boots. Then she heard the creaking of an opening door, and silence fell once more.

XXXII

CRY ALOUD FOR SORROW

Leto

She did as Mathias had bid—ducked beneath the final tapestry—and emerged mere moments later in the corridor that led to her rooms. She made sure to stamp her feet loudly as she entered, so Melantho would know precisely how furious she was.

"I swear," she announced, "Mathias is the most *infuriating*, cowardly—" She broke off abruptly as she laid eyes on Melantho.

Melantho's face was twisted wildly; her hair was a mess. Her hands were clenched into tight, furious fists. There was dried blood on her golden wrist. "You're here," she said. "Good."

Without another word, she brushed past Leto and marched out into the corridor. Bewildered, Leto followed.

Melantho's stride was purposeful, her sandals slapping rhythmically against the marble floors; she pulled her chiton up in one hand to avoid catching its hem beneath her feet.

Leto could hardly keep up with her. "What's the rush?"

"What's the rush?" Melantho spun around without warning; Leto walked straight into her.

"Tonight," said Melantho. "I hate this place, every wretched part of it. I cannot be here a moment longer. We try again tonight." She turned and resumed her frantic pace.

"Tonight? Melantho, what—" Leto tried to catch her by the

shoulder, to slow her, but Melantho shook her off. "Can you *wait*? I don't understand!"

Melantho did not stop until she had reached Mathias's rooms. There were no guards outside, which Leto suspected meant that there was probably no prince inside. Melantho paused there, allowing Leto to catch up to her, and then she flung the doors open.

The room was empty, as Leto had known it would be.

So was the next, hidden behind a gold curtain, and the next after that. Mathias was nowhere to be found. Some part of Leto was strangely relieved. They had seven days still—or six, now, since it was surely past midnight. They did not need to be *this* rash.

"He is not here, Melantho. We should go before he returns to find us snooping around his things again!"

"Again? I will remind you that *I* stayed in our chambers while you were off with your *half-dressed* prince. He must be here *somewhere*. He must be! Where else would the little rat go?"

"*Melantho.*" Something about the way that Melantho had spat the words *half-dressed* was beyond fury, beyond pain. Was it . . . *jealousy*? Leto caught her by the shoulder, hard, and forced her still. "*He is not here.* And even if we were to find him, I do not think you are in the state of mind to be trying anything! What is *wrong* with you?"

Melantho made a choking noise, a noise that sounded like a word. No, a name. A name that Leto had heard before, uttered by Melantho as she dreamed, her face screwed up in anguish.

Thalia.

Leto did not ask Melantho why Thalia's name was always the first from her lips. She did not ask Melantho if it was Thalia she dreamed of each and every night as she curled up beside Leto.

She merely took Melantho by the hand, drew her into her chest, and said, ever so quietly, "I am here, Melantho. You can tell me anything."

Melantho drew in a deep, gasping breath. "Leto," she said. "Leto, I cannot." She curled her fingers into Leto's skirts. "I cannot. I do not know what to say."

"Who is Thalia?"

Melantho's hands went still. She sighed, her shoulders dropping, but she did not move away. "Thalia was my lover," she said.

Leto had almost expected it. Still, it *hurt*. "I—What happened to her?"

"She was one of us. And then she died," said Melantho shortly. "Struck down with a spear, wielded by one of the king's guards. It went straight through her. She found her way to Pandou just in time to tell me, just in time to *die*." The word was all but lost in a gasping, painful breath. There were tears streaking Melantho's cheeks. "Even the power of the sea in her couldn't heal a wound like that. Stupid girl, she always got too close, took too many risks. She wouldn't plan, wouldn't think, wouldn't let me try to protect her. Not that I could, really, but I could have tried. She always wanted to be the one to break the curse. She was never satisfied, even after she'd killed so many. . . ." Melantho trailed off. "She knew there was one left. She wanted . . . she wanted to see it through."

"Right," said Leto. A question bubbled over her lips before she could stop it. "How did she *know*, though? That there was one left? How do *you* know, if so many of the girls set off and never came back?"

"I *feel* it," said Melantho. Her eyes were burning. "It feels—it feels like exhaling after holding my breath for an age. It should hurt; it should feel awful because a man lies *dead* each time. But it doesn't. It is always a relief, and it is terrible. And of course, if that wasn't enough—" She thrust her wrist into Leto's face. "Look."

It took Leto a moment to understand what she was meant to be looking at. What she had assumed to be a beauty mark, a perfect circle on the inside of Melantho's wrist, was a tiny black scale.

"There were twelve of them once," said Melantho quietly. "And now, there is one. See?"

"I see," said Leto.

A pause.

"So I *know*," said Melantho, "that this will work. But—but that isn't all. *Thalia* isn't all. There is one other you should know of. Her name was Timo, and I loved her more than I had loved anyone before. Or since."

Oh. Hurt reared in Leto's chest.

"I failed her," said Melantho. "Timo was—Timo is—the first and last in my heart. I loved her as a sister more than anything. She was tiny and frightened and unfailingly gentle. If you met her, you could wish only to protect her."

I loved her as a sister. Leto would not admit it, of course, but Melantho's words loosened the coils of a knot she had not known was bound within her.

"I'm sorry," she said. "What happened to her?"

"She was one of us." Melantho's smile was bitter. "So I'm sure that you can guess. But I shall tell you anyway. There was a king, a long time ago. He was a romantic, a fool, and—you must understand—the curse demanded that he must die."

"I understand," said Leto.

"Good," said Melantho. "Good, because I will not have you judge her. It was the king's fault, you see; the evening that it happened, he took his wife out rowing on the ocean. Alone, unprotected, it was an opportunity that could not be passed by. Timo tipped the boat, dragged him down, and drowned him. She left the wife with the wreck."

Leto listened silently.

"Timo resurfaced to find the wife screaming, crying, hysterical and splashing about in the water. Searching for something. Her child."

"No," said Leto softly.

"Timo took her to the shore. She was fighting her the whole time—she left nail marks all over Timo's body—and when Timo returned to the boat, she found the body of her son. He couldn't have been more than three years old, blue in the face and already so far beyond saving it would have been hopeless to try. But Timo tried. She commanded the water from his lungs, tried to force his little heart to beat, but he had died with his father."

"She didn't do it on purpose, though. She couldn't have known."

"Perhaps she would have done it anyway," said Melantho. "The child was a prince, he was of royal blood, and he was given to the sea as the curse required. Still, whatever she had intended, Timo said that she had done her part."

She did not have to say what Timo had done, then. Leto could see it in her eyes, and she knew the truth.

"Come," she said even softer. "It does no good to dwell on such things. We should leave—we don't want to be discovered here."

Melantho laughed. "I do not care. There is nowhere in this palace I can go. Timo follows me everywhere."

Leto thought suddenly of her mother. How her scent, her signature, her very *essence* had clung to the house, to the little room where she used to sell her prophecies. After her father died, Leto should have stayed there. But she had spent days hauling all their possessions across Vathi, into the house she had lived in since. Sometimes, there were parts of her past that she could not erase. She could only run, run, run from it and hope it did not follow.

"The sea, then?" Leto wanted to feel the water between her fingers, the surge of power that came with it. "They will not stop us. We will tell them we are going to pray."

"The sea?" Melantho sighed. "I will never be free of it, will I? But you are right. We should pray to Poseidon, I suppose, that he will look kindly on us the next time we make an attempt to . . . well, to break the curse." Leto was glad that she did not mention Mathias's name; she did not wish to think of his death tonight. Not when Melantho's tale had clenched her heart into a tight little fist and not let go.

Melantho had not noticed her trepidation. She rambled on, her grief and her pain set aside somehow. For now. "And *gods*, it has been so long. We should *practice*. Perhaps you can make me another bird. Given that you ruthlessly murdered my last one."

"They are not *alive*," said Leto.

"I know," said Melantho, "but I should like another, all the same."

XXXIII

THE GOING DOWN OF THE SUN

Leto

Melantho had spoken of prayer and practice, but when they reached the beach at last—having stammered their excuses to a nearby servant and sprinted from the castle before anyone could stop them—she merely sighed and spread herself out on the damp sand at the water's edge, eyes closed. The moisture turned her thin gown sheer.

Within moments, moonlight played off the emerald scales which rose from where she sat. They covered her from navel to hip then cascaded over the tops of her legs—splayed like jeweled seaweeds in the shallows and moving gently up and down with the tides. More scales peppered the bony tops of her feet and toes and dissolved into muted sage in the soft creases of her knees and thighs and the achingly tantalizing space between them.

The bronzed skin of her torso blossomed with a spray of mossy freckles. They shifted in and out of existence as splashes of salt water settled and then dried in the warm night air. Amongst the strands of black and jade in her hair were glossy threads of gold, which caught in the wind, glowing, and then vanished like wrasse startled in the reefs.

Leto leaned over and caught up a stray golden ringlet on her little finger. Melantho's eyes fluttered open for an instant and then closed again as she tilted her head back slightly. Curls fell away to expose her slender neck, with its ring of terrible black scales, risen from the sea with the rest. Leto had not thought much of them—beyond that once, at the Ithacan harbor, as they prepared themselves for the palace—but she wondered again now why Melantho's came and went with the tides. Why her own never did.

"What are you thinking of?" asked Leto abruptly.

Melantho didn't open her eyes. "You."

"Oh."

"I wouldn't have been able to leave without you," said Melantho. "Even now, I can barely believe that I am here."

"You are here," said Leto. "You're free."

"I will never be free," said Melantho.

A flash of anger twisted itself around Leto's throat. "Don't say that," she snapped. "Don't you ever say that to me, Melantho. You must know that your freedom is as fine a prize to me as Ithaca's. The future I dream of, the future in which the girls of Ithaca do not face death each year, you are *part* of that future. We are friends, you and I, are we not? You know that I will not leave this place without you. You have to be free. You have to be."

Melantho was quiet. Then, opening her eyes at last: "We are friends, then, in this future of yours? That is what you long for?"

No. "Yes," said Leto. "Yes. I will not be able to face the world without you."

"You may have to."

Leto glared at her. "I will *not*."

"You seem very sure of that." Melantho's eyes would not meet hers. They traced a path over Leto's cheeks and down, across her lips.

"I have to be," said Leto. And then, though it was impulsive, and ridiculous, and could have ruined every part of the precious tapestry of true companionship that had woven itself between them, Leto leaned over and kissed her.

She wasn't sure what she had expected. Perhaps Melantho would jerk away with an expression of surprise and distaste. Perhaps she would simply freeze under Leto's touch. Perhaps, worst of all, she would half-heartedly humor the advance for a few moments, then draw back, icy and unaffected.

But Melantho did nothing of the sort. The instant that Leto touched her, she was curving her body up from the sand in a tight arc to fit it perfectly against Leto's chest, bringing her knees up to trap Leto's waist. Her arms encircled Leto's shoulders even as her mouth opened against Leto's and she made the softest of sounds. She smelled of woodsmoke; she tasted of ripe figs.

Leto let her eyes flutter closed. She was kissing *Melantho*. It was all too astounding. Every nerve in her body was prickling, and her heart had begun to thrum so rapidly in her chest that she was almost worried it would fly out of her altogether. Melantho's lips were warm and soft. She cupped Leto's jaw with one hand and pulled her closer, closer, closer.

Finally, Melantho said, not with words, but through the movement of hands and legs and lips. *Finally*, Leto replied, though her mouth was occupied. She said it with tugging of hair and clutching of hips and the slow, luxurious dragging of her tongue over the curve of Melantho's neck and the shallow pool of sun-flushed flesh above her collarbone.

The sound of the ocean faded into the background as Melantho twisted and arched and sighed underneath Leto's touch, feather-light at first and then bolder. It was quite wonderful to discover that there was a spot on her left shoulder which, when scratched with the edge of cut-short fingernails *just so*, would send her jerking up with a muffled cry, and that her taut stomach rolled with waves of tension when, at last, at long last, Leto pressed her hand sweetly between shaking thighs and began where far-fetched and impossible fantasies had always left off.

⟋⟍⟋⟍⟋⟍

Later they lay curled together, half-asleep, like cats in patches of bright sunshine. Leto lay sprawled across Melantho with her head nestled above her breasts. She threaded her hand absentmindedly through Melantho's tangled tresses, pausing occasionally to unpick a knot or to fish out grains of sand or the odd twig. A beach, upon reflection, might not have been the best choice of location for amorous happenings. There was sand in Leto's hair, under her fingernails, in between her toes, and most uncomfortably—

"There is sand *inside* me," deadpanned Melantho. "I have endured it tolerably thus far, but it is migrating to areas I have to deem unacceptable."

Leto laughed. She felt like she was too full of happiness—her chest was light with it. "Shall we go back?"

Melantho nodded and offered Leto her cheek. Such a small, natural gesture that made every part of Leto's heart thrum with joy. She kissed Melantho on top of her golden cheekbone and got to her feet.

"Come on then. I'll race you."

⟋⟍⟋⟍⟋⟍

They returned to the palace in the early morning, slipping through the door that they had left unlocked. In the half dark, Leto leaned against the stone wall of the narrow passageway they had entered, heart thrumming in her chest. She lifted a hand and gently traced her lower lip, reveling in the memory of Melantho's mouth there and felt herself smiling without quite meaning to. She could hear Melantho's quiet breathing at her side.

"—yes, I am *trying*, Olympia. But there are other things to do—we have had five more reports of marked girls. I will have to collect them tonight, or early tomorrow morning if I cannot rouse some lazy bastard to come help me. We have to be efficient about it. Visitors will start arriving for the festival soon, and we don't want them seeing more than they need to . . ."

Leto started at the sound of Alexios's voice echoing around the corner. She pressed herself against the wall swiftly, ducking into the shadows thrown by the bracketed torches as best she could. Melantho was a rustle of skirts at her side, wide eyes caught in firelight. Leto pressed a finger to her lips.

She had caught Alexios's unfriendly glances more than once. He'd shown no sign of recognizing her, but she could not escape the creeping, choking fear that he might. She held her breath, praying that he would not continue on and discover their hiding place; it was a far better thing to keep a safe distance.

Especially now, as he spoke of the marked girls, as he plotted their retrievals and their deaths. Leto swallowed hard. She knew firsthand what he was capable of, could still hear the harsh, cracking sound of her flesh as he slapped her, his spittle-flecked face distorted with fury. It was not long until twelve more girls were at his mercy.

And his sister was really not much better. The look on her face as she had fired her perfect shot was not so easy to forget.

"It is hard to catch her in any suspicious act when I can so rarely locate her at all," Alexios continued furiously. Leto and Melantho had clearly stumbled upon an argument between the siblings. "It is only the prince that interacts with her at all, though I wish he would not."

"Nasty foreigner," agreed Olympia. "Why Mathias does not see the quality in the women of *Ithaca*, I don't know. What could Adrasteia, with her silly makeup and unkempt hair, *possibly* offer him? I bet *she* cannot string a bow." Leto's mouth fell open in outrage. Melantho caught her hand and squeezed it. Tightly. A warning.

"There's something I don't like about her," Alexios continued, interrupting Olympia as she continued to rattle off a substantial, and rather chastening, list of Leto's flaws. "I feel as if I recognize her, though I can't think from where. . . ."

As silently as possible, Leto groped behind her for the bolt of the door she had just shut. Perhaps if they were very fast, they could slip back through before Alexios saw them. She tugged. The door stuck fast and she swore under her breath.

The sound of Alexios's and Olympia's footfalls stopped abruptly. "Did you hear that?" Olympia asked.

At Leto's side, Melantho straightened and reached out for one of the torches.

"Stay behind me," said Alexios. "Whoever it is—" She heard the distinctive sound of sliding metal as he drew his sword. "Who's there?" he called out.

Leto gave the door a last fruitless tug. It stayed stubbornly put. Right. With a warning look at Melantho, she took a deep breath, squared her shoulders, and marched up the passageway toward Alexios and Olympia. She was a princess. She could do as she pleased. "Who is asking?" she called back, hoping she sounded imperiously haughty and not like a disobedient child.

She heard a mutter pass between the siblings; then she rounded the corner and they were almost face-to-face. The two couldn't have looked more different; if Mathias hadn't told Leto of their relation, she would never have put it together. Alexios was huge—he took up more than half of the space in the passage. Olympia stood next to him in a sweeping purple gown, with a face like sour milk. Her hair was still pulled up, though a handful of wispy curls had come loose at the front, framing her perfectly balanced features. Both her fierceness and her loveliness were even more pronounced up close. If she did have designs on Mathias, it wouldn't have been the most unreasonable match. The thought did not sit well in Leto's stomach.

"Hello," said Olympia stiffly.

"Hello," said Leto. "I was—" She racked her brain for an excuse and came up with nothing but the memory of Melantho. Her lips, her eyes, her thighs—

"Visiting the kitchen, were you?" sniffed Olympia. "I notice that you did not eat much at dinner."

"How delightful that you noticed," said Leto.

"It was a relief," said Olympia. "You do chew so *very* loudly."

Leto frowned. The other girl's boldness was startling.

"You should ask your maids to alter that gown," said Olympia. "It is not flattering at all. I hope you have something for the festival that is more . . . befitting of your position. Now, if you will excuse us, my brother and I have somewhere to be."

She seized the silent Alexios by his sleeve and marched him forward. Leto sucked in a fearful breath—would they discover Melantho too, and wonder what a princess and her maid could have been doing alone in the dark? Suspect what they *had* been doing?— but they moved toward a door she had not noticed, hidden in the shadows where the corridor curved. As they passed Leto—she had to flatten herself against the stone wall to make room—Olympia shot her a look of open contempt. "Good night," she said.

"Good night," said Leto politely, wishing furiously that she, too, had been trained in the art of insult. The real Adrasteia would have known exactly what to say. Surely she could make some scathing remark about being Mathias's fiancée, a clever reminder that she had what Olympia coveted.

But her mind was still blank as Olympia and Alexios stepped through the door and closed it behind them with a deliberate snap.

Leto scowled after them.

Melantho, quiet as a mouse, rounded the corner and curled her fingers through Leto's. She pressed her mouth to Leto's neck. "Oh, she's so jealous."

"Hmm?" Leto could think of little but the brush of Melantho's lips.

"Olympia. She sounded like she was walking on nails. The sight of you must be *agonizing* to her; she must know she looks like a child next to you. Gods, it took everything in me not to laugh."

Leto managed a grin. "So *you* do not mind my silly makeup and unkempt hair?"

Now Melantho did laugh, reaching out and tugging one of Leto's loose curls. "The makeup is very silly," she said. "But it serves a purpose. As for your hair . . . well, I do not mind it being unkempt, so long as *I* am the one who made it so."

"Oh?" Leto leaned into her.

"*Oh*," said Melantho. "In fact, I think it's looking a little neat, maybe I should—"

Leto did not let her finish the sentence; she was already pushing the door open and dragging Melantho back to their rooms, all thoughts of Olympia and Alexios cast from her racing mind.

XXXIV

OUT TO SEA AGAIN

Leto

Ithaca would not permit Leto to be happy. Mathias summoned her
the very next morning to meet him in the room that, in his letter,
he called "the war room."

"Romantic," snorted Melantho, tearing open a warm bread roll
and slathering it with oil. It was raining outside, the droplets lash-
ing against the walls and spilling through the gaps between the
shutters.

"I have to go," said Leto dully, regarding her own breakfast—a
handful of grapes and a generous slab of goat's cheese—with dismay. She had been hoping to use the day to plan, to consider, to
devise another scheme to lure Mathias to the sea. She knew she
should be serious, but she felt buoyant, dizzy with delight. "Oh
gods, do you think he's planning a *war*?" she asked Melantho.
"Will you go ahead for me, see what he intends, and *try* to make it
less terrible? I am not even dressed."

Besides, she was not sure she could face Mathias alone. The
last time she'd seen him, she'd made it clear how little she thought
of his kingdom and his crown. The time before that, she'd tried to
kill him.

"You don't need my help getting dressed?" Melantho winked.
The night on the beach—and then, in the bed they shared

afterward—had changed everything between them. Melantho was almost giddy.

Heat rushed into Leto's face. What was this? What *were* they? Waking up together had been like lying in the summer sun: warm, comforting, familiar. Looking at Melantho now made her thoughts stutter and grind to a halt. "I don't need you *distracting* me. Not right now, anyway. Please, will you go for me?"

Melantho shrugged, taking a bite of bread. She spoke with her mouth full. "As you command, *Princess.*"

Leto threw the grapes at her.

9 9 9

The war room was in a part of the palace that Leto had not been to before; she walked past it twice before a helpful manservant showed her where to go.

The heavy wooden door was slightly ajar. She stepped inside and pulled it shut behind her.

The room was bigger than she had expected, the walls lined with marble columns that all but groaned under the weight of the high, sweeping ceilings. It was as lavishly decorated as her own, a dizzying display of extravagance in intricately embroidered tapestries and amphoras atop little display columns and a great circular table cast from marble. Someone had carved tightly spiraling patterns over its surface and filled them with rivers of molten gold.

When Leto stepped closer, she saw that the spiraling patterns came together in perfect cohesion, forming a shape she knew all too well: Ithaca, the coasts and contours of the kingdom in glittering gold.

Mathias stood behind it. "Leto," he said. His tanned cheeks

were flushed, and his hair was damp, the perfect curls pasted to his forehead. He must have come in from outside; even from across the room, Leto could smell the rain on him—wet grass and something sweet. She was not sure what she had expected from the prince besides jewels and undeserved airs, but she had certainly not predicted that he would be so . . . outdoorsy. Mathias smiled. His teeth were perfect. "You came."

"You asked me to," she said with some surprise. It had only just occurred to her that this request could have been refused. She was a princess now, after all, not a starving girl from Vathi bound to honor the queen and her ridiculous son. She tore her gaze from his face—something about his wide, black eyes and the sharp jut of his jaw made it impossible to think properly—and looked around the room again. "Where is Melantho?"

"Oh." Mathias smiled again, beyond lovely. "I dismissed her. She did not mind."

"You dismissed her." Not a question—a flat, irritable statement. Leto fought down the flare of panic that had sparked in her chest, the prickle of trepidation that marched its way up her spine and whispered, *You cannot do this without her.* Was this not what she had wanted? To do it herself? To lift the burden from Melantho's shoulders, to be Atlas and carry her skies for the merest moment?

Mathias's smile slipped. "She did not mind," he said again, rather hastily. "Leto, I thought—"

"Your grace." Leto interrupted him, abruptly formal. She never should have told him her true name, should not have blurted it out to him in bewilderment that first night. Every time it passed his lips, traitorous instinct had her turning to him, her eyes wide and searching. She injected an extra drop of venom into her voice as she replied, determined not to let him rattle her, "I was not aware that Melantho was your maid to dismiss."

Mathias looked truly admonished now; his shoulders had come up and his brows were furrowed above his dark eyes. "I thought—" he tried again.

"Where did you send her?"

"The kitchens. I—"

"Melantho is *not* a kitchen maid," snapped Leto. "She is *my* maid. You would do well to remember that, my *prince*."

He was not even looking at her now; he had fixed his eyes upon some invisible blemish upon the tabletop. "I wish you would call me Mathias," he mumbled.

Perhaps she had been a little harsh. She could not forget that, betrothed or not, Mathias had the power to do more than dismiss Melantho from a room. He could send her, and Leto with her, from Ithaca itself if he was so inclined. There was not so much time left; she should be endearing herself to him. Or at least, she should not be shouting at him. She softened her tone. "If, as you said, Melantho did not mind, then I suppose I will forgive you. Still, I trust it will not happen again." She paused deliberately before adding, as if it were an afterthought, "Mathias."

He lifted his head at the sound of his own name. She indulged him with a small smile, a symbol of her generous forgiveness.

"I will remember it," said Mathias, meeting her gaze with unblinking sincerity. "You will apologize to her for me, won't you? And I will do it myself, the next time our paths cross."

Leto felt her smile slip into something that might have been genuine as she lied to him. "I am sure that Melantho will forgive you your indiscretion."

"I hope so," said Mathias. "Truly, I do."

"Well then," said Leto. Within six days, he would be dead and she would be the one that had killed him. She could indulge him for now. "What are we going to do?"

⌒⌒⌒

Knucklebones. It was stupid and childish and a complete distraction from her inevitable task. Somehow, though, Leto was actually enjoying herself.

She did not know the rules so Mathias had explained them slowly, carefully—as carefully as one could explain the concept of tossing chicken vertebrae into the air, scrabbling around on the table for those that were not thrown, and trying to catch the rest one-handed. She had caught herself smiling when he recounted playing with his father, and she had scowled quite dangerously when he had suggested inviting Olympia, who *apparently* had an affinity for the game.

"You are cheating," declared Leto as he succeeded and she failed for the fifth time.

"I have practiced," said Mathias. There was a jar full of fresh daffodils on the table. He pulled one loose and stuck the stem behind his ear. It was a burst of gold against his dark hair. "That is the only difference between us."

Leto frowned and tossed a bone into the air, scrabbling at the table to collect the rest before the first fell. When she succeeded at last, she whooped so loudly that an alarmed servant ducked into the room to check on them.

"Sorry," she said, knowing that she did not sound very sorry at all.

"Don't be," he said, scooping up the pieces. "Again?"

Mathias had added more of the bones as they played. Where

there had once been five, it was now a collection of nine bones that spilled into the air. He caught seven one-handed.

"Impressive," said Leto. "But that isn't the game."

He grinned, all straight white teeth and flashing black eyes and perfect little dimples at the corners of his mouth. It was impossible not to find him lovely—even a fool could have seen that he was as pretty as a nymph with that stupid daffodil tucked behind his ear. "You were impressed. That is the game."

No, decided Leto firmly. She could not allow herself to slip into this charade again, so she looked up into his face and said, very coolly, "I did not know that my affections were a game to you."

He paled. "I—I did not mean—"

"I know," she said. She had thrown the bones up idly as they spoke, and now the little ivory-colored pieces fell to the table with a clatter. Mathias barely seemed to notice the sound. Leto cast them a cursory, sideways look.

She froze.

The bones had landed in the shape of a skull.

Leto was on her feet before she knew it, scattering them with a hard sweep of her hand. "It is getting late," she blurted. How could she *do* this? Sit around playing games with the boy she wanted to see dead? The gods were not pleased with her, clearly. Was it a warning? A threat?

Mathias blinked up at her. "It is—what? Leto, it is barely the afternoon."

She remembered then the hushed conversation she had over-heard the night before. There was an opportunity to be cruel; she seized it. "I heard that more girls were brought in last night—or was it this morning? Should you not be planning their executions?"

He took an audible breath, then said, "That is not fair."

"What is not *fair* is that you are here playing knucklebones and they are staring down Hades. Where is your shame?"

"I—"

"Last night, you told me that you cared. I do not think you do. I think you are content to make grand speeches and say that you would do *anything* to see Ithaca liberated, but you will *not*. What have you ever done to prove yourself?"

"You judge me too harshly," snapped Mathias.

"Do I? Why should I not?"

"Because I am trying my best!" His hands were clenched into fists. "I have *tried*. I have spent hours, alone, in the library, sorting through festering records and maps and myths, *searching* for something that will help me. I have been up to the temples on the hills, I have—" He broke off. His cheeks were patchy and red. "My apologies. I should not have raised my voice."

Leto stared at him wordlessly. "Why did you not tell me any of that before?"

He raised his shoulders in a half shrug. "What does it matter? I have failed."

"What does it *matter*?" It mattered for so many reasons: because it meant that he was not so selfish, not so cowardly as she had thought. It meant that killing him would not feel like justice. "I hope you are not lying to me."

Mathias looked miserable. He pulled the daffodil from behind his ear and replaced it in the jar. "I wish you would not think that of me. Most of what I have found is in the library. Will you—would you come with me, and let me prove it to you? That I am sincere?"

The library was at the other end of the palace, and they walked there in silence. They were passing the great hall when they heard the sound of the queen's voice—sharp, imperious—and Mathias pivoted so abruptly that Leto almost walked into him. "This way," he said quickly, shooting her a desperate sideways look.

She did not question the diversion; she wanted to see the queen about as much as she suspected he did.

The next corridor was empty but for a single maid, cupping a lit candle in her palms. She looked up as they rounded the corner, went very pink, and then all but ran through the door at the far end of the passage.

"Not far now," said Mathias quietly.

"Good," said Leto. She snuck a sideways look at him, and a peculiar guilt surged within her at the sight of his sad, crumpled expression. She swallowed. "Look, Mathias, I didn't mean to shout at you like that. I just thought—"

She broke off as the sound of voices issued from ahead once again. "You think *that* is clean? I can assure you, it is *not*." Alexios. Typical. Of course he was here.

"I am sorry, sir. Truly."

A girl's voice, anxious and high-pitched and . . . strangely familiar. Leto frowned. Where had she heard it before?

"I have heard your excuses before. They convince me less each time. Do not think I have forgotten about last spring."

"A mistake, sir."

"That is what you told me, but a pair of shears is not so easy to forget, is it? Perhaps you are lying to me. Perhaps you wanted her to escape, hmm?"

Oh. *Oh.* A memory flashed in Leto's mind: a girl with wide

doll-like eyes and shaking hands. Hands that held little white flowers, hands that had woven those flowers into Leto's hair.

This maid knew who Leto was. They had spent hours together as the maid carefully pinned her gown into place and pulled her curls into braids. And for Alexios to see them *together*—he would remember exactly where he recognized her from. His words from the previous night had made his suspicion clear.

Leto could not let them catch sight of her. Not when it would be the end of it all.

The voices were coming closer; she had to hide.

She flailed about for an escape and, seeing none but the nearest door, flung it open and yanked Mathias inside.

He was much bigger than she was, and far stronger too, but the suddenness of her actions must have surprised him so entirely that he barely resisted at all but for a rather muffled, "Leto!" as she shoved him into the corner. There came an earthy, clattering noise—they were in a storeroom stacked with clay pots. Wine, maybe, or heavy jars of olives.

"Shhh!" said Leto, pulling the door shut behind them. Her heart was racing in her chest, and there was a tension in her stomach that would not release.

"What are you *doing*?" demanded Mathias as he extracted himself from the corner. The tiny room was barely big enough for the both of them; they were pressed together in a manner that sent heat rushing to Leto's cheeks. She shoved Mathias angrily against the stone wall again, so she could peek through the keyhole.

"I thought I saw—" she started, then broke off. There was no explaining it to him without revealing herself. "A maid I wish to avoid," she finished weakly, still squinting through the little gap at the lock. "I—uh—spilled tea on her by mistake and I doubt very much that she intends to forgive me." A lie, though she had spilled tea on Melantho the previous morning. The look of startled outrage on Melantho's face had faded in seconds; she'd grinned as she used her pouch of fountain water to soothe her reddened skin.

"Tea?" echoed Mathias. Was that *relief* she detected in his voice? He must be grateful she was not still raging at him. "She can hardly be upset about some *tea*."

"It was very hot," invented Leto.

"Well, I daresay she will heal," said Mathias, "unlike my leg, which appears to be impaled on this jar."

"What?" Leto turned to see Mathias looking down rather mournfully at the spot where a shard of terra-cotta, jutting dangerously from a broken handle, had firmly inserted itself in his thigh. A thin stream of blood was beginning to stain his tunic. "Oh gods," she managed faintly. "I am *so* sorry. Let me look at that. I didn't mean to—"

"I am quite all right," said Mathias firmly, "and I rather think you have done enough."

They were face-to-face now, with very little room between them, and Mathias was looking down at her with an expression of exasperation. "There is a cobweb in your hair," he said after a pause, with a small smile, and he reached out to brush it away. Leto found that she was holding her breath. Her muscles had gone all tense; she did not seem to know whether to move away or to lean in closer.

The door banged open and they both jumped, Mathias with a cry of pain as the movement yanked at the shard of pottery and tore open his tunic. Alexios was standing in the doorway with a face like thunder.

His eyes slowly took in their position. Mathias had his hand curved against Leto's face, which was hot with the sudden peculiar anxiety of the moment. His touch was featherlight on her cheek, and they really were standing *very* close to each other.

"Alexios," Mathias began, but the guard was already turning away.

"Excuse me, your grace," he said stiffly, and then slammed the door in their faces.

XXXV

HEART, BE STILL

Mathias

"Well," said Mathias into the darkness. He did not know what else to say. It was not every day that he was shut into a storeroom with a girl—a very *beautiful* girl at that, with long brown hair and grey-brown eyes that seemed to allow her to observe his every thought. A girl who had returned to hating him again. "I suppose that could have been worse."

"Could have been worse?" echoed Leto. *"How?"*

"We could have been found in a much more compromising position," said Mathias reasonably. They were, after all, engaged to be married, and married people quite frequently engaged in the sort of activities that Mathias certainly would *not* want to be caught doing. He found himself thinking about doing those things—about doing those things with Leto—and was grateful that the darkness hid the flush of heat that had rushed up his neck and set his cheeks aflame.

The space was much smaller than he had first realized; they were pressed very closely together. The curve of a jar was pushed uncomfortably against the backs of his legs. He could feel the hammering of Leto's heart—or was that his own?—and hear the soft pull of air each time she inhaled.

She laughed, a short, derisive sound. "I think that is my cue to leave. Good afternoon, Mathias." The door rattled as she tugged on it. It was a rattle that grew rather louder and more rapid as she twisted and pushed at it with increasing desperation.

"It's locked," she said, appalled. "We're locked in here."

"Oh dear," said Mathias.

Leto's breathing was louder now, each inhale and furious exhale rasped in Mathias's ear. Without warning, he felt her throw herself against the door. She collided with the wood with a dull thud.

"*Somebody help!*" she howled. "*Let us out!*"

Mathias did not move. A month ago, they had been forced to let another lot of servants go. Their everyday costs were high enough, but with the gold spent on the betrothal feast and then the upcoming festival . . . Well, the palace corridors were all but empty now, with the bulk of the staff spending their time in the kitchens. The lady's maids were always attached to the hip of whichever noble girl they served, and the guards tended to patrol the perimeters, not some narrow hallway lined with storerooms.

And the fact that Alexios had been here already and would most certainly *not* be returning . . . Mathias did not think anyone would be coming for a long time. He kept this thought private, though, as Leto hurled herself against the door again with a shriek of rage. His fiancée always managed to conduct herself with such hostility, and he wasn't convinced that she was familiar with the phrase *don't shoot the messenger.*

"Ow," said Mathias mildly as she stumbled back into him, sending a sharp flare of pain up from his thigh. "Careful. There's a hole in my leg, and I think it's probably still bleeding."

Leto froze. "Sorry," she said eventually. "I had forgotten."

"Easily done." He would forgive her. Frankly, he would forgive her anything. He had not realized, not truly, how *lonely* he had been with Selene gone, Hekate oceans away on Crete, and his father dead in his grave. Furious, scathing Leto seemed to want nothing at all from him; it made him want everything from her.

She simmered for a moment in the still darkness. "Well, I suppose we shall have to wait here."

"Yes, I suppose so."

There was a long pause. Then, "We should have brought the knucklebones," said Leto dryly. "I am already bored. And it smells in here—I hope that is the contents of these jars and not you."

Mathias decided not to respond to that.

XXXVI

AMONG THE ASHES

Leto

It had been hours, Leto was sure of it.

Perhaps they would die here, and someone would discover their unfortunate corpses some ten years in the future and wonder how on earth they'd managed it.

"You have a sister," she blurted. It was the one thing she remembered from their previous conversations. Or was it two sisters? She had always wanted a sibling, a brother especially; soon, Mathias's sisters would want for a brother too. The thought left a bitter taste in her mouth.

"Yes," said Mathias. "I do. Hekate."

One sister, then, though she could have sworn . . . No matter. "Where is she?"

She felt the warmth of his breath as he exhaled. "She is on Crete," he said. "My mother's cousin is the queen there and Hekate is betrothed to her son; it is all very convenient, you see." There was something like bitterness in his voice. "It protects her, keeps her safe from Ithaca and its . . ." He paused. "Well, she is safe there. That is all."

The understanding dawned slowly on Leto. "The curse cannot reach her there?"

His hair rustled in the near-darkness as he shook his head.

"The smallest of blessings. The curse controls us, compels us. But it does not call us home."

Leto chewed on her lip. When she spoke, her voice sounded hesitant, wary, even to herself. "If the curse can be escaped . . . why do you not then leave?"

"Leave?" He laughed. There it was again, that bitterness. "Do you know how many people live here? How many *poor* people, Leto? Who would take them? Where would they get the money for passage? They are trapped here, I'm afraid. As am I."

He said this last part quietly. She was not sure whether he wanted her to hear it or not.

She had not known that the curse had bounds. That she could simply have run away and never had to face the rope. Why had her mother not taken her? Her father?

"Leto?" Mathias's voice was hardly a whisper.

"Yes?"

"I meant what I said. This curse is a vicious, ugly thing. I would do—*I am* doing everything I can to break it. I admit I have not found much, but I have been *trying*. I go to the library every night that I can. I would do anything to see it end. Anything, you understand?"

She did. She hated that she did, but it was an undeniable truth. It made it so much harder to know what she must do, what she must do to *him*. "So would I," she said.

"Good," said Mathias.

This time, when he kissed her, she did not push him away.

If kisses were words, it would have been a whisper. So softly did Mathias's lips touch her own that Leto was only half sure they had touched at all. His mouth brushed over hers with such tenderness that she was rendered temporarily breathless.

Leto had wondered about this ever since the cliffside. And now here they were, those lips on hers, that lovely face impossibly close. *What would Melantho say?* But of course, Melantho would not have to know. If Leto did not tell her.

It took all Leto's strength not to groan in sheer frustration. She was weak, she was traitorous, she was kissing him back.

Mathias was gentler than she ever would have thought. He did not press his body against hers as she might have wished him to but melted against her as he reached up to cup her jaw and pull her face ever so slightly closer.

His lips were parted under hers, his breath sweet and warm.

At last, he pulled away. "Gods," he whispered reverently.

"Gods," she echoed, leaning back against the wall. Something metallic clattered as she brushed against it and knocked it to the floor. "Damn it, what was that?"

"Let me," offered Mathias. She felt him drop to his knees, reach carefully past her ankles to pat at the floor. The clattering noise came again. "Ah," said Mathias.

"What is it?"

"The key," said Mathias. "It appears that we were not so stuck after all."

꩜

Once Mathias had unlocked the door, Leto had fled. What else was there to do? She could not go to the library with him after that, could not risk him endearing himself to her any more. And he had said himself that his research had not turned up any answer. She had to kill him. She had to kill him soon. She walked back to her rooms in a haze, her mind spinning.

She could hardly believe it, but there it was, painted with irremovable brushstrokes in her memory: Mathias's lips on hers, his hands cupping her face, the air steeped with the scent of him. She could still smell it now, clinging to her clothes and hair: expensive leather and elderflower.

It would not do to dwell on it; she forced it from her mind as she reached her rooms and pushed the door open tentatively. "Melantho?"

The beautiful room was empty, the embellished chairs unoccupied, and half-open shutters shivered in the humid wind. From beyond the screen of gold silk that shielded the bedchamber there came the soft, familiar sound of . . . water?

The door shut behind Leto with a thud. "Melantho?" she tried again.

This time, she got an answer. "In here." Melantho's voice was low and husky.

Leto followed the sound to the little bath chamber they shared. She came to an abrupt stop in the doorway. The Melantho she had expected to see had hair and skin like golden sand, eyes the shade of the first tufts of spring grass. The Melantho before her—laid back in the bath, her legs crossed over the side and dripping water onto the tiled floor—had hair like the sea and eyes like ink. Her skin was the mottled grey of a pebble left so long at the water's edge that moss had crept across its surface and settled there.

The copper bath had been filled to the brim with water. Leto could feel the tug of it, almost *hear* it humming to her, felt something flickering in the palm of her hands. "Is that seawater?" She frowned. "Please do not tell me that you convinced some poor maid to drag a barrel of *seawater* up the hill for you."

Melantho laughed and grinned, showing pearlescent teeth and canines that were just a *little* too sharp. "If there were a maid to be found anywhere in this abominable place," she said, "I doubt very much that she would listen to me. *I* am the maid, remember?"

Leto narrowed her eyes. "Do not tell me that *you* dragged a barrel of seawater up the hill."

Melantho moved her hand across the water's surface. Leto was suddenly grateful for the fog of salt and the swirling of the lazy currents that always collected about Melantho. She knew what lay beneath the surface, *ached* for it. And right now, she was supposed to be berating Melantho, not gazing, transfixed, at the curve of her thigh and the arch of her neck and—

"It's from the fountain," said Melantho. Her black eyes gleamed in the torchlight. From a distance, she could have been a normal human girl, dipped in molten clay and adorned with swirls of mossy-green ink. "Join me?"

Leto could not say no. She shrugged off her chiton with a practiced ease, allowing herself a moment to savor the curl of Melantho's lips as she dragged her gaze over Leto's body. She stood at the edge of the bathtub longer than was strictly necessary. No one had ever looked at her like *that*. It was like a featherlight touch on her bare skin.

"Was that blood on your chiton?"

Ah. *It is probably still bleeding.* It was blood, and she knew exactly whose it was. And how it had got there. But what good would it do her to be truthful, to admit such treachery now? It would not matter soon, what she thought of Mathias. "No," she said. "Wine. Move over."

Melantho shifted obediently.

Leto dipped a toe into the water and felt the familiar shivers of change begin to twist up her legs. "It's warm," she blurted out. She had braced herself for cold, but the water was temperate, a little hot even.

Melantho grinned. "Ask me how."

Leto sank into the water and sat between Melantho's legs. The bronze mirror that stood beside the bath had clouded with steam, but Leto knew what would have been looking back at her had it been clear: herself and Melantho, Poseidon's creatures, mirror images of green and grey. Melantho was watching her eagerly, practically thrumming with self-satisfaction. "How?" asked Leto, indulging her. It was the least she could do.

"Watch," said Melantho, and she ran her fingers over the surface of the water. Bubbles erupted beneath her fingertips and Leto jerked her legs away at the sudden flare of heat.

"How?" Leto leaned forward, her interest sincere this time, and peered at the last of the bubbles as they faded away.

"I knew you'd be impressed," said Melantho smugly. "Thalia would use it to heat the sea on Pandou, to catch fish. I'd forgotten. While you were off with the prince all day, I spent a lot of time wandering around aimlessly." She nodded toward the bedchamber. "I raided the kitchens for snacks, and I saw them boiling fish and it reminded me of it. Then I spent two hours filling jugs up from the fountain and bringing them here. I thought we could continue your training, if you're not too busy with your prince."

"We've barely been here a week. You don't think very highly of me if you worry that I'll have forgotten our training already." Leto raised her brows deliberately, pushed all traitorous thoughts of Mathias from her mind. "And he is not *my* prince. Besides, last I recall, you were not so very eager to train."

"You were not either," Melantho pointed out.

"You were sad," said Leto. They had not discussed Melantho's peculiar rage again, her consuming air of tragedy. "You were so, so sad."

Melantho said nothing for a moment. She traced patterns over the water's surface. "I am often sad," she said. "So are you, I think."

"Perhaps," said Leto.

"Will you tell me why?" Melantho leaned forward. "Perhaps I may be able to help. I have known much sadness, and sometimes, I have watched it as it leaves."

Leto sighed. "All right, then," she said. "I will tell you. But I will tell you in front of the fire, when we are both dressed, because I cannot talk of sadness whilst you are"—she waved her hand idly in Melantho's direction—"like that."

Melantho arched her back so that her breasts cleared the water. Water dripped from her shoulder, carving a path over the curve of her collarbone and—

"I will tell you another time, then," said Leto. "I promise."

"Another time," agreed Melantho.

As Melantho's hands made their way to Leto's waist, as her mouth brushed over Leto's neck, Leto managed to forget about Mathias. She forgot the warmth of his touch and the press of his lips against hers and the way he'd smiled at her—like she was the loveliest thing he'd ever seen.

XXXVII

THE LONG WATCHES OF THE NIGHT

Leto

Later, dressed and warm and sitting in front of the hearth, Leto remembered her promise. She had not spoken of her past to anyone before, of her mother's death and her father's self-destruction and the way it had suddenly, irreparably changed everything.

"This is a dangerous place," she ventured. Her mother had lived here once, and it had destroyed her. Had Melantho's short life been the same?

"Hmm? Oh, yes." Melantho was embroidering daffodils onto the sleeve of a chiton. She did not seem to notice the seriousness in Leto's tone. "I was bitten by a snake today."

The words did not fully register in Leto's mind; she frowned at Melantho. This was not the conversation she'd expected. "What?"

"Yes, I forgot to tell you. It was in your cloak pocket, with one of your notes. I smacked it with a shoe, then stuck my hand in the fountain." She looked very pleased with herself as she offered Leto the aforementioned hand. "It went green, and I was briefly concerned I was going lose the hand, but it's fine now. See, the bite marks are almost gone."

Leto stared at her. "One of my notes? Which one?"

"Oh, I don't know. A scrap of papyrus. It was in black ink and—"

Leto lurched to her feet. She had written no note. "Which cloak?"

Melantho looked up, alarmed. "The green. What are you—"

Leto all but dived for it, thrusting her hand into the hidden pocket and snatching at the little slip of papyrus inside. One glance at the messy scrawl told her that it was not her handwriting. A second, that something was very, very wrong.

"Melantho," she said quietly. "Did anyone come in here today? Anyone who could have left this?"

Melantho shook her head, peered nervously into Leto's face, "No, I—like I said, I was in and out. What does it say?"

Leto could not meet her eye. "It says *the venom shouldn't be fatal. If you live, you should leave.* It's a threat."

Something dawned on her, slowly, gradually. She was not certain of it at first, but the more she thought on it, the surer she felt. "Melantho," she said. "Did you cut my saddlecloth strap?"

"Did I—what?"

Of course she hadn't. Of *course.* Leto should have known. "My saddlecloth," she repeated. "When I fell from the horse. It was cut—I assumed that it was you, that you intended it for Mathias."

"The strap was *cut?*" asked Melantho. "And you choose to tell me this *now*? Why on earth would I cut your saddlecloth strap? What were you *thinking*? Are you so desperate to be killed that—" She paused, her eyes filling with the question that had now pushed itself to the front of Leto's mind. "Who cut it, then?"

"Who put the snake there?" asked Leto.

"You think someone is trying to kill us."

"That's rather self-important," said Leto mildly. "I think someone is trying to kill *me,* and it just so happened that you were . . . caught in the crossfire, so to speak." The snake had been in the pocket of *her* cloak, after all. And the strap had been cut on *her* saddlecloth. The princess of Athens, it seemed, was not as welcome on Ithaca as she had thought.

"Thank you," said Melantho. "You do know how to make me feel special."

Leto looked at her, fixed her gaze on the green of Melantho's eyes. "If you died," she said carefully, "I would die with you." She had lost everything once, twice before. She could not do it again.

Melantho's brows arched upward. "Perhaps that is a little far."

"It isn't," said Leto. "That is how my father went. Dying from heartbreak is in my blood."

"I do not wish to know what is in *my* blood," said Melantho. She carefully pulled through another stitch in her embroidery, a streak of yellow cotton and the silver flash of the needle. "I do not think we are defined by it, that our destinies are not our own. I do not believe, as others do, that the Fates decide the circumstances of our lives, of our deaths. My life is not a strand of yarn for Lachesis to measure, for Atropos to cut."

Leto blinked at her; she had not heard the Moirai spoken of for many years, the three Fates working to spin, measure, cut short the lives of mortals. Perhaps Ithaca had drawn from the gods far further than she had realized.

"I believe my actions *change* things," said Melantho. "Otherwise, what is the point of me at all?"

"We are more than our actions," said Leto. "We are the way we love others and the way they love us back." *And the way that others will ruin themselves in our absence, the way that no one else will ever be good enough for life to be worth living.*

"That's very philosophical," said Melantho. "You are thinking of your father, aren't you?"

His wide mouth, his broad, suntanned hands. His vacant, grey eyes fixed on a place just past Leto's face. Yes, she was thinking of her father, even if he had never spared a thought for her.

Leto took a deep breath. "After my mother died, my father might as well have died with her. He just . . . gave up. Stopped working, stopped bathing, stopped *eating*. I used to spend hours convincing him to take a sip from a cup of godsdamned water."

Melantho's stitching slowed. She laid down the embroidery at last and looked up. Her cheeks were flushed with the warmth of the evening air, her pupils blown huge in the dark. A strand of gold had slipped free from her braids; Leto longed to tuck it back behind her ear, to pull their faces together and forget that they had a purpose here. A purpose that would end in slaughter, whether they succeeded or not. One life, or twelve, time and time again. "Grief does peculiar things to people," said Melantho quietly.

"It made me hate him," said Leto. "I hated my own *father* because he made me hate *her*. Because I had to wake up every day and know that I was not as good as her. Not as interesting as her, not as kind as her, not as clever or talented or *worthwhile*. I had to look into my father's face as he wasted away, as he decided that there was no point to it all without her there and know that I was not worth living for. That if I were a little braver, a little stronger, I could have saved him."

"No, you couldn't," said Melantho. "You cannot save someone who does not *want* to be saved."

Leto had not wanted to be saved. She remembered the relief of death, the way the pain had fallen away, had let her drop peacefully into nothingness. The agony of the rope had been nothing; it had felt like going home. And yet—

"That's a lie," said Leto. "You know that's a lie."

"We need to try again tonight," said Melantho later, quietly. The sky had fallen into a soft twilight, peppered with stars. "If we are right, and someone is targeting you, then I doubt they will wait too long to try again." She paused. "Or perhaps we should tell him. He might know who—"

"*Tell him?*" Leto stared at her. "What could he do? It is Alexios or his awful sister. I am sure of it. They *both* have the queen's ear, and she would know the second we told Mathias. Which means they would too."

"Then the only alternative is to finish it," said Melantho. "You know that as well as I do."

"Mathias might be in the library," said Leto. Her chest was tight; she had wanted to do this herself, had not wanted Melantho to worry. Instead, she'd been careless and distracted and Melantho had been *attacked*. Even if Leto *had* been the intended target, it could not be allowed to happen again. Besides—the thought dawned on her slowly, terribly—she was a *princess*. Her murder would be an international incident. But Melantho's—

"The library," she said again. *I go to the library every night that I can.* Where else would he go? "He'll be there. Should we find him?" The thought of it was strangely repulsive to her, the very idea of forcing their way into the room that was Mathias's sanctuary, the place where he had hoped and dreamed and *tried* to break the curse. It would be poetic, then.

It was too late for Mathias, but it didn't have to be too late for the twelve girls that bore Poseidon's mark, the twelve girls who would face the rope in just six days' time.

"No," said Melantho, and Leto was grateful for it. "No, not

there. He must die in the water, remember? Poseidon must be able to claim him. You should send him a message, invite him to the sea somehow."

"What possible reason could there be for that? It is nighttime."

"What else can we do?"

Leto remembered Melantho laughing in the copper bathtub, sending the water bubbling up under her fingers. It was not the same, but surely it was worth an attempt. "The fountain," she said. "The fountain is Poseidon's. Do you think it will work?"

Mathias's smile, Mathias's laugh, Mathias's mouth on hers. She would never see it, hear it, feel it again. She did not allow herself to linger on the thought. There were only six days left till the equinox, they were halfway through and still, he lived. They could not delay any longer.

Melantho's smile was dark, dangerous. "Yes."

❧❧❧

Leto sent the letter to Mathias as Melantho directed, and his reply came back shortly. *Anything*, it read, *for you.*

She would meet him at midnight in the courtyard that held the fountain.

She would plunge him into the water.

She would end it all.

❧❧❧

Leto slipped between the shadows of the columns that lined the edges of the courtyard, hiding herself from Mathias's gaze as he walked circles around the fountain and waited for her to come to him. Melantho was a silent wraith at her side. She had slipped her hand into Leto's and woven their fingers together.

Leto took one last look at Mathias: at the soft curve of his cheeks and the way they shone like gold in the narrow beams of torchlight, at the black curls that fell over his forehead, at the nervous fluttering of his fingertips as he paced up and down and tugged at his numerous rings. He was lovely; he was afraid. He did not deserve this.

Leto pulled her own hands free from Melantho's grasp and raised them. She reached out to the water of the fountain, said a silent prayer, and asked it to drown the prince of Ithaca.

Mathias did not notice as the first tendrils of water began to creep toward him. He did not startle or shout, alarmed, when one wrapped itself, delicately, about his wrist. Instead, when he looked down at it, nothing changed at all in his posture or his face, except that his lips—his full, perfect, lips—parted in innocent surprise.

The next caught him by the other wrist, then his neck, then his chest, striking him hard over his heart and pulling him backwards. He flailed at the stone edge of the fountain. Slowly, as if time itself had thickened around him, he fell in, and the water rushed to fill his lungs.

At Leto's side, Melantho made a small sound.

Leto could not look away; the water would not allow it. It controlled her now as much as she controlled it, plunging itself through Mathias with a joyful fervor. Any doubts that Leto had harbored, that the fountain would not work, that it *had* to be the sea, had been entirely unfounded. The ocean sang in her blood; *this* was what it had been waiting for all along.

She could not stop; she was as helpless as a marionette as the water surged and Mathias struggled and gasped. She felt him drowning. She wanted to scream but she could make no sound. But there was something else there too. Some*one* else. The feel of their pain cascaded down on her even as Mathias's dulled, as he stilled.

She knew that feeling. She took too long to realize it.

Melantho crumpled.

She slumped against Leto's legs, sending them both sprawling to the ground.

The ocean's grip loosened, and Leto thrust it away from her with all the strength she could muster. Melantho was gasping beside her, her face ashen as she clawed at her throat.

She was *drowning*. Leto remembered the cliff top. How Melantho had stumbled as Mathias had, how she said that someone had *pushed* her.

Was this what love was? Throwing away the chance to do something great, something *important*, because Melantho was in danger?

"Melantho." Leto caught at her, pulled her into her arms. "Melantho, *no*. What are you doing?" She did not know what else to ask, she could not understand. This was not supposed to happen; Mathias was supposed to be dead by now; the curse was meant to be broken by now. Melantho was meant to be free by now. Not gasping for air as slowly, slowly, the color returned to her face. The realization came all at once—her stumbling on the cliffside, her gasping and panting now. Mathias's fate echoed onto Melantho's.

"Melantho," said Leto again.

Melantho's lips shaped words but the sound did not come. She was crying, her eyes huge and panicked as she fixed them on Leto's face. She tried to speak again, and this time she managed it, clutching at Leto's wrist. "Go . . . Go to—" She choked on the words and pulled in a desperate breath. *"Him."*

"Him?"

"Mathias. Kill—" Satisfied, Melantho sagged again. Her face

was tight with pain, but each ragged breath she took sounded a little clearer. Whatever it was that had been killing her, it was gone now. When Leto did not move, Melantho tightened her grip on Leto's wrist and dug her nails in. It was not a request; it was a command.

Leto stood and stepped, hesitant, into the courtyard. What she saw there took her breath away.

She had not just forced the ocean from herself; she had flung it from the fountain entirely. Every stone, every column about her was drenched in salt water. The fountain itself was empty, Mathias lying prone in its basin.

He was heavier than she had expected. There was no elegance to her movement as she dragged him out and laid him on the court-yard flagstones. Somehow, impossibly, he was breathing. Each drag of air was ragged, infrequent, but he clung to life with a relentless determination.

Melantho had said *kill.* But looking down into his lovely face, Leto hesitated. If she did nothing, he would survive. The curse would endure. And yet, she could not finish it. Not while some-thing, *someone,* bound his fate to Melantho's, not while his death might also mean hers. Leto left him there.

Shaking from the effort, terrified that it would take hold of her as it had before, she reached out with her power and pulled the water back into its basin. She held her breath until the last drop was returned, and it was steadily bubbling again as if nothing untoward had happened at all.

Leto exhaled. She knelt at Melantho's side, sobbed as she pressed her lips to Melantho's brow, and tried not to dwell on the terrible truth that was slowly occurring to her—the truth that if Melantho had not knocked into her as she collapsed, had not severed the connection for long enough for Leto to take control of herself again, then she would not have been able to stop at all. That Melantho would have—

No. She could not think such things.

She clutched Melantho tight and listened to the gasps of her breathing. "You're safe," she murmured, only half sure that she was speaking to Melantho and not to herself. It was past midnight; there were five days left. Five days to kill Mathias before twelve more girls were condemned. But if that meant Melantho would be gone too . . .

She did not think she would be able to do it.

She pushed the curls back from Melantho's face, pressed a kiss to her clammy forehead.

"You're not leaving me. I won't let anything happen to you."

XXXVIII
THROUGH PATHS OF DARKNESS

Melantho

Back in their rooms, Melantho and Leto held their silence for a long while. They had dragged Mathias to his bed—Melantho, still dizzy and afraid, had not really helped much—then tucked him in beneath the heavy coverlet and left, hoping only that he had not glimpsed them lurking at the edge of the courtyard, that he would not know what they had attempted. What they had failed to do.

Would he remember what had happened? They had dried his clothes, brushed out his messy curls. Melantho hoped—*prayed*, though she was not one to place her faith in the gods—that he would awaken to nothing but the memory of a bad dream.

Melantho took another deep breath. She would not take the action for granted again; those moments on the ground, clutching at her throat, feeling her chest heave desperately as her lungs fought for air, had been the longest, most painful moments of her life.

Her throat still felt raw and ragged, and her fingers trembled in her lap.

Somehow, despite it all, the overwhelming feeling in her heart was not of pain, or fear, but grim satisfaction. She had known Poseidon would not let her go so easily; here was the proof.

She shivered.

Perhaps, *perhaps,* it would not have killed her. Some small part of her wished that Leto had not stopped, so that, at least, Melantho's own fate was certain. And if it was death that awaited her—well, some part of her might even welcome it. Some part of her knew she deserved it.

"I will not do it," said Leto.

Melantho looked up. Leto's face was ashen, her grey eyes dulled and bloodshot. Her fingers were claws in the upholstered arms of her chair and she had bitten hard into her bottom lip so that blood trickled from the center of her mouth and over her narrow chin. "Do what?" asked Melantho, though she was as certain of the answer as of her own name.

"*That.*" Leto took a rattling breath. "Not after what just happened." A pause. "What *did* happen?"

Melantho forced herself to shrug. "I don't know."

"I don't *understand.* Perhaps we were wrong—the fountain water *is* salt water, but it isn't *sea*water. It is not *enough.* Yes, that must be it, mustn't it? There is no other way to explain it. Or perhaps I can't use my powers when I do it—perhaps he must be hanged, like the girls are. But, no, you told me Timo drowned hers. How did Thalia kill them? Did she use her powers? Maybe that is it."

Melantho sighed. She was exhausted to the very bone; her body chose that moment to protest against her relentless abuse of it by giving her a splitting headache. "I don't know," she said. "I never went with them."

"Well, how did *you* do it, then?"

I didn't. I never did. Pandou has always been my prison—it was meant to keep me forever. The words were so close to the tip of her tongue, but she bit them back. That would open the door to so many questions, with answers Melantho was not ready to reveal quite yet. Perhaps she never would be. "The only condition is that they must die in Poseidon's domain. Perhaps you are right. Perhaps the fountain is not enough for this one thing."

Leto was clearly not satisfied with this answer. She huffed and wrung her hands together. "I don't understand why you were affected. *Only* you."

Melantho looked at her hands. "Does it matter?"

"What? Of course it matters."

"No, it doesn't. It *mustn't*." Melantho looked into her face. "If the choice arises again, if you can kill him, you *must*. You heard Alexios—they are finding the marked girls; they are going to *kill* them. You cannot stop because of me. I am not worth twelve. I am not worth hundreds."

"*What?*" hissed Leto. "You are worth *everything*. And I will not risk you, not until it is the very last option." Her posture shifted alarmingly; before, she had been hunched over, frightened, but now she straightened, widened her stance, set her jaw. "No, we must find another way, and we don't have much time. Which means, I suppose, that there is only one thing left to do."

"Which is?"

Leto's smile was grim. "You are not going to like it."

XXXIX

CURIOUS AND UNACCOUNTABLE THINGS

Mathias

There were not many things that frightened Mathias, but looking up from a scroll—his fourteenth of the afternoon—to find his fiancée standing, arms folded, in the entrance to his library was one of them. When he'd finally mustered the courage to remove the bolts over the doors, he had thought his greatest issue would be his mother. Leto was a far more terrifying prospect.

He swallowed. Whatever she was here to say, he suspected that it was not good.

He had not been able to shake the persistent cloud of foreboding that had hung over him since early that morning. It had still been dark; he had awoken in his bed with no idea of how he had got there and his whole body drenched in a feverish sweat. His chest had been gripped by an incomparable terror, his mind racing with the memory of *something* that slipped away every time he reached for it. *Drowning*—that was all he could remember of it.

After that, he had not been able to fall asleep again.

And now this.

It was not so much the fact that Leto looked angry—which she did—that perturbed him so greatly, but that he had not noticed her arrival. She could have been standing there for hours, a silent apparition in her soft gold chiton.

He eyed her cautiously. She had not followed him to the library before. She'd fled from him after the storeroom. Whatever she had come here to say, it must have been important; she was still dressed for the outdoors. Her cheeks were pink, her eyes bright, and the pin of her navy-blue cloak had slipped off-center to expose the sharp edge of her collarbone. At her side, as always, stood Melantho, her cascades of golden hair a wild mess. She glared at him.

Mathias carefully set down the scroll and willed his racing heart to calm.

"Hello," he said. He was exhausted; it was all he could think to say.

Leto took a step forward. "Hello, Mathias," she said. The sound of his name on her lips set his heart aflutter again. Since that last kiss—and the expression on Leto's face when she had hurried away from him—he had begun to think that maybe she would *never* love him, that their marriage would not be the sort that he had always hoped for. She was still impossibly beautiful, though, still drew him into a haze of joy in her rare moments of kindness. He could sustain himself for a lifetime on those moments alone.

Belatedly, he remembered that he had agreed to meet her last night. Had he made it there? Had she fixed him with those huge, grey-brown eyes as she did now? She did not seem angry. Perhaps he had dreamed every part of it.

"We," said Leto, her eyes darting to Melantho, "were hoping to speak to you. Now, if you have the time. It's about something rather important, you see, and we need your help."

Melantho looked like she was in pain.

Mathias could not help it; he raised his eyebrows. "You need help . . . from me?"

He had not realized that it was possible but, somehow, Melantho's expression became even more murderous. "I told you," she hissed, barely bothering to lower her voice. "We shouldn't have come. We're wasting our time."

Leto frowned back at her. "Melantho—"

"Wait." Mathias was on his feet, hand outstretched, before he realized it. "I'm sorry. I didn't mean to insult you. I just . . ." He was just *what*, exactly? Surprised? Alarmed? Or was he carefully, tentatively hopeful that something, at last, was about to change between them? He settled for something less intense. "I assumed you didn't want to come here." *Not after yesterday.*

"Well," said Melantho, sniffing. "That's because it's filthy."

Leto smacked her arm. Not in the way that Mathias's mother had so often struck her own maids—hard, across the cheek, leaving a mark—but in an affable, mild sort of way that spoke of the existence of a genuine affection. "Melantho," she said. "Do I need to remind you that we came here uninvited? And look." She waved a hand at the mess of scrolls on the tables, the heaps of them on the floor. Mathias felt a stab of embarrassment. "He's trying. *I* for one would like to hear what he's learned."

She did not always speak in this stilted, formal way; Mathias had overheard her laughing, joking, as she walked the gardens at Melantho's side. She had hurled insults directly in his face without a hint of apprehension. He saw now the tension in the lines of her face, the tight fists her hands had made against her skirts. She was *nervous.*

"Sit down," he offered.

"Where?" asked Melantho.

It was not a terrible question. Every surface lay beneath a heaped pile of scrolls, hollowed out kalamos, and the dried blocks of ink that would fill them. There were at least four apple cores buried amongst the clutter too, and half a pastry that Mathias had misplaced a week ago. He could imagine the look of triumphant disdain on Melantho's face if she found it.

"Take my chair," he said hastily, indicating the singular vacant space. It was clear that Melantho was going to be a permanent fixture in his life—Leto had made it clear that she would never permit her dismissal and, in truth, Mathias wasn't convinced that he would want it himself—so it was in his best interests to convince her to tolerate him at the very least.

"There are *two* of us, Mathias." But Leto was smiling as she tugged Melantho across the dusty flagstones. She was lovely. Beyond lovely. His heart skipped like a giddy child. He forced down his unease, that awful, choking feeling, and found himself returning her smile with a hopeful, tentative one of his own. He would not ask whether she had come to meet him at the fountain the previous night, whether she had waited for him there.

"It's a big chair," said Mathias.

Leto laughed. "Find us another, will you? Then we can talk."

He did as she asked. He tucked the scroll he'd been reading into his pocket, then, after hastily clearing its surface of papyrus scraps, dragged a heavy wooden stool across the floor. That one was not research; it was a note from one of the advisors—the pirates on the strait had not been seen for some time. Maybe they had been sated by their raid on the Athenian ship, by the gold that had been destined for Ithaca. Gold that Mathias sorely needed.

Still, it would do no good to dwell on that. If this was what he hoped it was—an olive branch, extended from Leto to him—then perhaps Ithaca would not have to worry about gold much longer.

XL

AS LEAVES AND BLOOMS IN SUMMER

Melantho

"You want to . . . work with me?"

Melantho tried not to shriek in frustration as Mathias blinked stupidly at Leto, his long, dark eyelashes fluttering with each quick, bewildered movement. The stool he'd found for himself was far too small; the seat was barely wide enough for one of his thighs. Melantho glared at one of the precariously narrow legs and willed it to break. What she wouldn't give to see the doe-eyed princeling sprawled on the dusty flagstones in all his finery. Again.

But the wooden legs, somehow, held fast as Mathias continued to gaze at them—at Leto, realistically, since he never seemed to be able to tear his gaze away from her—with his mouth half-open. He had been like that as they'd carried him back to his chambers the night before, barely conscious, his head lolling with every step. Melantho had felt just as wretched, she was sure of it, but *she* hadn't needed to be so unceremoniously lifted.

She clicked her tongue impatiently and leaned back on the legs of her own chair. "Were you not listening to *anything* we—"

Leto leaned over and elbowed her sharply in the ribs.

"*Ow.*"

"Melantho's in a bad mood," said Leto firmly. "Don't let it put you off."

"Isn't she always?" Mathias threw Leto a secretive smile, a smile that slipped the moment that he caught Melantho glowering at him.

He was wrong.

Melantho was not *always* this miserable; her ribs did not always feel this tight, like a cage about her lungs that kept her breaths fast and shallow. As much as she batted away Leto's concern with a toss of her curls and a laugh that rang false even to herself, the events of the previous night, the night with the full moon, had shaken her badly. Whenever she closed her eyes, she was standing in the shadows of the palace again with freezing water rushing into her lungs. She was clawing at her throat, she was gasping for air that would not come.

She smacked the legs of her chair back onto the stone floor. "If Leto is to be your queen," she said flatly, "she would rather not be queen of a dying kingdom that murders its citizens on an annual basis."

How easy it was to place that blame on his shoulders. As if he had a choice. As if Melantho herself was not a killer too. As if every innocent death on Ithaca for the last three centuries had not been her fault.

A dull flush had risen in Mathias's cheeks. "You speak as if we do it for sport."

"No, I don't," said Melantho. She took a deep, calming breath and tried to avoid the furious look Leto was aiming at her. It was in moments like these that she longed for Thalia. Thalia had walked these halls time and time again, had dragged so many of its princes to their deaths. She would know what to do. She would not be afraid to die, as Melantho was.

Leto cleared her throat. "I know that you wish this curse broken as much as we do—"

Mathias cut her off with an uncharacteristically curt, humorless laugh. "As much as you do? You must excuse me for speaking frankly, Leto, but you are not of this kingdom. You may be my betrothed, you may be destined to be queen, but you do not know what we have suffered, the pain we have felt for—gods." In a sudden move that set the circlet on his brow crooked, he dropped his head into his hands. When he spoke again his voice was muffled. "For *centuries*. No one—no one at all—wishes to see this curse gone more than I do."

Melantho doubted very much that that was true. Still, she said nothing. She had known grief all her life, and the pain in Mathias's voice was an echo of her own. It reached down her throat and stoked with gentle hands the glowing embers that burned within her still.

"Well then," said Leto, breaking the silence that had stiffened the air. "I suppose we are in agreement. The curse must be broken."

Mathias raised his head enough to watch through his fingers as Leto reached for the table of scrolls and pulled one free. A moth, stirred from its slumber, flew up in a cloud of dust. Leto's face twisted for a moment—with a surprise that was soft and sad—but then her expression was open and warm again.

"You said that you have been working at this for a while. Tell us everything you know so far."

◎◎◎

"Nothing!" exploded Melantho when she and Leto finally returned to their rooms. It was early evening; the sun had fallen and the moon bathed Melantho's skin in a silvery light as she threw herself down on the bed and tore her shoes off, avoiding her reflection in the mirror hung up at the bedside. Dark, purplish circles had dusted themselves beneath her eyes. She had never seen herself look so *tired*.

Leto ducked good-naturedly as Melantho tossed her shoe at the wall. "He knew *nothing!*"

"That's not true," said Leto mildly, perching herself on the edge of the bed and reaching for one of Melantho's hands. Melantho gave it to her, still scowling, and they sat in silence as Leto traced swirling patterns over her skin. "He has found the story of the maids," she said after a moment. This was true; she had been unable to hide her surprise when he began to recount it to them, delighted in his recent discovery. "That means he is making progress, doesn't it? That story had been lost to Ithaca."

Melantho sniffed. "It wasn't lost to me."

"Give him time," said Leto. "Perhaps he will find something we didn't know." She squeezed Melantho's hand. Her fingers were cold. "Perhaps he will find another way. A better way."

Melantho looked up at her. In the low light, Leto's eyes were more grey than brown—the pelt of a wolf, the shine of a flint spear tip. "And if he doesn't?"

The answer hung in the air between them. Even as they spoke, innocent girls were huddled in sparse cells in remote guard towers. Perhaps some of them were even here, in the palace—out of reach and perfectly within it all at once. Melantho would not let them die, so if Mathias could not save them, she would. Leto would. They would take him to the sea, lead him into the churning water, and they would kill him. Cut his throat, perhaps. A far kinder death than drowning: quicker, cleaner.

And then Melantho would learn the truth of her own fate. Would the blade drag across her own throat too? Would her blood mix with his in the shallows, would she slump down next to him as the sea dragged them both to its depths?

She would not admit it, did not *deserve* to feel it, but she was afraid.

Leto held her gaze. "Not yet, Melantho," she said quietly. There was an edge to her voice, a dulled blade made sharp for the briefest of moments. "Don't ask me that yet. Not when you know the answer."

XLI

TO LIE IN SECRET

Leto

The air in the room was still and frigid when Leto retired to bed, nestled in Melantho's arms, so she did what she had always wanted to do when Melantho's eyes looked like that—cold, wistful, old, fixed on the ceiling above them—she leaned in and kissed her.

The kiss was soft and sweet for the first few moments, until Melantho shifted her body, tipping Leto off balance. Leto toppled onto her. Melantho lay back, her golden hair fanned out about her face, looked up, and said, "I did that on purpose."

"Good," said Leto.

The kiss that followed was harder. Leto pushed Melantho's hips into the quilts with the weight of her body. When Melantho moved again, rolling them so it was her body over Leto's, her stomach was taut and solid. Leto ran her hands over Melantho's back, delighting in the way the muscle rippled with tension as Melantho gasped against her mouth.

"Leto?" It was a request; Melantho's kisses were becoming deeper, more frantic. Her hands had begun the desperate journey down to Leto's waist, pulling at the sash there until the knot loosened, and then further. A breeze had sprung up around them. It sent Melantho's hair swirling wildly above her and cooled Leto's burning brow. Her whole body was on fire, and she was damp with sweat.

"Yes," said Leto simply, and she felt Melantho smiling before she pulled away, yanking Leto's skirt up to her hips and ducking between her exposed thighs to—

They broke apart at the sound of a sharp knock on the door.

Shit. *Shit.* Mathias could not find them like this. None of his servants could find them like this.

"One moment!" Leto called out hurriedly, throwing Melantho off. Melantho let out a furious yelp as she landed.

Leto hardly heard her. She could not be so careless; she was betrothed to the prince, after all. There was already so much at stake, to risk it like this was beyond irresponsible. But it was intoxicating too, impossible to resist. She threw a desperate, longing glance back at Melantho. Her hair was a wild mess of gold. She was achingly lovely.

"Sorry," hissed Leto, pulling the sash of her chiton into a hasty knot and running her hands over her curls to soothe them down.

"If that is Mathias," said Melantho, "I will castrate him like a horse."

Leto cocked her head. "Have you ever castrated a horse?"

"No," said Melantho darkly. "But I'm sure that I could if I wanted to."

"Well, then, let's hope it never comes to that." Leto padded into the central room and crossed over to the door. She eased it open a crack and peered through the narrow gap at the servant standing outside. It was dark in the corridor beyond. "Can I help you?"

"A message, your grace," stammered the girl, thrusting it up for Leto to examine.

Leto opened the door a little further. "From?"

"Prince Mathias, his grace," said the girl. "Your grace."

"Wonderful," said Leto dryly, because she knew Melantho was

listening and because she knew that it was what Melantho was thinking. That and, *What is so urgent that he could not wait until tomorrow?* She plucked the scroll from the girl's hand. The papyrus was thin; under the flickering light of the corridor's torch brackets, she could see through to Mathias's careful, looping scrawl. "Thank you."

The girl fled and Leto eased the door shut again.

"Wise of him not to come himself." Melantho's voice floated to her through the gauzy curtain that separated them. "He must have sensed his impending doom."

Leto laughed, allowed herself to relax her shoulders and be *happy* for a moment. She walked back into the bedchamber and grinned at Melantho. "You are all bluster," she said.

"Oh, *am I?*" Melantho's teeth flashed white. She smiled like a predator, a panther stalking its oblivious prey. "Why don't I tell you *exactly* what I intend to do to you, and you can decide for yourself if it is . . ." She leaned back, letting the light play off the arches of her collarbones. She hadn't bothered to retie her own chiton; Leto watched it fall slowly open. Something in her stomach coiled itself into a knot as Melantho's lips shaped the words. ". . . all bluster."

Leto cleared her throat and looked away before her eyes betrayed her every thought. "Read this, will you?" She tossed the scroll at Melantho.

Melantho caught it and threw it back, hard. It bounced off the side of Leto's head. *"Ow."*

"Read it yourself. I am not your servant."

"Technically—"

"Don't try," warned Melantho, but she was smiling. "Leave it to the morning, won't you? We were in the middle of something." She tossed herself back on the pillows and lifted her chin, arching her brows in that familiar, teasing way. Her eyes glittered in the half-light. "Now," she drawled. The chiton fell completely open. "Where *exactly* were we?"

Mathias could not have learned anything new in those few short hours. And with Melantho smiling like *that*, her golden hair spread out in ringlets over the pillows . . . The prince's message could wait.

Leto left the scroll where it had fallen and crossed to the bed, climbing over the creased linens. She leaned down over Melantho, so that their lips were barely a whisper apart. Melantho brought her hands up to cup Leto's face and Leto smiled.

"About here, I think," she said as Melantho inclined her face up to kiss her.

෧ ෧ ෧

The scroll lay on the floor, unread, until midmorning of the following day, when the sunlight filtering in through the windows roused Leto at last.

She extracted herself from the tangle of Melantho's arms and legs and reached out to snatch it up, easing the ribbon apart. Melantho stirred and murmured something softly. Her hair was a spray of gold on the pillows. At times like this—her face scrubbed clean, her eyes closed, and her pale lashes fluttering against her cheeks—it was easy to forget who she was and what she had suffered, that she was not just a girl of seventeen asleep in a patch of the morning sun.

Leto could not help but smile.

It slipped from her face as she read the few lines of curling script.

My dear Leto, it read.

I cannot convey enough how grateful I am for your help,

*and for that of Melantho. Perhaps, together, we will be able
to bring this shameful chapter in Ithaca's history to a close.
I hope you—both of you—will agree to breakfast with me
tomorrow. I will be waiting in the library an hour after the
sun rises.*

My sincerest thanks again,
Mathias

He signed his name elegantly, the letters flowing easily into one
another. Leto blinked at it owlishly for a moment, then she turned
her gaze to the window and the sun that had risen beyond it. Well
over an hour ago.

"*Shit*," she said loudly.

Melantho started awake. Her arms had been thrown wide on
the pillows—she had a notable habit of taking up far more than her
fair share of the bed—but now she brought one hand up sharply
to protect her face as the other plunged beneath the cushions and
emerged holding a knife.

"Zeus, Melantho!" Leto sprang to her feet as Melantho sat up
and blinked blearily at her. "I didn't even know that was there!" It
wasn't exactly a comforting thought.

Melantho squinted at her. "That's because you never change
the sheets," she said. "I thought we were being attacked."

Leto waved the scroll at her. "We're supposed to be meeting
Mathias. We're late."

Melantho picked up a pillow and pulled it over her face. The
goose-down stuffing muffled her voice. "I don't care."

Leto picked up one of Melantho's discarded shoes—the other
was lying where she had tossed it the previous night, on the opposite side of the room—and threw it at her. "Get up," she said, not
unkindly. "And brush your hair. It's all knotted."

Melantho peered at her from behind the pillow, her grass-green eyes narrowed. "I hate you."

She would be justified in it if she did. If she knew Leto's thoughts, sometimes, her thoughts of Mathias, of letting him live, then perhaps she *would*. But Leto would not allow those thoughts to be the loudest, would not let herself waver in her task.

She smiled, "No, you don't."

XLII

OF THE SUN AND MOON

Melantho

When Melantho and Leto hurried into the library, the relief was visible on Mathias's face. Melantho stayed quiet as Leto panted her apologies, her hand on Mathias's arm. Either she was exceptionally good at faking it, or she was genuinely ashamed.

Mathias waved off her excuses. "No, no," he said firmly. In his white chiton, a gold cloak thrown over his shoulders, he was every inch the benevolent future king. "It is my fault—I should not have expected you to read my correspondence immediately. It was presumptuous."

Melantho rolled her eyes. The air still carried the musky, decaying scent of the library, but there was something else there too, something sweeter. Leto had smelled it too. She lifted her face to Mathias and asked, her voice full of delight, "Is that honey cake?"

It was. And dried apricots and figs and a dozen other things spread out over the table in little stone bowls painted and glazed to look as if they were made of sea-foam. Melantho's stomach growled. To his credit, Mathias said nothing, though she saw his eyes dart momentarily to her before he returned to gazing adoringly at Leto.

"I thought we could start over," said Mathias, offering Leto a platter of neatly sliced baklava. "I care deeply for my people. I hope that one day you will too." He looked at Melantho now and smiled. He was beautiful, truly, with his high cheekbones and perfect curls falling over his forehead. He even had *dimples*.

Melantho looked away. She had known a prince like that once, a prince who was all gold and honey and sweetness until one day he wasn't. It was easy to distrust beautiful people; after all, Pandora's jar had been glorious to behold. A work of art, despite the horrors that it contained, the monsters that it had unleashed on the world.

When he offered her the baklava, she waved it away without looking at him.

They sat about the table under the flickering lights of a half dozen torches. Melantho picked apart a dried fig with her nails as Mathias, animated and almost illuminated by the sheer *joy* of company, explained—in meticulous detail—his new system for filing the scrolls.

"This is *wonderful*," said Leto when he'd finished. She examined the labels on a basket of scrolls—the papers that had littered the place in blatant disarray were now arranged neatly by content—and beamed at Mathias. "How long did this take you?"

Mathias ran a hand through his curls and shot her a sheepish smile. "Oh, not too long," he said. "I've been meaning to do it for some months, so it was all planned out. And I suppose I was here for some time last night. I couldn't sleep. And then an hour this morning, while I waited."

Leto looked distinctly guilty.

"Look," he said, lifting a basket up from the floor and placing it in front of her. "This is my attempt at collating Ithaca's history. The oldest scrolls are mostly destroyed, but some of them were copied out. Here." He pulled one loose and shook it at her. "This is barely thirty years old, but it speaks of events dating back centuries.

And this"—he retrieved another—"is from the time of King Odysseus himself; it's where I found the account of the hanged maids. You seemed interested in that yesterday, so I wanted to show you."

"Yes," said Leto eagerly. "I think that is a good place to start."

Somewhere amongst the rotting scrolls, there would also be accounts of the deaths of eleven princes, Melantho was sure of that. She tried to catch Leto's eye; they could not let Mathias discover them. They did not need him to connect the dots, to flee in the night or barricade himself in his chambers or any other such foolishness. But Leto was not looking at her. She had picked up a hunk of honey cake, buried herself in one of the scrolls, and was devouring them both. Her eyes raced across the aged papyrus.

Mathias pushed a scroll across the table toward Melantho. "Here," he said, beaming at her. "I haven't read this one; it's labeled 'curses' but it could be anything, really."

Melantho looked at it. She longed to snatch it up, pull it open, tear through the words, and prove that she was not out of her depth, that she was not afraid, that she was *useful*. But she knew that she could not. She forced her voice to be quiet and calm and cold. "I can't read."

Leto choked on her cake.

Melantho looked down at the table as Mathias jumped to his feet to fuss about with the pitcher of wine, pushing a cup into Leto's hands and watching her closely as she took an audible gulp. She could not bear to look into Leto's face, to see the bewilderment that she knew would be written all over it.

Her cheeks burned with shame.

She had avoided the subject as best she could, using any excuse she could find, unable to return to the memory of a life where she had been *just a maid*. Just an *illiterate* maid—her queen had liked to keep her maids ignorant; it meant that they could be relied upon not to snoop.

"It is not an issue," she declared hurriedly, once Leto had ceased choking. "I can do . . ." She cast around for something, *anything.* "Well, I am sure we will find something."

Mathias's face lit up. He was like a child, always so *desperate* to please. "I have just the thing!" He dived beneath the table and emerged with yet another basket. "These are illuminated—if there are words they are mainly titles of the pieces. Here." He offered the basket to her.

Melantho took it from him, grateful, for the first time, for his presence. He distracted Leto at the very least. Her sad, searching eyes had moved away from Melantho's face at last and were now fixed on the basket of scrolls that Melantho held.

She was smiling. "My mother loved myths like these," she said, leaning over to pull one free. She slipped the ribbon off and held the delicate parchment open for Mathias to peer at. "Look, Persephone and Hades. She told me this one. It was one of the few things we would do together, when there was time for it. She was always so busy, and when she *wasn't* busy, she was always *tired.*"

"The perils of having a queen for a mother," said Mathias.

"I—yes." A flush rose in Leto's cheeks. She was a terrible liar. "Yes, I suppose that was it. But when there was a moment of peace, a time when—when there were not taxes to review and all that sort of thing—"

Melantho reached for another fig and set about pulverizing it. Mathias was still looking at Leto with those wide, black eyes of his, his lips parted as she lied to him.

"We would sit together by the fire," Leto continued. "And she would tell me stories of the gods, all the ancient heroes. She would put on all the voices too. It was magical." She drew in a deep breath, her next words tumbling from her lips as if unbidden. "People always listened when she spoke. She was captivating. *Beyond* captivating. And clever too, and beautiful."

"You speak of her as if she is gone," said Mathias. "She is not so very far away, Leto. You can go back to Athens anytime you like when we are married."

The mangled fig in Melantho's hands slipped onto the table with a soft thump.

Leto's eyes darted to hers. A small, almost imperceptible movement that should have calmed Melantho but did quite the opposite. There was grief there, but her cheeks were red, and she looked flustered. Melantho looked away pointedly.

Was Leto *blushing* at the thought of marrying Mathias?

Leto returned to pulling illuminated scrolls from another basket. "Oh, look at *these.* These are *wonderful.*"

Mathias leaned over to look. "Oh, yes," he said. "Aren't they? I just grouped together all the ones that the last oracle wrote and—"

"The oracle?" Leto's voice was sharp. Too sharp. A princess from Athens should not have such a reaction to an Ithacan oracle. But of course, Leto was not a princess from Athens, and she was coming dangerously close to betraying this fact.

"There are no oracles in Athens," said Melantho. Adrasteia had said as much, as she'd begged them to let her go, to find her own future on the island of Delphi. "Leto has a special interest in them."

Leto didn't even look at her. "My mother had a particular interest in them, you see," she said, leaning into Mathias.

Why was she doing that? She did not need to be that close to him, did she? There was just no reason for it. As Mathias opened his mouth to reply, Melantho cut in.

"I never knew my mother," she said pleasantly. Her heart was racing. She hated feeling like this: out of control, afraid, impatient, and impulsive. She had always been the patient one, the cautious one, the one that waited too long, too late. "Not that I remember, anyway. She sold me to the queen when I was six for a gold piece."

Mathias and Leto stayed silent, their faces identical masks of discomfort. Melantho plowed onward, her voice full of a false brightness. "That was quite a lot, you know. I suppose I was a pretty child."

"Melantho," said Leto. As it tumbled from her tongue, the name sounded like a warning.

It was more than Melantho could take. She scraped her chair back with the harsh, grating sound of wood against stone, and stood. "You're right," she said shortly. "I'm not much help here, am I? I'll just go do something more suited to my *station*. Scrub a few floors, perhaps?"

Mathias watched her quietly. Leto's face was crumpled and bewildered. "Melantho," she said again.

"Don't bother," said Melantho. "I'll leave you to it. But a word of advice. Silly legends aren't going to help you much. Why don't you look for something *relevant*? Like records of *your* family's wrongdoings." Who knew what other secrets were hidden here? That would keep them busy. She turned and strode from the room, her cheeks burning, her eyes prickling in the dusty air, her heart heavy with the peculiar sense that she had lost something precious.

XLIII

IN SPITE OF SORROW

Leto

Leto had known from the expression on Melantho's face that she did not want to be followed. Still, she would have done so had it not been for the prince sitting before her, peering at her through his lashes. Her mind was wild with bewilderment; she had never seen Melantho act so rashly, so furiously. And why had Melantho never told her that she did not know how to read? Leto would have taught her.

She shook her head, cleared her thoughts. There were more important things to think of now. Like the fact that there were four days remaining before Mathias had to die.

Before Leto had to kill him.

Unless they could find another way. But that was almost too much to hope for. She could not forget what lay on the table between them, the pile of scrolls that spoke of prophecies. Of her *mother's* prophecies.

"This oracle," she said casually, picking up another roll of parchment and shaking the dust from its seal. "What else do you know about her?"

Mathias looked down at his own sheet of parchment. "Not much, if I am to be honest. I know that she retired from her position shortly after I was born. If I ever met her, I'm afraid that I don't remember it at all."

The wave of disappointment hurt more than Leto expected. She had not realized how much hope she still carried that someday, one day, she would find out what happened to her mother. Nor, in truth, how much of that hoped she had pinned on the boy sitting before her. He chewed absentmindedly on a piece of honey cake, dropping golden crumbs onto the table.

"That's a shame," she said.

Mathias looked up. "Is it?" he asked through a mouthful of cake.

Leto raised an eyebrow and he flushed, his cheeks flaring with red.

He swallowed hastily and tried again. "Is it?"

"Well," she said, keeping her voice carefully level, betraying as little as she could, "oracles make prophecies, do they not?" *Yes,* said the voice in the back of her mind, *prophecies that show them Melantho's death. Prophecies they ignore because they are too dim-witted to work out what they mean.* She plowed on: "Perhaps something about the curse, even?"

"I searched Apollo's temple. There was nothing there we could use." He did not seem to be listening, really, his eyes were already shifting back to his papers. "Ugh, look at this. Narcissus . . . Crocus . . ." He shuffled through the scrolls on the table. "A lot of unfortunate mortals seem to end up as flowers, don't they?"

"Well," said Leto. "At least we remember them."

"Hmm." Mathias lifted one of the illuminations to his face and squinted at it. "Which flower would you be?"

"I'm sorry?"

"If the gods killed you." He looked up with a bright, lovely smile. "What do you think you'd turn into?"

"I thought the point was that they make a *new* flower. I'd be a Leto flower."

He didn't seem pleased with that answer. "That's not the point. That doesn't *mean* anything." A pause. "I'd be a daffodil."

"Really?"

"Why not? I like daffodils."

"I—" She narrowed her eyes at him. "Look, back to the oracle a moment. She existed beyond the temple, surely. She was the *royal* oracle, no? Where did she live? Was it *here?* Maybe she would have left clues behind. Or if you'd known where her rooms were, perhaps. We could search them."

"Oh, well," said Mathias, perking up visibly. One of his curls had fallen over his eyes; he tucked it behind his ear and beamed at her. "If she had rooms, it shouldn't be too hard to discover where they were. I've found maps, lots of them. There are so many hidden passages in this place, it's ridiculous." He rifled through a nearby basket until he found what he was looking for. "Let's see . . . servants' quarters . . . stable master. Here! You're right—I can't believe I didn't think of that before. The oracle's rooms are on the eastern side of the palace, and I am sure they have not been touched since she left."

"You—you are?"

"Of course. In fact, I'll take you there," he said, scraping his chair back and jumping to his feet. He seemed suddenly to thrum with purpose, a relief that *at last* he could do something of worth. She could see his impatience in the way he shifted his weight from one foot to another and back again as he reached for her hand. "Come on."

She took it, lacing her fingers with his, and allowed him to lead her from the room.

Her mother's chambers were in the east wing of the palace, hidden somewhere amongst the twisting labyrinth of identical, marble-walled corridors and tightly coiled staircases. They blurred together in Leto's mind as she hurried to keep up with Mathias and the insistent pull of his hand on hers. When he came to a halt at last—in front of a smooth, wooden door branded with a spiraling insignia—she walked straight into him.

"Careful," he said, steadying her.

"This is it?"

"It is."

She peered at the door. The pattern resolved itself into a flurry of swirling wings that tugged at Leto's memories and brought with them the sweet smell of incense. Incense and ash.

"This is it," she said again. This time, it was not a question.

"Yes," said Mathias. He pressed the tips of his fingers against the door and pushed. There came a long, awful squeaking noise as the wood resisted for a moment and—

The door fell off.

"Oh—" Mathias swore, loudly, the words echoing about the corridor. As they left his lips, he clapped a hand to his face, looking appalled. "*Gods,* I am *sorry.* I did not—"

Leto laughed. The sound of it—bright, ringing—surprised her. She had not expected to laugh like that with Mathias, had not expected to feel so comfortable, so at *home* with him. "I am made of stronger stuff than you seem to think, Mathias," she said. "I will not shatter into fragments of indignity every time you say something remotely improper."

Mathias fixed his eyes on the floor. There was a high red flush in his cheeks. "Indignant or not, you must accept my apologies. And my compliments. I did not mention it earlier, but you look lovely today. As dazzling as the moon."

"I will not accept your compliments, they are ridiculous. Are we going inside?" Her face was hot; she pushed him aside and entered the room, navigating carefully about the broken door. Her heart felt like glass, like ice, as if it could shatter at any moment. Her mother had been here.

Her *mother*. How easy it had been to forget her amidst all the plotting and scheming. How it hurt to remember again.

"Oh," said Mathias. He had followed her; he lingered at her shoulder like a shadow. He brushed the back of his hand over hers, and when she did not pull away, he carefully slipped his fingers between hers. His thumb swept an arc over her palm. "It is beautiful."

It was.

The room had fallen into an appalling state of disrepair and yet—Mathias was right. It was as exquisite as it was broken.

One wall was devoted entirely to a sheet of hammered bronze that served as a huge distorted mirror. Swathes of its polished surface had all but vanished under layers of dust and detritus. Something glimmered dully on the little table at its side. A great dent seemed to cleave it in two; the reflections that looked back at Leto—a girl and a boy, their hands entwined—shimmered and fractured. If she was the moon, he was always, always the sun. A blazing, beautiful boy, destined to burn. She met his eyes in the reflection and looked away.

"What happened?" she asked him. Her mother had lived in these rooms, had gazed out of these very same windows. Had laughed here, perhaps loved here. And now it was a rotting shell. The air was thick with the smell of decay, and the only sound was that of the wind as it stirred up dust.

Mathias gazed upon it with anguish in every line of his beautiful face. "Nothing," he said quietly. "Nothing at all—it is exactly as it always was. Just look at the dust. I think we must be the first to step foot in here for more than a decade."

More than a decade. For more than *ten years* her mother's legacy had slowly but surely deteriorated into nothing. Leto should have felt angry, should have hated the boy standing beside her in all his finery. But she just felt hollow. If she had pressed a finger to her wrist, she would not have been surprised to find that there was no pulse there. Her mother was gone from this place; it meant nothing now.

"It is not just here," she said. "It is everywhere. The library is falling to pieces. There are corridors, staircases that lead to *nothing;* there is so much *emptiness* here." She looked up at Mathias. He was still staring blankly at the dusty bronze. "It cannot have always been like this, surely?"

"No," said Mathias. "You are right, of course."

"What changed?"

"Money," said Mathias. "We have none. Our treasury is all but empty, we can barely afford the few servants we have kept on, our people are starving, and we're about to *hemorrhage* funds on this ridiculous equinox festival. And time. Tomorrow is the last *full* day we'll have." He aimed a half-hearted kick at a dust-covered chair. They collided with a dull thump and Mathias's face twisted.

"That looked like it hurt."

"Not too badly." The anguish remained in his face though. His eyes were always black, of course, but somehow, they looked darker now.

Leto endeavored to keep her tone light. "You look positively morbid. Surely the prospect of the festival isn't *so* bad."

"This room—" he began haltingly, then broke off.

"What is it?" Something in his tone gave her pause. She turned away from examining the battered lock of a rotting chest and peered up at him.

He shook his head. "It is nothing. You will laugh at me."

"I will not." Whatever it was he had seen, had heard, she must know it.

"It's just—" He broke off again and looked away. When he spoke again his voice was soft and careful. "I do not think that the oracle was a happy woman. This room reeks of sadness. I can . . . I can hardly bear to be in here. Do you understand what I mean? It is—"

"Yes," Leto interrupted him. Something about Mathias saying it made it true, and she could not bear to hear it. "Yes, I do. You are right. It is awful here and I cannot stand it, either. Come on." She took his hand. His skin was feverish. He clutched at her as if he were a drowning man, and she was the siren pulling him to his death. "There is nothing for us here."

As she left, she swept her hand idly over the filthy table and pocketed the tiny bottle that had been concealed in the dirt there, the bottle that had caught her eye with its glimmer, so that there was nothing left in the room for her but the dusty air, thick with the grief of her dead mother.

XLIV

AGAIN BY TORCH LIGHT

Melantho

When Leto returned at last from her romantic escapades with Mathias—because, of course, Melantho could not imagine that they were doing anything else—her face was pale and drawn. The hem of her chiton and the tips of her fingers were sticky with dust.

"I am going to the sea," she announced.

Melantho looked up with deliberate slowness. Was that all that Leto had to say? No apology, no attempt to make amends for what had occurred in the library? Melantho said nothing.

Leto stood up straight and spoke to the air above Melantho's head. "I am going to find the wreck of the Athenian ship." A pause. "I hope," she added, and Melantho was relieved to hear the crack in her voice, "that you will come with me."

Melantho stayed quiet for as long as she knew Leto would be able to stand. When she spoke, she was direct and succinct. "Why?"

"The wreck of the ship," said Leto again. "I need to find it. I need to find the *gold* that went down with it. And when I do, I am going to take every last gold piece from the seabed and bring it here. But I cannot do it without you." Her voice was full of pleading.

Melantho's eyes snagged on the protective curve of one of Leto's hands, the set of her fingers that meant she was hiding something within. Melantho liked secrets. She liked hearing them and keeping them and using them for herself when the time came. Whatever secret Leto was hiding now, Melantho wanted it.

"I will come with you," she said, and she smiled as Leto did, as surprise and joy flashed across Leto's face in equal measure. "*But*, first, you must show me what you have in your hand."

"Agreed," said Leto without a moment's pause. Perhaps it was not such a secret, then. "Yes. Thank you, Melantho, thank you—"

"All right. Don't be like that; you knew I would say yes." She allowed her voice to soften. "I would do anything for you."

"As I would for you," said Leto, her eyes warm and sincere. She walked to Melantho, knelt at her side, and pressed something small and cold into her hand.

Melantho looked down at the vial.

The bottle was thick with dust, but the stopper had held true; the liquid inside, cloudy as it was, was uncorrupted.

When she pulled the stopper out carefully, she could smell the musk of decay on the bottle, and beyond it a sweetness that tugged at the threads of her memory. It was a peculiar, automatic instinct that had her placing her littlest finger over the top of the bottle and inverting it quickly, leaving a fat milky droplet on her skin.

"Melantho." Leto had started to her feet, was reaching toward Melantho with an expression of fearful wariness in her hazel eyes. "What are you—"

Melantho touched the drop to her tongue.

Yes. There was the memory, tearing itself out and presenting its awful contents to her.

It was as if three centuries meant nothing. With the taste of poppy—of opium, because, of course, that was what the bottle held—she was seventeen years old, pinned against the wall of a secluded corridor as Eurymachus panted in her ear, his greasy hair pressed against her cheek.

Melantho tried to pull away and he caught her wrist in his hand, yanked at it insistently.

"Melantho," said a girl's voice. It was coming from very far away.

Eurymachus was on her, in her, she could not break free, she could not breathe, she could not—

"Melantho."

The memory shattered.

Leto's face, her eyes a soft grey in the low light, swam into focus. Melantho gazed at her, hands shaking, twitching with the pain and the anger of the memory. Her wretched heart did not care that the memory was over now; it drummed out a frantic beat inside her chest.

"Melantho?" said Leto, for the third time. She wrapped her fingers over Melantho's wrists and squeezed. "What is that? Is it—is it poison? Do we need to go to the fountain? Can you hear me?"

"It is tears of Hypnos," said Melantho. "It is a drug. I—I have seen it used by women when they—" She could not go on. If Eurymachus was long dead, how could she still hear his piglike grunting, how did he still breathe on her neck like this and run clammy fingers over the soft flesh above her hips? She shivered, a sudden, violent jerking of her limbs.

"Melantho?" Leto leaned into her, eyes wide, lips parted.

Leto would not hurt her; Melantho knew it to be true, and yet . . . something scrabbled at her lungs, traced an icy finger across the bones of her rib cage. Her whole body was screaming at Leto's touch upon her wrist.

"I cannot breathe," she said, and found that it was true.

"Is there an antidote?"

Melantho shook her head wordlessly. *It is not the drug that is causing this.* She should have been clearer in her gesture—the alarm on Leto's face intensified.

"There's no antidote?"

Melantho forced the words through. "It isn't a poison. It is . . . something else."

Leto frowned. At last, she let go. "I don't understand."

"You do not need to." Melantho yanked her hand away and stood abruptly. The sea would help. It would wash away her memories, bury them beneath the sand. It had done so before. "Come," she said. "The light is fading. We should leave if we wish to be back before the sun rises again."

"Very well," said Leto, but her expression was still tentative, unsure. "Let us go, then."

୭ ୭ ୭

It was a great relief to plunge into the cool water, to let the pull of the ocean wash over her and change her from a weak, human girl. Monster, creature, it did not matter so long as she was *strong*, so long as she could kill a man that looked at her and saw only a prize to be won, a bounty to be taken.

Melantho smiled, felt the razor points of her teeth cut into her lips, tasted the blood.

Leto tugged at her arm. The implication was clear: *we've got a ship to find.*

That would be easy. Melantho was good at finding things that were lost at sea; it had been her singular task for centuries. To find the lost things, to clean the grit and the dirt from their slack faces, to set them carefully beneath the soil of Pandou and bid them good fortune in their journeys onward.

❦❦❦

Later, they deposited the great heap of gold in front of Mathias's door. They had barely spoken at all as they methodically ferried it from the wreck to the beach, nor as they'd dragged it up the path to the palace.

Leto broke the silence back in their chambers.

"Sit." She pushed Melantho into a chair and set about pulling out pieces of papyrus from an astoundingly varied collection of hiding places. The last she tugged out from the place where a torch bracket had been hammered into the walls.

"What are you doing?" asked Melantho as Leto smacked down the mess of papyrus in front of her and ducked under the table.

"Teaching you to read," said Leto shortly, reemerging with a length of reed in her hand. She smoothed out the papyrus. Melantho could think of nothing to say; she gaped at Leto. No one had even *offered* to teach her before, let alone commanded it.

"To read?"

"Yes," said Leto. "The festival is in two days' time—one really, given the hour—and there's still so much to do. We will work through the scrolls much faster if there are three of us, don't you think?" She tipped ink into the hollow of the reed and made a stark, black mark on the paper. She smiled, satisfied. "What would you like to learn first? Your name?"

"Your name," said Melantho; her answer was automatic and immediate. It did not matter that in four days they would have to kill together. For now, they could be normal, human. For now, she was just a girl, leaning into another and wishing she could stay in this precious moment forever. "If I am writing to anyone, I am writing to you."

XLV

THE CHILD OF ANGER

Mathias

Mathias had not been surprised when Leto made her excuses after they had left the oracle's rooms and slipped away back to her own chambers. He should not have discussed the Ithacan treasuries with her; it was both improper and foolish beyond belief. What princess—what princess of *Athens*, with its military prowess and its coffers heaving with coin—would want to marry into such a poor family? He could not provide her with the comforts he knew she must desire, not while his people starved in the streets.

He could not give her jewels or gold, and he knew she was fond of them; she always wore that thick gold collar, studded with gemstones. On the rare occasion she did not, there would be a ribbon around her neck and diamonds in her ears. He could not help but wonder what it was that she hated so much about her neck. Did she have a scar there, a birthmark? Some peculiar secret she wished to conceal from him? Whatever it was, he doubted she would lose her taste for necklaces. No, Leto would not wish to marry him when he could not pay for such things.

He should have kept his godsdamned mouth shut.

He had messed this up time and time again; time and time over he had insulted her—without meaning to, of course, but the intent did not matter here and the expression on Leto's face *did*— and yet she had stayed. His mother had been awful to her, and she had stayed. One of his horses had thrown her from its back, and she had stayed. He had confessed to her that his kingdom killed innocents, and she had not only stayed but endeavored to help him end it.

He did not deserve her.

But he would. He would break this curse, *prove* to her, once and for all, what he was willing to do for her. For Ithaca. He could only hope that it would be enough.

For once, just once, perhaps he could do something right.

Perhaps Ithaca would forgive him; perhaps he would have earned it.

*   *   *

Melantho was slouched outside Leto's chambers when Mathias arrived at last to collect her for the festival. It had been a mere day since he had awoken to a knock in the night and an astonishing mound of gold on the doorstop. There had been no note, but every coin had been stamped with Athenian insignia, so he had known it must come from Leto. At first, he had thought it was a dream—a manifestation which surely must disappear the next time he closed his eyes. But it had not, and now he almost dared to assume it was a token of her forgiveness, her understanding. A commitment to do what she could to save his kingdom, hidden safely away in her chambers until she decided he had earned it.

"Melantho," he said. He knew the maid did not like him; being alone with her made him feel peculiarly self-conscious, aware suddenly of every slightest thing. His posture, the drape of his chiton, the awkward way he knew he held his hands. "Hello."

Melantho looked him up and down slowly. He did not miss the way her eyes darted up to the circlet of gold resting atop his brow, how they lingered on the rubies in his ears and the shining cuffs at each of his wrists. "Hello," she said. "You look nice."

It could have been a compliment. It probably wasn't. Still, he decided to take it as one. "Thank you. As do you."

Melantho raised her eyebrows. "I look the same as always."

"You always look nice." Melantho's brows climbed even higher. She probably thought that he was lying or spewing niceties for the sake of politeness, but he really *did* mean it. She was not lovely in the way Leto was—all sharp contrast, her skin and hair like the moon against the night sky—but Melantho's suntanned skin was barely a shade away from her waves of shining yellow curls. She could have been a statuette cast in gold.

"Why are you out here?"

She scowled. "I've been banished. She says I'm too *judgmental.* Can you believe it?"

Yes. "No," said Mathias.

"You are lying," said Melantho lightly. Her lips were lifted in a half smile. Something—something other than Mathias—had put her in an uncharacteristically good mood. "Deceptive wretch."

He should not have allowed her to speak to him this way, but he found that he simply did not *care.* Besides, it was nice to speak to Melantho no matter her tone—she spent so much of their time together scowling and destroying pieces of fruit or scraps of paper. Just that morning, she had turned one discarded sheet of papyrus—a blank one, thank the gods, because Mathias had strong opinions about the destruction of literature—into careful strips. Then, she had braided them together into something that had *distinctly* resembled an effigy before she had thrown it on the fire. She'd even given it a little crown.

When she'd caught Mathias watching her, she had smiled.

He would have sworn that her canines were longer than they had been before, peculiar and *other,* but he'd blinked and Melantho's glittering smile had been human again. Threatening and full of animosity, but human.

"How long is she going to *be*?" he asked, drumming his foot impatiently against the stones. "Is she braiding her eyebrows?" He wasn't sure why he'd said it; it was what his father had always said when Selene took too long to get dressed and Mathias had always found it distinctly unfunny. But Melantho laughed, loudly. Her eyes flared, mirroring his own surprise, then softened. She threw him a wide, genuine smile. He gazed at her. That might have been the first time she had looked at him with anything other than animosity.

Tentatively, he smiled back.

XLVI
A BIRD IN THE AIR

Leto

Melantho was laughing. The sound issued from the corridor beyond Leto's rooms. A moment later, Mathias's laugh joined her—a rich baritone. Perhaps he had fallen over or embarrassed himself in some other fashion; Leto could think of no other reason for their mirth.

She gazed at herself in the mirror and tried to swallow down the nervous knot in her throat. In the festival chiton, with its fussy gold embellishments and plunging, beaded neckline, she felt almost princess-like. Adrasteia, of course, had been taller and more distinguished in frame, but something about the gown made her feel truly lovely. Perhaps it was the bodice—it dipped low enough to show off a truly alarming portion of her breasts, cleverly supported by overlapping straps of fabric, pulled very tight. A veil cascaded from her braided hair; she pulled the sheer material over her chest.

This was as good as it was going to get. She sucked in a deep breath, turned sharply on one silk-slipper-clad heel, and marched toward the door.

Melantho and Mathias ceased their laughing the moment that Leto thrust the doors open and stepped into the corridor beyond.

They had actually been *doubled over*—they straightened at the same time, their faces equally guilty. It was not the reception Leto had hoped for.

Mathias recovered first. "Leto," he said, hurriedly taking her

hands and brushing a kiss over her knuckles. "you look radiant." He was dressed in rich plum; the fine quality of the embroidery marked his wealth, the narrow band of gold around his head marked his rank.

"You look uncomfortable," said Melantho. "But exquisite, of course. Like royalty." There was a wry half smile on her face, but the set of her eyes and her brows said that she meant it.

"As she should," said Mathias. He offered her his arm. "Shall we?"

She took it, caught Melantho's laughing eyes. Perhaps she had preferred it when they were snapping at each other, when she had known that Melantho would step forward to strike any blow that Leto could not.

Two days left before the true equinox. There was just not enough *time*. The truth of it had not quite sunk in. She still clung to the useless hope that they *would* discover something in the hours they had remaining, that Mathias might yet escape unscathed.

She could enjoy tonight, perhaps, before the illusion shattered.

The courtyard had been made splendid.

Leto frowned out at the stone floor; it had been scrubbed by servants until it was almost shining. There might have been a hundred guests there; they milled about in their finery, drinking and laughing, or perched on the edge of the fountain and trailed elegant fingers in the water. Clearly, they were all long acquainted. Though some shot Leto occasional appraising looks as they strolled past, none approached her.

This was not surprising; Melantho and Mathias flanked her like a personal guard.

A touch on the shoulder brought her out of her thoughts. "Do not be frightened now." It was Mathias, smiling shyly at her. A single black curl had liberated itself from the rest and hung off center over his forehead. She resisted the urge to brush it away—she could feel eyes watching them, boring into Mathias's back.

"This looks beautiful," she said.

"It would be nothing without you," he said softly. "And not just because it is Athens' gold that will pay for it. Or at least, that ensured that our people will not starve at the end of it."

"Oh," she managed. She did not want to say too much, lest he catch her in a lie. At any moment, he might ask how she had recovered the gold, and that was a question she knew she could not answer.

He beamed at her. "Would you like to dance?"

Leto stole a glance around the courtyard. Several ladies quickly ducked their heads, plunging into conversations that were rather louder than strictly necessary. Nearby, Alexios stood to attention by a great platter of figs and cheese. He met her eyes and glowered. She turned swiftly back to Mathias and forced herself to smile. "Of course."

Melantho brushed a finger over her waist, a touch that said, *Go. I will wait for you.* When Leto turned to look at her, she was already gone, working her way toward the edges of the room. She had the sort of presence that meant people moved out of her way instinctively, then paused, looking bewildered, as they realized they had just cleared a path for a mere maid.

Mathias beamed and placed his hand on her elbow. "This way," he said, steering her across the bustling space. A walkway appeared for them like magic as ladies and their gentlemen stepped smoothly out of his way.

When they found the perfect place, right in the center of the courtyard, Leto allowed him to nudge her into the correct position. They swayed together in the soft evening light. The last light of the setting sun—how apt a metaphor.

"Everyone is staring at us," she murmured.

"Yes," said Mathias. "I do not think they know what else to do."

"Wonderful." A servant was passing with a tray of chalices, brimming with ruby-red wine. Leto snagged two, careful to keep them steady. A single drop would destroy her gown, and she was peculiarly attached to it already, but she could not last the night without *something* to fog the relentless churning of her mind, to help her bear the ridiculous pageantry.

Mathias made to take a cup from her.

"Excuse me," she said, forcing herself to be light, teasing, "get your own."

"You have two."

"And they are both for me. Go on." She batted at him with an elbow.

"The wine will keep coming, Leto." He reached for the chalice again. "Come *on,* let me have it. I will have to dance with every lady here, you know. I *need* it."

"And I will have to dance with every man, I suppose? So *I* need it."

"Not Alexios," said Mathias. "That is one."

"With all the rest to go." In one movement, Leto drained one of the chalices and handed it to him.

He took it automatically. "What is this for?"

The wine was strong, sharp. She smiled at Mathias and shrugged. "If you cannot protect me from the hordes of noblemen, the least you can do is hold my cup."

"But it is *empty.*"

"Exactly." She drained the other, savoring the heady rush that came with it.

"Mathias!" Olympia materialized from the crowd and forced herself between them. The great loops of polished metal around her neck and wrists clattered together as she moved. Leto bit back a smile. The sound was close to that of the little bell the cat at Vathi's bakery always wore, jangling as he prowled around trying to steal pastries.

Olympia smiled up at Mathias. "You owe me a dance, remember?" she said in a wheedling voice, studiously ignoring Leto's presence. "Do not tell me you had forgotten!"

Mathias returned her smile—though Leto did not feel his heart was fully in the gesture—and inclined his head. "Of course not," he said. "How could I have forgotten to dance with my dearest friend?" Olympia's smile stagnated slightly at this description of herself. "Indeed," Mathias plowed on, "I believe the musician Linos has composed an ode on the cithara later, an original for the occasion. I would be honored to stand up with you for such a fine piece. I will come and find you before it."

The dismissal in his voice was clear. Olympia, with an expression like sour milk, dropped a curtsy and turned to Leto. "Adrasteia," she said.

"Your grace," corrected Leto pleasantly. She was being unkind, and it was deliberate. This girl had planted a snake in her room, she was sure of it.

"Your *grace*." Olympia's face twisted. "The queen wishes to see you."

A peculiar prickling sensation slithered its way along Leto's spine. What could the queen—who had made her disdain so very clear—*possibly* have to say to her?

Mathias's face reflected the question; his eyebrows had shot up, his mouth was half-open. "What, now? But the festival—"

Olympia smiled tightly. "I believe it is a delicate topic, and one requiring some urgency."

Mathias turned helplessly to Leto. She schooled her features into an expression of dutiful obedience and gritted her teeth in a smile. She could handle the queen's hostility for a few minutes. "I suppose I'll see you later, then."

"Oh," said Mathias. "Yes, I suppose so, then." He caught up her hand in his and pressed his lips to her wrist, where the tracery of blue was visible beneath her skin. "Hurry."

If Leto hadn't been listening for it, she might not have heard Olympia's furious huff. She fought back a smile. "You'll hardly miss me," she promised him. "It is probably a discussion of jewelry or a letter from my kingdom. I'll be back before you know it."

XLVII

CHILDREN OF THE GROVES
AND FOUNTAINS

Melantho

From her position—half-hidden beneath the leaves of a palm—Melantho watched as Leto left Mathias alone. A moment later, Alexios had materialized at his side and muttered something to him. Mathias's face had fallen in an instant. Now she tracked the prince with her eyes as he crossed the dance floor, snatched up a platter of charred meat, and disappeared through a curtain leading back into the east wing.

She debated leaving him there, letting him wander the corridors with his plate of meat. But if Melantho was anything, she was irredeemably nosy. She followed him.

She found him easily; he was not a light walker and his sandals slapped against the stone floor as he went. She turned a corner just in time to watch him slip into an innocuous side room and shut the battered wooden door behind him. Clearly, he wanted to be alone.

Melantho did not particularly care what he wanted. Something drew her to this melancholy boy, so different from the prince she had known so many hundreds of years ago. If he knew the truth, what would he say? Would he welcome death for the sake of his people, or run from it? She pushed the door open and entered.

Mathias had been crouching in front of a fireplace. He started at the sound of her entrance and turned, hurriedly, from the flames.

His skin—usually tanned and smooth—was pink and patchy, and he hastily wiped his eyes with the sleeve of his chiton.

Gods, was he *crying?* Melantho felt abruptly awkward.

"Um," she said.

"Melantho," sniffed Mathias. "Hello, come in." He was relentlessly polite. He did not mention that she had already come in, without his invitation.

"Are you drunk?" she asked hopefully. She had seen men cry over the most idiotic of matters when drunk. If Mathias was drunk, he might not be *actually* sad, and Melantho wouldn't have to feel quite so wretched for barging in on his misery.

He frowned. "Why would I be drunk?"

She shrugged. "Why did you leave the festival?"

"They found the twelfth girl," he said flatly. "The last marked girl. So that is all of them now. Their families will all be grieving, so I do not understand how we can be *celebrating*. There will be prayers to Poseidon tonight, you know? As if he has not caused us centuries of pain. As if he will not cause us centuries more."

I know.

You can stop it.

Melantho could have said it to him. The twelfth girl found; how little time Mathias had left. Two days. Just two. Instead she said, "A kingdom cannot be in mourning for centuries." She meant it, somehow. Ithaca should have not had to bear this grief for so long, should not have suffered and suffered and suffered. Not when the blame was so easily traced: a silver thread that led back to Melantho.

"It *should* be." His hands were clenched into fists, his voice was harder than she had ever heard it. Melantho decided not to push it, occupying herself with examining the small room they were in instead.

It was remarkably plain, empty of furniture but for the fireplace and the mantel above it. A single little statue stood atop it; Melantho peered at it.

The statuette was brightly painted and remarkably lifelike. It depicted a girl with long flowing hair and eyes that, even cut from marble, seemed to follow Melantho. "Oh, I like these," she said, taking it up in her hands. "They're for remembering the dead, aren't they?"

"Yes." Moving with a pointed deliberateness, Mathias took it from her. "They are."

His tone was not sharp exactly, but there was an edge to it. Pain, perhaps. Or grief—

Oh. She was an idiot. The food he had taken from the festival smoldered in the grate. An offering. At last, she understood. "You lost someone." It was not a question.

Mathias exhaled. "My sister. Selene." He stumbled over the words, like he had left them unsaid so long that he had forgotten how they should sound.

Melantho's surprise was sharp, startling; it unfurled in her chest and bloomed into something else. She wanted to hate him, to despise him viciously for the way he looked at Leto. But of course, it was the way *she* looked at Leto and the way that his voice shook now was achingly familiar to Melantho. Loss was Melantho's constant companion—it never left her side.

The room was very quiet. Melantho shook her head. "I'm sorry." There was so much more she wanted to say; she wanted to grip his hands and look into his pretty face and tell him *I understand.* To tell him how sometimes, she would close her eyes and all she could see was Thalia, pulling a spear from her chest. She had watched it play out a hundred times in her mind and Thalia's expression was always, *always* the same. Surprise. And the first hint of fear, the creeping realization that she was going to die.

She wanted to close her eyes and tell him that the other times, she saw Sofia, falling to her knees on the sand and screaming. Slitting her throat with a flint that was not sharp enough to make it *quick*.

Or Timo. Eyes closed, floating in the water, her little hands slack.

"She was sixteen," said Mathias, jolting Melantho from her memories. He was watching her closely, curiously, his dark brows furrowed.

When she had first met him, she had thought he looked like the queen; he had her smooth, tanned skin, and her black curls, and her full, feminine lips. Now, though, they seemed to her as different as night and day. The queen's eyes were cold, empty, shut off to the rest of the world. Mathias let every thought play out over his face. Even now, he leaned in to Melantho and said, "I was fourteen, believing myself to be on the cusp of adulthood, just coming into my own inflated sense of self-importance. An *idiot*."

"A fourteen-year-old is a child," said Melantho.

Mathias shook his head. "I was a *prince*. A prince is never just a child. My every whim had to be indulged, whatever I wanted, whatever I asked for, it had to be done. So when I saw that ring of scales on her neck—" He broke off and Melantho realized, with an unpleasant lurching in her stomach, that he was crying. "I forbade it," he choked out. "I would not let her go. My mother had protested, and my father had her locked away. He never listened to her, but he listened to *me*. And he should not have. Selene didn't. And when the sea came for her, she did for me what I could not do myself. She *made* me let go."

"It wasn't your fault. Whatever you think—" said Melantho, but Mathias cut her off with a wave of his ring-laden hands.

"There is a fountain in the courtyard," he said. "Salt water. The legends say that Poseidon himself raised it from the earth. It is his."

I know.

"Selene knew it. One of her maids volunteered to go to the gallows in her place. They had grown up together. They were close, closer than I think I'd ever realized a princess could be with her maid. And she died for nothing."

That admission stunned the breath from her. But the grief on Mathias's face was too much, and he was still talking, stumbling over the desperate words. "I locked her in her room as the storm raged beyond it, and she had to watch as the sea destroyed everything that lay between it and her. I was standing outside, with some ridiculous pretention of protecting her if anyone tried to stop it, to do what we should have done from the start." The tears were streaking his cheeks, shining in the flickering torchlight. "She called for me and I ran inside, expecting to find some—some villain or other such nonsense—threatening her, forcing her toward the sea. But there was no one there, just Selene, standing in the window with her hair blowing about her face and she was *smiling*."

Melantho's chest tightened. Even if she had not known that Selene must be dead, had not seen it written in every line of Mathias's face, she would have known what that smile had looked like. Would have known what it meant.

Thalia had smiled too, at the last moment. Melantho had known then that it was over.

"She was smiling," said Mathias again. "And it rooted me in place. I could not speak, could not move even as she turned to face the ocean. Even when she looked back over her shoulder and spoke to me, the last words she would ever say." He bit his lip hard enough to draw blood.

"You don't have to tell me," said Melantho softly. "I will not make you."

"The words are branded into my mind. I cannot forget them: 'When I see you again, we will have much to tell each other. I know you will make me proud.' And then she jumped." His voice broke. "I suppose she was aiming for the fountain, for the water within. But she hit the edge. The *sound*—"

Melantho could not listen any longer. "You were just a *child*," she said again, and this time she did not push down the impulse to comfort him. She caught up his hands in hers and shook them. "Look at me, you idiot."

Mathias laughed, a brief, bright sound that fell off into a choking sob. "The water in the fountain reached out and *took her*. And then she was gone."

"It wasn't your fault," said Melantho.

"What if it was?"

"I don't like you," said Melantho. "I don't like the way you talk, the way you hold a fork, that *stupid* crown of yours. It's ridiculous." She stopped here, the words *and I don't like the way you look at Leto* dissolving into nothing on the tip of her tongue.

Mathias had raised a hand to the gold atop his brow, his mouth curled down in an expression of great injury.

"But," she continued pointedly, "I reserve the right to dislike you because you are an adult. You make your own decisions. You have the potential for rational, measured thought. Even if you do not always use it."

Mathias smiled, then, a weak little half smile as he wiped his shining cheeks with the sleeves of his tunic. Melantho had never thought much of boys, had not thought much of the girls that did, but Mathias infuriated her because she knew exactly why Leto liked him. He was not just lovely, but kind and gentle and good humored. Sometimes, she just wanted to shake him and shout at him, *Why couldn't you just be terrible? Why couldn't you make this easy on her?*

"Five years ago," she said, "when your sister died, you were not an adult. You were a stupid, immature child. A powerful child, perhaps, but a child nonetheless. You were surrounded by adults who should have stopped you, who should have known better. Adults who were supposed to protect you and did an *awful* job of it."

"A child with power is a dangerous thing," said Mathias.

Melantho thought then of Telemachus. *Trust me,* she could have said. *I know.*

"He is dangerous because he is afraid," she said. "You shouldn't have had to be afraid."

"What about you, Melantho?"

She hadn't expected that. *"What?"*

His black eyes were fixed on her face. She shifted uncomfortably. "Do not think I have forgotten what you said about your mother," he said, "and the queen who bought you. I am familiar with guilt; I carry it with me every day."

"I—"

"I will not make you tell me," he said. "But, Melantho, you cannot be older than eighteen. Whatever happened to you happened when you were a child too, and you should not have had to be afraid. Someone was meant to protect you. You cannot say these things to me and have them be untrue for you. I will not allow it."

Melantho gaped at him. "I . . ."

She did not know what to say. He was wrong, of course he was wrong. Melantho had betrayed her queen; of course that queen had not stepped in to save her. Melantho had cursed a kingdom—why should anyone help her? Yet here was Mathias, telling her that it was not her fault.

He was *wrong*.

Still, it was peculiar to have someone say such things to her; her whole life had been a string of scared girls, appalled by the atrocities they knew they must commit. Melantho had comforted them, convinced them, taken their guilt and made it hers. But no one had ever comforted *her*. Not like this. "You don't know what I have done," she managed at last.

"I know what you are *doing*," he said. "You are trying to break a curse that was inflicted upon us by a god. You are just a girl, Melantho, and you have taken it upon yourself to intervene in the rages and whims of a being far greater than either of us. I believe—I *know*—that you are good. Whatever you did in the past, I do not doubt that you did it with nothing but the best intentions."

"Intentions do not always matter," Melantho choked out. Gods, was she *crying*? She hated this stupid boy.

"Of course they do," said Mathias. "I loved my sister. I love her still. When I kept her from her fate, I did not think that it would cause death and destruction because I could not see beyond the thought of saving her. If I had kept her with the *intent* to destroy, I would be evil. Do you think I am evil, Melantho?"

"No." She wished he was, wished he were a wicked little thing that did not need so desperately to be protected. From *her*.

"I do not think you are evil, either." He stood, then paused with his hand on the door. "You are aware that no one has ever spoken to me like you have before."

Melantho shrugged. "I suppose they were probably too scared."

"My mother would have you whipped," he said. It might have been a threat had it come from anyone else. But Mathias said it so thoughtfully, so *lightly*, as if it were a hypothetical that could never truly happen, that Melantho did not feel afraid at all.

"You wouldn't allow it," she said. "For *her*."

"No," he said. "I suppose you are right." A pause. Then, "Melantho?"

"Yes?"

"Why do you care? About breaking the curse, I mean."

She blinked at him. Why did she *care*? How could she *not* care? His sister was dead, his sister was dead because of *her*. Belatedly, she remembered her guise—the servant from Athens, the stranger. "I—I suppose because it isn't *fair*."

Mathias's smile was wry. "What in life is?"

"That doesn't mean unfairness should be tolerated. That it should be *expected*. We should not—we should not be playthings for the gods." She drew a sharp breath and let the words tumble from her lips. "A god who is bored, who has more power than he knows what to do with, a god who is *vengeful* should not destroy a kingdom *full of people* to settle his petty scores with its ruler. The girls on this island are *innocent*. Why should we fear the sea? I am a person; I am not a bargaining chip. I am not . . . not a *martyr*, made to suffer so that others might live. Did anyone ask me what I wanted? *I* want to survive. I want to live, and I want to be unafraid."

The room was silent but for the gentle crackling of the fireplace. "I see," said Mathias at last.

"Do you?"

"I don't know." He paused. "Melantho?"

"Yes?"

"I know that you do not like me, but I hope you know that I

like you very much." And with that, he pulled the door open and strode out into the corridor beyond.

Melantho sat at Selene's shrine and stared into the flickering coals. Mathias's voice would not stop ringing in her ears. *I could not see beyond the thought of saving her.*

She had thought she was saving Timo, and instead she had destroyed her. But she had tried. She had done what she had thought was right, had tried, desperately, to hold on to Timo just as Mathias had held on to Selene.

If she could forgive him that, she could forgive herself the same.

"I'm sorry, Timo."

She spoke the words out loud; they hung in the air as she pushed herself to her feet and made to leave the room. She had a murder to plan.

Still, she left it there, that single regret, for Selene, and pushed down the thought that had arisen, unbidden, in her mind: Selene had not died in the sea. Her body had fallen into the *fountain*, its waters had claimed her, and her death had calmed the vengeful tides. But the sacrificed girls were given to Poseidon.

Which meant the water in the fountain truly was Poseidon's, was as much his as the sea itself. Wherever Mathias met his end, the result would be the same. For him—and for Melantho.

XLVIII
THE GATES OF THE SUN

Leto

Olympia led Leto to the edge of the courtyard, where they waited a minute or two before she was unceremoniously handed over to Alexios.

She followed him—tense, keeping her face turned away from him as much as she could, her eyes darting down every corridor as she searched for some weapon, some escape route should she need it. The noise from the festival faded into naught but a distant buzzing. Even that was all but drowned out by the heavy thudding of Alexios's footsteps and Leto's own, lighter and faster, as she followed a little farther behind him than was strictly necessary for propriety. Her breath came in rapid pants. Had he finally recognized her? Was she about to be confronted, exposed?

"Here." He stopped in front of a small, elegant door and rapped on the wood with one huge fist.

"Enter." Soft as it was, the queen's voice never lost its steel edge.

Alexios pushed open the door. Once Leto had ducked past him, her face still pointedly turned away, he slammed it shut behind her, leaving her alone with Mathias's mother.

The queen wore green. Whichever of her maids had advised her to do so was a clever maid indeed; it was as if she had been born to wear the color. Her dark hair was twisted into braids atop her head, woven through with little metallic leaves and strands of shining gold. Her skin was flushed and lovely; she might have been a dryad, escaped from her woods and brought into a prison of stone.

Not that the queen could have been considered a prisoner. If anything, she was the jailer, leaning back in her great oak chair with a practiced arrogance. She beckoned Leto forward with a single imperious finger. "Sit." She indicated the only other chair in the room.

Leto sat.

For a moment, they stayed like that, facing each other across the queen's broad wooden desk in perfect silence. When Leto could stand it no longer, she opened her mouth to speak.

"I suppose you are wondering why I asked you here," interrupted the queen before the first syllable could pass Leto's lips.

Asked was not so strong a word as the one Leto might have used. Commanded, perhaps. Demanded. She ducked her head. "Yes, your grace."

"I have a warning for you," said the queen. "And you would do well to heed it."

The peculiar prickling sensation had returned. It was all Leto could do not to shiver. "Your grace?"

The queen leaned forward with a lovely smile. She had Mathias's mouth; it was not so gentle in her narrow face. *"Leave."*

Leto blinked. "I'm—I'm sorry?"

"We have visitors from the mainland here tonight," said the queen smoothly. "I have secured you passage with those from Thrace—not under your own name, of course, you will have to travel as a serving girl or some other such unnoticeable thing. If you are a clever girl, and I believe that you are, you will go with them."

Leave. Once, long ago, leaving Ithaca had been all Leto had ever wanted. Now though—

"Why would I do that?" she said. "I'm engaged. I'm engaged to your son. You would have me jilt him?"

The queen was still smiling. "A word of advice," she said, "from one princess to another. I from Sparta, and you from Athens—happy, prosperous countries. *You cannot be happy here.* Ithaca is rotting. No, don't interrupt me."

Leto had opened her mouth to speak. She shut it again.

"Don't think I don't know your story, Princess. Young, lovely—I'm sure your father was thrilled when you grew into such a valuable little gem. To strengthen alliances, to clear the way for one of your brothers to take the throne without you being bothersome. They wanted me out of the way too, you see. And I was grateful to come. Sparta is not always kind. It took so much from me. But *Ithaca*"—her face twisted violently, her dark eyes flashed—"*Ithaca has taken everything.*"

"I don't think—"

"We are the *same*. And I am offering you a way out, so you do not end up like me—a bitter old woman who has lost everything she loves."

Leto frowned. The queen could hardly have been described as *old*, and then there was that peculiar assertion—

"Mathias?" she suggested haltingly.

The queen laughed. "Mathias? You are right that I love him, but my son has not loved me in return for many years. No, he was always his *father's* boy and his sisters were mine. But his sisters are gone—one dead, one sent away so that she cannot meet the same fate. No, I have no child that loves me anymore."

Leto became aware that her mouth was hanging open. She shut it with a snap. Dead. Mathias's sister was *dead*. And of course she was; how could she have forgotten the rumors that had flown through Vathi so many years ago, when the sea had risen up to ravage the hills? They had said that a girl working at the palace had hidden Poseidon's mark, had hidden from her fate, had doomed them all. But that was a lie.

How the queen had kept it a secret, she did not know. "I—"

"I see that Mathias failed to inform you." The queen smiled grimly. "Allow me to fill in the gaps." She opened a drawer in the desk and pulled out a curl of papyrus. She handled it with uncharacteristic care, cradling it between her fingertips as if it were a kitten, smoothing out the well-worn creases. "Do you know what this is?"

Leto shook her head wordlessly. So this was why the queen had treated her so coldly. She saw in Leto—in Adrasteia, really—everything she had once possessed and everything she had lost.

"It is a prophecy," said the queen. "Made by my husband's oracle, on the occasion of the birth of his daughter."

Leto froze. She had eyed the parchment with some interest before these words, but now it was all she could do to tear her gaze away, to meet the queen's own and to say "Oracle?"

"Wicked, deceptive creature," snapped the queen. "We fed her, clothed her, housed her, and *this* is how she repaid us." She thrust the parchment at Leto.

Tentatively, Leto took it.

The hand was not her mother's—she supposed some assistant must have transcribed the words—but there was something in the flow, the structure, that stirred some ancient memory within her. Of her mother, muttering in front of the fireplace, her eyes wide and blank.

This one has been touched by a god, it read. *He has seen her, and he is pleased.*

He has laid claim to her,
So that none other may harm her.

"None *other*," spat the queen. "You see? When I heard it first I was *pleased*. I thought, here is a future *worthy* of a daughter of mine. Gods touched, indeed. But Poseidon would not protect my Selene from himself, from *his* mark. Poseidon did not stop her leaping to her death—" She broke off with a gasp.

Gently, Leto laid her mother's prophecy down. "An oracle speaks only the truth she is shown," she said. "Perhaps she did not know, perhaps—"

"I tried to stop it. The women of Sparta do not embrace death, and I would not let my daughter go easily. My husband had me dragged away, screaming." She smiled coldly. "I was allowed out in time to watch the waves carry her still body away. And *then*. Then, I had to hide my pain, had to hide her death. Had to blame some hapless servant for the rising of the sea and pretend that Selene was gone to Crete with her sister, so the people would not rise up against us. My husband had me announce her death months later, pretend it was wholly unconnected. You cannot *imagine*." She sucked in a deep breath. "And do you want to know the future she saw for Mathias? Do you want to know the future she saw for my son? For my son and for *you*. Let us see if you think her so innocent then."

"For me?" Her mother had always refused to ask for Leto's future, had grown snappish and irritated whenever Leto asked. *It is not for us to know our fates.* Was this why? Was there something written in a spidering hand that spelled Leto's demise? Or was it Adrasteia's fortune contained there?

"Oh yes," said the queen. She drew out a second piece of parchment. This one, she did not offer to Leto—she read its contents aloud in an anguished, forced cadence.

"This one is gods-touched also.

"As twelve are cast out, so one returns,

"To bring flames to the shadow that smothers us."

Leto stared at her. *As twelve are cast out, so one returns.* And the flames to the shadow—could she dare to hope that it meant she would succeed? Yes, it was her fortune. *Hers.* Not Adrasteia's, which meant— "I fail to see how it concerns me," she said carefully. Surely the queen could not know her true identity. She'd have been arrested by now. Or—she amended, meeting the queen's blazing stare—executed. "There is no mention of a princess, a wedding. Not even a betrothal."

"Twelve are cast out," said the queen significantly. "Twelve ships, you see, sent out by my late husband in the summer following our son's birth. Sent to every kingdom we deemed useful, with an offer of marriage."

"Oh," said Leto.

"Oh *indeed*," said the queen. "I knew at once the meaning and sent twelve of my own ships to stop them. But one was wrecked in a storm. Its target escaped. Its target reached *Athens.*"

If not for the present company, Leto might have laughed. That was the way of prophecies—they could mean anyone, anything, if they were only read a little differently. But they always came true, from one path or another. "You cannot change your fate," she said automatically. How many times had she said that to customers over the years? Eventually, she had stopped haltingly relaying whatever Apollo *had* shown her and just told her patrons what they wished to hear. "No matter what you wish, the end is always the same. That is the way of the Moirai—"

"Do not speak to me of the fates, *child*," snapped the queen. "Do not presume that I do not *know*. Do not presume that *you* would not have done the same for your own child. This is the only copy of the prophecy that remains—I have burned the rest. No one else knows of it. No one *will*. I will protect my children from those who seek to execute the will of the gods."

Here, Leto had no reply. She knew little of what parents would do for their children. Leave them forever without a word? Wither away into nothing? "But," she managed, "what of that prophecy was so very awful? Flames to a shadow—I believe they must be speaking of Ithaca's curse, no? Surely—"

"I asked the oracle the very same question," said the queen. "I had heard her prophecy, and though I must confess I wondered at it, I did not see how it could relate to Mathias. So I asked her. See, the scribe has written it down—"

Leto followed the queen's trembling finger to a line of curling script. "And what of my son?" she read aloud.

"And what of my son?" echoed the queen. "Do you want to know what she said?"

Leto had no answer. There was a weight in the air, a pressure on her heart. She could see in the queen's twisted features that Mathias's destiny had not been a kind one.

"*Who will feed the flames? Your boy has eyes like coal.*" The last word was barely intelligible; she shrieked it. Her eyes had filled with tears. "Those were her wretched words, as she condemned my son to his death. A death at your hand, a death the scribe most helpfully noted as she recorded the prophecy. *The oracle has foretold the prince's death*, that is what she wrote. No, don't stand—"

Leto had gripped the arms of her chair, ready to push herself away if she needed to. She did not move.

"You are the one of twelve," said the queen. She returned the prophecy to its drawer. As she shut it, Leto caught a glimpse of something else that lay within—a little gold locket, marked with a swirling insignia. Leto knew that sign: it was the mark of Delphi. She knew that locket. It had belonged to her mother. Why was it here?

She clenched a fist in her lap as the queen went on. "I am sure of it. You see now why you must go, you *must*."

"It will not change his fate," said Leto quietly. "You know it cannot."

"I have changed it once before. The oracle thought the words referred to *her*, you know. She told me herself—she was one of twelve initiates, offered by Ithaca to be trained at the temples of Delphi. She was the victor, that wretched creature returned to serve her crown. Twelve cast out, one returned, you see? She told me *herself*, eight years ago, as she stood at the bedside of my son *with a knife in her hand* and told me that the gods had chosen her. That she could not shy from her fate."

"What?" Leto was almost startled by the sound of her own voice. She had not known she had a voice at all; she had thought perhaps the queen's words had simply rendered her into nothing. Her mother had tried to kill Mathias. Had been *caught*.

"Alexios stopped her himself," said the queen. "Barely twelve years old, but already so loyal that he launched himself at a madwoman without a care. Earned himself that scar, you know."

"He killed her?"

"Oh, no." The queen bared her teeth. "No, that pleasure was all mine. She had thought to break the curse, you see, to prevent another year of death. But with that year's equinox a mere day away, it was so *easy* to have her vanish. I told her family Poseidon had claimed her. Then I chained her to a wall in the dungeons and left her there. Maybe it was starvation that killed her. Maybe the rats tore her still-beating heart from her chest. It is what she deserved, for destroying my family, for tearing out *my* heart. You know, I almost commanded the death of *her* daughter. But when I sent my men to the house, they told me she was a useless little thing, stumbling over her pathetic prophecies, possessing a mere fraction of her mother's power. A crueler fate to leave her alive, I thought—but Poseidon claimed her in the end. It's almost poetic."

Leto lurched to her feet. "Stop it," she said viciously. "*Stop it.*" She wanted to throw up, wanted to faint, wanted to launch herself across the desk and throttle the queen with her bare hands.

She needed to leave. Blindly, she rushed for the door, the queen's words ringing in her ears. Not just the horror of her mother's fate, but how boldly she had gone to it. *She could not shy from her fate.* What would she have thought of Leto if she saw her now?

"I don't want to threaten you," said the queen as Leto fought, half-blind, to pull the door open. To get *out*. "But you know now what I do to those who endanger my family. I have lost Selene. I have all but lost Hekate too. Mathias is my chance—my *only* chance. I *will* make him into a king worthy of the line of Sparta. Save yourself, little Princess. When the company of Thrace sail away, make sure you are sailing with them."

〰〰〰

Mathias was waiting for her when she returned.

She knew she must look a wreck. She could not cast the queen from her mind, could not organize the thoughts reverberating through her skull. The queen's threats. Selene, Mathias, Alexios. Her mother.

Her mother had tried to break the curse—it should have been a *noble* thing. But if she had vanished when Leto was ten, a mere child, then her target must also have been a child. Eleven years old himself, or thereabouts.

Would Leto have done it? It was a question she could not answer. It was hard not to remember how Timo had met her end; killing a child was not an easy thing to do, nor to live with the memory of.

Mathias smiled at her giddily. His eyes were bright. "Follow me," he said. "I have something to tell you." He led her swiftly to a curtain-covered door, pulling the fabric aside to reveal a tightly spiraling staircase. Would he look at her like that, beaming and hopeful and open, as she thrust her blade through his chest or forced his head down beneath the surface of the sea? Her chest ached with some nameless, hopeless sorrow. They had not made enough progress; they were not going to figure out a way to save him in time.

It did not matter what he felt for her. If his heart beat faster for her, it made no difference. It would stutter and still all the same as Poseidon rose to claim him. Two days left. Just two. She swallowed. "Up there?" No torches burned ahead.

"It is safe, I promise. I will go first." Their hands were entwined, and he pulled her up behind him.

Mathias said nothing more until they emerged onto a broad stone balcony lit dimly from below by the courtyard torches.

"It's cold," she said automatically. Away from the fires, the night was cool and quiet.

"Here." Mathias's fingers went to the tie of his cloak.

Leto put out a hand to stop him. "Leave it on." She wrapped her veil over her shoulders, though the thin material did little to warm her. "What did you have to tell me?"

"Leto," sighed Mathias. "How can you ask me that—do you truly not know the answer?"

"I—what?"

Mathias placed two fingers under her chin and brought her face to his. "Leto, you are an impossible creature." He kissed her.

Perhaps it was the music, the cool night air, the wine, but all of a sudden Leto was kissing him back, reaching up to thread her fingers through his smooth, dark hair. She felt the golden circlet he wore slipping, though he made no move to right it.

Instead, he ran long, gentle fingers over the bunching fabric at her waist, then trailed them in delicious spirals on the outside of her thigh. Her stomach contracted and she felt herself twitch against him.

He laughed. Low, sultry, lovely, against her mouth. "Did I tell you," he asked between featherlight kisses, "how beautiful you look tonight?" He moved his mouth to the side of her jaw and kissed down the length of her throat.

"You did." Leto tilted her head back. Mathias's hands circled up to her waist as he pulled her ever closer.

"Then let me tell you again," he said. His mouth returned to meet hers and he kissed her again, soft and undemanding. "You are the most beautiful girl I have ever seen."

Several things happened at once then. One of his hands moved to Leto's waist to pull her harder against him, and she twisted her hips to meet him, closed her eyes, and exhaled with a sharp *"Oh."*

Then, Mathias's other hand was moving to unclasp the thick gold necklace wrapped tightly around her throat. One second her body was curling traitorously against him, and the next her lust-fogged brain caught up with her and she was tearing herself back from him in a panic, ring-laden hand flying to cover her throat before the necklace could slip away and reveal what lay beneath.

She collided painfully with the stone balustrade and leaned

there, chest heaving, eyes fixed wide and incredulous on Mathias. *"Mathias."* The necklace had not fallen. She was safe.

"Leto?" The sound of her name did not come from Mathias— it came from the top of the stairs. Leto's heart had been pounding in her chest. It dropped abruptly into her stomach as she raised her eyes. *No, not now. Please.* But of course, the gods did not answer her prayer.

Melantho stood at the entrance to the balcony, her trembling hand pressed to her mouth. She had seen everything, clearly; it was written all over her face. She looked faintly nauseous.

"Melantho?" Mathias turned.

"Mathias," said Melantho.

He spun back to face Leto. "Leto?" It was a helpless question. His pupils had been blown wide; now they contracted. His smile had well and truly disappeared. He straightened his clothes and the circlet which had almost entirely slipped off his brow.

She did not know what to say. Her mind had gone utterly blank; she could think of nothing but the curious ringing that had begun to sound in her ears and the lingering taste of Mathias on her lips.

Melantho turned and ran down the stairs.

"Melantho?" said Mathias again. He turned back to Leto. "What's wrong?"

Leto could only shake her head. She wanted to flee, to run after Melantho and catch her by the hand and say, *No, no. You don't understand.*

"Leto, please." He advanced on her with a look of open, helpless concern. "I am sorry. I should never have presumed that you wished . . . that you wanted—what I mean to say is that you can have all the time you need. I can wait—" He reached out for her.

"Don't." It came out much harsher than she expected. Mathias froze where he stood, arm outstretched. They gazed at each other in silence for a moment.

"Leto?" said Mathias. "Please, I—"

"I cannot." The words tumbled from her lips. The expression on his face was unbearable. It was like kicking a puppy. A shadow shifted in the entrance to the stairway and slipped away, but Leto was so focused on Mathias that she barely allowed herself to acknowledge it. If Melantho had decided to eavesdrop, Leto would not stop her. "We are trying to break the curse, Mathias. We do not have time for . . . for this."

"Why not?" In the moonlight, his eyes shone dark as the sea—she could have drowned in them. "I was speaking to Melantho. She helped me *understand* something: that I cannot punish myself forever, that Sel—that the people I've lost would not *want* me to. They would have loved you. Do we not deserve to be happy?"

Selene. He was talking about Selene. "Happy? There are people that are *dying*, Mathias! There are bigger things out there to worry about than whether or not we are *happy*."

"And you think being miserable will stop them dying?"

"You are very arrogant to think that you will make me happy." She should not have said it. She did not even *mean* it; she just wanted the conversation to end so she could leave, could find Melantho and hold her close, but the way Mathias's mouth dropped open, the way his shoulders crumpled inward, told her that it did not matter. He had believed her.

"Oh," he said. "Well, I suppose that makes it a rather different situation."

"Mathias—"

"Excuse me, Leto." He cut her off smoothly. "I think this

conversation is over. Good night." He turned sharply on his heel and marched down the staircase.

"*Shit.*" Leto gathered her skirts and hurried after him.

By the time she returned to the courtyard—it was incredibly difficult to navigate the steep, winding staircase with her chiton catching under her sandals with every step she took—Mathias was dancing with Olympia. Olympia looked delighted; Mathias looked like he had eaten something poisonous.

She could have marched over to him, tugged him out of Olympia's arms and into hers. She longed to run to him, to pull him close, to whisper her adoration. But that would leave Melantho alone, would leave Melantho to invent a hundred scenarios in her head in which Leto chose Mathias over her.

Leto skirted the courtyard. The music had begun in earnest— the crowds of courtiers danced in time, knocking into Leto rhythmically as she struggled past. It was some small mercy that she did not see Alexios—clearly, he had found somewhere more suitably depressing to skulk about. The queen was standing with one of the guests from Thrace, marked as such by the particular shade of green of his chiton. Leto looked away before she could catch her eye.

At last, she was clear of the crowds. She threw a final, desperate look back at Mathias, then ducked through the door that led back into the palace again. If she was lucky, Alexios would not be guarding the queen's office. If she was lucky, she could slip in and out without being noticed.

Time was almost up, but there was one thing Leto could not leave without.

Leto threw open the doors to her chambers and marched inside. The queen's office had, as she'd hoped, been unguarded. Her mother's necklace was tucked safely beneath the neckline of her chiton. The copy of Mathias's prophecy was hidden in one of the draped pockets. Something had compelled her to take it, though she did not quite know what. It was not as if she could show it to him.

Melantho was standing at the window, gazing out onto the courtyard beyond, at the cobbles bathed in torchlight and the whirling dancers. She had pulled her hair out of its ribbons; it fell down her back in a cascade of molten gold. Her hands were fists at her side.

"Melantho—" Leto began.

"If it weren't for me," interrupted Melantho, her voice dangerously soft, "you could marry him."

Leto gaped. She had not been expecting *that*.

Incredulous, she laughed. "Marry Mathias? Don't be ridiculous." A kiss was one thing. Marriage was quite another, especially while the curse continued, while the next hangings were just two days away and they had yet to find a *single* alternative to Mathias's death.

Melantho's shoulders tensed. "Don't laugh at me. It is not as if you haven't considered it yourself. You and Mathias, cuddled up *reading* and *bonding* for the rest of your lives."

"Because that means anything. Who hasn't dreamed of being a princess?" It was the wrong thing to say, she knew it. But Melantho looked so *angry*, it set the hairs on Leto's arms prickling. She felt jumpy, defenseless.

Melantho turned her head sharply. The skin of her cheeks was red and patchy, her nose pink. Her eyes were bright. "I served a queen once," she said sharply. "I was her favorite, her little *pet*. And

I loved her. I had a foolish, childish hope that she returned that love, and I was wrong. When I was condemned to the rope, she did *nothing*."

"What could she do? The curse—"

"She did *nothing*," repeated Melantho. "It was like she didn't care. She didn't even *watch*. My dream was a ridiculous thing that could never have come true. But *you*"—she sucked in a furious breath—"I have seen the way he looks at you. He could be yours if you wanted him."

"I *don't* want him," said Leto hotly. "If I married him, I would condemn hundreds of girls to die."

"Thousands," said Melantho.

"Exactly!" Leto threw her hands up. "There's no question of it! If I were truly that selfish, to think that my happiness was worth even *one* life, I—"

"But that's what I meant," said Melantho. "If it weren't for me, you wouldn't have to make that choice."

"I'd be dead! If I hadn't met you, I'd be *dead*, Melantho."

"That's not what I—" Melantho shook her head. "I'm just—I just want you to know that I'd understand. Mathias is a prince, and I'm just a *maid*. He can offer you the world, Leto, and I want you to know that you can have it if you want."

"The curse—" began Leto.

"Damn the curse!" Melantho actually stamped her foot. "That is not what I'm trying to say, Leto!"

"Then what are you saying? That I have your *permission* to, what? Go stick my tongue down Mathias's throat in some gilded corner of his damned palace?"

"Yes!" shouted Melantho. "That is exactly what I'm saying!"

Leto stared at her, chest heaving. "What is *happening*?" she asked, more of a question to herself than to Melantho.

"I love you," said Melantho. "How could I not? But you owe me nothing. And I want to make sure you know that. Mathias loves you."

"But I don't love him," said Leto. "I love you." It was a peculiar realization. One she had not quite known herself until this very moment. But saying it like this—out loud, without hesitation—settled it in her heart. She loved Melantho. Truly, entirely, with every fiber of her being. It had to be enough.

Melantho laughed, a bitter, awful sound. "What have I ever done to deserve it?"

Leto stared at her. Melantho had *loved* her; it had been a long time since anyone had done so. Melantho had laughed with her, cried with her, walked to the sea with her and coaxed the power from her trembling fingers. What had Leto been before this? A scared little girl, motherless, fatherless, friendless. She was irreversibly changed now.

"Everything," she said at last.

Whatever came next, she knew that this one thing was the truth.

☙☙☙

The next day was their last. The following noon, twelve girls would fall from twelve nooses, and their bodies would be given to the sea. Leto could not allow it.

So, mortified as she was, she had to face Mathias. She owed him that much. He did not know it, but his time was almost up—this was their last chance to find an alternative, *any* alternative. The thought of seeing him again was not an appealing one.

"He is going to hate me," she said mournfully. She had scorned him, rejected him outright. Still, she cared for him, even if she would not have dared to speak the thought aloud.

"No, he won't," said Melantho. "He was drunk and caught up in the celebration, as were you. He will forgive you, as you well know."

Leto shot her a sharp look. "And if he doesn't?"

Melantho's only reply was a weary shake of her golden head. Something still hung between them, the knowledge of what Leto had done and what Melantho had seen.

Leto had been dressed for hours, her mother's necklace safe around her neck, the prophecy hidden within the folds of her chiton. Still, she could not push aside the feeling that she was missing something, that she was not prepared for what lay ahead.

"Come on then," she sighed at last. "We don't want to be late."

◎◎◎

Leto had been right to be concerned. When they finally made their way down to the library, Mathias greeted her coolly.

"There is not much left to read," he said.

"We are wasting our time," said Melantho. "The answers are not going to be contained in some ridiculous little scroll. If there is another way to break the curse, we will need to *search* it out. Actively."

"Another way?" said Mathias. He frowned. "Did we find *one*?"

Melantho shot Leto a panicked look. "You misheard me," she said quickly. It was not the most believable of lies, but then again, Leto knew Melantho far better than Mathias did. Perhaps he would not notice the twitch of her eyes or the unnatural set of her jaw.

"I don't think—" began Mathias.

"Melantho is right," interrupted Leto hastily. She did not necessarily believe this to be true, but it was likely the best way to distract Mathias from the truth that Melantho had almost let slip. "We should search farther down—the cellars. There must be hundreds of rooms down there. You said there were secret passageways all over the maps you found—have you been through them all, Mathias?"

He ducked his head. "I don't disagree with you. Where should we start, then?"

Leto shrugged her shoulders. "Is there an entrance to the cellars nearby?"

"Relatively," said Mathias.

"Then take us there."

෨෨෨

They became very lost, very quickly.

The corridors looked identical, and even Mathias—who had lived there his entire life—was squinting around them in poorly concealed bewilderment. Leto watched him peer at a fraying tapestry as if it would reveal to him the way to escape this labyrinth.

"It must be this way," he said, sounding unconvinced, pointing down a shadowy passageway. "This will take us toward the kitchens. I think."

Melantho eyed him dubiously. "You think."

It was at that moment that voices sounded from up ahead.

A quiet, hesitant voice and another that was louder, sharper, and instantly familiar.

The queen.

The queen, who would be very interested to know why exactly

they were snooping around in the cellars. The queen, who had burned the prophecy that Leto's mother had made. The queen, who had promised death to Leto if she did not leave the kingdom.

And Leto had not left.

Leto swore under her breath and grabbed Mathias's arm. "*In here*," she hissed, then yanked him through the nearest door— unlocked, as if the gods had finally decided to bless her with *something* like luck—and into the chamber beyond. He toppled through, followed shortly by Melantho. Leto fought back the wild urge to laugh; this was not the first time that she had yanked Mathias through an unfamiliar door. At least this one was not a storeroom; the thought of the three of them pressed together in the dark was an unimaginable horror.

"What the hell did you do that for?" Melantho snarled. She rubbed at a red mark on her wrist, the place where his fingers had dug in as he'd pulled her after him.

"Be *quiet*," said Leto. Then, "Is it *raining* in here?" A drop of water had splashed onto the top of her head. Automatically, she looked up, and what lay above her took her breath away.

The single, curved wall of the chamber was lined with statues. Carved from white marble, twelve figures towered over them, their faces turned upward. Their outstretched hands cupped pools of water, catching the drips which fell rhythmically from a careful system of channels above. And in each pool floated a tiny candle.

Leto took an involuntary step forward. "How are those still burning?"

Behind her, Melantho made a small, horrified noise. Her eyes were fixed on one of the statues: the smallest but one, a tiny little thing whose crown of soft curls had been carefully cut from the marble. Melantho's lips were moving wordlessly. She sucked in harsh, awful breaths.

"Melantho?" said Leto softly. "What is it?"

"We should leave here," said Melantho. "Now."

"What?" Leto squinted at the statue again. It was a girl. It was not frightening, nor malevolent; it was just a girl. "Why?"

"Please." She had never heard Melantho's voice sound like that: thin, frail, panicked. "Will you trust me, Leto? Leave with me, *please*. This place is not for us." Her eyes darted across the room and snagged on something else. A heartbeat, and her eyes were flicking back to Leto. She looked desperate; her chest heaved as she breathed in and out. She looked again at the *something*, then away. "This is a shrine to the first maids. We should not be here."

But Melantho knew of the first maids already. What had she seen in this place that was new, that was not something they had pored over a hundred times before? Leto could not help it; she turned to see what on earth could be disconcerting Melantho so thoroughly.

The moment her eyes fell on it, she understood.

It was another of the statues, another girl carved from marble, half-illuminated in candlelight as the others were. But this one was different—this one sent a shock of recognition through her.

It was a statue of Melantho.

The artist had been a skilled one; it was a near-perfect likeness, from the loose curls tucked behind a rounded ear, to the curve of her jaw and the smooth sweep of her waist into her narrow hips. The marble Melantho was smiling serenely upwards. There were dimples in her stone cheeks where the salt water fell from above and spilled onto the floor.

The real Melantho was not smiling. She was staring, appalled, at Leto. Leto stared back.

The statues were of the first maids. Which meant that Melantho had been one of the first maids. When Melantho had spoken of them, she had been speaking of girls she had known. Girls she had worked with, girls she had loved, girls who had been violated and betrayed and murdered.

"This is *fantastic*," said Mathias.

Leto had all but forgotten about Mathias, and she could tell from the way that Melantho nearly jumped at the sound that she had too.

His voice was full of delight. "This must be something important, mustn't it? Look at the *candles* and the salt. And these statues are exquisite. It's the maids, isn't it? There are twelve, and they look young. And look"—he raised a hand to point at the closest statue; Melantho flinched—"the noose marks. It *is* them. There must be something to learn here!" He moved forward, peering at the marble as if it would reveal every secret of Ithaca to him.

Leto did not move. Something did not make sense. Melantho had told Leto of the maids, had told their tale unabashedly. And she was one of them. She had lied. *Why* had she lied?

She opened her mouth to say something, but before her lips could shape the first words, there came a sudden clatter from the corridor beyond the door, and low voices sounded directly outside.

The queen thrust the door open and swept into the room. Olympia, her coils of black hair bound into a braid atop her head, hovered at her shoulder.

"*Mother*," said Mathias.

"Mathias," said the queen. "Oh, and the princess is here too. And her maid." She shot Leto a tight, forced smile. Her eyes were flashing with a deadly fury. She didn't even look at Melantho.

"Mother," said Mathias again. "What is this place? Why was I never told of it before? And why on earth have you brought *Olympia* here when you would not bring your own son?"

Olympia looked wounded. "Why should I not come?"

"Hush, child," said the queen. "Mathias is not angry at you, he is angry at me. Why don't you leave this to me, hmm? You remember what we talked about?"

Olympia nodded, pouted, and fell silent.

"What were you talking about?" asked Mathias. "Your plotting is embarrassing, Mother."

Melantho was edging toward the door. The tilt of her head hid her face, her eyes, but Leto could see her anguish in the set of her narrow shoulders, in the almost imperceptible shake of her clenched fists.

She longed to go to her, to hold her close, to say, *I do not know why you lied to me, but I do not care. I trust you. I love you.*

Melantho slipped through the open door and vanished. A heartbeat later, Olympia followed suit with an unintelligible, mumbled excuse. Leto, stepping as slowly and quietly as she could, made to follow.

"*Adrasteia,*" the queen said, dropping a hand on her shoulder. "You are leaving?" There was a peculiar satisfaction in her voice.

"You can leave, Leto," said Mathias. "My mother has nothing of significance to say to you."

"Oh," said Leto. She did not know how to navigate a situation like this. She could not insult the queen, not without severe consequences, but she did not wish to stay, either. Not with Melantho gone, not after the truth that had been so unceremoniously uncovered. "Mathias, I am sure that isn't true." The queen's hand tightened on her shoulder, the bands of her rings pressed hard against Leto's skin.

"You flatter me," she said.

"Adrasteia has things to attend to, Mother," said Mathias. "And I have things I wish to discuss with you. Such as *what is this place* and *why on earth did you not tell me about it?*"

This seemed like a good time for Leto to make her escape.

She shook the queen's hand from her shoulder as politely as she could and dropped into a curtsy. "I will not intrude on your conversation any longer. Excuse me, your grace."

From the look on the queen's face, she was most certainly *not* excused, but she could not find it within herself to care as she slammed the door behind her, pulled her skirts clear of her ankles, and sprinted after Melantho.

XLIX

A WILD BEAST IN THE FOREST

Melantho

Clear at last of the basements, Melantho leaned against a pillar, panting.

Her mind was full of the rushing of the ocean, each tide bringing in Leto, Leto, Leto. Leto's eyes, sparking with *something* before she kissed Melantho for the first time, the open longing on Leto's face as she leaned into Mathias over stacks of open scrolls, Leto's mouth falling open as she looked up at the statues—at Melantho, rendered in pale stone.

Melantho's eyes were prickling with tears, her ears ringing so loudly that she did not hear the footsteps behind her, did not turn until someone yanked her back by the hood of her cloak. Alarmed, she pulled back, twisted, felt *something* rake over her ribs. The pain it brought with it was sharp, startling.

She flailed, wild, and caught at a thin arm.

There was a moment where she almost thought she was safe, where she felt the someone fumble and stagger and topple onto her. But then there was pain—brighter, harder this time—as they relinquished their grip on her cloak and sank a knife into her stomach.

"*A message,*" hissed a familiar voice, "*for your mistress. She should leave if she does not wish to meet the same fate.*"

L

THE END OF THIS MOON

Leto

The corridors should not have been so silent.

The only sound was the rhythmic slapping of Leto's shoes as she ran toward her chambers. That was the only place Melantho could have gone, surely, unless she was headed for the ocean. If it was that, then Leto would never catch up with her. Not until Melantho wanted her to.

She skidded around a corner and almost collided with a lithe, dark-haired girl. Olympia raised her head in alarm as Leto threw out an arm to steady herself, catching hold of a groove in the wall and pulling herself to a standstill.

"Sorry," she panted. "I just—" She broke off. Olympia was looking at her as if she had seen a spirit. "Olympia?" she said. "Are you all right?"

Olympia opened her mouth and closed it again. "Mmph," she said eventually. She held her arm awkwardly, twisted beneath her cloak. There was something strange about the shape of it and . . . Leto narrowed her eyes at the pale material.

"Olympia," she said, "are you *bleeding*?"

"No," said Olympia, despite the fact that it was now very clear to Leto that she *was*.

"Are you sure?" Leto reached for her, for the spray of crimson, harsh against the yellow of the cloak.

"I am *sure*, Princess!" snapped Olympia, jerking away. "Now if you will excuse me—" Without another word, she shoved her way past Leto and disappeared down a narrow passageway. Her steps echoed through the corridor, regular at first, and then hard and fast as she began to run.

Leto frowned after her. Something was not right; something had happened. She could taste it in the air.

"Show me," she whispered. Her mother had made the same request in these very halls, had heard the gods answer. *"Show me."*

꩓꩓꩓

The vision was a nightmare.

There was blood everywhere. It was in Leto's nose, her mouth, her eyes. Her hands were slick with it. The air was full of its stench. Rust. Rust and death.

Through the sheen of red came a reaching hand: golden skin with rounded nails and rough grazes over the backs of clenched knuckles.

Melantho, whispered Apollo.

Melantho.

꩓꩓꩓

The vision was gone as soon as it had come, though the memory of it; the smell; the claustrophobic, choking feel of it hung in a cloud over Leto. Half-blind with panic, she called out, *"Melantho!"*

There came a small sound ahead. Leto jerked her head up, scouring the corridor for Melantho's familiar golden hair, the flush of her cheeks. For a moment, she thought that the corridor was empty.

And then she saw her.

Melantho was slumped on the floor. She had tucked herself into an alcove—or someone had done their very best to hide her there. She did not look up as Leto barreled toward her. "Melantho," she said. "*Melantho, are you hurt?*"

Melantho's head lolled. Her arm slipped off her belly and hit the floor with a soft thump. Leto barely registered the sound—her mind had frozen the instant that Melantho's hands had uncovered what laid beneath them.

Blood, just as she had seen.

A dark pool of it that crept out over Melantho's chiton, turning the pale pink to a red so deep it was almost black. Her lips were moving; she gasped out words that were weak whispers of breath.

Leto threw herself down at Melantho's side, pressed her own hands into the wound that must be there. Her fingertips found it—an ugly, ragged gash. It had been a clumsy blow, and the knife had been wrenched free without care. "*Who did this to you?*"

Melantho shook her head. There were tears in her eyes, always startlingly green. She looked afraid. Truly afraid, and never further from the wild creature that had first yanked Leto from the sea. Her sharp, clever face was no longer flushed gold; it was greyish and tight with pain. Her bloodless lips shaped words that would not come.

She sagged against the wall.

"No," said Leto out loud. "No, *no. Melantho.*"

She tried to lift Melantho, tried to scoop her up into her arms, but she was as limp as a doll. The dead weight of her—no, not dead, not *dead*, because Melantho was not allowed to die—was too much for Leto to carry alone. There was no one else around and the corridors that she had once rejoiced to find empty now felt more like a tomb. She would not find a servant here. *Mathias.* She needed Mathias.

She lifted her head and screamed his name. The sound echoed, piercing and awful, through the corridors as Leto doubled over Melantho again, clutching at the vicious wound in her belly, fingers scrabbling in the spreading pool of blood as if she could force back the relentless tide of it.

"Hold on," she whispered, rocking Melantho back and forth in her arms. "Mathias will be here soon. He will help us. You just need to hold on, Melantho."

Melantho's eyes had glazed over slightly. They were fixed, blankly, on thin air. Her lips trembled; Leto could hear a high, keening noise and she took a moment too long to realize that it was coming from her. Melantho's whispers were hardly whispers anymore, and then they were nothing at all.

"Melantho," Leto said again. Quietly, desperately: "Do not leave me. Do you understand? *Do not leave me.*"

If Melantho heard her, she made no sign of it. She merely continued to stare into nothingness, to murmur silent words as she bled out, ruby and rust.

LI

THE BEGINNING OF THE NEXT

Mathias

Mathias watched Leto go with an aching resignation. He longed to follow, but first, he had other business.

He turned to his mother. She was standing very still, back straight, with one hand rested upon her hip and an expression on her face that he had not seen since he was a child and she had caught him misbehaving.

He tried to match her stare, painfully aware of the fact that he was certainly failing to do so. "Why haven't I been here before?"

"I don't know." She raised a delicate shoulder. "You tell me."

"You didn't bring me here. But you'll take Olympia? She is not your child—*I* am."

"Ah, Mathias, so chastising. You always were your father's son."

"And what do you mean by that?" The words were out before he could stop them. He wanted to cringe at the petulance in his own voice, the childish fury. He knew the truth, so why did he continue to deny it? His parents' marriage had been as his would be: a political match, formed without any feeling but greed. Leto, at least, had made her own indifference very clear.

Besides, loveless marriages, he knew, were often unkind. And a queen, brought in like so many bolts of silk from across the sea, was not always well protected. A memory stirred within him: his mother's screams as the king's men locked her in her rooms. Selene, sobbing as the queen called her name over and over and over.

The queen regarded him evenly. "A king should be sensible of his own flaws—and those of his predecessors."

"I wasn't meant to be king," he snapped.

"As if I needed reminding."

They glared at each other across the small, dim space. His mother's lips were pursed. He gave in first, as he always did. "Fine." He turned and strode toward the door. He had moved barely three paces before he was yanked to a stop. Slowly, deliberately, he turned his gaze to his mother's fingers, looking very small, wrapped around his wrist.

"Let me go," he snarled. "Leto—Adrasteia, I mean. I should go after her."

His mother did not release her hold on him. Something twitched in her face—the hatred she had always held for his Athenian fiancée bubbled to the surface and spilled over. "Funny," she hissed. "That you call her *Leto*. Shall I tell you what happened to the last Leto I knew?"

He pried himself free, ignoring the dig of her nails into his skin. "You had her killed, I suppose? Or had her hands smashed to pieces—don't think I didn't hear about that one."

The queen smiled. There was not a single crack in her composure; clearly, she had no wish to hide the truth from him, did not think it *wrong* enough to be ashamed of. She had been a princess of Sparta once, and they were not well known for their gentleness. "Mathias, darling, I am not a killer if I can avoid it. But in this case, Poseidon did it for me. Although." She paused, examined the curve of her nails. "I suppose that you yourself must have given the order, no?"

"I—what?" Mathias fixed her with his blankest stare.

"Oh, come now, Mathias. You cannot have forgotten so easily. It does happen every year."

What? For a moment, he could do nothing but narrow his eyes at her. Then—Oh. *Oh.* Abruptly, there was a dry, bitter taste in his mouth: salt and sand and the green-brown plants that grew in pitiful clumps along the shoreline. His chest shuddered as he inhaled, and he had a peculiar feeling of *something*—though he did not know quite what it was—falling heavily into place. "One of the . . . the chosen girls. The hanged girls."

"She was *spirited* too. Just like your Leto. She almost got away, but Alexios caught her." Her smile widened, and she leaned in as if they were sharing some private joke. "I'm surprised she didn't see *that* coming."

He frowned. The punch line lingered somewhere beyond his reach. She always made him feel stupid, slow, a lame foal stumbling behind the herd. "But how would she see it coming? Poseidon's choices are random."

Her brows arched. "I thought Olympia told you?"

At the mention of her, he instinctively looked for Olympia. But the room was empty but for him and his mother, and the twelve silent statues towering above them, their empty stone eyes cast upwards, as if they could see straight through the dripping marble ceiling and on to the stars beyond.

His mother took his searching silence as a denial. "Well, never mind, I'm sure you'll remember her. I heard that she made quite an impression on you, that you gave a darling little *speech* just for her."

The memories came obligingly forward: the girl with her hollow cheeks and blackened eyes, the furious mouth bound shut. And beyond that, the ragged beggar in Vathi grinning at him through broken teeth, offering him the name *Ophelia*, and that distinctive feeling of missing something. The feeling that he had been lied to. "The oracle girl," said Mathias flatly. "The girl who tried to run. Her name was Leto."

His mother only nodded. There was a hard glint in her eye; she knew that she had won this one, even if she did not quite know why.

"But . . ." He scrambled for understanding. "He—I mean, I was told that her name was Ophelia. When I asked—I asked the name of the oracle who had lived there, and he told me—"

"Ophelia *was* the oracle that lived there. The last royal oracle, with her worthless husband and their worthless daughter. If Leto was anything, she was but a pale imitation of her mother." She waved a dismissive hand. "I sent men to investigate her and they assured me that her prophecies were little more than childish fancies."

"She's dead. There is no need to speak of her like that."

"I will speak of the dead as I please."

There was a subtle shift in the air. His mother's eyes darkened, her posture softened, and she seemed to curl in on herself. They were not speaking of the dead oracle girl anymore, Mathias was sure of that. "Mother," he said quietly.

"Our evils do not leave with us when we go," she said. Her fingers twitched at her side as if she had meant to reach for him, then reconsidered. "Sometimes the dead deserve to be spoken ill of, for all the suffering they inflicted in life. Dying is not so difficult a task as to earn *my* forgiveness."

Candlelight flickered off her features. There was an echo of Selene there, in her dark eyes, the tightness of her jaw, and the high slant of her cheeks. It was easy to forget sometimes, for all her fierceness, all the things she had given up, all the things that had been taken from her. She gave him one last searching, disappointed

look; made a quiet, sighing sound that might have been his name; and swept from the room.

Alone, Mathias found himself gazing up into the stone face of the nearest statue.

Even with his mother gone, the feeling of inadequacy she brought out in him still lingered. He drummed his fingers restlessly against his thigh and frowned hard at the statue. What was he missing? What was this place—why had it been made, who maintained it? Who lit the candles, how did they burn on even as water dripped from the ceiling in an endless stream? There was something—he could *feel* it—hovering just beyond his reach.

He stepped closer to the stone maid. Then, on some mad instinct, he pulled himself up onto the plinth with her.

Up here, the top of his head was level with her chin. The candle in her cupped hands was warm. Careful not to fall, he picked it up and cradled it against his chest. "Who left this here, hmm?" he spoke into the emptiness. There was no answer but the echo of his own voice.

Feeling suddenly foolish, he clambered down. The flame in his hand jumped, the flickering light bouncing off. . . . What *was* that? He frowned and carefully knelt so that his face was level with the stone girl's feet.

There was an inscription there, carved into the plinth that she stood upon, but the years had worn it away to illegibility. The dripping water from above had carved channels through the words.

He ran a reverent finger over one of the grooves. The destruction was thorough; underneath, he could barely make out a single word. *That* one might have said "twelve," and another might have been "chance." Or was it "choice"? Mathias moved even closer. What had the inscription said? Who had carved it there? Why?

Perhaps he would have been able to read more, understand more, if not for what came next: from somewhere far away, Leto screamed.

She had never screamed like that before, not that he had heard, but somehow, Mathias knew that it was her. The sound was raw with pain, full of an incomparable grief that kept coming and coming and coming as the scream echoed through the halls around him. His heart contracted, hard enough that it hurt, then leapt into a frantic beating.

Mathias sprinted toward the source of the sound. Toward Leto.

He did not know where he was going; she could have been down any number of the corridors that spread out before him. Somehow, though, his feet seemed to know where to take him, led him down stairs and through archways and past tapestry after tapestry after tapestry until he found her.

He smelled the blood before he saw it, that thick metallic stench of slaughter. Mathias's father had smelled like that toward the end of his life, when he had begun to cough up great wads of crimson. The maids had ushered Mathias away when they caught him watching, but they could not erase the memory from his mind: his father, doubled over, spitting a clot the size of Mathias's little fist into a polished silver bowl.

Leto was dying. There was no other explanation for it.

She looked up at the sound of his footsteps, paused in her helpless efforts to drag the something slumped in her lap across the floor. Her eyes were panicked and full of anguish, but they were bright. She was safe. He was ashamed of the relief that spread through him along with the realization that it was not Leto that was dying, but Melantho.

Fear followed it. Melantho—furious, hate-filled Melantho who had spoken to him so softly as he wept over Selene. Melantho could not die. He had not thought her capable of it.

"Mathias." Leto's voice was a bare whisper. "Help me."

He crouched at her side. Melantho was a mess of blood, of weakly fluttering eyelashes and harsh, panting breaths. "How?"

"Do you think you can lift her?"

"Can I lift her?" he echoed. Melantho was tall, but she was narrow hipped and slender. Mathias would be able to carry her with ease. But where would they take her? There was no palace physician anymore, and it was too far, surely, to the nearest village.

"I can help you if you need—"

"I can lift her," he said firmly. "But where—"

"Good," Leto said, interrupting him. "Follow me."

Inexplicably, she led him down the steep stairs to the courtyard. Melantho was limp in his arms and alarmingly cold as he held her close to his chest. When they stepped out into the courtyard, the warm evening air was a welcome rush.

Leto stood in front of the fountain. "Put her in the water."

"What?" What good could that do? He had heard of putting salt in wounds—to inhibit infection, to seal the wound—but the *fountain*? It would only accelerate the bleeding, wouldn't it?

"*Do it*," Leto snarled. Her fingers were tight little fists at her sides, and her shoulders were drawn in and shaking with tension.

He did as she said, easing Melantho over the edge of the fountain so the water covered her to the waist. Where she had been pressed against him, his chiton was a mess of red.

"Lower," said Leto. "Over her ribs." She was suddenly beside him, leaning past him to push her hands against Melantho's bloody belly. She smelled of violets. Violets and blood.

Mathias dipped Melantho lower. He looked anxiously at Leto, seeking her approval, but she did not spare him a glance. She had bitten through her lower lip, sucking in her cheeks and furrowing her brow. He had not realized she was crying, but the tears trailed over her cheekbones and dripped from her chin.

He shifted his grip on Melantho, feeling her chiton slip beneath his hands. It was improper to touch a lady—even a lady's maid—on her bare skin, and he made to pull away—

His fingers met something that was not flesh.

The sensation of it sent him flinching back in wordless horror. Where he had expected to find Melantho's legs was not smooth skin. Instead, his fingers had brushed over a layer of supple, sharp-edged scales.

Gods. He pictured very suddenly the scrolls from the library, illuminated with vivid depictions of lore and myth. Scrolls his mother had left to rot. *Circe transforms Scylla* had branded itself into his mind: a graphic scene of the nymph Scylla writhing in agony as dogs' heads burst from her waist and reptilian scales bloomed on her neck as it began to split into six.

He could not help it—his eyes flickered to Melantho's waist. No dogs—only the spreading spill of blood about her wound, turning the pale pink of her chiton into crimson. And Leto's hands, slipping on the wetness as she tried desperately to stem the flow, to hold Melantho together as she bled out.

Then he looked at Melantho's face and everything fell apart.

LII

TERRIBLE ARE THE SEAS

Leto

Leto knew the moment that Melantho changed because Mathias made an awful, fearful sound in his throat and lurched away.

"Mathias," she said through gritted teeth. There was blood everywhere: a spreading pool in the water, a smell that lay thick in the air, a stain that turned the golden ends of Melantho's hair to ruby red and then to emerald and obsidian as the ocean took hold of her. Her arms and legs were grey and green; only her face and throat, clear of the water, remained human—almost. Her eyes were half-open and a flat, insectile black. "Not now, *please.*"

"*Look at her,*" he said.

"I *know.*" She looked up at last, into Mathias's terror-stricken face. His tanned skin had a sheen of grey to it now; his eyes were wide and his lips trembled. "But please, *please.* I need your help." The fountain wasn't healing Melantho as quickly as she wanted. She needed time, lots of it. Perhaps taking her to the sea would have drawn less attention, but Leto would not be able to get her there alone; she would need Mathias, and she would need him to trust her.

Mathias shook his head wordlessly. He was a mess, disheveled and nearly as bloodstained as Leto herself.

"*Help me, Mathias.*"

He jerked, opened his mouth, and then closed it again.

"*Mathias.*"

"All right, all right." She didn't know if he was speaking to her or to himself. She was hardly listening anyway, too busy coaxing the water away from her own fingertips, forcing down the green and grey that bloomed as the water washed over them. "We should take that necklace off," Mathias was still muttering. "She can't breathe."

Leto took a second too long to react. *Wait.*

By the time she had looked up, horrified, at Mathias, he had already reached over and torn Melantho's necklace free, tossing the strip of bronze aside.

"What—?" he began, then broke off abruptly, his shoulders stiffening. Leto didn't have to follow his gaze to know what he had seen. Melantho's throat, laid bare in the dying light, and the raw scar that encircled it.

She should have said something, invented some wild excuse as to why Melantho bore the mark of the rope, but she could find nothing. Perhaps Mathias would not understand. Perhaps he would attribute it to some freak accident, some long-forgotten misstep and narrow escape from the law.

He looked up.

His eyes were flat, unreadable but for a terrible kind of recognition, the look of a man who has seen something he never thought possible. She remembered his face as he had stood in the shrine of the maids, how he had brushed his fingers over Timo's stone hands. He must have noticed that one of the statues looked just like Melantho. He must be making the link between them now. His hands were clenched into fists at his side as he stared at her, as his lips shaped the words that would be her undoing.

"Take off your necklace, Leto," said Mathias. Her name in his mouth, said like *that*, like it was unbearably precious, sent Leto's heart racing faster. Traitorous thing.

She shook her head. "Mathias, I—I can explain."

"Take off your necklace." She had never heard him raise his voice before, not even once. Not when Melantho had snapped at him over some ridiculous, petty little thing for the tenth time in an evening, not when Leto had kissed him, then cursed him in the same breath. But now, his voice rang clear as a bell through the courtyard. His chest heaved. He sounded like a prince.

He sounded like the future king.

"No," said Leto.

"Take it off," said Mathias. "Or I will tear it from you myself."

She had begun to shiver, though the night air was warm. "You would do well not to threaten me, Mathias. I am not just your betrothed. I am a daughter of Athens and I—"

He was on her in an instant, catching her by the shoulders and forcing her still, staring at her so intently that it was as if he was looking *through* her. His pupils were blown huge, his teeth were bared as he ground out the words "Take. It. Off."

Leto reached her trembling hands to the clasp and flicked it open. The necklace slipped and then fell to the ground between them with a clatter, but Leto barely registered the sound. Her mind was full of the rushing of water as Mathias looked slowly, deliberately downward at the ragged scar from the rope and then lower, to the ring of black scales that slashed her throat in two.

He let go of her wordlessly.

His rage had vanished as quickly as it had come, every emotion sapped from his features as he gazed at her.

"Mathias," Leto whispered.

"Leto," he said flatly. "The girl that was hanged, her name was Leto. And you—how could I have *missed* it?" Then, his voice thick with a terrible anguish: "How are you here?"

"It's not what you think," she said. "I swear to you—"

"Get out," said Mathias.

"What?"

"Go to the stables," said Mathias. "Take a horse, any horse, I do not care. And then *get out.*"

"You don't understand," she said desperately. "Mathias, *please.*"

He would not even look at her. "I don't need to understand everything," he said. "I need only to know that you lied to me, *Leto*, and I have little sympathy for liars. Look at you—did you even wish to break the curse? Clearly, it has not burdened you as it has burdened so many others. Were those marks there when you berated me for allowing it to continue, when it is clear now that you knew how to evade it? Did you really look me in the face and tell me that I was to blame when you have Poseidon's mark about your throat and *you are still alive*? When *my sister is dead.*"

"Mathias, I didn't—"

"How did you do it? Tell me, or *leave.*"

"I can't—" Every word caught in her throat.

"Must I do it myself?" he snapped. "Very well, I will get the horse. And you will get on it, and you will leave this place and you *will not come back.*"

He shouldered past her and marched toward the stables, shaking the pinkish water from his hands as he went.

Leto watched him go wordlessly. The hangings were *tomorrow*; it could not all be over now, not like this. Mathias would change his mind.

He had to.

She returned to Melantho's side. She had slipped under the water now; her face was blurred beneath a shifting layer of water and blood. And though she was healing, it was not fast enough.

She needed the sea, where Poseidon was stronger. But Leto could not move her. Not without risking her life.

"Leto." It was Mathias, returned with a mare.

"Mathias." She could not bear to look at him. "Consider what you are doing, please."

"If you need my help lifting her, you should tell me now," he said. His voice was peculiarly flat.

"Mathias—"

"Do you? I can leave her like this if you wish. You leave alone, and Melantho can remain here. You should know this, though, Leto, I will not try to save her." He meant it. Somehow, he meant it. He was truly prepared to banish her, to never see her again. She could beg him, try to convince him, if only there were time.

"Yes," she said. Her voice broke. "Yes, help me. Please."

"Get on the horse."

She did as he commanded, pulling herself up without any pretense of grace. The mare shifted under her weight and then again as Mathias heaved Melantho up after her. She was limp, her eyes closed. Her breath stirred the damp, bloodstained ends of Leto's hair; it was the only indication that there was life in her at all.

"Go," said Mathias.

Leto wanted to weep, wanted to clutch his hands in hers. She wanted to shout at him *Melantho's death will not bring Selene back.*

She remembered the prophecy crumpled in her pocket. "Please," she said, tearing it free and thrusting it toward Mathias. "Please, read this. Perhaps you will understand."

He did not make any move to take it. Eventually, she leaned so far off the horse she might have fallen, pushed it into his palm herself, and closed his fingers around it. "Please," she said again. "For me."

He would not look at her. "Go."

She didn't have a choice. She kicked her heels clumsily into the horse's side and it broke into a trot, slowed by the weight of their bodies.

She turned, at the last moment, just in time to see Mathias loosen his grip on the scrap of papyrus. It fell into the mess of salt water and blood and boot filth at his feet. He stared at it blankly for a moment, then turned and walked away.

With Melantho sagging in her arms, eyes closed, and the coppery tang of blood on the wind, Leto rode hard for the sea.

LIII

A NAME IN STORY

Mathias

As a child, Mathias had always loved stories.

He would hound his nursemaids relentlessly for them, his sister, his mother—and then, when they had all rebuked him for the fifth or the sixth time that evening, he would pad down the uneven steps to the rooms that lay below the palace, the rooms that made up his father's library.

There, he would spend hours, sitting cross-legged on the floor by his father's chair, lost in a haze of delight as he devoured stories of Zeus, of Apollo, of Persephone. Sometimes, his father would read them aloud, in his soft, clever voice, with Mathias perched on his knee. Mathias loved those stories the best.

He had lost some of that love after Selene's death and then again after his father's. He had trapped the memories deep down within himself to be left untouched. One, though, had found its way to the surface. Days ago—though in truth, it felt more like an age now—leaning into Leto as she told him of her mother, he had remembered it.

The memory of a conversation: sitting in bed with his father, leaning against the king's shoulder as he told him the story of Odysseus. When his father had broken off to cough, as he struggled to regain his breath, Mathias had asked if people would tell stories about *him* one day.

"I hope not" had been his father's response.

Mathias had scowled, had demanded to know why.

"Happy people do not make good stories," he had said, each word an effort. "The times we care about are times of change, times of unrest. You cannot have a story without a conflict, and you cannot have a conflict without hurting someone. Stories are borne of unhappiness, loneliness, loss. Heroes never have happy endings."

Mathias had been twelve years old, and it was that youthful naivete that had allowed him to dismiss his father's words with ease. He would much rather be a hero than happy, he had thought, even when the maids had come to him, years later, to brush his curls back and tell him that his father had died.

Now though, leaning against the door of his rooms with Melantho's blood smeared across his fingertips, Mathias understood.

He had always loved stories.

But stories came to an end, and for there to be an ending, a hero had to fall.

LIV

OF EVERY WIND THAT BLOWS

Leto

Leto did not often pray, but she prayed now, galloping across the hillsides toward the sea. She prayed more sincerely than she had ever done before.

She did not ride well, but fear, desperation, *love* gave her the strength to cling on. It did not matter that the equinox was tomorrow. It did not matter that twelve lives would be lost unless she went back tonight and ended it all. Nothing mattered but Melantho.

Leto did not allow herself pause, to breathe or think, until the mare's hooves hit sand and she was at last able to slide from her back, to lower Melantho into the shallows and let the tides wash in over her.

LV

UNWAKED AND UNBURIED

Melantho

Consciousness returned slowly to Melantho.

With it came the pain, persistent and throbbing and so awful that it consumed her every thought. She was vaguely aware of someone with her, someone smoothing the hair back from her face and pulling the torn material of her chiton out of the way of the ocean as it ran its familiar fingers over her.

She wanted to sleep but the pain would not let her. It rose and fell as if with the tides; from a great distance away, she heard someone cry out. And then, a voice in her ear, low and soft and familiar. "Melantho? Can you hear me?"

Go away. Let me sleep.

"Melantho." The voice was louder. "You need to wake up, Melantho. You are healing, you're going to be fine. But we cannot stay here. We will be seen. You need to walk with me. Can you do that?"

No, Melantho tried to say. *No, I cannot. Let me go.* Hands caught her beneath her armpits, hauled her from the water, lay her on the sand, and shook her by the shoulders.

"*Melantho*," said Leto. "*Wake up.*"

She would do anything for that voice. Even move toward the light as it burned and burned and burned. *Leto is waiting.*

But it hurts.

She is waiting for you.

Melantho opened her eyes.

LVI
TELL ME AND TELL ME TRUE

Leto

The streets of Vathi were dark but for the dim light of the crescent moon as Leto dragged Melantho toward the little house that had once been her home. She could only hope that it had not been claimed by someone else; it was the only place she could think to go. It might have been easier to ride, but by the time they reemerged from the waves, the mare had vanished. Stolen, perhaps, or wandered back to her home in the palace. Leto pictured her clattering into the courtyard, the reins hanging loose from her head. Mathias would take one look at her and assume them long gone.

Mathias. The mere thought of him was a dagger to the chest. Leto swallowed hard and returned her attention to Vathi. Her eyes were far keener than they had been; the town seemed smaller now, the colors harsher, the edges sharper. It even seemed to move more slowly.

More than once she caught the movement of an errant sandal or a flailing arm in the near distance and was able to flatten herself in a doorway, hand over her throat before the straggler, usually swinging a flask, passed by without noticing her.

She had spent her time living here hidden behind scarves and incense, a vain attempt to conceal her age from fortune-seekers who would be skeptical of a teenaged oracle, but there was still a chance she might be recognized. And with the mark on her throat, with the sacrifices looming so near . . . she could not let them see her.

Besides, Melantho, feverishly warm in her arms, could barely stand with Leto's support. If one of these wretched passersby decided that the two of them—ragged, exhausted pair that they made— were an easy target, she would be able to do little to stop them.

The streets were comfortingly ordinary. Leto had no idea where they would go from here, when the new day brought death in one way or another, but she knew where they could go for tonight. Vathi settled her heart with its familiarity; here was the shoe smith, the school, the weaver's shop. The rickety shack belonging to the strange old man who said he had once been a hero.

Most of the island folk may have abandoned them, but the shrines to the gods persisted. Fountains dripped salt water into roughly carved basins, and the ashy remains of burned offerings smoldered in grates. Ahead, amongst a row of low white buildings, a candle flickered in a doorway.

She glanced up the hill toward the palace. The paths toward it were still and silent. Dawn was still hours upon hours away, and though soon the road would be bustling with merchants and servants, for now, she and Melantho were alone. Unseen. She pulled the hood of her cloak further over her face and together they staggered down the familiar cobbles that led to her home.

She knew every inch of the little street. Knew where the uneven stones would trip her, knew the places where water would pool after a rainstorm. Nothing had changed. The old man in the second house still had the same broken shutters. His fat orange cat dozed on the windowsill. When Leto and Melantho passed, it cracked open a shining yellow eye and watched them, unmoving.

At last, she stood in front of her own house again. She could see where the door had been carefully reattached to its hinges. A strip of wood had been nailed over the splintering marks where the guards had kicked it in. Some villager, someone who knew what had become of her, must have done it—this small act of kindness for a girl they believed was dead. Had they mourned her? she wondered. Had anyone missed her at all? The lock must have been unsalvageable—the door swung open at her touch.

The smell of rosemary hit her. Bunches of dried herbs had been strung up and piled on every free surface. The floor had been swept clean—another kindness for a dead girl. Her breath caught in her throat.

Besides the bed and the battered trunk that had once held her clothes, the room was empty but for a cracked basin. A pool of stale water still sat in its bottom.

She led Melantho to the bed, carefully unhooked her arm from beneath Melantho's, and lowered her gently down. Melantho winced. The blood had stopped pouring from her belly, the wound had scabbed over, and she had slowly regained lucidity as Leto had dragged her from the beach and into Vathi.

"Stay still," she said. She flipped the trunk open with some trepidation—believing her dead, would the villagers have left anything here for her?—and pulled out an ancient chiton. *Gods.* The last time she had worn this, she had been a different girl. Faking prophecies, scrambling for the morsels that the gods would drop to her. As she turned back to Melantho, something caught under her foot and skittered away, glittering. An obol—the shape was unmistakable. Automatically, she stooped down and scooped it up, wiping some of the grime off on her skirt.

When had she found this? It must have been years ago. Battered and dusty as it was, some part of Leto must have been unable to leave it; a coin was a coin and could always be traded for a cup of stew from the cold and congealing dregs of the pot. Leto had learned that quickly after her father's death. Leftovers weren't always pretty, but they eased the knot of hunger in her belly.

She shook her head clear of the memory and set about tearing the chiton into strips.

"What are you doing?" Melantho's voice was soft.

"Bandages," said Leto. She chewed her lip. "I don't know how much use they'll be, but perhaps they'll help stave off infection or promote healing or . . . oh, I don't know. It's just what I've seen done. I don't know what else I can do."

Melantho must have heard the crack in her voice. "It is a good idea," she said gently. "Will you do it for me?"

She stayed quiet as Leto carefully bound the knife wound, wincing whenever Leto's hands brushed too close to the angry red gash. When it was done, and Leto had knotted the loose ends together, she took one of the remaining pieces of the chiton in her hands and said, "You have to go back, you know."

This had occurred to Leto a hundred times—as she'd ridden from the palace, as she'd lain in the shallows at Melantho's side, waiting for the ocean to breathe life into her again. "I know," she said. "I know."

"You have to go back tonight," said Melantho. She reached up to lay her hand against Leto's cheek and then carefully wrapped the strip of fabric in her hand around Leto's throat. "You must. It is the last chance we will have. The hangings are *tomorrow*."

"Without you?" The thought of it was appalling.

"As it was always meant to be, I suppose," said Melantho with a wry smile. "Perhaps that is the sign the gods tried to give us when they—" She trailed off. Neither of them needed a reminder of the last time they had tried to kill Mathias, when Melantho had fallen as Mathias did, choking on air as if it were tar.

"And if I fail?"

"You cannot," said Melantho. "You *cannot*. I did not tell you this before, Leto, I suppose because I was afraid. But I will tell you now. You are the last."

"The last?"

"The last that Poseidon lets free, the last girl that falls to the sea and then rises again. He promised to grant me twelve, twelve *only*, and eleven girls have come and gone and died. You are the last. If you fail, tonight, then it is over."

She left the implications unspoken in the air between them. Hundreds upon hundreds of girls, hanged for the mere crime of existing on this miserable, cursed island. Leto could not fail them; she could not.

"All right," said Leto at last with wretched finality. It was not long ago that she had come ashore, without reservation, with only one goal in her mind. She wished she could return to that place, that killing Mathias would not break apart the last fragments of her heart. "You are right, of course. I will go back, and I will finish it."

"Good," said Melantho. She closed her eyes. "You should leave now. I will not die, not from this *scratch*." Leto could smell the blood on her still, from beneath the strips of bandaging. If the dagger wound was anything, it was most certainly not a *scratch*.

"Not yet," said Leto. "If Mathias has summoned up his guard, if they know what I am, they may try to stop me. I could die tonight."

Melantho said nothing. Her face twisted.

"I will not die in vain," said Leto. "Nor will I die ignorant. Before

I go, will you tell me what happened? The truth this time? How did the curse come to be, Melantho? And what part did you play in it?"

"A large one," said Melantho. Her eyes were full of the moonlight, her skin was pale gold, and she was as lovely as the first daffodil of spring. "Perhaps I played the greatest part of all."

LVII

A LEGACY OF SORROW

Melantho

"I was born to a slave woman in the village of Vathi," said Melantho. Each word sent a dull throb of pain through her stomach, the reminder of the not-quite-healed wound hidden beneath her bandages. "At least, that's what the queen who bought me from my mother told me."

It was easy to slip back into the memories. Melantho closed her eyes, and she was walking through the halls of the palace once again.

At that time, it was a wondrous thing to behold, a sprawling mass—a kingdom in itself—of marble columns and gold-threaded tapestries and narrow passageways that bustled with servants. A sea of faces as familiar to Melantho as the freckles and scars that marked the backs of her hands.

She had loved it here once.

The servants that passed her would not look her in the face. They skirted sideways to avoid her as she walked toward the queen's chambers with a basket of roughly spun goat's wool on her hip. They knew that Melantho held Penelope's ear, that she could be a wicked, dangerous thing if baited. They knew of the trinkets that Penelope bestowed upon her, the invitations to dine at her table in the evenings, that sometimes Melantho would kneel in front of Penelope's chair and the queen would braid her yellow hair as if

Melantho were her own child. They knew of the stable boy, dismissed at Melantho's bequest.

They knew nothing else.

Melantho turned a corner and collided with something solid, something warm. Something that let out a huff of surprise and stepped back, caught Melantho by the shoulders and steadied her. They had knocked into her basket; the pale threads had spilled onto the polished flagstones.

"Watch it," she snapped, shaking herself free and bending to gather the wool together again.

"Watch it?" repeated a voice—a male voice, smooth as honey and deep as the wells Melantho hauled water from each morning. The syllables dripped with amusement.

Melantho stiffened. "My apologies," she said carefully, keeping her eyes down. "I did not see you, my prince."

Telemachus laughed. "Melantho, my darling. Do not waste your pretty words on me. You know I would forgive you any transgression."

They had grown up together, Melantho and Telemachus, two golden-haired children in Penelope's chambers as she waited for her husband to return from the war that had burned Troy to the ground. The three years that separated them—for Telemachus was the senior of the two by so much—had not mattered, had not stopped them clinging together, giggling as they pulled Penelope's clothes from her wardrobes or raced their stocky ponies over the hillside. She had loved him.

Looking at him even now set her heart aching. She could not pinpoint the precise moment that it had changed, that they had gone from *Mel and Tel* to *Melantho the maid and Telemachus the prince*, but she knew that he did not look at her as a sister anymore.

Now twenty, his childhood shed for a blustering manhood, Telemachus would look at her and his black eyes would glitter with something harder, sharper. It was the same look she had seen on his face when the first of the suitors had arrived at the palace and presented him with a fine grey stallion for his stables.

Greed.

She had only had to turn him down once, but that once had been enough. She had heard Penelope shrieking at her son from two corridors down, the sharp sound of her hand meeting his cheek, splitting the skin of his face open with her rings. Any love that Telemachus held for Melantho had died that day. The puckered scar atop his cheekbone remained, a pale star, a reminder.

Melantho could see it now as his hand forced her chin up, and she looked at last into his lovely face.

"Eurymachus asks about you," he said. The words were casual, but his eyes darted a frantic dance over her face as he spoke of his mother's suitor. There were too many of them to count; they lazed around and fought amongst themselves as they waited for Penelope to choose one of them. Penelope herself spent each day weaving a shroud, the shroud that her husband's father would be buried in. Until it was finished, she would not choose. And her suitors—Eurymachus amongst them—would seek their entertainment elsewhere.

But it would never be finished because Melantho stayed up each night with eleven others and pulled the careful weave undone. She did not do it for duty; she did it for the love of a queen who had only ever treated her with kindness.

"Does he?" Melantho kept her voice level.

Eurymachus was in his thirties at least; Melantho had never given him a second thought until he had cornered her in the first weeks after her fifteenth birthday. His breath had been rank with wine and he had leaned into her with the confidence of a man who had never heard the word no.

Melantho shuddered and broke off in her tale. Leto was leaning into her, eyes wide.

"Did he—" she began, her mouth twisting. Melantho felt something knot in her stomach. Leto could not even *say* it.

"He had a friend," she said. "Named Antinous. You remember that I told you of Timo, do you not?"

The first and last in my heart, she had said. She saw in Leto's face that she remembered. That she remembered what had happened to Timo in the end.

"Antinous took a fancy to Timo, and he took what he wanted from her," she said. Timo had not cried out, had not shed a single tear. But her eyes had never sparked again with childish delight, and she did not smile so often if at all. It had been her first death that night. The first of three.

"The queen could not protect her—would not, perhaps. I could not protect her. I turned to someone who could."

Eurymachus's help came with a price.

When Melantho pushed the door open, he was slouched lazily in bed, waiting for her. "Look who it is," he said softly. "My little lark, come home to nest." His red tunic lay discarded on the floor with the jumbled mess that was the rest of his clothing. Melantho could see the spots of dried blood on the pale trousers. That would be a nightmare in the laundry rooms. He watched as she took it in, then gestured her forward.

Melantho stood her ground. Bloodstains proved nothing. "What of Antinous?"

Eurymachus waved a dismissive hand. "He won't touch her again. He knows now what I can, and will, do with a knife if he disobeys me. Timo can walk freely." He beckoned her toward him again, more impatiently.

Melantho bobbed her head. "Thank you," she said. Timo then, at least, was safe.

"Is that all you came for? To make sure I'd made good on my word?" Eurymachus sat up. The sheets fell away from his torso and gathered in his lap. Melantho's eyes caught on the sliver of the tops of his thighs that was visible. Dark hair pooled in between them and disappeared under the linen. "Because I have, little lark. I have done as I promised, and now it is your turn."

Timo was safe. She was safe because of this. Melantho swallowed, then reached up for the knot of fabric behind her neck. With a swift tug of her fingers, the tie unraveled and the chiton fell loose to her waist. Eurymachus's eyes widened with a desperation that might have been comical in any other place, any other time. His fingers twitched as his gaze devoured her, running hungrily over her breasts to the bottom of her stomach.

"It is cold," said Melantho quietly. She crossed the room and pulled the shutters closed over the room's wide window. The thought that no unfortunate passerby would happen to glance in was comforting. Perhaps even the gods would avert their eyes. *Hera forgive me.* She turned back to Eurymachus. The shutters blocked much of the light from the room. In the dark, he was just the shadowed shape of a man. A shadow could not harm her.

She squared her shoulders and pulled open the second knot in her chiton. It fell from her in a smooth movement and pooled around her feet. She stepped forward. As she moved, Eurymachus reached for her. His voice was like honey in the quiet. "My love."

If she closed her eyes, she could almost forget that he was lying. "Come here to me, my darling. My little lark."

Melantho went to him.

Later, as the pain bloomed between her legs, she lay on her back and blinked back tears. Eurymachus was snoring quietly at her side, his arm thrown over her waist. The weight and warmth of it was nauseating.

He had not been unkind to her. In fact, he'd been almost sweet. His kisses had been gentle, and his hands soft. As he had reached his pleasure, he had groaned her name, and afterward, he had swept the hair from her forehead and kissed it. "Lovely, lovely Melantho," he had crooned. "You will be the death of me."

If she had been a braver woman, she would have met his eyes and hissed, "Gods, I hope so." But she was not a braver woman, and there was Timo to consider—how would Timo survive if Melantho was strung up for murder?—so she had smiled, and whispered tender words in return, and hidden the agony from her eyes.

This arrangement lasted the better part of a year.

In the afternoons, Eurymachus took his pleasure. In the evenings, and well into the early hours of the following days, Melantho would sit—a little quieter, a little older now—with the queen and meticulously unpick her weaving. In the mornings, she would rise swiftly to retrieve the linen drying in the yard, to boil the water for the dirty laundry the other maids brought down by the armful, and to surreptitiously check the back gate for the queen's messenger. When he brought no news, the queen was restless, and the watchful Eurymachus was jubilant and generous. When the messenger brought good news, the delighted queen would dismiss Melantho to the suspicious and agitated Eurymachus.

"What is it that distracts her from her weaving?" he raged on one such day as he furiously paced his chambers. Melantho sat silently in the bed, nursing the hand-shaped bruises on her thighs. "Why is she weaving anyway? Does that wretch Laertes really need a shroud? He is still alive." He paused in his pacing. "Perhaps we should just kill him," he mused. "Then she'd have to finish the godsdamned thing."

Eurymachus did not know of the queen's trickery. He did not know that she bid her maids, bid *Melantho*, to unpick her weaving each night. The shroud would never be finished. Penelope would never choose a new husband. Nothing would ever change; Melantho would come here again and again and again and it would cease to hurt her. She would empty her soul out and become a shell, like so many of the other maids that wandered these halls.

"His wife, Anticlea, is dead," Melantho ventured. "His daughter, Ctimene, is married in Sami. His son is lost at sea. The queen feels the shroud weaving is a duty that can fall only to her. It would be improper for such a great hero—"

"Lost at sea?" interrupted Eurymachus. His usual charm had vanished. "Odysseus is dead. He is dead, do you hear me? And that bitch of his will have to remarry eventually and the sooner she realizes that, the better. Then I will have her, and the rest of these lazy oafs can clear off to trouble some other man's halls, instead of lounging around day after day eating my goats, drinking my wine, and making eyes at my queen—"

"She is not your queen yet. Nor are they your goats, nor your wine." No sooner had the words left her mouth than she was cringing away as Eurymachus stormed toward her, his face an ugly shade of puce. Melantho looked down, screwed her eyes shut. It was love that had loosened her tongue, but she could not regret it, not when Penelope loved her back like her own child.

"Shut your whore mouth," spat Eurymachus. "You think your precious queen would hesitate for one second to cast you out if she knew where it is you disappear to? If she knew you were spreading your legs for every nobleman who can promise you something?"

"I never—" Melantho tried to protest but Eurymachus's diatribe was unstoppable.

"You think you're so good, do you?" he screamed. "Graciously martyring yourself for the sake of little Timo, are you? I see through you, whore. I know what you really want." Spittle flew from his lips; his eyes were wild. "Oh, you'll be so happy the second my seed plants itself a bastard in your belly. You think you'll have me in your reach then, but you won't." He stopped, breathing heavily. "That ever happens, I'll beat it out of you myself and throw you in a boat to join Ctimene in Sami. Or just skip the inevitable middle-men and throw you in the sea."

Melantho sat frozen. A wrong word would earn her a dozen more bruises.

"Get out," he said at last. "Don't come back."

Melantho didn't need any encouragement. She hugged her chiton to her chest and fled the room.

Antinous went to Timo again that day. Melantho knew that Eurymachus had permitted it. He had not stopped it, this violation of the rules that bound a guest to decency. But nor had Penelope. Penelope had not protected Timo and she had not protected Melantho.

She never would. Penelope might have loved her, but she was a clever queen. She would not endanger herself, her kingdom, for a mere slave girl. Melantho had nothing to offer her. But she had something more to offer Eurymachus.

The next night, Melantho told him Penelope's secret. She sold out her queen to the dogs, ensured that soon Penelope would take Melantho's place in Eurymachus's grasp.

The next night was the last.

∽∽∽

This was all that Melantho could bear to recount. "You know how it goes from here," she said.

Leto was watching her closely with those wide, brown eyes. "I do. Odysseus returned to Ithaca. He punished you—punished you all—for your betrayal, your impurity. But then—how did *this* happen? I don't understand."

Of course she didn't understand. Melantho wanted to take her by the hands, to look into her face and say *That is a good thing. It means you have not known the pain that I have known, the anguish I have suffered. You do not know what it is like to be desperate, to feel as if there is nowhere left for you to turn, and I am glad that you do not. It would change you, as it has changed me.*

She sighed.

"You know so much already, I am sure you can guess what happened. What I did—and the reason. I loved Timo, and she was raped and then she was hanged because it had *sullied* her. I called upon Poseidon the first time I watched Timo die." She laughed bitterly. "It is not a mistake I would make again. But I remember, even as they strung me up, how sincerely I believed that they would spare her. And I remember realizing they would not; I remember the sight of two reaching palms swimming in and out of hazy definition, desperately familiar to me. They were hands I had held for ten years. Hands whose shapes and scars and scrapes I knew as my

own. Hands I had taught to sew and weave and throw and strike. They were Timo's hands, reaching out for me as she died, and I knew then that I must avenge her."

She clenched her fists in her lap. "And so I made my request to the gods. I sent the plea skyward, seaward. Sent it plummeting into the very depths of the earths to shake the halls of the Unseen God. 'Save us. Avenge us,' I begged them, 'hurt them as they have hurt us.'" She broke off. "If I was wrong to do so by your judgment, then tell me now. I have told you what happened to Timo. You know how she died. You know that I have been punished enough."

"You were not wrong," said Leto. "You were afraid, and you should not have had to be. I am sorry."

Melantho had not realized that she was crying. Some griefs, some memories, would never leave her. She could still remember—indeed, she could hardly forget—the first time she had beheld Pandou's shoreline. The dead girls in the water, the horror as she looked upon herself and saw a monster. And Timo—tiny, innocent Timo—stood before her, blank eyed and shaking as Poseidon's words, his curse, spilled from her lips. As Melantho had listened, had *understood* what it was that she had set in motion, she had thought that nothing could be worse. But then Timo had opened her eyes again, her *own* horrified, accusatory eyes and had begun her own change even as she beheld the bodies that surrounded them, and it had been the fiercest pain that Melantho had ever felt.

I am sorry, Leto had said. Melantho took a sharp breath. "So am I. I have been since I woke on Pandou, with ten bodies in the water with me, and Timo—Timo looking at me with horror as the scales crept over her skin. I could *feel* Poseidon watching. He had granted my wish. He had saved her. But he had destroyed her too."

LVIII

MAKE TRIAL OF THE BOW

Leto

Leto returned to the palace for what she knew would be the last time. Dusk had stolen across the sky, turning every tree root and loose stone into a shadowed and lethal trap. In her pocket was concealed a little bottle, and inside the bottle were ten drops of milky white liquid. Hypnos's tears. Enough to knock a man out cold for hours. Melantho had the rest; Leto had taken the only knife they could find, and she could not bear to leave Melantho utterly undefended. She would see her again soon; they would meet on the Vathi shore as the sun rose. This would not go wrong.

She pulled her cloak down over her face and slipped toward the servant's gate. There was only one guard on the gate when she arrived, but even that was unusual. She was used to strolling through easily.

She rooted around the base of the wall for a piece of rock. Once she had located one that was sufficiently large—not too difficult, since the wall was ancient, and pieces of it were strewn all around her—she picked it up, weighted it thoughtfully in one hand, then tossed it hard in the direction of the guard.

There came a yell of surprise. Leto poked her head around the corner. The guard was facing away from her, the rock at his feet, examining the crumbling wall for its source. Before he had time to lose interest and return to his post, Leto stole through the gate and into the palace.

The corridors were deserted, and Leto reached the passageway leading toward Mathias's chambers without meeting a soul. The few torches left alight were burning low in their brackets. Mathias must have lit them when he last passed through. Leto could have sworn his scent clung to the still air, sending her pulse racing and her fingers twitching with nerves.

The air was cool here, and the curtains on all the windows were pulled open. Through the gaps she could see the glittering movement of the fountain in the courtyard. The door to Mathias's bedroom was up ahead and unguarded.

Leto paused, turning her head from side to side, straining for the slightest noise.

She took another step forward.

"Stop right there, *Adrasteia*."

No. Not now. Leto froze as Alexios stepped into the passageway.

"Let me through," said Leto. Her eyes darted across the narrow space, searching for a way out or a weapon. Except for the flickering torches, the tapestries, and the amphoras that flanked each entrance, the corridor was bare. Her gaze caught again on the light that glistened off the water of the fountain.

"No," said Alexios.

Leto took a deep, calming breath. Olympia and Alexios had tried to kill Melantho, had probably tried to kill *her* too. Or at least to seriously injure her. Leto had come to this place prepared to commit a murder; what was one more?

"Fine," said Leto. Something must have shifted in her countenance. The arrogance melted away from Alexios's face and he reached for his blade.

He moved fast. But Leto was faster.

His fingers had barely closed on the hilt before she was sprinting down the hallway toward him. He yanked the blade free clumsily, moonlight flashing off its polished edges.

Leto refused to let herself falter.

She knew he had years of fighting experience. Knew, if he swung it back, that his blade would catch her square in the chest. Knew that he watched her every move so closely that he would miss nothing she tried. He met Leto's eyes and smiled, safe in the knowledge that no human on the island would have been able to best him.

That was his mistake. Because Leto was not human. Not anymore. She reached out with her power, felt a sudden *surge* as something reached back.

She belonged to the water; the water belonged to her.

She smiled, giddy and victorious, and summoned forth the contents of the fountain.

The water smashed into him with the force of a galloping mare. It raised him right off his feet and sent him flying. The spray soaked Leto; it sent power rippling through her. She was on Alexios a second later, knocking his blade away easily and driving him to the ground. The water was in his throat, in his eyes and ears, and he fell like a missed knucklebone, arms flailing wildly.

Leto forced the water further into his lungs.

Alexios convulsed. One of his hands caught Leto by the throat and he threw her away from him. She slid on the wet floor, smashing into an ornamental jug before collapsing into a pitiful heap.

Get up. She could not fail now.

The water had already fallen into a glistening sheet by the time she had staggered to her feet. At the other end of the corridor, Alexios was doing the same, expelling great, choking lungfuls of water.

"*You little bitch,*" he spat. She'd thought he would be surprised,

but there was nothing in his eyes but hatred, fury. "I should have tried harder to kill you."

She had lost the element of surprise now. Alexios kept his mouth shut as he advanced, batting away the water with his huge arms as Leto sent it spiraling hopelessly toward him. It was too spread out, harder to control all at once. She retreated until her back hit a wall. She was trapped.

Alexios covered the remaining distance between them in a few short steps. Leto commanded the water to surround his head, one final, desperate attempt to suffocate him as he reached out and lifted her up by the throat, tearing the knotted strip of fabric away with his thick fingers.

It was a pain she had known before, that ripping, that tearing. Alexios's grip was tight enough to crush her throat; she wondered whether it could kill her. She closed her eyes and scrabbled helplessly at her thigh for her dagger. It slipped from her twitching fingers.

There came the sound of smashing ceramic and Alexios released her. Leto's eyes flew open as, with a great look of surprise on his face and shards of pottery in his dark hair, Alexios fell to his knees and then smashed face-first into the floor. The amphora that Leto had thrown at him—that the water had carried to splinter against his skull—was a mess of broken pieces around him.

Someone gasped.

Leto lifted her head and her eyes met Olympia's.

Or rather, her eyes met the tip of Olympia's arrow.

She was standing at the far end of the corridor, her face screwed up into an expression that was equal parts pain and fury. But her hands were steady, and the sleek antelope-horn bow she clutched in them was drawn. The arrow was aimed at Leto's heart.

"Is he dead?" Olympia's voice quivered as she looked at her brother, splayed out at Leto's feet. Blood trickled from his cheeks where he had fallen onto the shattered pieces of the jug. In sleep—because his unconsciousness could, generously, be referred to as a slumber—he looked younger, softer.

Leto had watched Olympia shoot before. She remembered how Olympia had met her eye and fired, her arrow finding its mark. How Olympia had smiled. If Olympia loosed her arrow, it would not miss.

She offered the girl her palms. *Look, I am unarmed.* "No," she said. "He's unconscious."

Olympia said nothing. She flexed her grip and shifted her feet into a stance that Leto recognized.

"Olympia," she said. "Have you killed a person before?"

"I have killed," said Olympia.

"It is different," said Leto. "A person is not like a rabbit, Olympia. You are fifteen."

It was the wrong thing to say. "My brother killed his first man at twelve," snarled Olympia. "Those of us who are not nobility are not permitted the luxury of youth. We have to claw our way up; we have to deserve everything a hundred times over. What have you done to deserve him?"

She truly was in love with Mathias. It was written all over her features, in the harsh curl of her lips and the sharp line of her clenched jaw. She could have had him if it were not for Leto, for Adrasteia.

Nothing, Leto could have said. *I have done nothing to deserve him.* But instead, she said, "Olympia," in the softest of voices and reached as surreptitiously as she could for the dagger at her hip. Her aim wasn't good enough to strike the girl down from such a

distance, but perhaps she could knock her arrows from the air. Her reactions were fast; her eyes were sharp. "What are you doing?"

"What I should have done the day you arrived," said Olympia. "What the *queen* asked me to do if you graced our halls any longer." She let her arrow loose.

Too late, Leto's fingers closed on the empty leather sheath that had held her dagger. Too late, she remembered that the little blade lay at her feet.

Too far away.

Leto threw herself sideways and Olympia's arrow buried itself in the tapestry that hung behind her, pinning it to the stone underneath.

Leto scrambled to her feet, her chiton soaked in the water that still covered the floors in a thin film. Her legs were thrumming with change; the water that had trickled away between the tiles of the floor shivered. It was not seeping into the ground anymore, but upward in tiny streams that snaked toward Leto and wrapped their freezing fingers about her ankles.

Leto took a sharp breath. The water made her stronger, faster; perhaps she would survive the first arrow to hit her. The second, though? The third? The dagger was still too far away, and Olympia had already drawn another arrow, was pulling the bowstring taut—

"Olympia," said Leto desperately. "Please—"

Olympia noticed the water at last. Her eyes flared wide, fearful, and she let the second arrow fly.

It slammed into the grey-green skin of Leto's thigh and lodged there, vibrating.

Leto howled in pain.

Olympia had drawn a third arrow. "This one is going to kill you," she said.

Leto did not doubt her. There was no way to stop it, surely. She was going to die here, on the floor, barely a room away from where Mathias was sleeping. Time seemed to slow as Olympia pulled the bowstring back, aimed, and let go.

A memory tugged at Leto's mind. Melantho, grinning. *"Ask me how."* Water boiling in a copper bath. And if she could get it to boil . . .

Leto raised her hands. The water surged into a wall, cutting the corridor in half so that Olympia was little but a foggy silhouette at the other end. As the arrow hit the wall, Leto froze it solid.

The arrow stuck fast.

Olympia's blurred outline turned and ran.

It was easy, now that she had done it once. Now that the water knew what to do. The ice melted in an instant. Leto ripped the arrow free from her leg, ignoring the pain as best she could, and threw the water at Olympia. She was not as strong as her brother; it caught her up and tossed her with ease against the door she had been trying to open.

The water plunged down Olympia's throat. Leto was at her side in an instant, catching the girl before she fell. Olympia was smaller than she had thought, lithe and muscular but still just a girl; there was so little substance to her. Her eyes were huge and childish, her cheeks rounded.

Leto held Olympia to her chest as she choked, as the sea surged into her lungs with vicious joy and turned her first red, then purplish, then an awful grey. Leto was careful this time. She did not allow herself to be caught up; the moment that Olympia fell unconscious, she pulled the water from her lungs. As it retreated, it curled over Leto's legs, healing the wound the arrow had left behind. She had been lucky—the shaft had not gone as deep as it might have, and the pain was a mere throbbing as she got to her feet.

She smoothed Olympia's hair back from her face, checked that the girl was breathing, and left her there.

※ ※ ※

The door to Mathias's bedchamber creaked softly as Leto eased it open. She had been here only once before; she almost stumbled over a table she had not noticed. All was dark and still inside.

She advanced slowly toward the bed and the hunched shape of Mathias lying within it. Her fingers shook on the little bottle she held in one hand. The other rested on the hilt of the dagger at her hip. She imagined bringing it down on Mathias, not enough to kill, just enough to stun, and felt instantly, violently ill.

No, she told herself sternly. She would not have to use it. The remnants of the drug within the bottle would be enough to subdue him. It had to be. She reached the bed and uncapped the bottle, holding her breath.

"What are you going to do with that, *Princess*?"

LIX

MANY A WEARY WAVE

Leto

Leto started as light flared from the opposite corner of the room.

She spun around, dropping into a half crouch. She drew the knife from her belt and leveled it shakily at Mathias.

He watched her steadily from where he sat, very still, in a high-backed chair. His hands were folded in his lap. A single lamp burned beside him. He was fully dressed and armed—his sword leaned against the side of the chair and the blade of a knife was just visible, peeking from the cuffs of his ornate sleeves. "But I suppose," he said, "that you aren't *really* a princess, are you?"

Leto didn't move a muscle.

"And the knife?" continued Mathias calmly. "Were you going to use that on me too?"

"If I had to." The words fell, unbidden, from Leto's tongue. She straightened slowly. "Which has suddenly become a whole lot more likely." She forced a smile, mind racing, "You couldn't have just made it easy, could you?"

"My own murder?" queried Mathias. "No, unfortunately not."

Leto kept her blade pointed at him. "That's a shame."

He laughed, the humor stopping before it reached his eyes. "What are you going to do, gut me here? One shout from me and half the Ithacan guard will be on you. I don't think you'd get far."

It was strange to speak to him so frankly. Normally their conversations were all half-concealed implications and double entendres. But now Mathias was looking at her with stark challenge.

"I will cut your throat," said Leto quietly. Her hand was shaking, the movements sending the tip of the knife shifting, flinging the lamplight away in all directions. "You don't know what I am capable of. The things I've done. The things I'm willing to do. But I assure you that I will cut your throat and leave you to bleed out on the floor as I escape." It was a lie—if Mathias died here, out of the sea, she would lose everything and gain nothing. The pressure, the *pain* in her chest was incomparable, but she tugged on her powers, curled just below the surface of her skin, and smiled, forcing her teeth to lengthen and sharpen.

Mathias was on his feet in an instant. "What—" he managed. "It is not just the scales, then. You are like her, you are . . . you are something not human. Something else."

"I am alive," said Leto. "I was saved—I was *chosen*. And my purpose is to end the scourge on this land. To save hundreds upon hundreds of innocent girls from slaughter."

Mathias shook his head. "You're lying," he said. His fingers were slowly moving toward the knife hidden in his sleeve.

"Touch that blade," said Leto, "and I will kill you where you stand." She could not waver. This was her last chance, her *only* chance. Mathias's life was not the only one at stake here and she could not allow herself to forget it. Hundreds of girls. Girls like her, girls like Melantho and Timo and Thalia. The next time the sun reached its peak there would be twelve more. Twelve more if she did not *stop it now*.

Mathias stopped moving. He took in a sharp, audible breath. There was a long, awful pause, in which the only sound was the humming of the wind and the distant rush of the waves on the shore. It filled Leto with longing as the pain in her leg flared yet again.

"I have never thought of you as cruel," said Mathias at last. "I see that I was wrong."

He had never looked at her like that before. Like she was the enemy. Like he hated her. It was as if Leto's ribs were made of glass; her chest was tight and hard and cold and oh so close to just *shattering*. "I need a prince," she said. "To break the curse."

"I was ready to marry you," said Mathias. "I was ready to love you. I thought—I hoped—that you could love me."

Everything holding Leto together broke at once.

"Don't," she snarled. "Don't you *dare* make this harder than it already is. I *know* that you are good, and kind, and gentle, and it will hurt me so deeply the moment that you are gone to know that I was responsible." Her heart was thrumming madly in her chest, desperate to break free from its broken cage. She curled her hands into fists at her side and forced her voice down.

"But," she said. "The girls that you'll see hang will be good, and kind, and gentle too. Or maybe they'll be snide, and bitter, and angry. But not a single one of them will deserve to die. They'll have lovers and friends and families that adore them. The children that I've seen die were blameless. *I* was blameless." She had run out of air and it forced her to pause, to suck in another breath and whisper on the exhale, *"Do you know what that's like?"*

"No," said Mathias. "No, you're right. I don't. Of course I don't." He paused. "I was right, wasn't I? That you are Leto, sacrifice to Poseidon, daughter of Ophelia. The girl who tried to run. The girl I saw hang."

"You were right." There was nothing else she could say.

"Leto," said Mathias musingly. "At least that was not a lie. It is

a very pretty name. As lovely as you yourself are."

Leto laughed softly. "You don't need to flatter me. I'm about to kill you, Mathias."

"No, you aren't." Mathias's smile was bitter. He lifted a hand and what Leto saw in it sent a thrill of relief—followed swiftly by a great surge of grief—running through her. The prophecy. Bloodied, muddied, and damp, but curled within Mathias's fingers. "You can't, can you? Not like this."

She blinked at him. His voice had wavered before, but now it rang with certainty. He must know, then, that his death only mattered to Poseidon if it came about in the sea. But *how*? She strained to remember the precise phrasing of the prophecy. "I—what?"

"*You* can't kill me. I have to choose it," he said. "Don't I? That's how it works."

No? Leto bit down the incredulous word. Instead, she repeated, "Choose it?"

"I have to make the choice. That's the answer we were searching for all along," he said. "Or that *I* was searching for all along—I suppose it would be foolish to think that you did not know."

Now she was so bewildered that she could do nothing but shake her head wordlessly. What had he found that had convinced him so strongly of something that was so far from the truth? She did not need his permission to drown him. And drowning him *would* work—that much had been made clear in the courtyard, when the salt water had surged down his throat and, as he fell, Melantho had crumpled at Leto's side.

Mathias made an exasperated noise. "*Look*," he said. He snatched up a mess of papyrus sheets from the table at his side. "Selene's journal," he explained. "Her notes, everything she learned about breaking the curse before she—before she died. There's something that always struck me as odd, but I didn't understand it until now," he said. "Look, the same words, all the way through. Written over and over again. She must have found something or sought an oracle or . . . well. It doesn't matter now." He offered Leto the battered bundle.

She did not need to look beyond the first page. Written there—no, *scrawled* there, with a hand that must have trembled with each word—were three lines.

Twelve by chance to stay the tides.
Twelve by force to stop them, or—
One by choice to sate them.

Selene had underlined one word half a dozen times, until the tip of her reed pen had torn through the ink-sodden sheet. *Choice.*

"One by choice," said Leto. Something in her stomach had tied itself into an aching knot; she felt distinctly sick. One *what*? One girl? No, it would never have been that easy. And *to sate them*? The rest was clear enough: the twelve by chance must be the marked girls, whose deaths would stay the tides for a year, and the twelve by force were surely the twelve sons of Odysseus's line doomed to slaughter.

"Selene thought it meant *her*," said Mathias. "That must be why—" He paused, audibly swallowed. "Why she jumped. But she was wrong. It didn't mean her, did it? It means *me*. It always meant me."

"Mathias." Leto reached for him instinctively; she could not bear to see the raw pain in his eyes, in the set of his jaw. If what he said was true, that a single death through choice was all that was required, then Poseidon had never *needed* twelve of Odysseus's line; he had only needed one.

If only they had known before, if only this had happened three hundred years ago, if pain and fear had been put aside for just a moment to work together against a common enemy. A moment to talk, to comfort, to understand. How many lives could have been saved? But justice, or something close to it, had long rusted away into sharp-toothed vengeance. Eleven of Odysseus's line were dead. It was already over.

Leto gazed helplessly at Mathias. This was what all their searching and hoping had come to; they had found another way, but they had found it far too late.

Everything had changed, and nothing had changed at all.

"I was born to feed the flames," said Mathias. He brandished the wet, bloodstained prophecy. "That's what your mother said, wasn't it?"

"I suppose she did." She looked at him for a long moment, hoping the pain in her eyes would convey everything she needed to say and could not. "It is not your fault," she said at last.

"But it must happen?"

"It must."

"Will you tell me why?" Mathias asked. "I understand you may be pressed for time. But I—I think you know more than I do. I would like to know why my death is required. *If* it truly is." He straightened. "You're sure that it will free Ithaca?"

Leto nodded her head slowly. "It will," she said. "But I am not so pressed for time. For you, I have all the time in the world."

And so, she told him.

She told him of the maids and their deaths, of Melantho's anguish and her desperate plea. Told him of the curse, of the dead kings and their sons and then of her own hanging—the sorrow in his face then almost broke her heart—and of her awakening. Told him of her days spent in Melantho's company, and of Adrasteia.

And she told him of her arrival on Ithaca, and of the moment she realized that the boy she had been sent to kill was a boy she could not stand to be parted from.

"But this is not about me," she finished. She did not know when she had started to cry, but now the tears carved a warm path down her cheeks and dripped from her chin. "This is about the hundreds of girls who have died and the hundreds more that would. It is about the twelve who are languishing in cells as we speak. They have *hours* left to live. They are innocent, Mathias, and it is you that can save them."

⑤⑥⑥⑥

Mathias looked at her for a long time after that. "Very well," he said at last. "So I must die. But there is something I would like you to do for me before I do."

Leto offered him her upturned palms. "Anything," she said softly. "Anything at all for you."

"I want—" He stopped, a look of anguished uncertainty twisting his lovely face. Then he stepped forward, watching Leto for her reaction. Leto forced herself not to move, to trust him, as he took another step, then reached out to gently brush the tears from Leto's cheeks. The touch made her skin prickle and burn. "I would like very much," he corrected himself, "to kiss you once more."

Leto made a choking noise halfway between a laugh and a sob. She ducked her head into a nod—she did not think she could speak.

Mathias looked at her with shining eyes. He stepped forward and there was barely a space between them. He placed his hands uncertainly on her hips and drew her forward and then there truly was no space at all. "Leto," he said, as if trying the word out on his tongue. "I do believe I really am in love with you." And then, before she had time to think or to respond, he kissed her.

They both knew that she had kissed him before: that once on the cliff tops—a scene which had not left Leto's mind since it occurred—then, again, in the storeroom, and when he'd made his disastrous declaration of love at the festival, but all those kisses had barely been kisses at all. They had been interrupted or avoided or hastened and chastened by propriety. But this was no time to be proper.

His lips were warm and gentle as they had been before. For a few moments Leto allowed him to be soft and appropriate, to reassure himself with the familiarity of her embrace before taking whatever it was he wanted. When he did not, she took it for him. She pulled his body hard into her and dug her nails into his shoulders. When he gasped in surprise, she reveled in the sudden openness of his mouth.

Mathias responded beautifully. His hands left her hips and made their way to her waist, her thighs, the back of her neck in languid, stroking movements. His tongue brushed her lips like a question. She answered it with her own.

The pressure of his hands relented for a second and then they were tugging at the ridiculous lacing at the back of her chiton, the crossing strips of fabric which bound her into perfect shape.

"Damn fashion," he mumbled against her mouth. Finding the ribbons more tangled with each passing second, he drew back from her. His forehead creased between his eyebrows.

"Terribly sorry," he said. With one fluid motion he leant down, pulled a knife from where it had been strapped inside his boot, and pulled the blade down the full length of Leto's spine.

For a heart-stopping moment she thought he had cut her, had changed his mind and decided that Leto should be the one to die instead. Then the back of the gown fell open to the cool breeze beyond the open windows and the thought vanished. All she could think of was the boy in front of her, his curls mussed over his forehead, dark brown eyes bashfully averted.

"Look at me," she breathed.

He did. She took a half step forward and pulled at the bodice of the gown. It fell to the floor with a rustle. Then, with sharp tug from Leto's hand, the simple band of cloth which had covered her breasts joined it. She stood in front of him, completely bare, and reached for him wordlessly.

Mathias did not move. His gaze covered her like silks. "Beautiful," he breathed. Then he stepped forward and cupped her face in his hands. She tilted her chin up. He looked dizzy with desire; his lips were parted to rapid breaths and his pupils were huge. "Beautiful," he repeated.

He pulled her back toward him and they tumbled together onto the bed. His hands covered her with an unfamiliar urgency, and he kissed her with a furious intensity she would never have expected from him. In between kisses she managed to tug his tunic over his head. He freed himself with a wild shake of his dark curls. They plastered themselves to his forehead with sweat, and Leto was reminded vividly of the first time they had met—Mathias damp from bathing, and she herself falling in through the window sweaty and bedraggled and ridiculous.

Despite the urgency in his movements, there was a curious

gentleness to Mathias. He was so different from Melantho, who was frantic passion and nails and teeth. Mathias was soft, languishing strokes and long, burning kisses from her mouth to her collarbone then her stomach then her hip then—*oh*.

Leto closed her eyes and imagined that they could remain there forever.

LX

FROM BEYOND THE SEAS

Leto

Leto walked down the shore with Mathias's hand clutched in her own. Melantho—pale and shaken but alive, mercifully alive—waited for them there. Miles away, a note addressed to the queen rested on Mathias's cold pillows: an explanation, an apology. A goodbye.

No one would find it in time to stop them; Olympia and Alexios lay unconscious where they had fallen, and the tears of Hypnos that Leto had tipped into their slack mouths would keep them there awhile.

Leto was dressed in a pale green chiton borrowed from Mathias, and it fell to the middle of her calves. Once the sea lapped coolly at the hem, she stopped. It was not yet dawn; the sky was soft under the moon and the island was silent, the birds not yet awakened and calling.

The ocean seemed to be holding its breath—only the faintest tide tugged at her senses as she reached for its essence and let its power wash over her. Mathias's grip tightened for the briefest of moments; then he let go of her hand as color rushed up her limbs and painted them in the soft grey green of the shallows.

Automatically, she reached for Mathias's arm, wrapping her hand around his wrist.

"Here," she said quietly, aware of Melantho's eyes on them. She pulled a leather cord out from where it had lain against her chest, the cord that had held the obol that an Ithacan maid had given her so very long ago. Her mother's necklace swung below it. "This is for Charon," she said, and tore the coin free.

Mathias looked down at the coin. "An obol," he said, "so little." He turned the coin over in his hand, then said abruptly, "You've died. How much does it really cost?"

There was no lying to him. "Everything you have," said Leto.

"Not everything," said Melantho.

She was the girl she had been hundreds of years ago. The beautiful, hopeful girl, who walked the earth and loved the queen. Here was Melantho, not eternal but mortal. Her eyes were green, her hair was blonde, her skin was rosy and clear.

"Not everything," she repeated. "You leave much behind you, Mathias."

Melantho stretched out her arm and opened her fist to offer the little bottle that lay within. The last of the tears of Hypnos. It would sedate him; his death would be quick, painless.

Mathias tried to take a step forward. "Leto," he said softly, "you need to let me go now."

"I don't want to," she choked out.

"You have to. Think about what this is *for*. The Fates brought us together, I think. But it was always meant to end."

"Not like this," she said.

"Always like this." He smiled. He was so beautiful it hurt. "I've been dead since the moment you met me."

Leto looked down at her hand on his arm. So tightly was she gripping that her knuckles had gone white and Mathias's skin had reddened underneath them. She released him wordlessly.

He moved forward until he was standing in front of Melantho. He gazed down at her for an instant, then dropped to one knee in front of her in the surf, his beautiful dark head bowed.

"I hope you will forgive me," he murmured, eyes down, "for the sins of my family."

Melantho cupped his jaw with one delicate hand. "I hope you will forgive me for mine."

Mathias nodded. Leto could see the tension in his shoulders. She longed to kneel with him, to kiss him softly, to run her hands through his spray-dampened curls. She balled her hands into fists and stayed back.

Her eyes flickered across and met Melantho's. She had looked up from Mathias and was watching Leto intently, her head tilted to the side. She flashed Leto a tense, close-lipped smile. Her trepidation and fear were written in every line of her face.

"So," said Mathias. "Should we—should we get this over with?" His voice shook almost imperceptibly.

Melantho's smile was sad as she offered him the vial. It would knock him unconscious in minutes. He wouldn't even feel it as the waves drowned him, as the water rushed into his waiting lungs, as his heart pumped out its final, wavering beat.

Something broke inside Leto. She took one staggering step, then another.

She allowed herself to run clumsily through the shallow water to Mathias. She collapsed next to him and twisted her arms around his body. He embraced her gently, pressing a kiss to the top of her head. "Don't cry," he said as Leto's shoulders began to shake. "I'll be fine."

He gently untangled them and rose to his feet, pulling Leto up with him. "Goodbye, Leto." he said. "I am very glad that we met." He cupped her face with his hands and brought it up to meet his. He kissed her. It was a long, lingering kiss. His mouth was warm and soft against hers; she could feel his heart beating against her

chest. Behind him, Leto saw Melantho look away.

This was how she would remember him. Warm and vibrant and beautiful and *alive*. She pulled away and smiled at him. "Goodbye, Mathias," she whispered, taking a half step back. "I love you."

He turned back to Melantho, one hand still entwined in Leto's, and took the bottle from her. She had removed the stopper for him. All he had to do was bring it to his mouth and tip it back. His throat moved as he swallowed.

His lips shone with the drug. Leto wiped the tears away with the back of her hand and smiled at him fiercely.

"It's all right," he said, answering the unasked question she knew was in her eyes. "I'll see you again one day."

She led him out into the bay. At last they reached the point where the sand ended and plunged steeply down to the open ocean.

His eyes fluttered closed, and he sagged against her. She brushed his hair back from his face with one hand. "I'm sorry," she said. The wind whipped the words from her lips and carried them away.

But Mathias heard them. He returned her smile—he looked like a young god, reborn from his mortal life—and dipped his chin.

The water shuddered as he let go of consciousness. Then the ocean tore him from her, pulled him under, and dragged him away. The last she saw of him was his elegant wrists, the curl of his gentle hands, the pale tips of his fingers, and then they were gone too. Mathias was gone.

Only Melantho remained.

She walked slowly toward Leto. "We should go to the shore," she said once they stood together, side by side. She took Leto's hand and began to lead her back up to the sand. Numbly—with salt in her eyes, spilling down her cheeks, pooling where her lips met— Leto followed.

LXI

I MAY ENDURE STILL

Mathias

Mathias did not feel pain. He did not feel anything.

He was falling, sinking through an endless, empty ocean. Its waves cradled him tenderly as they bore him downward, as they pushed between his lips and forced the last gasps of air from his lungs. Or perhaps he was not falling; perhaps he was only suspended in the nothingness, unfeeling and unknowing, arms and legs flung wide, eyes closed and his head thrown back to expose his throat.

And then, from amongst the nothing, he felt something. A fleeting pressure across his palm, like sand spilling from his grasp, like the shade of a snake slipping through his slack fingers. Whatever it was, it was all that Mathias had left in the world, and he knew, even now, that he did not wish to be alone. With a great effort, with every bit of his dying strength, he forced his hand into a fist around it.

Ah; as if from very far away, a dull spark of pain thudded through him. His body shuddered and he became dimly aware of his chest convulsing as it fought for air.

So this was dying. He was grateful for the bitter taste of the drug on his lips. With it coursing through his veins, slowing his heart and his mind to the barest of flickers, Mathias was only a little afraid.

He knew what he should do now. Knew that he should be thinking back on a life of heroism, of greatness and bravery. He should be preparing to recount every reason that the Judges of the Underworld should not cast him into the meadows of Asphodel with every other wandering, wretched shade, but beckon him into Elysium, into paradise, into the fields where every hero was said to walk.

But Mathias had never been a hero. He had lived, and now he would die, but what had he ever done that was worthy of greatness?

So instead, he thought of Hekate, borne across the waves to Crete. He thought of Selene, bold and beautiful and breaking against the fountain's edge. He even thought of his mother, alone in the palace, as the sea stole the last of her children from her.

Mathias thought of Melantho, he thought of Olympia, he thought of Leto. He gripped tight to that inexplicable something, all that was left in the darkness with him, and did not let go.

Down,

    down,

        down he fell, through the endless nothingness.

And then, at last, there was something else. A stirring in the water that surrounded him, like a soul passing by near enough his to touch. The brush of a hand against his cheek, gentle fingers smoothing the curls back from his face. A familiar voice in his ear.

"Do not be afraid, little brother," said Selene. She was there and she was not; it did not matter. He was not alone anymore. "No one will hurt you. I am here."

Mathias smiled.

He let go.

LXII

THE STARS HAD SHIFTED THEIR PLACES

Leto

Each step Leto took seemed to last an eternity; it was only the familiar grip of Melantho's hand in hers that kept her from slumping onto her knees in the shallows, that kept her moving slowly, steadily toward the sand. They were mere feet away when something surged through the water, sending the both of them sprawling.

Leto choked on a mouthful of brine. She tried to use the water to pull herself back up. It lapped uselessly about her.

She frowned. "What—" She broke off abruptly at the look on Melantho's face. She looked drained, morose. Understanding dawned slowly on Leto. She tried to reach for the water again, but it felt strange and cold. It didn't respond to her touch at all.

She staggered to her feet. Her powers were gone. Mathias was gone. "He's dead." And Melantho was *not*. The realization stunned her. Poseidon had spared her, then. Had granted her, at last, a life where she was not just a piece in someone else's game of revenge. For once, for *once*, the gods had looked kindly upon her.

"The curse is broken," breathed Melantho. She pulled herself up to stand next to Leto and watched, with eyes full of wonder, as the last dark scale on her wrist fell away into the surf. "It is over. Ithaca is saved."

Leto looked at her blankly. She could find nothing to say. It was over. Melantho was going to *live*. So why did the realization feel so empty in her heart?

Something was missing. Something was yet to come.

LXIII

THERE IS DAWN AND SUN-RISE

Leto

Leto looked at Melantho for a long, long while.

"What now?" she asked eventually. Her voice sounded hollow. It was over. She had chosen Ithaca over Mathias. She had chosen *Melantho* over Mathias, and now she had to live with that choice. Even if it had cost Mathias his life.

"What now?" repeated Melantho softly. "Now I want to do everything. I want to stand on the beach and not feel the sea calling me back. I want to walk to the top of that hill"—she pointed inland—"and know that I am safe. I want to—" She broke off, stiffening suddenly, and then collapsed in the surf.

"Melantho." Leto caught her around the shoulders. Melantho's weight dragged her back to her knees. She pulled Melantho into a sitting position. "Melantho, what—" The words turned to ash on her tongue as she saw Melantho's face.

"Help me up," breathed Melantho. Her eyes were wild and afraid—and the clear, uninterrupted green of spring grass. The ring of black had vanished. Leto gaped at her.

"What's happening?" she whispered.

No. *No.* Her heart knew the answer; it stilled in her aching chest.

Melantho smiled without replying. Her lips were ever so slightly asymmetrical. Leto had never noticed it before. Nor had she noticed the scar under Melantho's ear, nor the fact that the blonde of her hair was threaded with grey at the roots.

She was changing. Her powers had vanished in their entirety and now she was human again. Entirely, wholly, devastatingly human.

Leto had grown used to unearthly beauty. This Melantho, with her softly creased skin and cascades of greying hair, was achingly real. "What's happening?" Leto repeated louder.

"The curse is broken," Melantho said simply. "And—and I'm dying." Her voice broke on the word, but she was smiling. "I'm human and I'm ancient and I'm dying." She closed her eyes.

"No." Leto tried to pull her upright. "Poseidon set you *free*. You're not dying. You're not allowed to." Panic stuck at the back of her throat even as Melantho grasped blindly for her. Something ran down her cheek and dripped into Melantho's hair. The grey was spreading further, eating into the gold, dimming the shine of it. It took Leto a moment to realize that she was crying.

"Take me out of the water," Melantho said. There was a sudden urgency in her wavering voice. "Leto, please. I do not wish to die in the ocean. It has already taken so much from me. Please, Leto. Help me." She was shaking, hysterical; when she opened her eyes, they were glassy and unfocussed. "I can't see," she said. "I can't get up. *Take me out of the water, Leto.*"

There was nothing else to do. Leto put an arm under Melantho's shoulders and hauled the dying girl from the water. Spray whipped up around them, threading salt through Melantho's thick curls and mingling with the silent tears that ran down Leto's cheeks. "I've got you," she murmured; when she could go no further they collapsed onto the sodden sand. She sat up straight and eased Melantho's head into her lap.

Melantho looked up into the grey sky. Her eyes fixed blindly on a point in the distance. "The sky is gone," she said. She sounded almost relieved. Then she tilted her face down. "Can I be honest with you?" she asked gravely.

Leto had never heard her so serious. There was no mocking, no cruelty, no lust in her tone. She nodded. "You can tell me anything."

Melantho smiled. She was so entirely, wholly, impossibly beautiful. "I really hate the sea."

Despite herself, Leto laughed. Tears spilled over her cheeks. "So do I," she said.

"Whatever hell I end up in," said Melantho, "I hope it's a *desert*."

Leto clutched Melantho to her. "You are not going to any hell," she said furiously. "You aren't going anywhere. You're staying right here." She pushed damp hair back from Melantho's face. *"Don't you dare leave me."*

"I've got to go," said Melantho sadly. "I have been here far longer than I ever intended. It is time to let go. Death doesn't frighten me."

Leto shook her head hard. "I—I have to know," she blurted. "I *have* to know. Did you always know it would kill you? The breaking of the curse? Even before—before the cliffs and the fountain."

"I suspected it," said Melantho simply. "I hoped it would not. Still, if this was always meant to be the end, I considered it a worthy price."

"Why didn't you tell me?"

"I could not charge you with that decision. The burden of choice was mine alone. And I bore it gladly if it would spare you. You had enough to face already."

"You should have told me," said Leto.

"Would it have changed anything?" Melantho's words had

grown weaker and softer, her eyes were filled with tears which welled over and slipped down her greying cheeks. "After everything," she said, breathless, "after it all, would you still choose me?"

"Always," said Leto. "Always."

Melantho swallowed, a visible, laborious movement. "Good," she managed. She put her shaking hands to Leto's face, carefully feeling the shape of her jaw. She leaned in and kissed her carefully on her forehead and each of her cheeks in turn.

"I love you." Then, with an aching sort of finality she pressed a last sweet kiss to Leto's mouth. The sea had receded from her body, and she tasted not of something sharp and deadly as before, not of woodsmoke and ripe figs, but of salt and of warm skin.

"Don't go," said Leto desperately. "I love you, Melantho." She gave Melantho's shoulder a little shake. "Stay."

But Melantho wasn't listening. Her eyes had glazed over again and she was gazing past Leto with an expression of incomparable delight. "*Oh,*" she said. Her face was full of wonder. "I can see fields."

"No," said Leto. "No no no no no no no. Stay here. Stay with me." Without realizing, she had begun to rock the two of them back and forth. Her hands stroked Melantho's face, memorizing the feel of her skin.

"I've got to go," said Melantho again. "They are waiting for me. I have to go." She clutched at Leto. "Let me go. They are waiting for me in Elysium, in all the beautiful places. *I can see the fields.*"

"All right," said Leto, "it's going to be all right." She leaned over Melantho, cradling her like a child. Tears dripped from her face onto Melantho's as she carefully pulled her mother's locket over her head and tucked it into Melantho's palm. Charon would accept it. He had to. "You should go. I love you."

Melantho smiled. Her eyes closed. And then sharp-tongued Melantho with the blooming cheeks, of the twelve hanged slave women, of the halls of Odysseus and Penelope, and—at last, at long last—of the shores of Ithaca, gave a small sigh of relief and died, dissolving into nothing but sand and shadows to be swept up in the swirling winds.

🌀🌀🌀

Leto lifted her hands to her face and gazed uncomprehendingly at her empty palms. Melantho was gone. Mathias was gone. She was completely and entirely alone.

"Give them back," she said.

She did not know who she was speaking to, her face turned helplessly toward the sea. The wind caught the words and whipped them away. But for the tides dragging it in and out again, the sea was still and quiet. She staggered to her feet and ran into the water, fighting against it until she stood submerged to the waist.

"Please," she sobbed. *"Please. Give them back to me."*

The water didn't respond to her. Where before she had felt its power surging about her, heard its call in her ears, she felt nothing now. She threw herself into the waves, diving to the shallow bed, and forced her eyes open. The world was foggy and blue around her. Every remnant of her power had gone.

She was just Leto again. Human, helpless. Her lungs burned, desperate for air.

She kicked to the surface and gasped for breath, scrambling to find her footing on the shifting sand. She forced herself to turn in the water and began to struggle back toward the beach.

The absence of her power was jarring. Every step was the hardest she had ever taken.

At last, she staggered ashore and crumpled into the sand. She had barely considered the effect of submerging herself in the sea, but as she shivered on the beach, she regretted leaving her gown on. It was drenched through and freezing.

She folded in on herself, her body wracked with sobs so agonizing that she wondered if the gods would hear her, her numb fingers searching in the sand for something that was already long gone.

Something that would not be returning.

LXIV

THERE FALLS NOT RAIN

Leto

It could have been hours, days, weeks before Leto dragged herself from the beach. She walked, numb, to the hills, the land that had been razed by the sea when Mathias had denied it his sister.

She fell to her knees on the barren soil and sank her fingertips into the clods of dirt. In the myths her father had whispered to her as she fell asleep, the stories that Mathias had unfurled again from the scrolls inked in her mother's hand, there was always *something* at the end. A spider, weaving lace in the spaces between the trees. Hope, fluttering from an open jar.

A titan, a mountain, an eagle.

Leto clenched her eyes shut and threw her head back.

This is the last time, she said to the gods, and though the words were not spoken aloud, they hung in the air for a moment, then faded like mist into nothing. She was not her mother; she was not an oracle. *I will not ask again.*

Show me what they were worth to you.

The gods did not always answer her. They were not kind; they were wild and fierce and *forever.* Leto was barely a star in the infinite sky to them. And yet—

A heartbeat. Not long enough to be sure of it, but long enough to *feel* it when the sea beyond the shore stilled, when the wind ceased its howling and the air softened, somehow. Leto took a gasping breath and it felt like waking up from a dream.

The gods answered her.

This.

The ground exploded. Trees surged from the soil, a riot of green and orange and brown. Flowers bloomed between their roots; birds sang into the still air. It was the clearest vision of the future she had ever been granted. Wooden gallows lay wrecked in the shallows, the nooses that had swung from them already lost to the tides. The sun shone brightly over Ithaca as little girls played in the streams and their mothers watched them, safe in the knowledge that their daughters would grow fat and strong, and flourish and *live*.

Leto tilted her head to the sky. She was half-blind with her tears, but she saw Melantho, a crown of flowers in her hair, a willowy girl with grey eyes at her side. Another, smaller, with olive skin and tousled black curls was half-tucked behind her.

She saw Mathias, a single bloom pushed behind his ear, clutching the hand of a young woman that could only have been his sister.

They smiled; they opened their mouths to speak.

Ithaca stilled for a moment.

And then, at last, pushing up through the earth to spread their leaves and unfurl their golden petals and drink in the last rays of the winter's sun—

Daffodils.

Thousands of them.

ACKNOWLEDGMENTS

Writing is often depicted as a very solitary career, but that has rarely been my experience of it. I am tremendously lucky to be surrounded by so many extraordinarily kind, generous, and supportive people.

I owe the world (and more) to my incomparable agent, Catherine Cho, who is unfailingly brilliant and drives the hardest bargain known to man. Thank you for dealing with my chaotic WhatsApps, for sending all the emails I don't want to, and for taking such a chance on a twenty-one-year-old writing in a genre you didn't represent; it has been a delight and a privilege to watch Paper Literary grow. Thank you also to Chris Rowlands and James Choi for that very first email.

Huge thank-yous to my film agent, Emily Hayward Whitlock, and to all our foreign language coagents: Anoukh Foerg and Maria Dürig from the Anoukh Foerg Agency, Catherine LaPautre of Agence LaPautre, Marco Vigeveni and Claire Sabatiegarat from the Italian Literary Agency, Lester Hekking at Sebes and Bisseling, Maria Ridao, Mònica Martin, Txell Torrent, Cristina Auladell, and Marta Gonzalez at MB Agencia Literaria, Efrat Lev from the Deborah Harris Agency, Dominika Bojanowska, Beata Glińska, and Zuzanna Brzezińska at the Anna Jarota Agency, Gray Tan of Grayhawk Agency, Miko Yamanouchi of Japan Uni, and Danny Hong and Alice Moon from the Danny Hong Agency.

Thank you to my editors, Sarah Levison and Stephanie Stein, and to Lindsey Heaven for making every single one of my dreams come true again and again. I am so lucky to work with you, and every part of this process has been made better and easier by your unfailing support and insight. Thank you for loving Leto, Melantho, and Mathias as much as I do.

Thank you to everyone else on the teams at Farshore and HarperTeen. It takes a village to publish and promote a book, and this is mine: Lucy Courtenay, Laura Bird, Olivia Carson, Sarah Bates, Hannah Penny, Pippa Poole, Ingrid Gilmore, Brogan Furey, Leah Woods, Anna Verghese, Charlotte Cooper, Sophie Schmidt, Jessica Berg, Gwen Morton, Gretchen Stelter, Rosanne Lauer, Corina Lupp, Alison Klapthor, Annabelle Sinoff, Nicole Moulaison, Michael D'Angelo, Sabrina Abballe, Sam Fox, Jennifer Corcoran, Cindy Hamilton, Olivia Adams, Susila Baybars, and everyone else who has had to deal with me and this book over the last twoish years. I am immeasurably grateful for all your hard work and generosity. Extra big thank-you to Jasveen Bansal and Ellie Bavester (RIP) (not actually dead, just changed jobs), who are the coolest marketing/PR duo in the world.

Thank you also to Jennie Roman for your very rigorous copyediting—I did not realize I had so many crutch words.

Thank you to Micaela Alcaino for designing my indescribably stunning covers. Every single version is so gorgeous and classic and classy; I still can hardly believe this beautiful book is mine. Also huge thanks to Daphne Lao Tonge and everyone at Illumicrate (!!!!!!!!!) and to Therese (Warickaart), for being the perfect artist to bring my characters alive every time. You are always such a joy to work with, even when I ask you to change Mathias' mouth three times in a row.

Lies We Sing to the Sea would not exist as it does without the relentless support and friendship of other writers. Thank you to Marisa Salvia and Ania Poranek, who were there since day one, and are here still. You are both so brilliant and talented, and I am so lucky to know you. To all the London writers, especially Kat Dunn, Kate Dylan, and Saara El-Arifi, and to every established author who made time for me when I needed it most, especially Natasha Bowen, Jennifer Saint, and Rebecca F. Kuang. Thank you to everyone in the UK debut group, which has been a wonderful little community (extra thanks to Lizzie Huxley-Jones and the Bonk Dog) and to Aleema Omotoni, who can make even plastic hygiene gloves into a look. Also to Zohra Nabi—I will be bragging forever how I knew you before you were famous.

Thank you to all the wonderful people who read early versions of *Lies* and pushed me onward, especially Bethany Baptiste, Miranda Sun, Kyla Zhao, Lujia Liu, Lyssa Mia Smith, Dana Chloe Draper, Kamilah Cole, and Trang Tanh Tran. You are all so wonderful and talented and kind, and it is an honor to know you. Thank you also to Joel Rochester, Ellie Thomas, Emma Finnerty, Clara Foster, and Harveen Khailany, publishing *professionals* and all-around wonderful people. Let's get dinner.

You hear a lot in publishing about how one moment changed the course of a writer's life. To Grace Li and Becca Mix, you are that moment. I love you both.

To everyone who has blurbed *Lies We Sing to the Sea*: Rebecca Ross, Allison Saft, Jamie Pacton, Laura Steven, and Heather Walter. I have fallen in love with all of your words time and time over; thank you for sparing some for me.

Thank you to Tracy Alexander, John Carter, and everyone else behind the Honiton & District Young Writer's Award, and to Caroline Ambrose and the Bath Novel Awards. Also, thanks to Kate Cavanaugh—I wrote most of the first draft of *Lies* during your writing sprints.

Above all, this is a book about love. Thank you to Amar, Andrew, Ric, Emily, Sid, George, Tara, Max, Cherizza, Annabelle, George, Juli, Maddy, Sophie, David, Daisy, Dan, Hugh, Tom, and all my other wonderful, wonderful friends at Imperial and Cambridge, who are the reason I did not drop out of university and also of existence. Also to Lauren, who doesn't neatly slot into any other group (inconsiderate), and to Jemma, Rosie, Tasha, Kendall, Susan, Iain, Marianna, and everyone else who makes home home. And thank you to Alex (of "Sarah has one close friend (Alex)" fame) for all your kindness, enthusiasm and friendship.

Thank you, always, to my parents, who told me that I could do anything I wanted (but definitely didn't mean this), and my sisters, Natalie and Helen: I am a far better person because of you. Also to my brother-in-law-to-be, Balaj (I am possibly a worse person because of you).

And to my boyfriend, James. I love you when you're here; I love you when you're a thousand miles away.